separations

SEPARATIONS

two novels of
mothers and children

massimo bontempelli

translated by estelle gilson

mcpherson & company
kingston, new york
2000

Published by McPherson & Company, Publishers
Post Office Box 1126, Kingston, New York 12402.
www.mcphersonco.com
Manufactured in the United States of America.
Design by Bruce McPherson. Typeset in Fairfield.
First Edition.
1 3 5 7 9 10 8 6 4 2   2000 2001 2002 2003 2004

Library of Congress Cataloging-in-Publication Data

Bontempelli, Massimo, 1878-1960.
[Due storie di madri e figli. English]
Separations : two novels of mothers and children, Massimo Bontempelli ;
translated by Estelle Gilson.
p. cm.
ISBN 0-929701-61-5
1. Bontempelli, Massimo, 1878-1960—Translations into English. I. Gilson,
Estelle. II. Bontempelli, Massimo, 1878-1960. Figlio di due madri. English.
III. Bontempelli, Massimo, 1878-1960. Vita e morte di Adria e dei suoi figli.
English. IV. Title: Figlio di due madri. V. Title: Vita e morte di Adria e dei
suoi figli. VI. Title.

PQ4807.O65 D8513 2000
853'.912—dc21
99-088837

Publication of this book has been made possible by a grant from the
Literature Program of the New York State Council on the Arts.

This book is printed on acid-free paper to ensure permanence.

contents

preface

W HEN I CAME ACROSS MASSIMO BONTEMPELLI'S collected fiction more than two decades ago, I knew nothing about the man, his literary theories, or the controversies that surrounded his public life. I knew only that I was reading stories I wished all my friends could read, and that, surprisingly, the stories were not available in English. My decision to translate some of these tales proved to be the fateful first step on one of those long journeys from which there is no retreat. My goal often receded even as I advanced, yet the more of Bontempelli I translated, and the more I learned about his life, the more convinced I became of its importance, not only to lovers of good fiction but also to literary historians.

Long before the advent of the fantastic fiction we associate with Latin American writers—particularly Jorge Luis Borges and Alejo Carpentier—it was Massimo Bontempelli (twenty-one years Borges' senior, twenty-six Carpentier's) who defined a new literary style he called *realismo magico*. Bontempelli believed that the 20th century was ushering in a new kind of literature which would replace classicism and futurism, and had begun experimenting with fantasy in his own fiction. "[It] is the essence of the 20th century," he wrote in 1926, "that rejects both reality as reality and fantasy as fantasy, and lives by the sense of magic discoverable in the daily lives of people and things."

For decades afterward the term "magic realism" was everywhere almost synonymous with his name. At his death in 1960, *The New York Times* described Bontempelli as the "leader of the futuristic school in the 1920s...whose goal it was to create a world of fantasy which would have the objectivity of the natural world."

As befits a man intent on uniting what to most of us would seem to be the irreconcilable worlds of magic and reality, Bontempelli was a person of enormous and intriguing contrasts. He led a public life as journalist, playwright, editor, translator, writer of fiction, and composer (he was a close friend of Pirandello's, and wrote music for one of his plays), yet was secretive about his personal life. In an ostensibly autobiographic work, *Mia vita, morte e miracoli (My Life, Death and Miracles)* published in 1931, the year after he was named to the Italian National Academy, Bontempelli promises a glimpse into the relationships between the realities of his life and his art, "Not once, not one time, not one single time," he tells his readers, "have I told another person's story. They're always my own." And almost immediately he delivers a Bontempellian miracle. "I was born of an act of my own will. I remember the moment precisely." Before the book ends he will die and be reborn.

Bontempelli's political views, like his literary views, were, as one critic put it, "poised between opposite tendencies." Although associated with the Fascist Party during its earliest days, he later became a staunch and open anti-Fascist. On November 27, 1938, speaking at a commemoration of Gabriele D'Annunzio's death at the late poet's birthplace in Pescara, Bontempelli took the occasion to denounce the era's glorification of violence and conquest, its negation of virtue and fantasy, its renunciation of smiles and forgiveness. In such an era, he concluded, "ten years can destroy ten centuries." The speech earned Bontempelli a year of internal exile.

Massimo Bontempelli was born in Como on May 12, 1878 to Alfredo and Anna Cislaghi Bontempelli. His father was a railway construction engineer, and before completing secondary school, young Massimo had lived in eight different cities with three separate stays in Milan. Later, in Milan, he studied with Alfredo Panzini, Arturo Graf and Giuseppe Fraccoli and took degrees in philosophy and literature.

With the help of Pirandello, who was then himself a teacher,

8

Bontempelli obtained a teaching position, and spent several years as an instructor in various secondary schools before devoting himself entirely to writing. From the first he wrote frequently for newspapers and magazines, a practice he was to continue all his life. Bontempelli's first volume of poetry, *Eclogue,* appeared in 1904 and was followed by two others in rapid succession in 1905 and 1906, all in the classic tradition. His earliest collection of stories, *Socrate Moderno,* was published in 1908. By 1914, when the First World War broke out, he had produced five more volumes of prose and poetry. During the War Bontempelli served in the Italian army, earning several decorations. On completing military service he resumed all his literary activities. Between 1919 and 1925 he found time to sail the Mediterranean as correspondent for a publication on naval affairs, and to produce five volumes of fiction, two of essays, one of poetry, and three plays. By the end of this time, he had repudiated all his earlier works and had moved beyond classical forms and themes to produce works which prefigure magic realism. One of the most delightful is a children's book, *La scacchiera davanti allo specchio (The Chessboard Before the Mirror),* possibly written for his eleven-year-old son—also named Massimo—in 1922. (Bontempelli had married Amelia della Pergola in 1909; eventually they went on to live separate lives.) The book is a kind of *Alice Through the Looking Glass* in which a child, lured by a reflected White King, enters a mirrored world where every sound and sight that takes place before the mirror has been preserved.

In 1926 Bontempelli founded the literary review *'900: Cahiers d'Italie et d'Europe* with Curzio Malaparte. Malaparte, whose original name was Kurt Erich Suckert, was an Italian-born writer and journalist, who was also, though later than Bontempelli, to turn against Fascism. The review was intended to reflect modern day cultural and political renewal and European unity. To this end, it was published in French, and its editorial committee was deliberately composed of non-Italians. Members included Max Jacob, André Malraux, Rainer Maria Rilke and James Joyce (an excerpt of

Ulysses appeared in the first volume). Ilya Ehrenberg joined the committee in 1927. Among its foreign contributors were Virginia Woolf, D.H. Lawrence and Blaise Cendrars; among Italians, Marcello Gallian, Corrado Alvaro, Alberto Moravia, and Bontempelli's wife under the name of Diotima. Picasso, Carlo Carrà—and Bontempelli's teenage nephew, Corrado Cagli—were among the artist contributors. Bontempelli presented his literary hopes for the new century in the very first issue. (Though the title and the movement with which '900 is associated are often spelled out as *novecento* and *novecentismo*, the terms refer to the 20th century.) Bontempelli believed that society had passed through two long cultural eras: the Classical, which had ended with Christianity; and the Romantic, which the violence and upheavals of the First World War had brought to an end. Now it was on the threshold of a modern era that would bring fresh and free exchanges among writers and artists. The appearance of new Italian voices in French, he thought, would introduce Italian writers into the mainstream of European literature and allow them to take part in the creation of the new kind of universal art. Language was not a factor, because Bontempelli believed that it was the writer's task to create myths which transcended the writer's own life and times, and that the literature of the new era would therefore consist of translatable, transportable myths—effective in any language, any time, any place. "Translation does not mean distortion," Bontempelli wrote in response to challenges by Italian writers. "Translated Italian, if it is strong and representative, will retain its flavor—in spirit, construction and world view—just as Russian remains Russian." It did not take long, however, for the publication of a prestigious artistic and literary Italian journal in French to became a nagging issue in Italian cultural/political life. Malaparte withdrew from '900 in 1927 and joined the *strapaese* movement—writers and artists whose agenda was a kind of "rural Italy first." Despite the support of a small opposition group called *stracittà* which arose in response to *strapaese*, Bontempelli came under persistent pressure to publish '900 in Italian, and for a while it appeared in two languages.

It was '900, with its international group of readers and contributors—particularly during the period when it appeared in French and Italian—that helped spread the concept of magic realism throughout Europe. "Magic realism," Bontempelli wrote in its summer 1927 issue, stressing the interweaving of fantasy and reality, "has nothing to do with a thousand and one nights. More than fairy tales, we have a thirst for adventure. We want to see the most ordinary daily life as an exciting miracle, an unending risk."

In 1928 when Malaparte accused Bontempelli of being "ebreo and/or antifascista," and although strapaese and stracittà were both under the Fascist umbrella, Bontempelli was forced to discontinue publication in French and to resign his post as secretary of the Fascist writer's union. '900 discontinued publication in June 1929.

Bontempelli spent the following year in Paris. In 1927, after a long affair with French artist Mariette Lydis, he had met a young Italian writer, Paola Masino, who became his lifelong companion. For reasons not made clear in Masino's charming but highly selective memoir of their life together, Io, Massimo and gli altri, the two could not remain in Italy in 1930, and spent the year in Paris.

In or out of Italy, the years between the late 1920s and 1939 were among the most fruitful and successful of Bontempelli's literary career. He and Masino took up residence for various periods in Paris, Rome, Milan and other Italian cities, and made extensive trips through central Europe, as well as to Egypt, Greece, Spain, Belgium, and Scandinavia. They also traveled to Argentina and Brazil as cultural emissaries for the Italian government. Restless and rootless though he was, Bontempelli's literary theories found realization in an outpouring of articles, novels and plays. During this period he was a reviewer for numerous publications and became one of Italy's best-known, best-selling authors. Bontempelli's most noted plays, Nostra Dea and Minnie la candida ("Our Dea," and "Minnie, Who's Credulous") appeared in 1925 and 1928. Il figlio di due madri ("The Boy with Two Mothers") appeared in 1929 and was awarded the Premio dei trenta (so-called for its thirty judges).

It was followed in 1930 by *Vita e morte di Adria e del suoi figli* ("The Life and Death of Adria and Her Children"). Both works appeared in one volume in 1940 as *Due storie di madri e figli* ("Two Tales of Mothers and Children"). In 1933 Bontempelli founded *Quadrante*, with Pier Maria Bardi. Though essentially an architectural review to which Le Corbusier, Gropius, Breuer and Leger contributed, *Quadrante* was open to discussions of art, literature and music. Bontempelli's nephew, Corrado Cagli, by then an important Fascist artist, was a significant contributor on the future of modern art. In 1936 Bontempelli became the editor of *L'Italia Letteraria.*

Bontempelli's run-in with Fascist authorities in Pescara wasn't his only clash with the regime in 1938. That same year he was removed from the staff of the journal *Film* for not touting Italian movies. 1938 was also the year Italy's racial laws were passed, and shortly after the D'Annunzio incident Bontempelli refused the offer of the chair in Italian literature at the University of Florence vacated by the enforced departure of a Jew, Attilio Momigliano. It is thought by some that it was this incident, not the D'Annunzio speech, which resulted in Bontempelli's exile to Venice and the year of silence the regime imposed upon him. Both acts required conviction and courage. Momigliano described Bontempelli's gesture as one of "admirable generosity." Rosetta Loy, in her 1997 memoir, *La parola ebreo,* writes that although about three hunded faculty positions became available in Italy as a result of the racial laws, the only person known to have refused to replace a Jew was Bontempelli. In any event it is clear from a letter dated late in 1938 by Masino that the couple was already in the process of moving to Venice of their own choice. The restrictions against publishing, however, caused financial problems for Bontempelli, and in June 1939 he was forced to sell his "522," a Fiat auto which was the protagonist of an eponymous novel.

Without a full biography of Bontempelli we are forced to speculate about the writer's associations with the Fascist authorities. What was he expecting and getting from the regime? What did he offer it in return? What did his periodic disagreements and dissents mean to him and to it? Why were his dissensions in 1938 so much more overt? And why were they punished so lightly? At this moment there are very few answers. Masino offers a personal, if vague clue in a journal entry about some sweaters she gave Bontempelli in 1936, which he and Pirandello adopted as daily wear because they enabled the two friends to dispense with neckties. Recalling Bontempelli's disgust at having to don a uniform to speak at the commemoration of Pirandello's death later that year, she posits his real and metaphorical refusal to be constricted by Fascism from this time, and describes his reaction to the freedom that the sweaters offered as a new sense of dissent "which led directly to his speech on D'Annunzio in Pescara."

The path Italian Fascism took was undoubtedly a factor as well. From the moment Mussolini assumed power in 1922, the Fascist regime used every means possible to gain control of the Italian press. Repression of anti-Fascist publications was absolute and resolute. Art historian Emily Braun, however, presents a different picture of its approach to artistic expression. Fascist Italy, she writes, "unlike Nazi Germany, which it preceded in power by a decade...was not totalitarian in its cultural controls. Because of [its] beguiling margin of creative freedom, the large majority of artists and intellectuals co-existed with, if not openly supported the regime, at least until the anti-Semitic laws of 1938."

In this regard it would be interesting to know more about Bontempelli's relationship with his nephew, Corrado Cagli. Cagli, related to Bontempelli through Amelia della Pergola's family, was a Jew. Though in 1937 he had created a large mural entitled *Trionfo di Mussolini* for an International Exhibition, after passage of the racial laws the following year, he was forced to flee Italy. He arrived in the United States in 1939 and joined the United States army in 1941. Cagli was with the troops that entered Buchenwald, and he left sketches of that encounter. He returned to Italy in 1947 and died there in 1976.

It is not clear whether Bontempelli was ever again in the good graces of the Fascist party, but in 1939 he resumed writing for periodicals. One of his many regular columns, *Colloqui con Bontempelli*, became a popular favorite and ran until 1948. Among the most important fiction he subsequently produced was the collection *Giro del sole* in 1941. His last play, *Innocenza di Camillo* ("Camillo's Innocence"), appeared in 1949; and his last story collection, *L'Amante fedele* ("The Faithful Lover"), was awarded the Strega prize in 1954.

In the early 1940s Bontempelli completely disavowed Fascism and established contacts with Italian communists. In 1943 he was again in Rome, where a warrant for his arrest and death was issued by Alessandro Pavolini, the Fascist Party's cultural minister. Both Bontempelli and Masino spent time in hiding.

In 1944, immediately after the Germans, who had occupied Rome in 1943, were driven from the city, Bontempelli, Guido Piovene and Alberto Savinio began meeting on Sundays at the home of Maria and Goffredo Bellonci. Though the war was not yet over, the goal of the *Amici della domenica* (Sunday friends), as they called themselves, was to plan the renewal of Italian literature. They were joined the following year by Alberto Moravia, Elsa Morante, Giuseppe Ungaretti, and others. The group's efforts resulted in the creation of the Strega prize, which was first offered in 1947.

In the first post-war parliamentary elections, held in 1948, Bontempelli, then seventy, was elected Senator by Siena on the Popular Front (Communist) ticket. Shortly thereafter, however, his election was invalidated on the basis of his having contributed to Fascist literature via anthologies used in Italian schools. Devastated by the rejection, he retired from public life and, after a long illness, died in Rome in 1960.

One wants to think well of people whose work one loves. I was dismayed and disappointed to read about Bontempelli's involvement with Fascism—though ultimately relieved to learn that he had broken with it. If we have learned anything about any given artist's political views in this highly politicized century, it is that they are mutable, no better thought out than those of the general population's, and no gauge of the importance of the art or the pleasure it can bring.

The Boy with Two Mothers and *The Life and Death of Adria and Her Children*, written when Bontempelli was in mid-career, represent the essence of a style honed on short forms. Descriptions are generally brief and pithy, events move crisply, dialogue is clear and to the point. Both novels are driven by "magic" and document catastrophic family events. In *The Boy with Two Mothers*, the magic world lies outside the characters, in events they cannot understand or control. In *The Life and Death of Adria and Her Children*, the magic world lies within the astonishing Adria. Both tales are told with irony and humor, and the narrator's presence is explicit. In fact, it is the author's presence in his works that creates the distance required for the irony and humor to be effective, and that marks them unmistakably as Bontempellian. From the first page of *The Boy with Two Mothers*, in which Bontempelli offers readers his "magic cloak" as storyteller to whisk them to the time and location of his choice—to the last page of *The Life and Death of Adria and Her Children*, in which he reflects on the fate of Adria's soul— Bontempelli inserts himself in varying degrees between magic and reader, between characters and events, to fulfill what he believed was the writer's ultimate goal, "to tell a dream as if it were reality and reality as if it were a dream."

Perhaps one measure of Bontempelli's success in creating myths that survive his own time, place and language, is the fact that the struggles of his extravagant yet sympathetic creatures, against the unfathomable magic that drive their lives, persist in the reader's memory.

We must leave to critics and historians the evaluation of Bontempelli's place in literary history. His is a large body of work to explore, but it is an exploration worth pursuing. As distant as he seems to us now, "Massimo Bontempelli," critic Fernando Tempesti wrote, "is like one of those stars astronomers know has disappeared, but whose light continues to reach the earth."

❖ ❖ ❖ ❖ ❖

I WISH TO THANK THE LITERATURE programs of the National Endowment on the Arts and the New York State Council on the Arts for assistance in making this translation possible. I'd also like to thank Signor Alvise Memmo for permission to translate these and other Bontempelli works; and Professor Emerita Sister Juliana D'Amato, O.P., who made her doctoral thesis on Bontempelli available to me. I owe a debt as well to my editor and publisher, Bruce McPherson, for his commitment to the work; to my son, Michael, for his support during some of the dark moments along the way toward publication; and to my husband, Saul, for far too much to itemize.

—ESTELLE GILSON

the boy with
two mothers

1 THIS STRANGE STORY BEGINS IN
sunlight and happiness on a spring
day in the capital city of the world.
It starts at around one in the afternoon on the seventh of
May in the year 1900, the last of the century. The day was a
Monday, to which anyone with a calendar of the time can attest.
It was Monday in every nation of the civilized world which ad-
heres to the Gregorian calendar, and therefore Monday in Rome
as well, on via Abruzzi, the centermost of the streets on Ludovisio
Hill, named to honor the sixteen regions of Italy.

Having so quickly specified the moment and the place on
the earth's surface in which our tale commences, we can now
ascend—with the immunity and invisibility that God concedes
to storytellers—to the second floor of one of those modern houses
resembling villas that make up this most elegant quarter of the
Empire City. So without delay, and with perfect timing, we enter a cheerful dining room filled with sunlight, flowers, gleaming crystal, multicolored porcelains and silver.

Here, sitting around a white-clothed table, is a young family, the family of Mariano Parigi. Parigi is a man little known to
history, but one who plays a somewhat important role in life—
assuming it is important to earn a great deal of money annually
dealing in weighty matters, to use that money to provide well for
oneself and one's family, and to be the recipient of those honors
by which our society encourages its most industrious members.

The sun's rays entering through the wide-open window are

breaking upon decanters of red wine, sinking beneath the froth of white wine still left in goblets.

Parigi, the paterfamilias, is forty. Opposite him is his wife, Arianna, still young and attractive, at least to those who like small, plump, accommodating women with uninquiring minds. For such is signora Arianna. And because of these particular qualities, those closest to her have, understandably, sliced the head off her mythical and ethereal name, leaving behind the more prosaic Anna.

Between these two people, between Mariano and Arianna, between father and mother, enthroned on his chair, propped up on two plump cushions, sits their young son. Opposite him is his pale governess, also youthful though unsmiling. The sun's rays elude her. Two house maids in black and white are serving silently. This authentic portrait even includes a house cat. It is completely white and sits contentedly at the foot of the boy's chair. The cat is smug and satisfied because it has just finished its share of an unusually appetizing and festive meal. Throughout the room there is a lingering echo of toasts and barely concluded laughter.

But now a small shadow falls across that echo and darkens the room.

For precisely at the moment at which this story begins, as the boy, who had been diligently collecting the last crumbs of dessert from his plate and, assembling them in the palm of his hand, was about to pop them into his open mouth, a stern glance from his father, a timid gesture by his mother, and the sharp voice of his governess, Elena, stopped him in the middle of that voluptuous and innocent act.

Elena said, "Mario, we do not eat crumbs."

Mario stopped, stared at his elders with large stricken eyes, then asked. "Not even today, on my birthday?"

Mariano Parigi cast an angry, pitying glance at his son. Elena quivered with horror. But Arianna, moved by the boy's plight, placed her hand gently on his arm.

The father rose, tossed his napkin on the table and, with an utterly disconsolate look on his face, murmured, "We'll never make anything of this child."

Mario's large eyes filled with tears. Now Arianna stood up too. She bent over him, put her arm around his shoulders as though she were helping him down from his chair, then silently kissed the top of his head.

Everyone left the table.

The room was enormous and divided into two unequal parts by a vaulted arch. Beyond the arch, in the smaller part of the room, large glass doors were admitting the clamor of a Roman May.

In this luminous space stood Mariano Parigi's deep armchair, Arianna's small soft one and, on the thickly carpeted floor, Mario's and the cat's cushions. The cat was now walking, first in the family, tail straight up, solemnly heading for the spot on the carpet where the sun shone most fully. Behind him came Mario, still in his mother's embrace and almost supported by her.

The small shadow had dispersed toward the corners of the room and was nearly gone. After Mariano Parigi had very carefully selected the best cigar from a humidor and lit it with restrained pleasure, the sun was once more blazing everywhere—on the silver, in the air, along the walls—from which it sang happy birthday to Mario.

When each family member was thus restored to his customary place and the governess had silently disappeared, a new person entered the scene and was greeted joyously by all.

"Good day, doctor."

"Mario," the doctor called out, "I came to wish you happy birthday. This is the seventh time I'm doing it, no, the eighth, because I was right there when you were born in Milan seven years ago."

Mario looked up calmly at the doctor. The boy had a prominent forehead. His eyes were large, soft and filled with a strange uncertainty.

There was a brief silence. Perhaps everyone was waiting for Mario's reply. Instead, he asked a question.

"What time was it, when I was born?"

"Mario!" exclaimed his father, "don't ask silly questions."

Instantly Mario's face darkened. Gray clouds gathered on the walls and the air around him began quivering. His mother came to his aid and the sound of her voice quickly dissipated the chill. "During the day. At two, I think."

"That's right," the doctor agreed. "I remember it very well. The seventh of May, 1893, at precisely two o'clock."

"In that case," said Mario, "my birthday isn't for another hour."

"Exactly so," the doctor replied smiling. "Another hour. Right now, you weren't born. You're not here."

"I'm not here, but the presents I got this morning are here, and I want to show them to you. There's one from you too. Come take a look."

But at that moment the governess reappeared holding a hat and a veil. "It's time for our walk," she announced.

"Take him to Piazza di Siena," Arianna instructed.

Mario turned to his mother. "Aren't you coming, mamma? You promised me."

"Of course I'm coming. Wait for me there. I'll meet you in a little while and then we'll take a real walk"

"Where will we go?"

"Wherever you want, just as I promised."

"Mamma will go wherever I want today," Mario explained to the doctor, "because it's my birthday."

"And where do you want to go, you rascal? But then, how can you want anything, if you haven't been born yet?"

Mario replied with great seriousness, "But I'll be born in an hour and then I'll start doing whatever I want."

With Mario and Elena gone the conversation on the smoky veranda over cups of coffee slacked off quickly. Then Arianna left to change her clothes.

Mario, walking beside Elena along via Campania said to her, "Please let me know when an hour is up, because then I'll be born. The doctor explained it to me."

"He was only joking."

"No, he wasn't. He was perfectly serious. Anyway, even if you don't tell me, I'll know just the same."

Without further exchange, Mario and Elena skirted the Belisario walls, passed the Pinciana gate, left behind the muddy edge of the bridal path and reached the Piazza di Siena. At that time of day it was completely deserted.

Roman sunshine filled the air, proclaiming the glories of May to one and all. The meadows were emerald green, the shady areas were abysses of deep, dark blue.

Elena turned to the shade, chose a bench, dusted it and sat down.

Mario's voice was gentle, "You can stay here. But please hold my cap, the sun is good for me. I'm going to count those pine trees over there."

"That's fine, just don't go too far."

"And you know what," the boy added, "a lot of that hour must have passed by now. I'll tell you when I'm born."

Mario rushed away into the sunlit expanse. When he reached the pines he began counting them. He touched each as he did so, walking ever more slowly from one to another until he reached a tree at which he paused. He leaned against it and stood stock still.

Elena noticed nothing.

Everything surrounding the boy, light and shadow, air and

greenery, had stopped moving. The sun seemed fixed in the center of the sky.

When, about half an hour later, Arianna, slightly breathless, reached the Piazza di Siena, it was still fairly empty. Looking around she immediately saw Elena sitting stiffly on the bench with Mario's white cap in her lap. Arianna quickened her pace and Elena, seeing her, rose to meet her.

"Where's Mario?"

"Over there, signora," the young woman pointed to a tree across the green.

Arianna saw the child leaning against the tree as though submerged in its shadow, while all about him the air quivered with brilliant light.

He seemed absorbed. His head was bent somewhat toward the ground, though Arianna couldn't make out what he might be looking at. He leaned still further forward, and his head now protruded a little from the shadow, as if drawn down by that dazzling sight. The sun, striking his prominent forehead, exaggerated its shape.

Seeing him so engrossed didn't surprise Arianna. Mario often sat alone, lost in thought. Her immediate reaction was to start toward him across the edge of the meadow, almost at a run. But when she was just a few steps away and he still hadn't seen her or moved, another idea occurred to her. She stopped, smiled to herself, then changed direction. Although the grass was enough to have silenced her footsteps, began walking on her toes until she reached the back of the tree against which Mario was leaning.

Suddenly she put her hands around his head and covered his eyes.

"Guess who!"

Mario didn't react immediately. But after a moment he turned toward his mother and all at once raised his hands and tore hers from his eyes so quickly and forcibly, that it didn't occur to her to resist. And they remained that way, staring at each other, the mother bent toward him, the boy's face tilted up.

"What's the matter with you?"

"Nothing."

"Didn't you know it was me?"

"I don't know."

"What were you doing?"

"Nothing."

Arianna sought to rouse Mario from his distracted state. "Let's go for our walk now. We can still go. I know it's after two o'clock. I made you wait for me? But now I'm all yours. Shall we go?"

"Yes." The boy's voice was muted.

"Where do you want to go, darling?"

"Home."

"Home?" Anna was dumbstruck. "You don't feel well?"

"No, I just want to go home."

"But you just came from there."

"No."

"Darling, what are you talking about? What's the matter with you?" She bent over the boy, clasped his head tightly in her hands, feeling as if she were going to faint.

"I want to go home," he repeated. "Right now."

"Yes, of course, my love. We'll go home right away. But why?"

"I want to go to my own house, to my own mother."

Arianna fell upon Mario, circling him completely in her arms, as though he were about to fly off forever. "My God, what did you say, darling? I'm your mother."

"No."

"Mario," Arianna shouted and felt she was going crazy.

"And stop calling me Mario," the boy spoke severely. "Why do you keep doing it when you know it isn't my name?"

Trembling and sobbing, holding the boy tightly in her arms, Arianna now fell to her knees on the grass.

"You're sick, darling," she said. "Come, let's go. Let's go home. Elena, come over here. We have to get him home. What happened? What happened to him. What was he doing?"

"Nothing, signora. He just walked across the grass and was counting the trees. I don't know. Then he must have stopped there. But nothing happened. You know, yourself, he does that sometimes, stares at the ground as if he were in a trance. Just like now."

"Get me the carriage over there."

While Elena was across the street securing the carriage the boy's agitation subsided, though he still seemed oblivious of his surroundings and kept turning his eyes absently from one thing to another. A blue vein appeared down the center of his deeply troubled brow.

He didn't react again until he was in the carriage seated between his mother and the governess, and the carriage had begun moving. Perhaps he didn't remember entering it. For several minutes he'd felt nothing. But then, after looking about him with an air of quiet distraction, he suddenly asked suspiciously, "Where are we going?"

"Home, dear." His mother no longer had the heart to call him Mario.

"To my house?"

Arianna didn't dare answer. She put her hand on his forehead, but was so agitated that she couldn't tell whether it felt hot or cold to her touch. Over and over she asked herself what she was feeling, but her trembling hand was unable to relay the information to her mind.

By then the carriage was completing its short trip. It entered via Abruzzi and stopped in front of the house.

The governess descended and Arianna was about to rise from her seat when the boy suddenly shook violently and shouted, "No, not here. I want to go home. To my house. To my mother. Right now."

Arianna felt faint again. Elena, stunned, didn't even try to understand. Mario, his face dark and distraught, stared angrily at the walls of the house with his small fists pressed against his chest. Arianna, on the other hand, was deathly pale, as her world became silent and motionless for what seemed an eternity. Then the boy spoke in a strange, muffled and hostile voice. "Give him my address," he commanded.

It took superhuman strength for the mother to indulge him and to ask in a tiny voice, "What is it?"

His composure restored, the boy spoke quietly and calmly. "Number eighteen via del Muro Nuovo."

Once more it was the strength of her love that enabled Arianna to speak. "Via del Muro Nuovo," she murmured to the driver of the carriage, who had turned away while waiting for them to descend.

The driver muttered something under his breath, but didn't move. Arianna had to will herself to speak a second time. "Number eighteen," she said.

The driver frowned, turned back to her and was about to reply, when Mariano Parigi and the doctor appeared in the doorway.

Arianna stretched her arms toward them as if toward rescuers, but then was overcome by a strange fear and, without knowing why, lowered her arms and put them around the boy as if to protect him from imminent danger. The two men hurried toward the carriage. "What is it?" "What happened?" they asked.

Arianna stared at them blankly, too ashamed to explain. An anguished silence hung over the scene until, blushing and filled with fear, she finally whispered, "I think Mario is sick."

She thought she had spoken quietly, but the boy had heard her and protested furiously, "No, no, no, I am not sick. I just want to go home."

The doctor, perceiving the strange look in the child's eyes, called out to him. "Mario."

"Don't call me Mario. Use my right name. You know it's Ramiro. And take me home. I told you where, to via del Muro Nuovo."

Even the doctor was stunned. But Mariano Parigi, the man of action, took control of the situation. "Come on. Get down from the carriage and into the house, all of you. Beginning with you, Anna, get out."

Moving quickly he took the boy into his arms, lifted him out of the carriage, and was about to set him down when, still in his father's arms, the boy let out an inhuman scream and threw his head back violently. He became startlingly pale, his eyes rolled upward and he lost consciousness.

Carrying him into the elevator, they took him upstairs and into the apartment. When he awoke, his eyes shone and he was burning with fever, but he said nothing more. Breathlessly, Arianna recounted the child's strange utterances. Neither man could understand or explain them. Toward sunset Mario fell into a labored sleep that slowly and gradually became normal, quiet and deep. His forehead became cool again. Barely speaking, the three adults sat by his side for several hours.

"He's over it," the doctor finally said. "The crisis is past."

"What a relief," Mariano Parigi exclaimed. "I've got a business trip tomorrow. It would have been dreadful to leave a sick child behind. That was frightening. Come on now, Anna, you don't have worry about him anymore."

But Anna wasn't relieved. Her son's physical recovery was not enough for her. The insistent, inexplicable things he'd said to her, as cutting as knives, were still lodged in her heart. She wanted to talk about them, but couldn't bring herself to do so. She was hoping frantically that one of the men would raise the subject, but it appeared that her husband and the doctor had forgotten those words.

It was only when the doctor rose to take his leave that Arianna ventured to speak. "Those things, doctor, those things that Mario said, 'I want to go to my own house. I want my…'"

"It's all nonsense," Mariano interrupted her. "Can't you see he's better now?"

"It was a kind of hallucination," the doctor explained. "With the fever coming on and his temperature going up, he had some strange fantasies, perhaps things he remembered from books. It was a kind of delirium. Forget it. He won't remember any of it afterward. And don't you think about it anymore, either. I'll be back tomorrow morning to take another look at him."

Mario slept peacefully into the night. But Arianna, in her nearby room, couldn't fall asleep. She didn't believe that Mario had recovered from that strange fit of madness. She didn't believe that it had been a delirium, as the doctor said. But she couldn't go beyond those thoughts. Comprehending mystery was beyond the capacity of her modest spirit. She didn't know what to think, but suffered torments of anguish. She turned again and again in bed, and at each turn recalled the terrifying events of the afternoon. She reexamined their every detail from the moment she first saw Mario motionless under the pine trees, bent forward a little, with his head in the sun, totally absorbed by something on the ground. Sunstroke, that's it! Stupid Elena, to have exposed him like that! But it's not sunstroke. When I got there he was leaning against the tree. I went around behind him. It was me. I frightened him. Maybe it was that instant of fright that made him sick. Oh, Lord, I'm the one who made Mario.…

Instantly, Arianna was up, sitting at the edge of the bed and staring into the darkness with her eyes wide open. So wide that she felt as if they were shooting forth light. The sensation sickened her. But suddenly she understood that what happened wasn't her fault. Mario hadn't become ill from fright. She tried to recall the doctor's reassuring words. She decided she was clear-headed now, and though it frightened her to do so, she began to think again about the moment she'd arrived at that park. Mario is sitting there against the tree in the shade with his head slightly forward. I tip toe around behind him. Then, suddenly, I put my hands around his little head and over his eyes. I say, "Guess who?" But he doesn't move right away. It's only afterward that he reacts so violently.

The darkness about Arianna was filled with tiny gleaming atoms that spun about like planets and extinguished themselves in the corners of her weary eyes. She could hear the sound of Mario's quiet breathing from his room.

Just before dawn she fell asleep. Immediately she was caught up in a languid, dolorous dream. She is traveling in a slow moving train that jolts constantly—opposite her is Mariano Parigi, and on her lap Mario, still an infant. The unending jolts carry the train onto a road between stone walls, where a gray atmosphere weighs ever more heavily on Arianna and on the child she is clutching to her breast. Then a more powerful jolt causes her to drop the boy at her left side, the side near her heart, and he falls beneath her body. Moaning, she struggles to move, but can't. Terrified of suffocating the baby, she tries to scream and can't do that either.

Although Arianna awoke at this point, she couldn't escape the nightmare of helplessness, for no sooner did she turn to her other side than it was upon her again.

Because her imagination is limited, her husband is still there. He looks at her with his air of superiority. She feels ashamed and trembles. She cannot take her eyes from his, which grow ever larger, until only they exist in the gray world. As a result she cannot look down at the child, who is once again in her arms. But is he really still there? She cannot be sure. She feels a weight in her arms, but cannot move them. She is afraid they are empty, but cannot look down, cannot make herself look away from those proud, scornful eyes fixed on her. Will she ever know if the child is still in her arms?

Then Arianna manages to speak in her sleep, to mumble something. She knows she is mumbling, speaking, not understanding the words. She listens to her voice carefully, trying to catch the meaning, and instantly she understands and shudders. She understands and a moan escapes from the side of her mouth, from the very mouth that has been mumbling over and over, "I'm not your mother. I'm not your…"

In her dream Arianna frantically jams her fist into her mouth to keep herself from speaking the loathsome words, and imagines she's awake. She is about to sigh with relief when icy terror seizes her again. There in the furthest corner of her room the darkness has taken the form of a pine tree, an evil, cursed pine tree. Beyond it is its shadow, which speaks to Arianna and says, "Why do you call him Mario? Don't you know his name is not Mario?"

Arianna's body heaves and she screams like a beast in labor. She thinks she is awake, but she is sleeping and dreaming. She thinks she is dreaming, but now she is awake, sitting up in bed, her face ashen in the light which begins to filter through the window frame.

She had slept for four minutes.

Now fully awake, she remained still for a moment with her head raised and her attention strained, because it seemed to her that she no longer heard Mario breathing. Then she jumped up, ran to his room and bent over his small bed. He was sleeping soundly and breathing as quietly and regularly as the calm sea at dawn.

Several hours later Mario awoke smiling.

"Are you all right, darling?" Arianna tried to peer into the depths of his being.

"I'm fine," he answered simply.

"You weren't so well yesterday," said the doctor from the doorway.

Mario hadn't seen him. He turned toward him now and looked at him intently, but said nothing.

"I'll be in the study with Mariano," the doctor told Arianna and left the room.

Arianna waited for the boy to get out of bed. She went with him to the bathroom, then began to help him get dressed.

While he was putting on his second shoe Mario suddenly stopped and looked up at his mother. She caught her breath.

"I'm very hungry," he said, and Arianna breathed again.

Watching him eat calmly and with a hearty appetite, she forgot her fears. They joined the men in the study. Mariano was in a good mood.

"Mario, kiss papa good-bye, I'll be away for over a week. What would you like me to bring you from Zurich?"

Mario looked at his father, then laughed, but didn't answer.

"All right, you think about it and write to me. Are you leaving too, doctor? Come along with me to the station."

The two men embraced the child and left.

Mario was leaning against the entrance to the veranda, looking out toward the sun when Arianna, having accompanied the men to the door, reentered the room. She walked toward him. "Mario, I told Elena to give you the day off from lessons. Isn't that nice? Would you like to go with me for a walk to the Villa Borghese instead of doing lessons?"

The child turned to her, then looked at the doorway for a moment before turning back to her and speaking. "Look," he said, his voice serious and confidential, "I waited for them to leave because I don't understand what they're saying to me. But now, will you take me there, to my house?"

A veil of darkness suddenly dropped before Arianna's eyes. She grasped the arm of a chair to support herself and stood rigidly. When her vision cleared she found herself staring into her son's face, and saw that it had become hostile.

Still standing stiffly and controlling her every nerve lest she fall completely apart, she said, "Yes. Wait for me."

She managed to leave the room, but once out of it had to stop a moment to try to understand what was happening to her. Whatever it was, she vowed to follow the will of destiny no matter where it led. In quick succession she ordered a carriage, dressed and returned to the room.

"Darling," she called out, not wanting to hear her son tell her not to call him Mario again, "We can go now."

In the carriage she asked him, "Via del Muro Nuovo?"

"Yes, eighteen."

She repeated the entire address to the driver.

"I don't know where that is," he answered.

When he looked the street up in his directory, it wasn't listed.

Arianna was caught between hope and despair. She turned a frightened look at Mario, who had heard the conversation. He responded as though recalling a memory. "It's on the other side of the river. You pass a piazza, it's pretty big, and there's a kind of castle near there…it's piazza…wait a minute, it's in Trastevere… Piazza…"

"Trastevere," Arianna ordered the coachman.

They traveled in silence. Arianna didn't dare look at her son. Mario turned his head this way and that, going down the via Veneto as if he'd never seen it before. At the bottom of the hill, Arianna looked at him somewhat timidly and began, "Listen, Mar…listen, darling."

The boy interrupted her. "You can call me Mario if you like. It's enough that we're going to my mother's house."

Arianna could no longer utter a sound.

They had already descended almost the entire Tritone when Mario spoke again. "What were you going to say?"

Arianna's eyes were puffed and dry. She shook her head. "I don't remember anymore. Let's just go on."

Having crossed the center of the city, the carriage plunged into the streets behind piazza Montecitoria. Passing the Pantheon, Arianna, whose face was as white as paper, bent to the child and in a choked voice asked, "Then who am I?"

The boy looked at her for a moment and frowned. His brow cleared and he said simply, "I don't know."

They were silent again for a long time. But for Arianna, time no longer existed. When they reached the end of via Torre Argentina, Mario suddenly shouted with joy. "I remember. It's called piazza d'Italia."

Arianna asked the driver, "Is there a piazza d'Italia?"

"Yes, just past the Garibaldi bridge in Trastevere."

In all his seven years, Arianna thought, I've never left Mario alone for a day. We've only been in Rome one year. Until this very minute, I didn't even know piazza d'Italia existed, and I'm sure he's never been in this part of the city either. But there is a piazza d'Italia and it's in Trastevere. How did he know that? I'm going mad.

When they passed via Arenula and were facing the bridge, Mario was seized by a kind of joyous restlessness. "Down there. Down there," he shouted, "that's piazza d'Italia." He was pointing to a kind of red castle that had become visible on the other side of the bridge. That's what he described, thought Arianna, a kind of castle. I'm going to die.

In the few minutes that it took them to reach the piazza, Arianna was possessed by both hope and dread. She prayed that Mario was mistaken, that the address he had given wouldn't be found, and that all of this had come from some strange dream of his. At the same time, she was terrified to think of how a disappointment might crush him. And then, like a knife, there's that strange fact that Mario knows about this part of the city and the names of its streets even though he's never been here, and we don't know anyone from here, and no one ever told us about it.

Not only did Mario know the name of piazza d'Italia, which was just before them now, but he was looking all around him with warmth and certainty, as if at familiar sights.

And he was very happy. He stood up in the carriage and pointed to the right, toward the head of a street. "That way," he said.

"That way," repeated Arianna.

When the carriage reached that corner, the driver slowed and continued straight ahead.

"Turn, turn," shouted Mario impatiently.

There was a newspaper stand a little further on. The driver drove till he reached it. "Where's via del Muro Nuovo?" he asked the vendor.

"Never heard of it," was the answer. "Not likely around here."

"Yes, it is," said Mario, looking past the man. "It's that one. And number eighteen is where I live."

But the driver, having turned the corner, held up his whip to the street sign. Mario and Arianna read:

VIA GUSTAVO MODENA

Mario was silent. Arianna's face was red when she looked at him. The driver also turned to the boy. Below them the newspaper vendor was smiling. Mario's eyes were as wide as if he were beholding a miracle. "They're crazy. This is it," he insisted.

For the first time Arianna was convinced that her son had taken leave of his senses. He was still standing. She put her arm around his waist and, looking into his eyes as though to reach his soul, spoke softly.

"Mario, look, it's a mistake. You were never here in this part of the city, ever. This isn't the street you say it is. It just seems that way to you. Let's go home. You don't live here. Can't you see that there's no house like the one you're looking for? Listen to me...."

Mario interrupted her resolutely.

"That's it. That's the street. Let's take it. Let's go to number eighteen. I'll show you my house is there."

Arianna was in terror of letting him face further disillusionment. To see Mario sink ever deeper into fantasies was breaking her heart.

"Let's go," the boy repeated imperiously.

"All right," Arianna sighed.

The carriage turned the corner slowly and stopped. All of them looked up again at the implacable street sign.

VIA GUSTAVO MODENA

Mario was calm now. "It's wrong," he said. "This is via del Muro Nuovo, my street. Why don't we just go to number eighteen?"

Arianna still had her arm around him. At that moment a man with his hands in his pockets stepped out of a corner shop and looked up at them with curiosity. The driver stopped the carriage. "Is there a via del Muro Nuovo around here?" he asked.

"Via del Muro Nuovo?"

Arianna's heart was pounding.

"Via del Muro Nuovo," the man repeated quietly. "It's this one. That's what it used to be called. They changed the name two years ago."

Now Arianna tightened her grip around the boy not so much to hold him as to keep herself from falling. A great cloud closed around her head. She could no longer see anything. Through a buzzing that seemed to come from an infinite distance, she heard her son's voice.

"You see? Let's go. Let's go to number eighteen."

And from that same great distance she heard him clap his hands together and felt his body quivering. She heard the wheels begin turning on the pavement, then was enveloped in darkness and heard nothing more. When she opened her eyes again and raised her head, the carriage had stopped in front of number eighteen.

2 DESCENDING FROM THE CARRIAGE, she told the driver, "Wait for me." The concierge's door was locked, and while Arianna tried to locate someone, Mario became restless. "What do you need the concierge for?" he asked. "There's a staircase over there. We're on the third floor."

Mounting the stairs, Mario turned every so often to look back at Arianna. The climb was exhausting her. When they reached the first landing Mario said, "Don't bother to ring the bell that turns, just the electric one that mamma had them put in. She said the other one annoyed her, so they fixed it so it doesn't ring inside anymore."

When they reached the third floor Arianna saw the two bells. While she hesitated before them in confusion, Mario stood up on his toes and pressed one.

The sound of the bell roused Arianna from the torpor into which she had been sinking, but the silence that followed the ring frightened her. She felt as if she might fall into it, and she stepped back from the door as if from the edge of a precipice.

Mario, who was jumping up and down breathlessly, wanted to ring the bell again, but his mother restrained him.

From the mysterious depths beyond the door they heard distant footsteps approaching.

"Someone's coming," Mario shouted.

The steps became the dragging of slippers. Then they heard the sound of two locks turning and a deep rumble. Finally, the door opened and before them on the threshold stood an old woman wearing a kerchief tied under her chin.

Mario was stunned. "Who's she?" he whispered to his mother.

The old woman looked at them suspiciously.

Arianna put her hand on Mario's head. It was an effort for her to speak. "Is the signora in?" she asked.

"No."

Mario seemed ever more amazed. A long line was furrowing his brow.

"She's not here?"

"She left yesterday."

Arianna's voice pleaded. "I have a favor to ask of you," she began, then stopped. Regaining her courage, she reached into her handbag and took out some bills. She hesitated again, but the old woman had already extended her own hand.

"Here you are," Arianna said. "Could you please let us come in for a moment. I need to speak to you." The old woman stepped aside. Arianna entered and sat down on a low chest. Mario entered behind her. His face was glowing.

"Why don't we go back there?" he shouted and ran toward the doorway that led to an inner room. The door was open, but the room beyond it was dark. He stopped at the threshold.

"Where are you going, little boy?" the old woman shouted at him.

The expression on her face frightened the child and filled his mind with uncertainties. He frowned.

"Wait a minute, Mario. I have to speak to this lady for a few minutes first."

Mario leaned against the door post and, staring into the room, tried to pierce the shadows before him.

Arianna took the opportunity to draw close to the old woman and spoke to her in a rapid whisper. "Please," she said, "do me a favor. Help me. My son has gotten a strange idea in his head.

He thinks that his mother may live here. I beg you to let him take a look around. It sounds a little crazy, and I don't understand it myself. But help me prove to him, make him see...."

The old woman thought for a moment, then grumbled, "The lady was here yesterday. It's the day she comes every year. She left last night."

"Is she coming back soon?"

"Next year."

Arianna began to feel confused, as if she couldn't go on. She looked anxiously at Mario's back. The old woman followed her glance, then turned back to her and said somewhat aloofly, "All right. Go in. But wait till I open the window."

Mario moved aside to let the woman enter. She walked past him through the darkness, pulled aside the curtain and opened a glass door and its shutter. The room filled with light.

"Look, look," Mario shouted, clapping his hands.

It was a small cozy sitting room, well furnished with fabrics and cushions.

Mario turned to his mother who had remained in the doorway and, taking her by the hand almost like a host, urged her. "Come, take a look in here. All my notebooks are inside it. Now that I've recovered, I'll go back to school."

"Recovered?"

Mario had pulled her toward a cabinet. "Oh, it's locked. Then come over here. And look at that. That's my mother."

He was pointing to a portrait hung on the wall above the cabinet. It was a large pastel of a young woman with thick, dark hair parted gently into two bands coiled over her ears. Her eyes were large and blue, her face pale.

Mario addressed the old woman in a quiet voice, not daring to look at her. "When is mamma coming back?"

The old woman hesitated for a moment. Then instead of answering him she said, "I'll open the other room too."

As the two followed her, Mario explained to Arianna, "That's our bedroom."

Inside the room there was a large bed and beyond it a smaller one. Both were covered by heavy spreads.

"See how nicely my bed is made up now that I'm better? And my mother sleeps in this one. Oh, look, do you recognize him?"

Following Mario's gaze, Arianna turned to a photo on a night table next to the large bed. She leaned forward a moment to look at it, turned pale, shrieked and fainted.

The old woman barely had time to catch her. Though she'd lost consciousness, Arianna still held the hand of the now terrified boy. The old woman managed to get Arianna onto the bed. "Just a minute, just a minute. Oh my God," she said, and ran from the room.

Almost immediately the woman returned with a glass of water and began sprinkling it on Arianna's face.

Very slowly Arianna opened her eyes and relaxed her grip on Mario's hand. The old woman and the boy tried to make her more comfortable. Arianna raised her head and looked around, still unaware of where she was. When the color returned to her face, she suddenly grasped Mario's hand again.

Though she had recovered physically, her mind was still clouded. But soon the clouds began lifting and memories of the previous day and night returned. Then, tumbling one after another, she recalled the events of that morning: the strange carriage ride, the arrival at the house, the entry into that room, and last of all...

At this point Arianna closed her eyes tightly to gather courage enough to reopen them and take a second look.

She was hoping that she had been mistaken, dreaming or even hallucinating.

She wanted to be strong in order to be able to see clearly, to face the truth.

When she felt certain she could do so, she sat up at the edge of the bed and collected herself once again. Then slowly she turned her head. This time she didn't scream. She just sat staring at it. There before her on the night table, framed in silver, was a photograph of Mario.

It pleased the boy to see Arianna looking at his picture. "I had a sailor suit then, but these clothes fit me better."

Regarding his image with pleasure, he added, "Maybe I grew while I was sick."

He waited a moment, then with a look of surprise took her hand and asked, "Why don't you say something?"

Arianna roused herself. She looked away from the photograph to the child.

Once again it took an enormous effort of will for her to remain composed. She was walking through shadows. Once more she resolved to follow the way until the very end, no matter the cost. "Show me some other things," she said to the boy.

"Yes, sure," Mario responded happily. "Let's go see if my horse is still all right. If it is, we'll take it out on the terrace."

Behind her, Arianna heard a kind of sigh, almost a moan. The old woman was standing in the doorway watching the boy with a stunned expression on her face. Though Arianna couldn't speak because Mario was pulling her forward, she managed to signal the woman to remain silent and to wait for her.

Mario pulled her toward a large curtain that hung before an alcove in the corner of the room and drew the curtain back.

"Aren't they wonderful! Look at them all."

There were two large sets of shelves filled with toys of every description—trumpets, locomotives, sailboats, and boxes of all sizes. There was a half-completed structure of colored blocks; there were guns, puppets, regiments of tin soldiers, all of them brilliant, breathing, ready. In front of the shelves stood a pram, two very large puppets and the cherished rocking horse. It was dappled gray with a hard nose and small ears that stood straight up.

"Later we'll look at everything one at a time," Mario went on, "but now help me get the horse outside."

Though barely touched, the horse began rocking back and forth as though in agreement. Without awaiting Arianna's assistance, Mario grabbed it by the nose. Paying no heed to the now trembling old woman who stepped back to allow him to pass, he dragged the horse across the living room to the glass doors.

Arianna helped him open the second door and shutters, and they stepped out into the sunshine. The view was a jumble of other terraces, patches of white wall, balcony railings, a piece of sky, and the corners of red roofs.

No sooner had Mario gotten the horse outside than he was struck by another thought. "Where can the cat be?"

He looked around. It was midday. Every terrace, every window, every balcony was deserted.

Then he reassured Arianna. "He's always going off, but then he always comes back."

"Call him," Arianna said, "and stay out here with your horse for a little while. I have to talk to the lady. You'll wait for me here, all right?"

"All right," Mario agreed.

While Mario set out on his horseback ride, Arianna hurried inside. She found the old woman, who was still trembling.

"What's the matter?" Arianna asked her.

"I don't know. I don't know. You're the one who has to tell me."

"What can I tell you? I know less than you do. I must see the signora. Where is she?"

"At the seashore. She spends the whole year there."

"Is it far?"

"No. It's just before you get to Terracina. Here's the address."

She shuffled over to a large chest of drawers and from the corner of the mirror above it, withdrew a small card. It read:

Luciana Veracina
San Felice Circeo

"She's always there?"

"For the past seven years. Everybody around here can tell you her story. She lived here with her little boy. The boy died and she went to live there at a hotel. She wanted to keep this place like it was, so I stay here. I've been here ever since. I keep everything clean, but no one ever comes here, except the signora. Once a year on the day the boy died she comes back. Yesterday it was seven years. Then she locks herself in that room. She's never missed once. She leaves at night and doesn't come back until the next year."

Arianna was leaning one hand on the marble surface of the chest, crumpling Luciana's address in the other. She heard a buzzing in her head and ignored it. She was drained. All these occurrences surpassed her comprehension, were far more powerful than she.

The two women were silent, each awaiting some glimmer of light from the other.

Finally the old woman spoke. "She left me her address so I can write to her. I get the concierge or someone else to do it when I have to, because I don't know how. Do you want me to find somebody right away?"

Arianna stared in bewilderment for a moment. At last the question penetrated her brain, and rushed down to her heart where something within her, something completely beyond control, made her shout, "No!"

The look on her face combined with the force of her outburst frightened the old woman, who sought to calm her. "All right, no," she repeated. "Don't get so upset."

43

But Arianna had already regained control of herself. She spoke in a low voice. "Maybe we don't have to. It probably was just a case of sunstroke. I don't know what it could have been. I can't even remember. Don't say anything."

"All right."

Arianna seized the old woman's hand and looked pleadingly at her. "Nothing. Don't say anything to anyone. I'll think about it." Her expression was humble, her words ingratiating, and she had no idea how tightly she was gripping the old woman's hand.

The woman disengaged herself and repeated, "Don't worry. I won't. I won't."

There was another silence. Then Arianna suddenly stood up and rushed out to the terrace. The old woman followed her and stopped once more in the doorway.

"Did you have fun? Come along now. We're going...we're going to have lunch. Come along with me."

Mario was piling up bricks in a corner of the terrace. He turned quickly, his face filled with alarm. "Aren't we waiting for mamma?"

Arianna put her arm around his waist and picked him up. "We can't. Your mo... No, darling, she's far away. She can't come. She's not coming back for a long time. Come with me. Come along."

She had gotten him inside, but he let out a shriek and was kicking so hard that she almost fell. When he went on writhing she had to put him down, whereupon he leaped away and screamed, "No, I want my mother. You go away. I want to wait for her here. It's not true she's not coming back for a long time. Tell that woman that my mamma is coming back right away and I have to wait here for her."

The old woman looked at Arianna, but remained silent. Arianna started walking toward the boy again. This time he didn't shout but backed himself to a wall, threw himself to the floor, and whimpered like a beaten dog.

Arianna rushed to him. The old women did too. Together they lifted him up.

Exhausted, he let them, but the eyes he turned on Arianna were dark and angry. The enormous grief of seeing him in such a state was more than Arianna could bear. Impulsively, she reassured him. "Yes, darling, we'll write to your...to your ...mother telling her to come—that you're waiting for her. You'll write to her today, won't you?"

"Yes," the old woman said. "Immediately."

"In fact, send her a telegram."

"A telegram."

"Say that she must come immediately. All right, darling?"

Mario studied Arianna's face and sensed that the two women were sincere. His gaze became clearer. "All right," he said.

"Do you think she'll get here by tomorrow?" Arianna asked the old woman. "Possibly in the morning?"

"If she wants to, she can even come back tonight," was the answer. "The train she usually takes leaves there at six-thirty. It gets here around nine, nine-thirty at the latest."

As she prepared to leave, Arianna told the old woman, "Then you will tell her we'll be back tomorrow morning... "

A shout from Mario interrupted her. "No."

"What's the matter? Oh God, darling..."

"No, no! Why tomorrow if she's coming tonight? You're wicked, mean!"

Frightened again, Arianna gave up all hope of delay. She spoke quickly and resolutely.

"Yes, of course, you're right. Tonight. We'll come back tonight. Send the telegram immediately. Darling, you can come back later. You can come back. But for now, it would be better if you came home...to my house. And then this evening we'll come back here when...your mother gets here."

Mario thought for a moment, then agreed.

Before leaving, Arianna asked the old woman her name.

"Angelica, "she replied.

Reaching for Arianna's hand to show her that his faith in her was restored. Mario suddenly called out, "Wait a minute. Let's look in that box up there. It's always full of chocolate."

He couldn't reach it. Arianna took the box down. It was empty.

"That's too bad because I wanted to give you one," the boy said. "But when we go out we'll stop at Giacomo's and get some there."

"Who's Giacomo?" asked Arianna as they left the apartment and began down the stairs.

"He's the grocer near here. Augusto's father. Oh, I want to see Augusto and tell him I'm back."

"Augusto?"

"He's a boy, no, he's a little kid. He's my age, seven, so I can call him a kid, right?"

"Of course."

"He always comes to play on the terrace with me. It's been a while now since he's come. Since I got sick. But I'll tell him he can come again."

They were out on the street. Arianna was about to enter the waiting carriage, when Mario held her back. "The store's over there."

He pointed to a shop a few steps away in an adjacent street. Exhausted, Arianna somehow summoned up enough energy to tell the coachman to follow them, and walked meekly behind Mario.

They entered the shop Mario had pointed out. A distracted looking boy of fourteen or fifteen was behind the counter.

Mario asked him, "Is Augusto here?"

The boy looked at him as though dumbstruck. Then his mouth opened and after a few seconds he said, "I'm Augusto."

Mario laughed, "No, no. Another Augusto."

"Which other one?"

"Augusto, who's smaller, like me. Giacomo's son."

"But...I'm Giacomo's son."

Mario looked at his mother as though to say this boy is a fool. Arianna, quivering with impatience to be home alone with Mario, and to try to untangle the web of confusion spun by these strange events, felt as if she were walking through fire.

"I'd like some chocolates," she said.

Augusto opened his mouth again, then got the tin of chocolates and weighed them out slowly. Arianna placed a bill on the counter but Augusto was not yet permitted to take money. Turning toward the back of the store, he called out, "Papa!"

A curtain parted and a small, bearded man holding eyeglasses in his hand appeared.

"Oh, signor Giacomo," Mario exclaimed.

Signor Giacomo squinted, then carefully set his glasses on his eyes and took a few steps forward.

He stopped short, raised his hands and began to shout, "But...!"

He could neither breathe, nor speak, nor move, but remained leaning forward like someone possessed.

"I was sick. You knew it, signor Giacomo? Where's Augusto?"

The gray-faced man didn't answer, but his arms, still over his head, began trembling horribly. And from his mouth, bit by bit, the following words emerged, "The son of...the son of...of signora Luciana...oh no!"

His terror, which frightened Mario, frightened Arianna still more. Seizing the boy by the arm she called out, "Come on, come."

Mario permitted himself be led from the shop and placed into the waiting carriage. While Arianna stammered out her address on via Abruzzi, Mario felt confused and hurt, as though a dark problem lay before him. Then he tired of thinking about it. "Signor Giacomo must have lost his mind," he said to Arianna. "And who knows where Augusto is? I don't understand it."

Arianna took him in her arms. The anxieties lodged in Mario's heart made the embrace of this woman who was protecting him feel sweet. They drove along in silence. Arianna felt tears streaming down her cheeks but did nothing to dry them. Her mind seethed. Her soul was shattered.

After a while she realized that Mario was speaking to her. She strained to understand him. "You didn't tell me whether you like my house," he said.

Her voice was ghostly. "Yes, I like it."

"Did you see the picture of my mother? Did you see how pretty she is? But really she's even prettier. You'll see this evening."

"This evening." Arianna bent toward him and peered into his eyes as one peers into the night and whispered, "And your father?"

Mario answered quietly. "I don't remember my father. He must have died when I was very little."

Slowly, the carriage climbed via Tritone. With Mario half asleep in her arms, Arianna felt an enormous fatigue. It was lucky Mariano was away, for as soon as she got home, she thought she'd lie down in bed with her son in her arms and they would fall asleep together. Afterward, toward evening, they would awake in each other's arms and neither would remember anything about this insane afternoon.

At that very moment, old Angelica, having reclosed the windows and put the house in order once again, was wondering who to ask to write the telegram to signora Luciana Veracina at San Felice Circeo.

3 LUCIANA VERACINA WASN'T HER real name. Her own, much less melodious and not Italian, was a name she had decided to bury in oblivion at the age of twenty-one, when she believed she was beginning a new life and breaking all ties with her unhappily interrupted youth.

She was born to an Austrian gentleman named Frederico Stirner who, while visiting Naples, became acquainted with a Neapolitan woman and fathered the little girl. Then, presumably because Stirner felt himself more inclined to the role of parent than that of lover, he deserted the woman and took the child, who had been named Lucia, back to Austria with him.

Lucia Stirner was raised in comfortable surroundings and received little attention in her childhood. Her adolescence was an interminable string of days, weeks, months, years, spent almost all alone in the huge rooms of the Stirner apartment on the Herrengasse, during which she read anything she could get her hands on, or played the violin which she was studying with Professor Hellmesberger. Occasionally her father took her out evenings to the theater, to melodramas and to the more spectacular balls at the Opera. Her romantic and imaginative inclinations were thus allowed to develop without encumbrance.

When she was eighteen her father died, leaving her a substantial income. Shortly afterward Lucia took a lover, whom she tortured for almost three years with the workings of her restless imagination, her insane jealousies, and her need to dramatize everything. He bore the brunt of her long deprivation of close contact with other people. Her upbringing and temperament had equipped her only to be entirely submissive or in chaotic control. Since Giorgio was young and gentle, it was she who dominated him. Their love affair was a series of furious battles and reconciliations from which she derived ever greater strength and which weakened him a little more every day. Occasionally they would run off on sudden, impulsive journeys. Lucia led him on, quenching his love for her and for life itself, yet managing with precisely timed outbursts of despair and floods of tears to keep him from freeing himself. During the summer of 1885 they visited Italy. Rome thrilled her. Giorgio was at the limits of his suffering.

One day they walked along the Pontine marshes all the way to Terracina, and from there the following morning they went to see the promontory that ancient navigators believed was an island, the one on which Circe grew her roses and maintained her hospitable residence.

Just below the village of San Felice Circeo they climbed to the very top of a cliff that overlooked the sea. Pressing close to her lover, Lucia stared out for a long time, then said, "When you leave me, I'll come back here and jump off this rock."

They returned to Rome later that day, spent two hours of the evening engaged in one of their customary noisy quarrels, shed some tears, then went to sleep.

When she awoke late the following morning Lucia found herself alone. There was a note on Giorgio's side of the bed—a farewell note. It sounded final. Giorgio had left her. He hadn't even taken his things along, so as not to impede his flight. The end of this letter was mysterious. It read: "Don't bother about anything else, because I'm taking care of it."

Lucia didn't try to understand what that sentence meant, nor did she hesitate in the slightest about what to do next. She recalled her vow of the previous day. There was nothing for her to do but fulfill it. She left the hotel as though she were going for a walk and hurried to the railroad station to await the first train to Terracina. From there she took a carriage to San Felice Circeo.

When she reached the small town she found it in a complete uproar. An unknown man had arrived there that morning and jumped off a cliff into the sea. His body had just been recovered. Lucia raced down to the shore and recognized the dead man as Giorgio.

The blow was so enormous that she wasn't even concerned when several weeks later she discovered she was pregnant. She spent the following two months in a kind of torpor, then took permanent lodgings in Rome at 18 via del Muro Nuovo, where she settled down to wait.

During that period she slowly pieced together designs for her future life. She resumed playing the violin, which she had neglected during the three years of her love affair, and decided to become a great violinist. The first thing she did was to choose a stage name, Luciana Veracina, to honor Francesco Maria Veracini, the composer whose heavenly sonatas she had studied with Hellmesberger. And immediately upon taking the name she was certain she had erased her past life.

She didn't spend as much time studying as she spent absorbed in long, airy fantasies of her future life as an artist. Sometimes she imagined a triumph in one of the great concert halls of Berlin or Paris. A life of anonymity and sacrifice appealed to her and she saw herself performing in a gypsy orchestra at a hillside café along the Buda. Or she was on the high seas, on the deck of a transatlantic liner, holding both passengers and crew in thrall to her virtuosity, as sea gulls flew overhead.

Her unborn child didn't play much of a role in her fantasies. Nor did she think of love anymore. Like many quick-tempered women she was not very sensual and didn't take other lovers. Her brief past was rich enough in romance to completely satisfy all her emotional needs and to feed her inner life.

It was only after the child was born in Rome in the spring of 1886 that she found herself overwhelmed with a frantic love for the creature she had awaited with a kind of indifference.

She would spend her days and nights looking at him, dressing and undressing him. She washed him thirty times a day. She set him on every arm chair, carpet and cushion in the house to see him against every background and in every possible light. Sometimes she would wake him in the middle of the night, distraught because she couldn't recall the exact shade of his eyes. She nursed him herself and named him Ramiro.

Soon Ramiro began uttering his first sounds. He would stand up in his crib babbling, murmuring and twittering streams of sweet and happy sounds, from which bright clear syllables would detach themselves, rise in the air toward the window and take off in joyous flight. Luciana, in constant ecstasy, spent hours listening to him with a pen in her hand, trying to capture and record those sounds in a notebook.

Sometimes when he would begin to cry she would take her violin, stand in front of him and play. She played whatever came to mind—fragments of studies, impromptu passages, snatches of melody which rose to memory after almost five years in oblivion. Then the baby would scream and she would compete with his screams by prying higher and higher sounds out of the violin. Ramiro would get louder. She'd get shriller, until their sounds penetrated the very walls of the apartment. She was certain they were playing a game that was enormously entertaining to the child.

Luciana Veracina never stopped dreaming of an ever more vague, unreal and unattainable future. She built and rebuilt her dreams as one builds a house of cards, without believing in its substance for even one moment. She began a search for books and mementos of the great Veracini, having forgotten that it was a name she herself had selected. She was happily anticipating the discovery of some relationship between herself and the Florentine musician, some connection between his birth and her own, when she suddenly recalled—and it felt as if a vulgar lout had hit her in the face—that an unknown Neapolitan woman had conceived Lucia Stirner, thanks to an Austrian tourist. Nevertheless, the following day she began her search again. Finally there came a moment in which that insulting memory completely infuriated her and she took up her violin, ripped its strings from their pegs, and hung the instrument on the living room wall next to the old faded photo of Hellmesberger. She was careful, however, to arrange the four strands of broken string so that they drooped attractively like the branches of a mournful willow. Ramiro was just over a year old. It was the day he took his first step.

He lurched forward, staggered, and laughing wildly fell into his mother's arms. Lucia saw some kind of strange, puerile symbolism in that coincidence and, taking the child in her arms, raised him high toward the crucified fiddle.

Ramiro spend his first years in coddled solitude. Until he was six he knew only his mother. His greatest pleasure was to accompany her to dressmakers and milliners, and to watch as she chose hats and dresses from all she tried on. Luciana never had a new outfit made for herself without having one made for Ramiro at the same time, and she took particular care in combining the colors and fabrics of their garments.

Ramiro was a sweet and intelligent child. His forehead was wide, somewhat protruding and filled with shadows. Luciana had a tutor come to the house for the boy. Over the years she also acquired a number of useless books on the subject of raising children. The boy was six when, perhaps as a consequence of reading one of them, she decided that it would be harmful for him to remain so isolated from other children of his age. She introduced him to her neighbors' children, and when she sent him out into the street to play with these ordinary boys and girls she would spend hours at a time watching him from behind the shutters. When he was nearly seven years old Ramiro became ill with pleurisy. Luciana nursed him for ten days, but he died on the eleventh day—at two in the afternoon, on the seventh of May.

Luciana didn't cry.

On returning home from his funeral she locked herself in her apartment for twenty-four hours. Her neighbors had begun whispering worriedly to each other and one of them had climbed up to her floor, and was still trying to decide whether to knock at her door, when she stepped out, silent and veiled. No one dared address her. After a few hours, she returned in a carriage, accompanied by a servant woman to whom she entrusted the apartment, having arranged for the woman to live there on the condition that she not permit anyone else to enter until she herself, Luciana, returned. Then she had the trunks and valises she had previously packed taken down, and she left.

The old housekeeper's name was Angelica. After a few days Angelica received a short letter from Luciana which contained some instructions and the following address:

Luciana Veracina
San Felice Circeo

Thereafter her agreed-upon wages arrived punctually every month. Luciana returned a year later, on the sixth of May, the eve of the first anniversary of Ramiro's death. She spent all of the following day shut in the room in which Ramiro had died, and departed again that evening without having uttered more then ten words to Angelica. The next year she came back on the same date, and as before left after twenty-four hours. And so on, for seven years.

She spent those seven years in the most extraordinary solitude. She'd arranged to take two rooms in a tiny inn below Circe's promontory, at the bottom of a hill, which dropped precipitously from the town of San Felice Circeo. From one of her windows she could see Terracina, dazzlingly white, watched over by absurdly blunt Mount Pisco, itself topped by the arcaded Temple of Jupiter, behind which lay an ominous wall of red and white stones. From another window she could with one glance take in the entire Tyrrhenian sea. In the distance were the Pontine Islands and beyond them the ghostly shapes of Procida and Ischia. On the clearest of mornings, perhaps two or three times a year, a wisp of smoke would rise from one of these and dissipate slowly in the blue sky. All summer long the sea and sky formed a huge vault of intoxicating, motionless blue. The infinite heat of the sun pressed heavily upon the earth immobilizing everything —the surface of the sea, the leaves of the trees, the peaks and edges of the reefs, the margin of sea and sand, and the figure of Luciana, seated bareheaded on the beach. Winters, from behind her windows, Luciana watched that same world of sea and sky smash itself to bits. Reefs and crags shrieked in the gale winds and screamed at the assault of the sea as it came roaring forward in long, high waves that broke against the face of the cliffs. Nights, in her sleep, Luciana felt herself surrounded by a constant flow of music reaching her from the ends of the earth.

Every day, summer and winter, she would walk out to gaze at that cliff—so immutable beneath sun and storm—from which her lover had jumped after leaving her. The cliff from which she herself should have leapt.

It rose from the water's edge just past a structure known as the Astura tower. The tower is still there. The cliff was destroyed, as we shall see later. It was high and long, flat at its crest, and black. The cliff seemed to be a distant shadow of the tower. At low tide, two or three large stones were enough to form a walk-

way from the sea to the bottom of the cliff. From there it was
easy to climb the steps which had been cut into the cliffside to
the land above. Luciana had climbed them only once, with
Giorgio, that day of her oath. Now almost every time she reached
the tower she would look toward the wall of the cliff, perhaps to
reassure herself that it was still there ready to receive her.

Every once in a while she would arrange to go to Terracina
by carriage. Two or three times she ventured as far as Naples
by train, but she never managed to believe that she had been
born there. Often she would have someone take her out in a
rowboat, particularly on spring mornings at dawn when it was
coldest.

Thus all of Luciana's hours and years went by. Every day
was filled with memories of her entire life: her long, lonely childhood wandering the rooms on the Herrengasse, her three year
love affair as seething and furious as the Tyrrhenian sea, and
the seven years of her motherhood, every detail of it up to the
absurd day of Ramiro's death. And here Luciana has to stop. For
the memory of Ramiro lying still in his small bed, and all the
memories after that—when she places him in the small casket
and they close it and take it to be buried and she throws earth
on it with her own hands—those aren't true memories. They're
stupid imaginings that never really happened. Because if they
had happened she would be dead too. And so Luciana doesn't
believe them, and therefore doesn't understand why they keep
recurring to her, why they keep happening over and over again
before her eyes. Which is why she lives through one year, five
years, seven years, as if she were merely trying to get through a
long sleepless night, and why she begins all over again, for the
hundredth time, the thousandth, the millionth to review her
entire life, while staring into the blue sea, the white sea, the
leaden sea, staring into the motionless sea, the furious sea, recalling everything from her earliest days, from the time she was

even younger than Ramiro's seven years, to the part she finds impossible to understand. She begins again, forever awaiting the day she will understand.

Luciana needs such patience in order to understand what happened at two in the afternoon on the seventh of May, 1893.

And when she does comprehend, something else will happen. She will be able to do as Giorgio did. The cliff is still there waiting for her. Neither sun nor sea can destroy it. Though other things might occur. There is nothing for her to do but to wait.

Her yearly trips to Rome on the anniversary of Ramiro's death were the mile posts, bleak as head stones, of an unnatural life in which her eyes and soul were filled with sails, spume, mist and sea birds.

On the afternoon of May 6, 1900, the eve of the seventh anniversary of Ramiro's death, Luciana departed the seashore as she'd done every year on that date. She took a carriage from San Felice Circeo to Terracina and then a train to Rome. She reached the house on via Gustavo Modena toward seven in the evening and sent Angelica away until the following evening.

As usual she spent the entire twenty-four hours of the anniversary in the room in which Ramiro had died. Then she left for San Felice to face the eighth year.

The following day, Tuesday the eighth of May, shortly after noon, she took a walk along the shore toward the Astura tower and Giorgio's cliff. She was returning by a path of fine sand. On the sea side, thick shrubs blocked any glimpse of blue. Luciana brushed past sandy, anemic poppies and low-lying vines. Then the blue reappeared. A narrow strip of pebbles separated the path from the shoreline, beyond which lay the entire sea.

Shortly thereafter Luciana abandoned the walk to cross over mounds of smooth stones. In the middle of her way, broom weed was flowering in the blazing sunlight. She brushed against the bare trunk of a telegraph pole, then returned to the path because the crunch of her footsteps on the dry grass sounded depressing to her. When she reached the side of the cliff, she didn't feel like going back to the inn and decided to walk up to the town. The climb was difficult. Luciana mounted step by step and felt a strange distress in addition to her fatigue. She had never before noticed that a group of beech trees along the opposite slope cast such a dark shadow. She had never before noticed that a house on the other side, set among low fig trees, was so white. So clearly fixed were the colors and shapes around her, that they filled her with apprehension. Looking down, she avoided crushing the small conical anthills and hurriedly kicked at the straws lying in the shape of a cross, but there were too many of them. She walked with her head up for a while so that she wouldn't see them, and began stumbling. She was panting when she stopped. "Why do I keep climbing up here?"

Certainly it made more sense, considering how tired she was, to turn around and go back down to the hotel. But she didn't. She continued on the difficult walk. A swarm of flies briefly circled her head like a turban, then flew off. She followed their flight with her eyes. They buzzed happily when they settled on a large dung heap. Beyond them an old woman was looking after a skinny pig and a child dark as a potato.

By now Luciana didn't feel like going on. When she sat down on a stone at the edge of the road, icy sweat broke out on her forehead, and a strange anxiety gripped her heart. She shut her eyes, reopened them as if she were recovering from a swoon, then little by little everything around her became still and clear. "Why?" she wondered. Suddenly it occurred to her that she didn't remember her age. She did the arithmetic. She was thirty-six. But the answer meant nothing to her. She had never even thought about it before. Youth and old age had no real meaning to Luciana. Instead, she asked herself another question. "Why was I wondering how old I am?"

Then she stopped thinking of anything. At the next moment she heard someone calling her name. She looked up and saw a man bounding down from the town. He stopped in front of her and held out something to her.

"A telegram, signora."

It was the first time she had received a telegram at San Felice Circeo, but it didn't surprise her.

She stood up, took the telegram, walked back down to the shore and then into the hotel.

Upon entering her room she locked the door and settled herself in an armchair near the window. Only then did she open the telegram.

It read: "Kindly return immediately apartment Rome. Imperative do not fail. Angelica."

Luciana didn't wonder what the message meant, nor stop to think of why it had been sent. She didn't change her clothes, but left immediately and climbed the hill to town almost at a run without any sense of fatigue. A carriage brought her to the train station in Terracina. There was still an hour and a half before the train to Rome would depart. She spent that time standing next to a water pump for the engines. At six-thirty she boarded the train.

The air between heaven and earth seemed clouded and troubled. As soon as the train left the station, Luciana saw Circeo against the sky, an island once again. For the first time she felt its mystery. Its atmosphere seemed different from every other, as though the air circling it were not really touching it, and all its surfaces were surrounded by a void. A stream of air quivered all the way up to Circeo. Clouds cast fluid, disorienting and stunning shadows upon it. Then suddenly it was twilight, brilliantly luminous on high, thickly shadowed on the ground. Luciana turned her gaze to the depressing countryside: low, sulfate-green vines, two mules, a few miserable ruins. When she looked up again Circeo had leaped ahead of her. It had elongated and now appeared flat, a dark blue ghost lying just above the horizon. The countryside had softened, and was filled with silly looking colts. A large fig tree rose up from the edge of a roiling, glittering canal.

Circeo lay far behind now. Luciana moved to the seat across so that she could continue looking as it hid behind a curtain of poplars, then reappeared fixed in place as the sun's last rays struck its rim two or three times before dying. Then the island disappeared, evaporated. Luciana rocked in a kind of half sleep. Two or three buffalo, yellow fields, other things passed by. There were jolts, glidings. She fell asleep and awoke in Rome. She took a carriage. "Via Gustavo Modena, number eighteen," she said.

4 By the time Giacomo, the old
man in the grocery store on the side
street, overcame the shock that was
almost the death of him, and managed to produce a sound,
Arianna and Mario were in the carriage which, having exited
the narrow streets, was speeding across the Garibaldi bridge
toward the other side of the city.

The sound that Giacomo finally emitted was a scream. A
primeval scream. A rising scream which in that first moment of
terror had frozen on his gray lips. By now, however, the old man
had recovered enough to want to understand what he had seen.
Having screamed, he questioned his son.

"Think carefully, Augusto, when did they come into the store?
What were their first words? Did the boy say anything?"

But his specific questions notwithstanding, Giacomo's voice
was so filled with anxiety that the best Augusto could do was to
stretch his mouth beyond all measure, and to stand that way
without speaking. This in turn rekindled the old man's fear and
once again he raised his arms as he had when he first caught
sight of Ramiro. He emitted a moan that, sinking immediately,
filtered through his gray beard, dribbled to the ground and was
absorbed into the very earth.

Only then did Augusto speak.

"What's wrong, papa?"

Giacomo responded imperiously, "Keep your mouth shut and
stay right here until I come back."

The old man hurried out of the store and began running. He was so small and slight that it appeared as if a sackful of human bones was rushing down the street pressed closely to the building walls. His tiny suspicious eyes kept turning in every direction. When he reached number 18 on via Gustavo Modena he suddenly stopped in his tracks. For at that moment Angelica, her face ashen, had come out of the doorway and was peering warily up and down the street. Seeing the terrified old man stop in front of her, she stared hard at him and asked, "What's the matter with you, Giacomo?"

"Oh Angelica, did you see him? Did you?"

"Who?"

"The boy. Luciana's son. The one who died long ago."

Angelica paused before replying.

"I didn't know her son. I began working for her after he died. But if he's been dead so many years, how can you ask me if I saw him?"

"I saw him. Not two minutes ago. With my own eyes. He came into my store. Him. Just the way he looked seven years ago when he used to come in on the way home from school to buy candy, and lots of times Augusto would go home with him. They were about the same age; they'd play in his house and he recognized me. He called me, 'Signor Giacomo.' You do know something, Angelica."

"I don't know anything. But I don't want to play games with you. Listen to this. About an hour ago a woman came to see me. She looked scared, half dead, and she had a little boy with her who knew all about the house and could put his hands on everything. She told me to send a telegram to the signora. Once she fainted, and once the boy threw himself down on the floor like he was possessed. He looks just like that picture of the dead boy the signora keeps on the night table. And I want to send the telegram right away to get her to come back, because even though

I don't exactly understand what those other two want, I know it's something serious. So now you can help me write it."

Giacomo nodded. They walked on together in silence until they reached the small square two blocks away where the telegraph office was located. They found it arduous to compose a message to summon Luciana Veracina, and then having done so didn't know what to do next. When Giacomo looked at Angelica she turned away from him, and said, "Listen, Giacomo, I think the signora will come tonight, and that other one with the little boy, too. I have to be at the house, otherwise, believe me, I wouldn't stay there, but why don't you come over too? Make up some excuse and come. You never know...."

"Sure. In fact, I'll keep you company while you're waiting. When do you expect them?"

"She won't get here before nine. But I want to warn you first, don't say a word to anyone."

"That's exactly what I was going to tell you. I don't like these goings on. They stink of the Devil."

Angelica crossed herself. They parted, and Giacomo walked on with his eyes to the ground, muttering incomprehensibly to himself.

Despite the fact that the two of them were fairly faithful to their pledge of silence, via Gustavo Modena and every street around it was agog that evening. From behind every window-shade glittering eyes raked the streets.

Every so often a woman would walk out to borrow a little something—salt, thread, a cheese grater from a neighbor—and as she passed the house at number eighteen, would slow her steps to try to peer inside.

At eight o'clock, after having closed his shop and warned his wife not to let Augusto out, and above all not to say a word about anything to anyone (he'd had, of course, to tell *her* the whole story), Giacomo left for Angelica's as promised. In the course of his walk he was assailed more than once by "Where are you going, Giacomo?" in voices laden with innuendo. One woman passed very close to him and murmured, "Is it true that you saw him?" He remained silent and guarded his mystery.

Angelica saw him from a window. She hurried down to open the door and admit him. There was still more than an hour to wait. She described the events of the previous day at great length to him, and afterward he gave her a detailed account of the apparition in his shop. Then each began again. It made the time pass quickly. Pressed against the blinds like sentries, they watched all who approached the building. Every so often they would dash to the apartment door and press their ears against it, listening as footsteps mounted the stairs, slowed down and then descended. No one's curiosity that evening was ardent enough to knock at Luciana Veracina's door.

It was a little past nine when Angelica sounded the first alarm. Luciana's carriage had arrived.

Luciana walked in calmly, without any sign of concern about the strange summons she had received. Angelica began a confused, rambling narrative, which Luciana interrupted.

"Tell me clearly what happened."

"A woman and a little boy came to look for you."

"Did they give you their names?"

"Well, the woman looked half dead. She fainted once."

"Did she say why she wants to see me?"

"The little boy said that you…that you had been…"

Giacomo could no longer control himself. "I saw him, signora Luciana. It's your little boy, Ramiro. Ramiro, alive. It's him. I saw him with my own eyes. You know I'd recognize him."

Angelica was stunned at the old man's imprudence—blurting out the kind of awesome news for which she would have prepared with a lengthy explanation. She glanced at Luciana expecting some kind of outburst. Instead Luciana asked her quietly, "And what else?"

Angelica brightened. "She told me to send you the telegram, though at first she didn't want to do it. But the little boy had a tantrum and he looked at that photo of you and said, 'That's my mother, that's her.' They saw the picture of the little boy too. That's when the woman fainted and I thought she was dead. I was only trying to do the right thing."

"You did fine."

"Well, it's possible that both of them are a little crazy, so its better if they talk to you…"

"It's him. It's him. As soon as he saw me he called me signor Giacomo," Giacomo wailed, once again visualizing the scene in his store.

Angelica rebuked him. "How can you talk that way?"

But Luciana interrupted her with strange equanimity. "He's right. It's him. It's Ramiro. I've been waiting for him."

The two old people were stunned. Luciana started toward the other room. Behind her back, they looked at each other, but didn't dare speak.

From the threshold of the room Luciana issued instructions. "When they arrive bring them in here. Now you, Giacomo, go home. It's late. And Angelica, as soon as they get here you can go to bed." She entered the room, closed the door and sat down.

The two old people returned to the window in silence, their minds blank. Dimly, they sensed an ineffable terror in the air.

LUCIANA FELT CALM. Yet when she heard the sound of wheels in the street, then Angelica's hurried steps in the other room and her breathless voice calling from behind the door, "Signora, they're here!" followed by the click of the latch, she pressed a hand over her heart, shut her eyes tightly and for a moment was bereft of her senses.

When she reopened her eyes, Ramiro was rushing into her arms crying, "Mamma, mamma!"

They remained entwined for a long time, he curled in Luciana's lap with his head buried in her neck, for she hadn't had the strength to stand up and was holding him in her arms tightly enough to crush him, with her lips pressed into his hair as if to drink him in. They held each other for an immeasurable time, forever unaware whether for a day, a decade, or a second. At the first moment that Luciana felt completely reunited with the physical being of her son, she saw images of her life pass before her eyes at superhuman speed, just as the dying do. Perhaps for a few moments she really did die, bent so tightly over the child's head.

It was Ramiro who first loosened their close embrace. Choking and laughing, he raised his head from his mother's shoulder and shook himself. He wanted to sit up, but her arms held him like tentacles.

"You're hurting me, mamma." His voice was filled with happiness.

Then Luciana also released her grip. The shadow of a shadow passed before her eyes. The most transcendent moment of her life had just occurred, one in which she had been more than a human being, had been for an instant filled with the essence of which gods and miracles are made.

The boy jumped off Luciana Veracina's lap and shouted, "Now, I'm really cured. But where were you yesterday and the day before? Do you know it's two whole days since we saw each other?"

Standing before her, he was still holding her hand. Luciana was about to answer him when, looking up, she saw a woman a few steps behind him. Arianna, trembling, was leaning against the door post.

The boy followed Luciana's glance, turned back to her and said, "She's my friend. We took two carriage rides together." And in a lowered voice he added, "and she's very nice."

66

Then he spoke louder and joyously. "If you want to talk to her, I'll go and look at all my toys again."

He ran to the curtained alcove and began sorting through his playthings, examining them carefully and changing their places on the shelves.

Arianna had fallen to her knees.

"Signora, help me. I don't understand. I don't understand anything. That boy is Mario. He's my child, my son. He's seven years old. I gave birth to him seven years ago and he's never been out of my sight, not for one minute."

Luciana stood up, walked over to her and lifted her gently to her feet.

"Yes, get up, my dear. Sit down here. You're mistaken. You've made a mistake. He's Ramiro. Didn't you just hear him call me mamma? Don't you see his picture there? But you must have understood because you brought him back to me. Oh, thank you. How can I ever thank you?"

Arianna was at a loss to reply. "My God," she stammered, "let me explain. What are you thinking, that I want to steal your child? Why would I? If he weren't mine, why would I want him? Don't you understand?"

"You believe he's yours, I know, but you're wrong. That's all there is to it. Didn't you see? Didn't you hear?"

"Oh God! It's because I don't know what to say. It's all so incredible. You have to let me explain, tell you what happened."

"All right. Tell me."

They sat in two low armchairs facing each other. Luciana set about listening to Arianna with an air of benign patience. But anyone scrutinizing her face, looking at that central point between the eyes where human will is most clearly expressed, would have recognized determination, unflinching to the point of ferocity.

The other woman was struggling desperately for words. "My name is Arianna Parigi. I was married eight years ago in Milan and the boy was born in Milan the following year. On the seventh of May."

"On the seventh of May?"

"Yes, the seventh of May, 1893."

"May seventh, 1893."

"At two in the afternoon."

"At two..."

"We named him Mario. He's our only child, you know, and I nursed him myself. He was always with me, always. Every one of those days. I swear to you I never even left him with the governess. So there's no way there can be a mistake. We moved to Rome a year ago because of my husband's business. I'd never been here before. Mario traveled on the train with me. He liked the ride. We live on via Abruzzi in the Ludovisio section. Would you like to go see my house now? The only places we ever take Mario to are the Villa Borghese, the Pincio and the Pariolo. I've never been in this part of the city before and neither has he. Never, ever. This morning was the first time we ever came here."

"Why did you come?"

"Why? I don't know. Because he wanted to."

Arianna stopped speaking, sensing a trap ahead. But Luciana pursued the opening she'd been given. "Why did the boy want to come here?"

Arianna writhed as if she were in the grip of a tentacled monster.

Luciana struck her blow. "Why?"

Arianna struggled desperately, unable to utter the words that would describe how Mario had insisted on coming there. She flared suddenly and cruelly. "No, signora. No. Your son is dead. I'm very sorry, signora, I know what that must mean to you. But he's dead."

"No, he's not. He's right over there. He was sick. Now he's well. Look at him."

It suddenly occurred to Arianna that Luciana was crazy and she softened her voice. "But he did die. Seven years ago. Everyone knows it. It's true."

"So he died. What's the difference? Now he's alive. Therefore it's no longer true that he's dead. And it's no longer true that he's someone else."

"But...but if he hadn't died seven years ago, he'd be fourteen today. Look at him."

"You're wrong. That's the child I lost. And that's the child I've gotten back. I've already explained to you that you returned him to me. So what does seven years have to do with any of it? Seven years! What seven years?"

"These last seven years. From seven years ago until now. What do you call them?"

"Those seven years? Well, if it's no longer true that he's dead, then those seven years are no longer true either."

It was clearer than ever to Arianna that Luciana was mad. "You say those years aren't real?" she asked her. "How can they not be real? Please, dear signora, try to think it through for a minute. Let's be reasonable."

"You think I'm crazy? Well, I'm not. There's nothing to reason about. Do you think one can resolve something like this using reason, talking about the passage of years? This is a completely different matter. There's the boy. Let's ask him his name."

"No"

"He'll say, 'Ramiro.' Let's ask him who his mother is."

"No!"

"He'll say it's me. We'll tell him to walk around this house, all through it. He'll recognize everything. He knew that man from around here. Who taught him that? No one. You said it yourself, that he never spoke about any of this with anyone. No one told him how to get here. My guess is that he figured it out, found the street all by himself, am I right?"

Arianna was twisting her neck this way and that, as if she were suffocating.

"I'm basing this just on what you yourself told me," Luciana went on. "You think I'm crazy! And Ramiro, is he crazy too? We're both crazy. But how come he and I agree on the same things? When did we arrange that? So you see, it's true. Everything is true. Not just what I say, but what he, Ramiro says too. It's true that he's my son. It's true I'm his mother."

Once again Arianna felt crushed, as if she were struggling in vain against circumstances more powerful than she. Her mind was fevered, her heart gripped by cold. Suddenly, in a disembodied voice, she pleaded. "Then I...I'd have to...lose him? Why?"

Luciana answered with strange grandiloquence. "And I, why did I lose him?"

She waited a moment to see the effect of her words. But the other woman remained silent and her gaze revealed nothing.

"I thought I'd lost him forever. I was wrong. I waited for him to come back. That was right. You say it's been seven years. So for seven years I've told myself it wasn't true. And that's why now it is true that I've found him again. Why would I have waited hour after hour for seven long years, if he weren't coming back? And he is back."

Arianna thought she had a powerful rejoinder. "But he doesn't know it's seven years. He thinks he saw you two days ago."

"Haven't you yourself seen that Ramiro hasn't been wrong about anything? Therefore he's right about this too."

Arianna didn't reply. With her head turned upwards, she was twisting again in every direction, as if lost in a void.

Silence enveloped the two women. And in that silence, as though moved by a strange concord, both turned simultaneously to look at the boy.

In the alcove where the toys were kept, in the midst of a jumble of open boxes, horses, horns, soldiers and trains, where the celebrated horse with hard, straight ears stood under an electric light, as if it were traversing a desert beneath the glare of the sun—amidst swords, pistols, cannons, puppets, sailboats and boats with tin funnels, there appeared to be a child sorcerer, who at the clap of his hands had evoked a constantly moving world from the very center of the earth. The little sorcerer, seated in a tall chair, wore a tired but happy expression. One of his hands was dangling at his side, clutching the tail of a tiger. His head was nodding and his hair hung over his half-closed, radiant eyes.

"You're exhausted. Oh, my darling, I'm going to put you to bed right now," Luciana said, rushing to the boy's side. Instinctively, Arianna followed her—out of love, or fear, to help or to hinder—she wasn't sure. Luciana had already lifted the boy into her arms. Arianna took one of his hands. Without speaking, without dissension, the two women undressed him. Luciana was completely at ease. Arianna, almost ashamed. Her face was red and her eyes glassy. Just as Luciana was about to put the child into his bed, he reopened his eyes and murmured, "No. Your bed tonight, mamma."

Luciana set him into the large bed, pulled the covers up to his chin, tucked in the sheet, then turned off all the lights except for a shaded lamp on the bedside table. At the threshold of the room she paused for a moment to look back at the sleeping boy. It was only then she realized that Arianna was no longer at her side. She was sobbing wordlessly and violently on the little bed in which Ramiro had died.

Luciana returned, helped her up gently and led her into the next room. After leaving the bedroom door open and listening a moment for any sounds, she settled Arianna on a low couch. Briefly, with Luciana bent over her, Arianna sat inertly, then her entire body shook violently in a spasm of rebellion which spent itself quickly and left her feeling utterly desperate and helpless.

But she thrust Luciana away from her and suddenly stood up, for now the agony and enormity of her situation had created an anxiety within her that was transformed into energy, energy she never dreamed she possessed. She stood still in the center of the room and, speaking passionately yet quietly, struck her blow.

"Then why did I give birth to him? I felt him being born, here, felt him being torn from me. My husband heard my cries in the other room."

"I gave birth to him too. And I too felt him being torn from my womb, taking with him almost all my blood and my life. But in my home there was no father to hear me scream. And for that he is all the more mine."

"Why did I nurse him? For eleven months he had no sustenance from anyone but me."

"And from me. He suckled at my breast too, to the last of my milk, leaving me dry."

"And I watched him grow, year by year."

"...day by day, like a tiny precious plant that sets out leaves. Ah, signora, you suffered his birth as I did. You watched him grow as I did. But you...you..."

As she spoke, Luciana too, had risen. She looked at her distraught rival and was able to stop trembling at the words she had been about to utter. Now, standing upright and still, without taking her eyes from Arianna's, Luciana completed her sentence. "But you didn't see him die."

5 LUCIANA'S LAST WORDS SOUNDED
like a voice from another world, like
a judgment, an apotheosis, a scriptural truth. They made the very air of the room shake. Its light grew beyond bounds. Its shadows dispersed. And its walls receded into a silent depth, opening it to the heavens where night and day no longer existed. Luciana Veracina's small room had become an empyrean. And she, dressed completely in black, stood in the center of that silent splendor, a slim, austere goddess. Arianna felt the miracle. She sat down at the edge of the divan and lifted her face toward Luciana, then slid to her knees on the carpet, pressed her hands together and raised them aloft. Gentle Arianna, who a moment earlier had felt shattered, dissolved in pain, overwhelmed with humiliation and powerlessness, suddenly felt herself renewed and composed with a sense of pure miracle. The myriad of troubles that had afflicted her for two days had become one stunning sublime sorrow. She felt united with the universe, restored, as all of us are when, after lives filled with grievous sorrows, we are laid to our final rest. Arianna's suffering and her heart had become as enormous as all heaven and earth.

Luciana, sensing her advantage, remained motionless for a few moments.

When she moved, it was to sit down on the carpet next to Arianna. She put her arm around the other woman and spoke softly. "You mustn't be angry with me. It isn't my fault that you were chosen to restore him to me. I've already thanked you. I love you. Don't you realize how unique you are? There's no one like you for me in the entire world? Before this I had Ramiro. Now I have both you and Ramiro forever, for as long as I live. Ramiro is mine, you see, all mine. But if you would like, he's a little ours as well, all right? You said that your son is alive and that mine isn't, as if they were two. But they are one and the same. There is only this one, my son, whom you kept for me and have now returned. Did you hear me? Why don't you say something, Arianna? I wish my name were Arianna, it might suit me better. Though Luciana is pretty too. Luciana Veracina. Would you like me to tell you the story of my life? But I don't want to see you like this on your knees. Get up, that's right, on the couch, that's nice. Now lie down, dear. You're tired. You've suffered so much, I know. You're probably not accustomed to suffering. But I am. I've suffered a great deal. And I'm sure I'm older than you are. Do you realize I'm thirty-six? Thirty-six. That's a lot of years. It occurred to me just today that I hadn't thought of my age for quite a while. I had to stop and figure it out. It was just the moment before I got the telegram. Isn't that strange? Thirty-six years is a long, long time. But my longest years were those when I was a girl studying the violin and never saw a soul. That was in Vienna. I was born in Naples. My father was Viennese. I never had a mother. I think I was born not needing one. That's funny, isn't it? I'm sure you don't know about such things, Arianna. I never even had a husband and that must seem dreadful to you too."

"No, no," Arianna whispered, feeling confused, and anxious to console Luciana.

"And Ramiro doesn't have a father. His father wasn't much more than a boy himself. He died before Ramiro's birth. He killed himself by throwing himself off a cliff into the sea because he was tired of me."

"You poor dear," Arianna whispered, once more overwhelmed

with sympathy. "How you must have suffered. And how could he do it? You're so lovely."

"But he left me the child. He was born eight months after his father's death. And then I was happy, happy all the time, every hour, every minute, the happiest person in all the world. Until he became ill with pleurisy. His forehead was scorching. All he wanted to do was drink, drink. And all the time he wanted me to hold his hand, and it was hot as fire. He kept wanting to uncover himself and I didn't want him to, you see? Because he would catch cold and get worse. Then one time when I forced him to keep the cover all the way up to chin, he got angry at me. He said I was mean, trying to…to kill him."

Luciana's voice broke, and Arianna's eyes were filled with tears as she raised one hand timidly to stroke Luciana's face. "You poor thing," she said.

"And then at that moment—just at that moment, you see?— he started losing consciousness. While he was speaking his eyes began darting here and there. I was never able to look into them again. The doctor said it was nothing, but I knew right away it was all over. 'Ramiro, Ramiro,' I said to him, 'look at me, look at mamma, who'll make you better.' But he was looking up, past my head and was saying things that didn't make sense. I tried to take him in my arms. I put my body against his to give him life, but suddenly he twitched violently and turned his head aside. He never moved again."

Arianna was weeping bitterly. The two women embraced. They rested their heads on each other's shaking shoulders and their tears streamed together.

When their sobs subsided and they separated, Luciana smiled at Arianna, placed one hand beneath the nape of her friend's neck, leaned her head back and said with sudden joy, "And now he's come back. We don't have to cry anymore. He's in there, sleeping quietly. Why don't you go to sleep now too, Arianna?"

Arianna, exhausted and under the spell of Luciana's gaze, lost all sense of reality. Her mind wandered off into what seemed pale, distant clouds and her heart was no longer filled with torment and anxiety. All she sensed was a light pressure between her eyes that was almost pleasurable, and a relaxation of her entire being which seemed to dissolve her, to melt her into the fabric against which she was lying, into the very cushions enveloping her.

After that incredible day, Arianna fell asleep.

Luciana looked at her for a moment, stood up again to raise one of Arianna's feet that had been hanging over the edge of the couch, then, walking on her toes, turned off the light and left the room. She stopped in the doorway to look at Arianna once more, and shut the door. She undressed quickly and got into bed. In his sleep Ramiro felt her presence and reached for her. Luciana took him in her arms, pressed her lips to his forehead and shut her eyes.

AND SO ON THE EIGHTH NIGHT of May everyone in Luciana Veracina's home fell asleep as calmly, quietly and peacefully as in every other home on every night of the year.

ARIANNA HAD ROLLED DOWN a long incline, when a fit of coughing jolted her onto a soft surface. Her mind retained some shred of her dream—of a plume of yellowish smoke arising from a train. She opened her eyes into the deep blackness around her and stared into it, not knowing where she was, suddenly feeling infinite desolation in her heart.

She tried desperately to regain full consciousness, but the effort failed. Her eyelids closed again and she was forced back amid the fragments of her imaginings of dark eyes, of dizzyingly high gray wheelings in the sky where a hard cloud was rocking. Little by little she was trying to wake from her troubled sleep, but its last strands remained attached to that other existence and kept pulling at her, tearing at her flesh. All at once the dry despair encircling her heart ripped her free and she was sitting up in bed. But where was she? She put her hand out and felt a wall, remembered and was overcome by grief. She leapt to her feet and stood still. Terrified to find herself alone in the dark, Arianna sat down abruptly at the edge of Luciana Veracina's couch.

Here she regained her composure, felt almost calm, and recalled everything. She studied her surroundings. The darkness was unrelieved, not the merest sliver of light leaked from any source. She cupped her head in her hands and began a minute review of everything that had happened since two in the afternoon of the previous day, when she had come upon Mario under the pine trees. Was it a just a few hours ago, just one hour, perhaps not even that long ago, that she'd wept in Luciana's arms? For a few minutes longer Arianna felt cold and deliberate, capable of evaluating all that had happened, capable of determining what to do.

But the feeling was short lived because it isn't Luciana who matters. It is Mario. His words and behavior are the abyss Arianna cannot cross, the mystery she cannot confront. It's possible Luciana is crazy. One can cope with that, get rid of her, even kill her. But Mario calls her mamma and no longer recognizes his own mother. And he knows strange places and people. There's no way to change that, no way to get around it. Luciana is nothing, but Mario is the whole world. Mario, who declared, "You're not my mother"—who asked, "Why are you calling me Mario when you know my name is Ramiro?" And that is not only inexplicable to Arianna, it is insuperable. She's sure it's useless to tell her husband or the doctor anything. They won't be able to overcome Mario's conviction.

In the midst of her agonizing, she has a sudden bright hope. Everything revolves around Mario, and who is to say that Mario cannot change? Perhaps his delusions are temporary and at any minute he'll escape them. Then the problem will be over. The two days will be forgotten. He won't recognize Luciana and he'll call her, Arianna, "mamma" again. This enormous hope agitates her. How many times in the past seven years has she heard herself called mamma by her son, and now to desire it, to pray for it as though it were a miracle! But perhaps the miracle is already in progress. Perhaps his present sleep is restoring Mario to his senses, and when he wakes tomorrow morning, in a few hours—in how many hours?

At this point it occurred to Arianna that she'd lost all track of time. The darkness felt frightening again and she was beset by anxiety. She felt like calling out, shouting, but the thought of waking Mario from the slumber which might be curing him kept her silent. She stood up and began walking around the room, hoping to find a light to turn on, or a window to open. Though she moved cautiously, she walked into an armchair, then into the wall, whose coarse fabric covering she recognized. She took a few more steps, felt completely disoriented and longed to find the couch, which now seemed a safe place. She thought she was back at it, but when she put out her hand she felt the wall covering again. Once more overcome by fear, she tried to call out, but couldn't. She groped spasmodically around the edge of a small table. Again and again she circled the room like a frightened animal, bumping into furniture, imagining her bruises, terrified at the noise she was making. Her blood was scalding her veins when she fell to the ground, gasping.

She lay there perhaps for hours.

She was miserable and in pain when she came to and found herself lying on the bare floor with her forehead pressed against a piece of wooden furniture. She sat up with difficulty, raised her head, looked around, and there before her was a geometric pattern of pale light. The window. She felt like shouting for joy.

Out there the night had passed. She breathed quickly, almost rapturously, relieved of the physical weight of darkness. She managed to stand up and grope her way toward the light. She unlocked the glass door, opened the shutter and stepped out onto the terrace.

Dawn had just broken, meager and leaden over whitish rooftops, walls and railings. The air was soft and the sky unpleasantly spotted. Arianna reentered the apartment.

Standing once more in the middle of the room, she stared at the other door, the closed door behind which Mario was sleeping in the other woman's arms.

A hot rage rose from the very depths of her soul. It made her tremble and set her face ablaze with fury. Luciana must die. Almost instantly, however, she recalled Mario's hard, angry look the previous day at the thought of going back home with her. She couldn't kill Luciana. Mario was protecting her. And Arianna no longer believed in her miracle, but understood clearly that Mario would awaken as he had gone to sleep, as Ramiro. She doesn't understand why. Nor does she understand its significance, but she is now convinced that Mario is Ramiro.

Then suddenly she thought of home and the fact that she'd left the previous day without a word to anyone. What must the servants be thinking? How worried Elena must be! I'll write Mariano immediately and tell him everything. I'll get the doctor. Fevered yearnings to do something rise in her, but her imagination is feeble and cannot come to her aid.

Next she noticed her hat on a chair, but without recalling when she took it off, or how it got there. At first sight it seemed an inducement to depart immediately, but then she looked again at the bedroom door and knew she couldn't abandon Mario lest he fall into complete madness.

She jumped at a sudden noise and put her hands to her heart. It was the sound of dragging feet in the entry hall—the old servant woman. As the footsteps approached, Arianna hurried back to the divan, turned to the wall and pretended to be asleep.

She heard the old woman open the door quietly, pause for a moment, then close it softly and walk away.

Several minutes passed.

Now the day was filled with light and a strong breeze was blowing from the terrace. Impulsively, Arianna got up, ran to the bedroom door and pulled it open, Before her were the intertwined forms of Luciana and Ramiro. Ramiro was sleeping quietly. Luciana opened her eyes.

"My dear," she whispered. "Didn't you sleep? Why are you up so early? Come here," and she motioned Arianna closer to her. When Arianna was at her side, Luciana extended one arm to her, then slid her other arm out from under Ramiro and embraced Arianna. The two women kissed.

"See how well he's sleeping? But you look upset, dear. I'll run a bath for you."

Luciana got out of bed, threw a robe over her nightgown, and led Arianna by the hand to the bathroom where Angelica, having heard their voices, joined them.

"When you're done, I'll get dressed. By then he'll be up too. But while the tub is filling, go take a look at him. Come. Now we can open a shutter. See how beautiful he is. Go on, Arianna, kiss him, there on his head, but gently."

Within the hour all three were up and dressed, and Angelica was preparing morning coffee. By this time Arianna was numb.

Ramiro had greeted her with pleasure, but as his friend. When breakfast was over he hurried off to ride his horse and Arianna spoke to Luciana. "I must go back home now," she said, then lowered her eyes. "I'd like...I'd like the boy to come too. I want to see what he says."

"Of course, Arianna. We'll go with you."

Ramiro welcomed the idea with enthusiasm. "You'll see, mamma," he said, "she has a beautiful house with an elevator. We went there yesterday in a carriage, or was it the day before yesterday?"

"And before that?" Arianna bent anxiously over him. "What about the days before that?"

Mario frowned. "No," he said after a moment. "Before that I was sick."

Luciana sent Angelica out to the piazza d'Italia to get a carriage. When the two women and the child came downstairs, there was a crowd of people, mostly women gathered in the street, all talking at the same time. At the sight of the three, they fell into silent stares and, drawing closer to the sidewalk on each side of them, pointed out the boy to each other. Arianna became alarmed. Luciana's face darkened.

"What a lot of people," Mario said, "What are they doing?"

Even the windows were filled with heads.

Suddenly two or three women threw themselves on their knees and the others followed suit. From the two walls of bowed heads there arose the murmur of a hurried prayer.

Mario became agitated. "What are they doing?" he asked again.

No one answered him. Luciana pushed him and Arianna into the carriage and spoke brusquely to the coachman. "Drive toward the city and hurry."

Astonished and curious, the coachman set off reluctantly. From within the carriage Mario looked out in terror. The two women averted their gaze from the crowd.

Once the carriage reached the bridge, it moved swiftly.

6 ELENA, THE GOVERNESS, SPENT
the early morning hours in a state
of terror and alarm. The previous
evening, on leaving the house, Arianna had told her, "We're going out to visit some friends of the family. Don't wait up for
me and send the servants to bed. I have the keys." Mariano
Parigi, as we know, had left for Zurich.

Ordinarily the two maids were summoned at seven and Elena
began working at nine. This morning at nine, however, the three
women listened first at Arianna's door, then at Mario's, astonished at not yet having been called. The silence appalled them.
After a brief discussion they cautiously entered the rooms, find-
ing them empty and the beds unslept in. They became hysterical, debated sending a telegram, phoning the doctor or calling
the police. They gave a breathless account of their plight to the
maids in the apartment downstairs, but couldn't decide what to
do. Elena began crying quietly.

They were all out in the street when the carriage arrived.
Elena stared in astonishment at her employer. Then through
her tears her face took on a cold, reproving look.

Arianna tried to appear at ease as she descended the steps
of the carriage. "Were you worried? I'm terribly sorry. We stayed
so late at this lady's house last evening that we decided to spend
the night rather than drive through Rome at that hour. This way,
Luciana, come."

She was careful not to call the boy by his name, terrified lest any of the servants hear him call the other woman "mamma." But the child seemed to sense her tension and didn't speak at all. When they entered the apartment, the maids and Elena returned to their quarters. Arianna ushered Luciana and the boy into Mario's room, then rushed into her husband's study to phone the doctor. In her own home she felt stronger, less afraid to seize any possibility.

"Doctor, come at once. No, Mario is all right and I am too. It's something else, an emergency. Please. Oh, thank you."

She hurried back into Mario's room. "Do you remember this room?" she asked him.

Ramiro looked around. "Isn't it where I was yesterday morning before we went back to my house?"

"Yes. But do you know why you were here? Who brought you back there?"

Mario's looked troubled. He didn't remember. Arianna feared putting him under too much pressure. She took some boxes from a large chest and opened them. "Do you remember any of these things?"

"No, but they're very nice."

They were the presents Mario had received for his birthday. Luciana, feeling calm and secure, remained silent.

Arianna thought for a moment. Then overcoming her first reluctance, she rang the bell to summon the governess. Pointing to her, she asked Mario, "Do you recognize this lady?"

Mario studied Elena intently. "I think I met her once. Oh, yes, we did meet, do you remember? It was in a very large park. But you didn't tell me your name."

Elena's mouth dropped, her eyes rolled and her pale hair seemed to become still lighter, but Arianna went on. "Do you remember the name of the park? And how you got there?"

Mario turned to Luciana. "How can I remember? But you must know. I was sick, but wait, then I was cured. And you must have taken me to that park. Yes, with all those trees and all that grass. But first it was very dark, black as night…wait a minute. Then it felt like it does when you dream you're flying and the air is cool, so cool all around you."

As Mario recounted his memory, it seemed to Arianna and Luciana that for an instant, the light about him intensified, then dispersed. Luciana had risen and was looking at him in a kind of ecstasy.

The boy broke the momentary spell. "That's right," he said somewhat irritably. "It was a nice park. So why don't we go back there now? What are we doing here?"

The women, each casting about for an answer to suit her own purpose, were slow to reply.

The sound of the doorbell released them.

"You may leave now," Arianna told Elena, and hurried from the room to admit the doctor. She took him aside, told him quickly, clearly and in detail everything that had happened.

"What do you think, doctor? But come in now and take a look at him. What can all this mean?"

The doctor's scientific knowledge was sorely lacking in this matter. "A psychopathological phenomena, my dear. They aren't that unusual. This one, however, does seem to have some very strange aspects. Don't worry. We'll have a look now. There have also been unusual cases of children pretending…"

"No, no."

"It was absolutely wrong of you to take him there."

"Oh, doctor, if you had seen him, heard him."

Meanwhile Luciana and Ramiro, alone in the other room, were gazing at each other affectionately. Then Ramiro asked, "Mamma, are we going to leave here soon?"

"In a little while, darling. We don't want to make your friend unhappy. She's very nice. Didn't you tell me so yourself, yesterday?"

84

"But what's wrong with her, mamma?" And the boy lowered his voice to ask somewhat maliciously, "Is she a little crazy?"

Luciana's answer was a whisper as well. "Yes, but we mustn't let her know. You're a sensible child so I can tell you everything. She's gotten it into her head that she's your mother."

Instinctively Ramiro pressed closer to Luciana. "Oh, the poor lady!" he said, his eyes wide with wonder. "What will we do?"

Arianna and the doctor entered the room.

"Look, dear," Arianna said to the boy, and as always, not speaking his name left a great void in her heart. "Do you recognize this friend?"

By now Mario was on his guard. He looked up at the doctor and said, "Not really. But I think…Isn't he the one who was here yesterday morning with that other man? Your husband? And they left together. But I didn't hear his name."

The doctor whispered to Arianna. "Has he gone back into the dining room, since the day before yesterday?"

"No, yesterday we ate in my room and he slept a great deal before we went back to her house."

"Come with me, Mario," the doctor said out loud.

The boy let himself be led by the hand into the dining room. The two women followed. Ramiro looked around at the silver, the crystal and majolica sparkling on the console and reflecting from the walls. He looked at the vaulted arch of the ceiling and the glass doors open to the brilliant sunlight.

"A cat," he exclaimed.

In a spot of sunlight on the carpet at the foot of the glass doors, the white cat opened its eyes and turned its head toward the boy running forward to pet it. The cat looked at the boy distrustfully, then jerked its head, got up slowly, walked off and curled itself in another corner of the room.

Arianna was stunned. "It always used to go to him," she whispered to the doctor. "Why doesn't it recognize him?"

Mario was clearly annoyed by her whispering to the bearded man.

The latter responded to Arianna's anguished inquiry with a shrug of his shoulders. He had the boy sit down on the cushions which had been his favorite place, while he himself sat down opposite him in a wicker chair.

"You don't remember the day before yesterday, Mario? You were sitting there, just where you are now, and I was here? It was your birthday and you received a great many presents."

Anxiously the doctor awaited the boy's reply. Arianna was disheartened, once more giving up hope, while Luciana maintained her air of assurance and forbearance.

But now Ramiro was upset. "No, no, no, that's not true," he shouted and jumped to his feet. Standing there, with his fists curled tight against his body, with his face reddened and his voice breaking, he went on, "What do you...want...from me?" Unable to utter another sound, he broke into tears.

Arianna and Luciana ran to him, bent over him and put their arms around him.

"No, Ramiro, be a good boy."

"No, darling, don't cry."

They held him in their arms, dried his cheeks and his eyes. And each in turn cast almost murderous glances at the doctor. The doctor shook his head to indicate his disapproval of their behavior.

The child calmed down quickly and the doctor sought to reassert his authority.

"Arianna dear," he said, "perhaps you'd step into the study with me for a minute—if the signora doesn't mind," he added bowing vaguely and coldly in Luciana's direction. "We'll go over this matter again and I'll tell you...."

Arianna stood up again and without replying walked toward the doorway. Halfway there she stopped and turned to Mario and Luciana. "You'll wait for me here?" she asked.

She left the room with the doctor and began speaking as soon as they entered the study. "We must write and tell Mariano what happened. But he won't be able to do anything. It's hopeless. Did you see? Did you?"

"I saw nothing irremediable. The woman is an hysteric. Or perhaps an adventuress."

"But the child, doctor. Mario, my…"

"You're making everything worse with your behavior. Situations like this must be dealt with firmly. Don't be afraid to be ruthless. Send the woman off to an asylum immediately. Take Mario on a trip. And that will be that! We're dealing with a case of complete amnesia complicated by a pseudo-memory hallucination, which often takes on an hysterical quality and is not at all unusual at this stage of development."

"But how come he knew the name of via del Muro Nuova that was changed two years ago? And how come he knew everything in that apartment, and that man, Giacomo? And his picture was there. Or maybe I didn't tell you about the picture."

"You told me. You told me. In fact too many times. You dwell on all these sentimental details, on coincidences that I don't deny are curious, but are not essential to an accurate scientific diagnosis. In these illnesses of a psychophysiological nature…"

"And he went looking for the rocking horse. And there was a rocking horse. Behind a curtain."

The doctor lost his patience. "My Lord, almost every little boy has a rocking horse…and behind a curtain. You're not letting me speak or explain. Of course, when a scientist explains something, it doesn't mean he finds the event normal. Diagnosing a psychosis requires much more caution and care than…"

Arianna interrupted him again. "Nevertheless, I have to write to Mariano and tell him everything. You'll write to him too, I hope, doctor."

"I'll wire him to return immediately."

Although she didn't understand why, the idea frightened Arianna. But the doctor insisted upon it.

"Leave this to me," he said. "I'll send him a telegram, but I'll make it clear, of course, that it's not a matter of illness, that it's not even very serious. Maybe something like, 'All in good health, but best for family you return as soon as possible.' There. That's it. Now, don't worry. I'll take care of it."

In the last few minutes Arianna had become annoyed with the doctor. Nothing he had said had given her the slightest hope or comfort. She accompanied him to the front hall, opened the door for him and bade him farewell with a weak handshake.

Feeling utterly desolate, she shut the apartment door behind him with a sigh, and turned toward the dining room where she had left Luciana and the boy. The room was empty.

She hurried to the adjacent room. It too was empty. They weren't in the boy's room, nor her own, nor the bathroom, nor the study. She sounded bells as she ran from one room to another. Now she found herself back in the dining room, where Elena and the maids were gathered. She questioned them frantically. "Where are they? Did you see Mario and that woman?"

No one had seen them. No one had heard anything. They had all been in their rooms. Arianna began running through the house again, calling "Luciana!" She looked out the window, turned back from it. Her mind was blank and she had to make herself think. She pressed her hands against her forehead and ordered herself to concentrate. At once she left the apartment and flew down the stairs. At the concierge's desk she asked in a thin voice, "Did you see my little boy, Mario, go by?"

"Yes, signora. Not more than five minutes ago. With the lady who came in with you."

Arianna leaned against the door post and shut her eyes tightly for a moment.

"Which way did they go?"

"That way, signora, to the left, toward the Belisario walls."
Voices sounded behind Arianna.

"Do you want us to come with you, signora?" It was Elena
and one of the maids.

"No, stay here."

She hurried out toward the walls. Pressing close to the sides
of buildings, she ran along the street thinking she was walking
slowly and tried to make herself go faster. Sunlight reflecting off
the whitewashed walls dazzled her. When she passed beneath a
tree limb hanging over the side of a small garden, she bent her
head fearing that she would hit it. At the corner of via Campania,
she looked to the right and to the left but saw no one. Auto-
matically, she turned left, thinking of the Villa Borghese. She
continued running, this time along an iron fence, looking in every
direction as she did so. The Belisario wall frightened her with
its menacing surface of dull red bricks and its long empty grooves.
They're gone. Gone. She took him from me. What will I do?

The fence ended. She noticed someone in the doorway of a
tavern watching her, and crossed the street. She tried to slow
down and stumbled. On the other side of the street, she began
running along the dull red walls. The doctor, that idiot doctor,
talked and talked. He kept me in that room. And I...I left them
alone together out of my sight. Her right foot hurt her. She
stopped and bent to touch it through the leather shoe, then
loosened its lace because she would have to keep wearing it,
have to keep running, how much further she didn't know, maybe
all her life, pursuing that evil, thieving woman, pursuing her
own most precious treasure. There isn't even a carriage around.
But that woman would have found one. Not just one. She took
them all. Run, run. Maybe they were on the Villa's grounds hiding behind the trees like criminals. But not him. He wouldn't
have wanted to go. She made him do it. She forced him to leave.
Oh, she'll find a carriage somewhere. And I'll have to run after

them, across the river, to via del Muro Nuovo, via Gustavo Modena, to that miserable place. But no, they won't go there, they won't, because she knows she'd be found there. Who can tell where she took him? Because she knows he's mine and she wants him, and doesn't want me to have him. But you, you, my darling? I'm your mother, you must know that. Arianna's heart leapt at the sight of two people far ahead of her walking side by side. But they weren't the two she was seeking. Neither was a woman. They were a man and a boy. The boy threw a stone at the dusty trunk of an acacia tree. Who cares about dusty acacias? The wall ended and opened onto a roadway. She crossed to the other side, put her hand on the gate around the Villa. It was long. To the right, to the left, it went on forever. She took ten or twelve more steps, now dragging her feet. Then her vision became blurred and she staggered. Her hand was still holding the uprights of the gate. She had to go on. Her hand struck a rough surface. She had reached a pillar, perhaps an entrance to the Villa. She groped for it, felt nauseated, and again her eyes clouded. Holding on, she turned and felt her way along the side of the pillar. But now her knees were wobbling. She could no longer see, no longer stand. She felt herself falling, and had a split second to think, they're gone and I'm dying...will I ever see you again?...before her legs gave way.

Arianna's body never reached the ground.

Through the darkness of her fading senses she felt two hands catch her, two arms encircle and support her, and a voice call her name.

"Arianna, Arianna. What's the matter?"

She thought for a moment she was delirious, but as her vision cleared she saw a face before her. Luciana's. With her last ounce of strength she turned her head, and there too was Mario. In a frenzy she reached with one hand to touch the boy's hair, then lost consciousness.

When she came to, she was on a bench a few steps from where she had fallen. Luciana had loosened her collar and was sprinkling her with water from a cup that another woman was holding. Arianna's hand was still on Mario's head and she pulled him to her breast, whispering, "Is it you? Really you?"

"Where were you going, Arianna?"

"I was looking for you."

"You went into the room with that bearded man and you never came out. Ramiro wanted me to take him out for a walk. We were just on our way back."

"I thought you'd run away."

"Why should we run away?"

"Yes. Why?"

Arianna was exhausted. The woman who had helped Luciana now went to find a carriage. Luciana and Ramiro returned home with Arianna, saw to it that she was put to bed, and spent the rest of the day at her side.

When the doctor telephoned, Elena, who answered his call, told him that the signora was sleeping. He left a message. "Tell her," he said, "that I sent the telegram. She'll know what it's about."

That evening Arianna suggested to Luciana that she remain for the night and sleep in the guest room next to Mario's. The doors between the three rooms were left open so that when one or the other of the women woke during the night, she could hear the quiet breathing of her son in the middle room. The three spent the following day together. The two women got along well, yet neither wanted to be away from the child for even a moment, and neither fully trusted the other.

Toward evening Mariano Parigi returned from Zurich. The doctor, whom he had notified in advance by telegram, met him at the station and immediately brought him up to date on the extraordinary events. Sputtering with fury, Parigi arrived home determined to put an end to the matter, to override his wife's passivity, get rid of Luciana, and deal straight on with his son's mental illness. But the depth of Arianna's despair, Luciana's silent yet fanatical conviction, and the boy's extraordinary behavior shook his resolution and thwarted him at every turn. He didn't even succeed in ousting his unwanted guest, for he didn't dare cut the strange sad ties that bound the three creatures to each other. So Luciana spent a second night, as though it were the most natural occurrence in the world, at the Parigi home.

The following morning Mariano went to see his attorney, who cited a good number of cases of children claimed by two mothers. "The most famous one is that of Margherita Revel and Anna Lucas of Saint-Louis in Lorraine, which occurred in 1722," he explained while shuffling through a dossier. "But in all of those cases," he went on, "a nurse or someone else substituted another child for a newborn—a frequent theme in ancient dramas." Then the lawyer raised a shocking hypothesis. "What if your governess, Elena, for personal reasons, for gain, or for other motives which we can undoubtedly uncover, switched children when she was alone with the boy between the hours of one and two in the afternoon of May 7th at the Villa Borghese?"

Mariano shrugged his shoulders. The lawyer promised to study the matter closely and decide how to proceed. In the meantime he advised Mariano to have Luciana confined to a mental hospital, which was precisely the advice medical science had offered him. On his way home Parigi fretted about the difficulty, perhaps even the ineffectiveness of that undertaking. At his apartment door he encountered a group of ragged strangers trying to persuade the maid to admit them. They were a kind of deputation of Trasteverites, five or six men and women, Giacomo among them, who lived in and around via del Muro Nuovo. News of the miracle had roused the entire neighborhood and there was no way they were going to let it escape them. They had located the coachman easily enough at stall number 115, it was in their district, and had learned from him where he had taken the Veracina woman and the boy, who after seven years had returned from the dead.

Mariano Parigi vented all his unexpressed furies and frustrations upon them, and drove them off harshly.

But as a result of Elena's and the maids' gossiping, via Abruzzi, too, was alive with interest in the mysterious events of the past three days at the Parigi home. Having been sent away, the Trasteverites gathered in front of the building and before long were arguing the case with an assemblage of maids, doormen and other servants from up and down the street. The groups informed and confused each other with a melange of facts and opinions, but eventually two clearly delineated and popular schools of thought emerged. The Trasteverites believed that the boy was Ramiro resurrected. The Ludovisiites refused to give credence to the miracle and loudly proclaimed the boy's true identity to be Mario Parigi. The two groups were on the verge of coming to blows, but morning was not the time for serious brawls. The Trasteverites withdrew, promising to return. The youngest and angriest of them shouted things like, "You'll have to give him up to us," "We'll be back to get him!" and prophesied battles and bedlam.

7

AN IRKSOME WHIRLWIND OF CURI-
osities of every sort exploded. "The
Parigi Case" quickly achieved pub-
lic notoriety and attracted strange interests; the press seized
upon it, public officials and authorities of the most diverse kind
became involved in it.

The first fuse was lit by the Trasteverites who, having put
off their threatened march on via Abruzzi to take Ramiro back
by force, found momentary satisfaction in a more innocuous
pursuit. They persuaded the priest at Santa Maria in Trastevere
to celebrate a mass of gratitude to God for the miracle with
which He had deigned to honor their parish. The priest, caught
off guard by the astounding story of Ramiro's return, saw no
problem with the request and made no effort to stay the fanat-
ics' haste. On the morning of May 13th, the crowd in the church
overflowed into the square, from the square into the neighboring streets, then all the way back to the slopes of the Janicolo.
When the mass was over the zealots improvised a procession,
carrying the local congregational standards beneath the closed
windows of Luciana Veracina's home to do homage to the door
at number 18 which, within the span of seven years, had ushered out a dead child, then readmitted him miraculously restored to life.

The priest was immediately rebuked and punished by his
superiors. On the same evening *La Vera Roma* published a history of the entire affair and expressed outrage at the priest's grave

94

error. It explained that the Church cannot admit the resurrection of those not in the Gospel, much less their reincarnation. It deplored the fact that through the error of an unwary clergyman, their religion had become embroiled in a matter that was perhaps diabolical, certainly illusory, undoubtedly pernicious, and which in any case did not merit attention or discussion.

Thus, the religious press buried Ramiro a second time. But other newspapers threw themselves into the story like hungry ferrets attacking a chicken. They began printing the few facts they knew, expanding them and coloring them in an unrestrained competition of wild imaginings. They hurried off to interview the protagonists and lesser participants. Thrown out by Mariano, eluded by Luciana and Arianna, they had no trouble getting Elena, Angelica, Giacomo, the carriage drivers and concierges to talk. Every once in a while Mariano Parigi would deny some published detail, and the following day a more damaging one would appear. If, using his connections, he succeeded in silencing one paper, another would immediately take its place. And by now these were not only Roman journals, but newspapers throughout Italy. Even foreign publications, particularly those in England and America, were the recipients of regular reports. *The Messaggero*, instead of indulging in the hunt for and elaboration of the factual details, began a series of interpretations and observations, which they described as an inquiry into "The Parigi Case." Thus, the publication offered itself as a platform to theosophists, theologians, biologists, spiritualists, jurists, psychiatrists and the literati. Each preached his own interpretation in the daily column, bowed and left the stage to his successor. Photographic equipment worked overtime, multiplying the snapshots of Mario and his two mothers which had been garnered assiduously here and there. Via Gustavo Modena and the modest doorway of number 18 were also honored many times in reproduction. Fantastic captions surmounted the photos:

"Ramiro, the Revived," "The Lazarus Child," "Mario or Ramiro?" Some were tendentious: "Mario refuses to cede his soul to Ramiro." Other newspapers went to, or pretended to go to San Felice and published views of places where for seven years "the hopeful mother had lived in solitude." They recounted the history of Circeo from Ulysses through Luciana Veracina. One day a cultural journal featured a clever musical-metaphysical interpretation, which demonstrated that the three tempi of Francesco Veracina's sixth sonata were a miraculously prophetic illustration of the extraordinary fate that awaited the descendant of the supreme musician, "the great violinist, who had broken the strings of her instrument to offer herself completely, a new Orpheus, to the task of recalling her son from his early tomb."

The clamor of the press and public interest seemed to be waning when Arianna and Luciana began receiving indications of a more unusual kind of attention. Luciana received a letter from the European representative of the worldwide Theosophical Society. After a few preliminaries it informed her that "the boy the civil state called Mario Parigi, born at 2 PM on the 7th of May 1893 in Milan, is the direct reincarnation of your son, who died a few minutes earlier on the same day in Rome. We have been able to establish in the most certain manner, that he is one of the subjects well known to our observers, and we have the complete lists of all his earlier incarnations which we can make available to you. It will please you to know that he was incarnated for the first time twenty-three thousand seven hundred eighty-five years before Christ on the island of Hawaii. His latest reincarnation took place in the Christian year 1597 in Venice. The average interval between incarnations was 1017 years and nine months. The longest interval between one life and another occurred between an incarnation in 12090 in Peru and one in 9686 (still before Christ, of course) in China. This was an interval, as you can see, of two thousand four hundred and four years.

However, this present occurrence is not the first time he has been reincarnated almost immediately after death. There were two other such occurrences. These took place in the south of India. Dead in 21504 at the age of thirty-six (he was then a female), and reborn the same year, he lived another forty-eight years, died and was reborn again in 21456. When he was born to you in the year 1886 of the Christian era in Rome, he had been in Devachan (the lowest of the celestial worlds in which souls spend their time between incarnations) only since 1626 after Christ. It will interest you particularly to know that though you and he met each other as mother and child when he was recently born to you, you had previous close relationships many times before: in 22978 before Christ in Madagascar as brother and sister; he was the female then, you the male; in 19617 before Christ in Bactria, where he was a priest and you an abandoned baby girl found by him on the temple steps; and in 9686 before Christ in China, as lovers prevented from marrying by family dissension, both of whom died at a very early age. If you would like any further details, they are available through our General Headquarters; you have only to write to the following address: Recording Secretary of the Theosophical Society, Adyar, Madras, S. India."

Arianna, on the other hand, attracted spiritualists. One such circle wrote to say that in several seances they had called upon the spirit of Veracina's son and he had always responded. This made it clear that he had not returned to life and that his identity could in no way be confused with that of Mario Parigi. The group put itself at the signora's disposal and invited her to enroll as a regular member so that she could attend seances, which were important not only as demonstrations in support of her position, but also as a defense against the unjust claims of the person trying to take her son from her.

Scores, hundreds of mothers wrote strange and banal letters to Arianna and Luciana. Luciana refused every invitation to discuss the matter, but collected and organized all the material she received. Arianna, frightened by the enormous outcry at her dreadful misfortune, found it a cruel offense to her sense of privacy. With endless sorrow she recalled those first few days which, though filled with fear and suffering, were at least all her own—prodigiously tragic, celestial days untainted by ridicule, uncontaminated by contact with the bestiality and stupidity of the world.

Days passed by. And now Mariano, Arianna and Luciana began to find themselves allied in a strange way by their common distaste for that wild outbreak of human curiosity—like noble beasts caged in the midst of a circus, surrounded by loud-voiced, vulgar adults and rowdy children, whose entertainment it is to watch the lions eat, while high on a platform trumpets and drums, playing fanfares and marches, stir galling visions of dust-filled streets. The passions that were troubling each of them were blunted within that oppressive enclosure of malicious glances, gaping mouths, and wonder born of stupidity. Every one of their actions was diminished by it. A troubled inertia fell like a heavy cover upon the noble drama, deforming it and quenching its light.

Mariano, waiting with nervous impatience for his attorney and the legal advisors he had consulted to establish a possible course of action, had passively accepted the absurd and immutable presence of Luciana, and tolerated the sight of Mario living every moment of his day under the simultaneous, evenly divided watchfulness of his two mothers. Two or three times Luciana, who couldn't bear to leave Ramiro even for an hour, had to return to her home in Trastevere. Without a word Arianna would get dressed as well, and the three would leave and return together. It seemed to Mariano that this entanglement was monstrous and that every day that it went on would make it more difficult to undo. He felt ashamed before Elena, the maids and his friends. Often he arranged to be away from home at meal times, avoiding those strange encounters around the family table with that intrusive woman. For the first time in his life, he felt himself caught in a current which no act, no effort of will could overcome. Occasionally he insulted his attorney for his long delay in acting. But the attorney was unable to find any precedent on which to base legal action and failed to see the absurdity of using juridical means to resolve a situation that had nothing in the least bit juridical about it. Nights brought Mariano strange furies, which exhausted him and left him drained and weak at daybreak. One morning, when insomnia had driven him from his bed just after dawn and he was wandering through the house seeing specters, he encountered Luciana, who, having walked out to the terrace in a dressing gown to take the morning air, was staring into the clear and intensely dark light surrounding a row of pine trees. Impulsively, he addressed her:

"Signora, we need to resolve this situation and to do it as soon as possible. Please tell me what your plans are. And don't try to make me explain more clearly."

"I understand you very well. And you are right. I will be leaving. This morning, in fact."

Mariano seemed perplexed, unable to grasp the import of her words. Luciana spoke again. "I'm saying that I myself have decided to leave. And to do it this morning. When Arianna gets up, I'll say good-bye."

Her words kept Mariano silent. He was afraid to risk asking "What about the boy?"

Luciana was bolder. "I understand Arianna's feelings very well," she said, "even yours, signore, but especially Arianna's. That's only natural."

"What do you mean?

"I mean that I'm very fond of Arianna. I'll stay...that is, we'll stay in Rome for a while and Arianna can come see him whenever she wants."

"See him?"

"Unless you think it would be better for Arianna's sake to make a quick and complete break."

"From whom?"

"From Ramiro, of course."

Mariano's face turned dark red and a series of murderous replies formed in his mind. Straining from head to toe, he controlled himself, and closed his hand tightly around the edge of the balustrade.

His cheeks had regained their natural color and his voice was icy when he finally spoke. "The child is ours and will remain here," he said. But he didn't look directly at her.

She didn't move. Her pale face and black gown were luminous. She too thought of a number of replies before simply saying, "No."

For a moment they stared into each other's eyes.

As though by agreement, they both moved. Until that instant, they had been standing alongside the terrace railing. Now they turned and walked side by side in tense silence until they reached the glass door and the threshold of the room.

Here Mariano Parigi declared, "It is necessary. It is imperative that someone else judge this matter and resolve it."

This somewhat enigmatic phrase didn't disturb Luciana, who after a pause stepped away from him as though to conclude the conversation. Enunciating every syllable clearly, she said, "Then you don't want us to leave today?"

Mariano managed to find the dry tone and words that he often used to conclude a business conversation. "Do as you please."

A few hours later Mariano was back at his lawyer's office. The two then picked up the doctor and all three went on to visit some highly placed people. The three men had decided that the first thing to do was to get Luciana out of the way by putting her in a sanitarium, at least temporarily. The highly placed people would cut through the formalities and speed the process.

The most difficult part was to find a way to entice Luciana out of the house alone, because the idea of someone coming into his home to take her away in the presence of the child was repellent to Mariano. Also, it seemed wiser to say nothing to his wife until the deed was done.

The difficulties were considered and resolved, and the action scheduled for the following day, May 27th.

ON THE TWENTY-SEVENTH OF MAY at four in the afternoon Mario was playing on the terrace. Mariano joined him. He was holding the boy's hat in his hand. "Come along with me," he said to him, "We're going to take a carriage ride to the Villa Borghese."

"Oh, that's nice. I'll take my ball. And mamma?"

"She's outside waiting for us."

"Then let's go right now."

The apartment door was ajar. When they walked out Mariano shut it carefully and the two ran down the stairs. A carriage was waiting just in front of the entry with its door open. Mariano hurried the child into it.

"Where's mamma?" he asked.

Mariano was in the carriage by now and had closed the door. "I thought she was down here already," he replied. "Call her, she must still be in her room."

Luciana's room faced the street. Mario raised his head toward her window and called, "mamma."

Luciana looked out and her face suddenly filled with alarm.

"Come down, mamma. What are you waiting for?"

Luciana disappeared from the window.

The boy was still looking up when Mariano touched the

driver's back and the carriage suddenly began moving.

Mario screamed. "No, no, wait!"

Mariano calmed him down. "We'll turn down there and wait for her in the shade."

With the horses at a gallop the carriage quickly covered the short stretch of road to via Campania, where it turned left, then stopped. Mario was looking back, but once the carriage made its turn, via Abruzzi was out of his sight.

"We'll wait for her here," said Mariano.

At the sound of Mario's voice calling her from the street, Luciana had felt a sudden, incomprehensible fear but suppressed it. She began looking for her hat, was unable to find it and decided not to bother. Something told her to hurry. She ran through the apartment, had some trouble opening the door, then raced down the two flights into the street. The carriage was gone.

Her heart missed a beat and she raised her arms as though to call out, then she remembered the direction the carriage took and began running. At the crossing of via Sicilia another carriage emerged. It blocked her passage and stopped in front of her.

Luciana had to slow her pace in order to pass behind the carriage whose doors were closed. Just at that moment one of its doors opened and two men emerged. They approached her and one said, "Kindly come with us."

The street was deserted.

"No. Who are you? No, no."

"Don't shout, signora. Don't be afraid. We're police. Everything will be explained to you and in half an hour you'll be free."

"All right," Luciana said anxiously. "But please," she pleaded, "let me drive past there." She pointed to the end of a street under a dense group of trees. "My little boy is waiting for me there. He'll be very upset if I don't meet him. I just have to tell him before I go."

"Of course, signora."

The men helped her courteously into the carriage and shut the door behind her. Luciana noted that the windows were curtained. The two men seated themselves, one across from her and one next to her. The carriage began moving immediately, but instead of turning as Luciana had expected, it continued straight ahead along via Sicilia. "No, no, that way," Luciana shouted.

The man at her side took her arm, and the other spoke harshly.

"Stop yelling. We told you you'll be free in a half hour."

She struggled and was about to scream, but they were ready for her with a handkerchief which they tied over her mouth. Luciana's eyes rolled wildly and she fell to the side. It was clear that struggling would be useless. Exhausted and confused, she closed her eyes and tried to understand what was happening to her.

From the jumble of thoughts that filled her mind, one thing stood out clearly: the conversation she'd had with Mariano Parigi on the terrace. When was it?—yesterday morning, of course, though it seemed so much longer ago. There was a connection, she was sure, between that exchange and what was happening now. Once more she seemed to hear that sweet voice calling her from the street. "Mamma." Ramiro had called her. Therefore she'd had to come down. That was it. He had made Ramiro call her. But Ramiro, Ramiro, where had they taken him? No, he wasn't in danger. He had just been used to get to her, to make her leave the house, come down into the street. That much was clear. And by now they'd taken him back home and were trying to console him. They think he's their son. They won't hurt him.

But just as she came to this reassuring thought, other confusing thoughts, images, fragments of memory, closed in on her. She no longer dared to open her eyes for fear of seeing hideous sights. Where are they taking me? She couldn't even conceive of an answer. She recalled their promise, "In half an hour you'll be free." It had never occurred to her to doubt it. But the half hour had passed by now, perhaps ten, a thousand half hours had passed. The carriage, which for a while had bounced on cobblestones, was now running smoothly, as if over a well-traveled road. Luciana withdrew completely. She lost all sense of the presence of the two men, and now barely even sensed her own body against the seat and cushions. She felt lighter, as if she had risen straight into the middle of space. Oh, how had Ramiro described his return to earth? "When you dream you're flying and it's cool, so cool all around you."

The carriage slowed its pace and Luciana opened her eyes. The windows had been uncovered and lowered. There was green on all sides and the carriage was following the curve of an avenue. The avenue opened onto a lovely meadow, interrupted here and there with great clumps of oleander. Opposite the meadow was a scattering of small white houses.

The carriage moved slowly along the narrow road that ran between the surrounding expanses of greenery, from which it was separated by a high metal mesh fence. They came to a gate, passed through it and stopped in a small flat area covered with fine gravel and enclosed by a line of rose bushes. Beyond the roses, there were low flower beds and beyond these a large planting of laurel, which in turn was backed by a thick copse of oak trees which rose to the top of a hill. The blinds of the houses were all green and all of them were closed. Between the houses there were rows of espaliered myrtles. Not a soul was to be seen. In one corner of the meadow a revolving sprinkler was spraying water on the grass and plantings. Everywhere, as far as the eye could see, there was peace and order. The very air that hung above the houses and extended to the horizon where umbrellas of pines pressed against bright clouds seemed kind and tender.

Luciana felt as if she were dreaming, and in this state she

descended the carriage steps and followed the two men toward
the entrance of one of the houses. The door opened silently; a
woman wearing a very white apron and holding in one hand a
mass of keys smiled at her and invited her in. They crossed an
atrium; the woman chose a key from her collection, let Luciana
enter before her, then closed the door behind them both. Further along the passage they repeated the procedure at another
door and found themselves in a marble hall. They walked up a
few steps. The woman opened and closed a third door. Now
they were in a corridor onto which several other doors opened
and the woman took Luciana through one of these. The room
behind it was simply furnished and completely white. Waiting
for her within was a rosy-cheeked, golden-bearded young man
wearing a long white coat. The young man smiled pleasantly
and bade Luciana sit in an armchair. Luciana put her hands out
toward him and pleaded, "Tell me where I am."

"You are among friends, dear signora. I know you are a very
intelligent woman. You will live here as comfortably as in your
own home, just for a short time, I believe, until you're cured.
You are in a sanitarium."

"A madhouse!" Luciana shouted, jumping from the chair.

"Nothing of the kind, signora. This is a sanitarium for women.
There are no men here and only the finest people. Yes, it is a
psychiatric hospital, but if there is anything you want, you have
only to ask for it."

"I'm asking you to let me out, doctor, to let me go back home
to my child immediately. God knows how frightened he must
be. How he's crying for me."

"Your son? Oh yes, I know the situation. Everyone has been
talking about it and I consider it an extraordinary piece of good
fortune to be involved in such a celebrated case."

"But my son! Let me go to him! Or bring him here to me."

"A little boy in a psychiatric sanitarium for women!"

"Sanitarium! But if you know everything, what do you expect to cure me of?"

"Your imagination, dear signora. I believe that with an intelligent woman such as yourself, it is better to be honest. You have imagined that the boy Mario Parigi, born in Milan seven years ago, of the still living Mariano Parigi, is your son, a son who, though I am sorry to recall this to your memory, died in Rome at 2 PM on the seventh of May, 1893."

"Doctor, let me explain this to you. Let me tell you. No, better than that, talk to the boy, just once. Then decide who is right."

"That's not within my competence, dear signora. My responsibility is to cure, not to resolve legal issues."

"Then tell me what to do."

"In good time, signora. In good time and when you've settled down."

"How long will that take? My son…"

"Soon, signora, soon. Everything will work out for the best, the best for everyone concerned. I have to leave you right now. At the end of that hallway," he pointed to the door, "there's an attendant to respond to any of your requests. We'll see each other again soon, signora. Be of good cheer."

Luciana fell back into the chair. She remained that way for a long time, her mind blank, her strength gone. She roused herself finally, upon feeling her face drenched in tears. She looked toward the window. It was barred. Beyond it, she saw the black umbrella pines pressed against the pale sky. Then she heard light footsteps in the hall and the sound of keys opening and closing doors, moving ever farther away from her. She seemed to be hearing the opening and closing of all the innumerable keys that had locked her inside this place. Where was Ramiro? She got up from the chair, threw herself face down on the bed and broke into loud, desperate sobs.

8 MARIO'S LIFE, ONCE THOSE FIRST three strange days had passed and he and Luciana had settled in at Mariano Parigi's home, had resumed a normal course. Everyone was careful not to bother him any longer with the kind of questions and experiments that had so upset him. Only once or twice did he and Luciana talk about their new friend's crazy idea that he was her son. By now he was very fond of Arianna and if she sometimes happened to call him Mario, he understood the reason for it and tolerated her doing so. But her husband was forever telling him what to do, and he tried to avoid being alone with him. Elena's services as governess had been bypassed. Arianna and Luciana taught the boy his lessons without wearying him and took him out for his walks. They never returned to the piazza di Siena for fear he would meet his old playmates, but every day after lunch took him to play in an area south of the Villa Borghese where he made new friends. He didn't much like being with children his own age. Arianna and Luciana's company was enough to fill his young life. The few people who occasionally visited the Parigis at home were close friends. Elena and the maids had received strict orders not to speak to him of the past. And the shadow cast by those three days had quickly faded from his memory. He knew that his home was elsewhere, in via Gustavo Modena. He had gone there a few times with the two women and brought back toys which he'd mingled with those at the Parigi home that he'd happily made his own. But not one fleeting memory of his childhood in Milan, or of his past year on via Abruzzi, ever entered his head.

Two weeks had passed from the day of his return to the day when Mariano Parigi had suggested their trip to the Villa Borghese —the day Mario had called out "mamma" and seen Luciana appear at the window, then disappear, and the carriage had carried him past the corner which hid the entry of the house from view.

Standing in the carriage, the boy had begun to tremble, then tightening his hands into fists at his sides, he had cast such a dark look at Mariano that the man became alarmed.

"Just a minute," he said to the boy. "She's coming. What are you so upset about? Sit down."

The boy neither quieted down nor obeyed him. He stood still for about a minute, then shouted, "I want to get out," and tried to climb over the carriage door.

Mariano stopped him. "No, no. wait. We'll go back. We'll go meet her."

He had grasped the boy's arm. Mario turned and looked at him in fury.

"Turn around and take us back," Mariano told the driver at the same time that he was calculating whether his plan could already have been executed.

As the turn began, the horse rushed forward.

"Slowly," Mariano shouted at the driver. "What's your hurry?"

While he held Mario with one hand, Mariano reached out with the other to pull at the bridle on the side opposite to the turn. The horse stopped short and was about to rear up.

"What do you think you're doing?" the driver shouted.

But Parigi had gained another few minutes. He felt the boy trembling, as if he were about to explode.

"Go on," he told the driver. "Turn slowly and let's go back home."

They turned slowly. He let go of Mario's arm. They reentered via Abruzzi. No one was in it. At the intersection of via Sicilia, Mariano looked both ways, saw a black carriage disappearing in the distance and knew that the deed had been accomplished. When they got out of the carriage, Mario raced up the stairs. Mariano caught up with him.

The boy ran into the apartment shouting, "Mamma, mamma." Arianna appeared. The maids had told her that the others had left the house and she had dressed quickly to go looking for them.

"Where's my mother?"

Mariano tried to signal his wife that he had something to tell her, but when she looked at him, her eyes were wide with astonishment. She took Mario in her arms and held him tightly.

"Come here, Anna," Mariano said, "I have something to tell you."

He made another gesture indicating that she should release the boy, but the child saw it, understood, and was driven to a frenzy. He began shouting. Arianna was holding him in her arms, trying to console him, and looking up in terror at Mariano. The latter paced the room to regain his composure, then with a changed expression on his face, bent over the boy and spoke softly to him. "Listen, your mother had to go out, but she'll be back soon, tomorrow, I think."

"You're lying," shouted the boy. "You're bad. "You've sent her away someplace. Take me where she is right now."

"We'll go out right now and look for her, do you want to?"

"No. I don't believe you. And I wouldn't go with you. I'm afraid."

He clung to Arianna, who was ever more frightened and agitated by his suffering and didn't know what to do or say.

Mariano grabbed the boy around his waist, tore him from Arianna's arms and, lifting him bodily, carried him kicking and screaming into the next room where he virtually dropped him into Elena's arms. "Keep him here for a minute," he told her.

He returned quickly to the other room and locked the door behind him.

Briefly he told Arianna what had happened. The fleeting impulse of joy she felt was not enough to quiet her apprehensions. From behind the door they could hear angry cries, Elena's shrill screams, and furious crashings. Hurrying to open it, they were appalled by Mario's appearance; by his flaming, distorted face streaked with tears, by his body racked with convulsions, by his disheveled hair and his venom-filled eyes. They picked him up and carried him, still struggling, into his room and put him on his bed. He kicked Mariano in the stomach, put his arms around Arianna's neck and pulled her to him, shouting, "Get him out of here. Get him out."

Anna looked at Mariano, who retreated, telling her, "See if you can calm him down." In a whisper he added, "I'll be in the other room."

Alone with Arianna, Mario seemed calmer. "Tell me where my mother is," he demanded.

Arianna barely hesitated. "She had to go away for a day or so, then she'll be back."

Mario looked hard into her eyes. "Then it's true. Where did she go?"

"I didn't ask her. I don't really know. What's the difference?"

"But why didn't she tell me?"

"Because you would have wanted to go with her and she needed to be alone."

Mario thought for a moment, then said, "I don't understand."

Arianna had an inspiration. "Like the other time. Don't you remember?"

"What other time?"

"Don't you remember when you and I went to find her and she wasn't there, and then we went back in the evening?"

"Yes."

"Well, where was she before we got there?"

"Before? Before that I was sick. And so, so…I don't know."

"You were here with me."

"I was here with you. That's right. Then we went to find her."

"That's right. Just like now. She left you here with me for two or three days, maybe four."

"No! No!"

"All right. Three at the most. Then either she'll be back here or you and I will go get her."

"Three days? That means today, tomorrow and then one more after that, and she'll be back."

"That's right. And if she's not back in three days we'll go look for her. That will be Wednesday. I promise you. You can trust me. Didn't I take you to her before?"

"Yes. I trust you."

Arianna put her arms around him and held him close to her for a very long time. During their silence Mariano re-entered the room quietly. The boy raised his head and looked at him with residual suspicion, but said nothing.

Arianna spent the following two days in a state of deep apprehension. Though Mario was calm now, she knew that on Wednesday morning he would remember her promise and would be adamant about keeping it. She asked Mariano what he thought. His ideas were facile and wrongheaded.

"Now that that woman is gone, the worst is over. Now it's just a matter of gaining time, putting him off from one day to another. Little by little he'll forget, and once he's free of her influence he'll be himself again. In a few days you'll be able to go away with him, take a short trip someplace, maybe to the country or the shore."

"No, Mariano, it won't go like that. You'll see tomorrow morning."

And, indeed, on the morning of the 30th, after having calmly eaten his breakfast, Mario said simply. "Let's go."

Mariano, sitting somewhat apart from them, was silent. He had heard the resolution behind the boy's quiet voice.

Arianna, however, had a ready reply. "Darling," she told him, "you need just a little more patience. I have to go alone. You trust me, don't you?"

"Yes."

"I'm going by myself to see your…to see your mother. I'll be back before one o'clock."

"You'll bring her back?"

"I think so."

"Just think?"

"Be a good boy. I told you can trust me."

She told the maids to look after Mario and left the room with Mariano.

"I thing it's absolutely necessary to bring Luciana back," she said to him.

Mariano bit his lips. "No, We'd be right back where we started from. When you see him this afternoon, tell him that Luciana went away and that you and he are going to meet her in the country. Then you'll take him out to the country, and with some fresh air and exercise…"

"I don't think it will work. And anyway, I really do want to go to the sanitarium."

"Why?"

"Because I promised Mario. And because I think it's a good idea to speak to Luciana."

"I suppose. All right," he said and gave his wife instructions on how to reach the institution and a note for the doctor in charge.

Arianna had no specific plan. She didn't even ask herself why she was going to see Luciana. If she had asked, she wouldn't have been able to answer her own question. To pacify Mario, of course. But she knew full well that there would be great danger in returning without Luciana. Accustomed all her life to being dependent on someone, now that she couldn't rely on her husband's advice, it was to Luciana, her enemy, her extraordinary rival, to whom she was turning. And gradually, as the carriage proceeded on its way and she felt herself getting closer to Luciana, Arianna gained somewhat in confidence.

At the sanitarium, she asked to see the doctor and handed over her husband's note.

She was led into a reception room in the main pavilion. The blond doctor appeared almost immediately and at once began speaking.

"Signora Stirner is doing fine. After our first session and her first outburst of tears, which, of course is normal, she settled down quickly. The following day she listened quite calmly to my interpretation of her illness. I saw her again the same evening and under my skillful guidance she readily acknowledged that she could have had a prolonged hallucination. Please understand, signora, I don't like bragging, but it's almost a miracle to have reached this stage so quickly. Physically, she is very well. She sleeps a great deal, takes long walks out there," he said, pointing to the garden and the thickets of laurel. "It wouldn't be easy, signora," he added, "to find a sanitarium as pleasant and varied, or as magnificently attractive in terms of natural surroundings, as this one."

The tension in Arianna's face dissipated as the doctor spoke. When he said, "she acknowledged that she could have been having a prolonged hallucination," she felt herself flooded with light as well as with a rush of affection for Luciana, and a sudden impulse to find and embrace her and hear those miraculous words for herself. Therefore, she barely paid any heed to the doctor's subsequent words. But as he went on speaking a dark shadow crossed Arianna's mind and she felt a clutch at her heart. Luciana admits her error, she thought, but Mario? All her hopes suddenly collapsed. What difference does it make what Luciana says, if Mario still calls her mamma? She was seized by apprehension. The blond psychiatrist stopped speaking for a moment.

Anxiously, Arianna asked him, "What you say is fine. I appreciate it, but the child, professor, it's the child, who still thinks …Mario…"

The doctor seemed annoyed. "That is not the problem. Lucia Stirner, known as Luciana Veracina, is in my care and is my patient. It was my responsibility to resolve Lucia's problem, not Mario's. And believe me, I've succeeded brilliantly. Would you like to speak with her?"

"Yes, please."

The doctor summoned the nurse from pavilion C.

When she appeared he asked, "Number eight?"

"I haven't seen her yet, doctor. But yesterday morning she didn't get up until eleven. If she's asleep, do you want me to wake her?"

"Yes, and tell her that signora Parigi is here. We'll wait for her in the garden."

The nurse left.

The doctor led Arianna to a bower of glycinia near the rose garden. They sat down on a bench. A small reservoir of water, fed by a stream that came down from the woods, was gurgling nearby. The surroundings were filled with peace. To Arianna's surprise, she felt herself wishing she could spend time amid such peace.

After a few minutes, the nurse returned.

"Number eight must be out walking around here."

"What do you mean?"

"The orderly told me that she went out a while ago to walk in the garden. I was with fifteen. He says he saw her talking with ten for a bit. Then the two of them walked toward the woods."

Glowering somewhat and without responding, the doctor headed toward the thicket of laurel and entered it, followed by the nurse and Arianna. He called loudly, "Signora."

Impulsively Arianna called, "Luciana," then was frightened by the sound of her own voice.

Having crossed the thicket of laurel, they were surrounded by oaks, huge, venerable oaks with scraggly, powerful trunks, and high over head, thickly interlaced branches and leaves. They could have been entering a temple.

"She can't have gotten much beyond here."

They began calling again.

"Signora."

"Luciana."

The doctor stopped. "Did you look into any of the rooms around hers?" he asked the nurse gruffly.

"No, doctor."

"Well, take a look right now. And send number ten over here to me."

The nurse ran off. The doctor and Arianna returned to the bench under the glycinia bushes. Number ten arrived. She was a woman of about forty with clear, light eyes and a soft unctuous voice. She rubbed her hands together continuously.

"What did the woman in room eight talk to you about this morning?"

"She told me stories she remembered from when she was a little girl in Vienna," she said. "Then she told me she lives at the seashore and she described that to me. She talked about a witch called Circe, and about sailors and a lot of other things like that."

"Did she say anything about her life or her illness?"

"No, doctor, nothing. You know I'd tell you."

"She didn't talk about a son?"

"No."

"Where did the two of you go?"

"For a while we sat over there," she turned and pointed to the laurels.

"Take us there."

They all followed her.

"Right here. We sat here on the ground with our backs against that tree."

"And then?"

"Then I wanted to go back to my room and take a rest. She stayed there. She said she wanted to read."

"She had a book with her?"

The woman thought for a moment. "To tell you the truth I didn't see one. But now that I think of it, she had a handbag with her, a pretty big one. Maybe the book was in there."

"Let's go back."

They met the first nurse, a second nurse, the orderly and the caretaker, all in a state of consternation. There was no trace of Luciana.

"Then we just have to do a more thorough search. It's physically impossible that she left the premises. You and Pietro go through every pavilion, every storeroom. And we," he turned to the guard and the second nurse, "we'll go back there."

They returned to the base of the tree.

The small patch of grass seemed disturbed and packed down. Nearby the caretaker discovered a small footprint, most certainly made by Luciana. They found other prints, faint and intermittent because of the hardness of the soil, but clear enough to mark the woman's trail. Luciana's course seemed uncertain for a distance, as if she'd been wandering aimlessly. The caretaker, who was bending over to study the prints, seemed skilled in this kind of search. When the others thought that they had lost the track, he would study a tuft of grass or a clump of soil and unexpectedly turn up the imprint of a heel or a sole.

At one point Luciana's trail became decisive. It headed in a straight line for the first of the oak trees, then it made a large circle and turned back toward the glade of laurels. At just that point the ground was quite uneven, with twigs, thorns and rocky patches intermixed with the grass. There were no longer any footprints and the trail was irretrievably lost.

The doctor summed up the situation. "She got this far and then she turned back. Following in this direction she could not have missed returning to the last or next to last pavilion. We'll keep looking."

The search went on. It was intensive, exhausting, numbing and unsuccessful.

"Perhaps she went beyond the oak trees," Arianna suggested. "And then perhaps she got sick there and…"

"Impossible. The last prints indicate very clearly that as soon as she reached the oaks, she immediately turned back. Nevertheless we'll search through there too."

Along with the doctor, every female employee of the Sanitarium, among whom the grounds had been divided up, now scoured the woods all the way to the base of the hill. It was there that Arianna, who had followed them, saw to her enormous horror a long stretch of barbed wire which cut through the woods, ensuring that the Sanitarium was completely separated from the rest of the world.

The doctor explained anxiously. "Even if she got this far, which she didn't, you can see she couldn't get through. You'd have to blow a hole with explosives. And this barbed wire fence runs into that other one you may have noticed when you arrived here, which is high and secure and under constant observation. Therefore, it is a fact, a scientific fact, that the woman has not escaped, but is merely hiding someplace. We just have to start over."

They searched through every single building again. It was

getting late and Arianna was increasingly uneasy. She asked to telephone Mariano before leaving. The doctor hesitated. He had suspended the search for the time being, but wasn't ready to let it be known that a patient had disappeared. At the same time he couldn't keep a visitor confined within the institution.

"I can guarantee you with the utmost certainty that signora Stirner, who is assuredly within the precincts of this establishment, will be found before the day is over. Phone me toward evening and I will tell you the news. But you must promise me, swear it now, that until then you won't say a word about this to anyone."

"I promise. But I'd like to telephone my husband now just to reassure him about my being so late. If I don't he'll be out here before long to look for me. You can listen while I speak to him, doctor."

She phoned. "I was delayed. Nothing serious. I can't talk now. I'll be back in a few hours, maybe sooner. No, I'll tell you then. No, no. Don't worry. How's Mario? Please, do me a favor ... tell him everything is all right."

It was with great reluctance that the doctor watched her leave. Immediately thereafter he assembled his entire staff and urged them, for their own good as well as the good of the institution, not to let a word about this extraordinary event leak out. They resumed their search, but Luciana, who assuredly could not have left the enclosure, could not be found anywhere within it despite the fact that every corner of every building, every inch of the grounds, the gardens and the woods had been paced and beaten as if for a hunt. Luciana's room was in perfect order. All her possessions were still there, including the clothing Mariano had sent to her the evening of her confinement.

On leaving the sanitarium, Arianna, who had arranged for the carriage to wait for her, had the driver take her to via Gustavo Modena. Angelica opened the door. From her manner, Arianna understood that Luciana hadn't been there.

"The signora asked me to get one of the boy's toys," she told the old woman.

Angelica let her in. Arianna chose a fuzzy bear and returned home. Mario met her at the entryway. His face darkened when he saw she was alone.

"My mamma?"

"I went to her house. She had to leave for San Felice, but she sent you this bear because it was bored being all alone and unhappy that you didn't take it with you."

"Oh, I know. Did she tell you when she's coming back?"

"In two or three days."

When Arianna was finally alone with Mariano, he plied her with so many questions that she was forced to tell him about Luciana's disappearance. He found the news appalling. Toward evening Arianna telephoned the sanitarium. She was told that the doctor wasn't in. "How is the woman in number eight?" she asked.

"The doctor will telephone you when he comes back," was the reply.

Both Arianna and Mariano knew that Luciana had not been found.

THEY COULDN'T FIND HER BECAUSE, the psychiatrist's certainty notwithstanding, Luciana was no longer within the confines of the sanitarium.

We left her on Sunday afternoon lying across her bed in the sanitarium, weeping disconsolately. When her tears were exhausted she got up and looked around her. Everything in the room was very plain and very white, and she was overcome by a second, silent and deeper despair. She was alone, locked away. She felt as if she had lost Ramiro for the second and last time, and as if she would never escape from this cell that was blinding her with its whiteness and the harsh glare of every surface, this cell in which there was not a shadow or a grain of dust on which to rest her eyes. For some time she sat that way, dazzled and withdrawn. She roused only when the nurse entered to bring her dinner and distracted her with a few kind words. Somewhat later she was struck with a violent headache and had to lie down. She fell asleep and woke in the middle of the night with a sense of resolution and strength. She began thinking seriously of what she would do. She understood Mariano Parigi's game. She remembered every word the doctor had said to her and had no illusions. She alone would have to free herself. She resolved to do so as soon as possible, to find Ramiro and take him far away to safety. The first step, she decided, was to deceive the eminent psychiatrist.

When he came to see her the following morning, he found her composed and pleasant. They discussed her case again and he noted that she seemed less sure of herself and was smiling apologetically. The psychiatrist advised her to take frequent naps and walks, lauded the natural beauties of the sanitarium once more, and left the interview feeling quite pleased. That afternoon he saw her wandering near the rose hedge. He joined her and together they walked into the woods. He spoke to her at great length, trying to make her see reason. Luciana acquiesced in all his interpretations. The doctor was ecstatic about his new patient's intelligence. So intelligent was she, that at the end she told him, "No one has ever spoken to me the way you do, doctor. You're so good at helping me understand."

The following day she made a statement to him: "I seem to have forgotten my past life. It's as if it were no longer mine, but something I'd read in a book when I was a child. Now I feel as if my entire world is right here. I've never been as calm or as happy as I've been in the past few days here with you. I feel as if I'll be here a long, long time and that I'll be very unhappy when I have to leave."

The doctor glowed.

During these two days Luciana, wandering the grounds of the sanitarium as though aimlessly, had surveyed it completely, from the high fence along the meadow to the barbed wire fence at the side of the hill, and had calculated all the difficulties of an escape. On the night of the 30th she put the small sum of money she'd been allowed to keep into a large purse, along with some crackers she'd set aside at the end of each meal. Patients were not permitted to leave their rooms or enter the hallways before seven in the morning. At the stroke of seven Luciana walked into the hallway and asked that her breakfast be served at a small table among the flower beds, just past the roses. It was an innocent request. The door was opened and she went out. She was hungry, very hungry and ate a large meal. It was here that the woman from room ten joined her. Together they walked off to sit at the foot of a laurel. After some time, as we already know, the woman left Luciana alone.

Luciana looked around and saw no one.

She stood up, and wandered back and forth as though aimlessly, making her way to the edge of the woods, where the first oak trees stood. There she paused, bent to look at the ground behind her and noticed the footprints she'd left.

Now she studied the surrounding terrain. In a moment she began walking a wide arc which skimmed the edge of the oak grove and led deeper into the thicket of laurels, and carefully left clear prints. Once at the grove, however, she lengthened her stride as much as possible in order to leave fewer prints. At the same time she tried to make each print lighter and sought out stony tracts where, of course, there would be no footprints at all.

Her next task—to return to and enter the oak woods without leaving any tracks—would be more difficult.

She peered through the flecked shadows of the laurels and listened carefully. There was no sound from the pavilions, no movement anywhere. She sat down on some rocks and removed her shoes, then began her walk toward the oaks. She walked lightly and on her toes, choosing the hardest and roughest surfaces she could find. If a step left a trace, she'd turn back, bend and erase it, or cover it with leaves or twigs. Walking thus, with infinite caution, she managed to reach the woods and to cross most of it without leaving a single trace. She sat down on the knotty roots of an oak to put her shoes back on and rested with her back against its thick trunk. If by chance they came upon her now, nothing about her presence would arouse suspicion. Still, she was frightened at the idea of being found, of having to give up this plan and having to formulate a new one. She was sure this was the only possible escape route, and the one least likely to be detected. She figured the time to be no later than nine o'clock. Until eleven, at least, no one would be looking for her.

She got up and, walking with the same care, continued to the barbed wire fence that divided the woods.

Beyond it was freedom. Beyond it, the whole world and Ramiro.

The fence was jagged. There was no way she could get through it.

She began to study the trunks of the oak trees.

Instinctively she froze. From across the shadowed woods, as from an infinite distance, she heard voices, two voices calling. "Signora," one shouted. Then the other, higher pitched, called "Luciana." A hammer began pounding in her chest. She pressed her hands against it to keep it from breaking. Tense and icy cold from head to foot, she stood as still as the trees around her. The silence that followed was almost unnatural, and she thought perhaps she had dreamed the voices. But they called again, "Signora." And the higher pitched one, "Luciana!" A little closer now, just a little closer, so that she recognized the voices of the doctor and of Arianna. Arianna here! Why are they looking for me so early? Why is she here? Oh, maybe Ramiro is with her. Luciana started to rush out of hiding, to run toward the voices, then restrained herself. No, no, if Ramiro were with them, he would be calling her too. And Ramiro would know that his mother was there. He'd have come running right up to her. Ramiro was not here. He was out there in the world on the other side of that wall of spikes and nails. Luciana remained still as a statue. The voices did not call out again and she knew that the searchers had gone off in a different direction. But she knew, too, that if they didn't find her soon, they would come back and search the woods again. She no longer had any time to waste. She shut her eyes and held them tightly closed, telling herself to be cool and strong. She looked around again and saw a stream, the stream that ran through the woods to reach the basin near the roses. She knelt to drink from it, bathed her forehead and wrists, then drank again. She stood up, dripping and resolute. She looked at the trunks of the last oaks. The fence came right up to them, and high above, their branches hung beyond it. Beyond it—toward Ramiro. One of the oaks was somewhat bent. With some knots in its trunk and breaks in its old bark, it looked as if it wouldn't be too difficult to climb. She was sure that no one searching for her would ever dream that a women could plan such an escape. She removed her skirt, rolled it up and tied it across her back like a soldier's cape. She hung her handbag at her waist, then began to climb the tree. It wasn't easy work. The trunk was too thick for her to get her arms around. She had to steel her nerves to hold it tightly. She grabbed at knobs and cracks in its bark and clung to them with the tips of her toes and her fingernails. Two things kept her going, force of will and the feeling that she was performing wonders. Twice she had to stop to catch her breath. When she felt on the verge of discouragement, she spurred herself onward by thinking of Ramiro, who was waiting for her, and of Mariano Parigi. She had climbed almost to the first branch. By stretching her arm she could touch it with her fingertips. A piece of the tree bark broke off in her hand and instantly she felt afraid. If it fell to the ground at the foot of the tree it would be a clue to her presence. She grasped it between her teeth and held it there. One more pull and she was at the branch. She put one arm around it and, straining every muscle in her body, got the other one around it as well. Good girl, Luciana! She had trouble regaining her breath with the bark between her teeth. She looked down at the ground with immense satisfaction, a kind of pride, then she looked up at the many branches still above her head. There was more climbing to do, but now it would be easier. Seated on the branch she allowed herself a moment of rest and then resumed her way. She climbed past two more branches up to a fork in the tree that opened into a sort of hollow. It was wide and secure, an ideal refuge. She spit out the bark there, then settled into the tree, making herself comfortable with a kind of deep happiness. Looking down she couldn't see the ground and felt certain that the great branches and leaves below hid her completely from anyone who might get to the base of that tree. She curled into the concavity of her refuge as into a deep armchair. Now it made sense to wait, to let some time pass, perhaps even a few hours, because they would probably come back.

The tree held her enclosed in its arms. Luciana, who for three days had been a creature suspended in space above a world that had disappeared and with no place to rest, no place to go, now felt secure as though she were a living part of that solid tree, safely enclosed in a womb that would soon release her into light.

Every so often she listened for sounds.

The morning air around her was silent, but the tree itself was waking to a thousand small sounds and stirrings, to the bursting of buds, the quivering of leaves, the murmuring of insects and faint buzzings which, heard together, blended into a harmony filled with innocence. Luciana extended one hand to trace the hard edge of a leaf.

She reached into her bag for a mirror and comb, and tidied herself up. Then, the adventure stories she'd read in childhood flashed before her eyes, a flight of fancy, and vanished. She smiled to herself, once again leaned her head against the trunk and fell into a restful half-sleep.

In that half-sleeping state she saw in succession the Tyrrhenian sea beaten by the winds, Giorgio's cliff, four pine trees outlined in black against a pearl-colored sky, the balustrade of a box at the Vienna Opera, Ramiro calling *mamma* from the street, sun-filled terraces and, last, the peak of Mount Circe fixed to the sky. But now a jolt from the train loosens it and the island clings to the clouds to keep from falling into the sea—a flowing shadow in the midst of cool air.

She awakened to a sound that came from the distance and grew louder. Footsteps. Footsteps and voices. Footsteps on the woodland floor, voices that wound through the woods and rose to warn her. The searchers were at it again. Luciana felt the blood rush from her head, but immediately reassured herself; it would be impossible to detect her. She tried to hear the voices clearly. There seemed to be three of them, though not the doctor's, or Arianna's. Three men were combing the woods in different places and calling to locate each other. She knew she was safe, but her heart began beating harder as one set of steps approached her. The man must have stopped almost directly beneath the tree. If she had dared to move, she could have seen him. She was shuddering. The man had spoken, and his voice, rising from just below her, had exploded in her ears. He was calling out to the others. "Never! Not on your life."

Then two voices from different directions answered him, but she couldn't make out their words. The man under the tree called out, "Go to the right and then around. I'll go to the left."

His footsteps crunched frighteningly on fallen branches, then quickly disappeared.

Luciana held her breath, the better to hear whether quiet had returned to the woods. And now a ray of sunlight shining through the leaves made strange designs on the tree trunk and on her clothes.

After another few minutes, she began wondering why she was feeling so calm. Luciana, you're still inside this place, when the whole idea is to get out of it.

Moving cautiously on her perch, she got up on her knees. She pushed some small branches aside, managed to lean her chest against a large one and, stretching out from it, looked down.

What she saw horrified her. She was just above the barbed wire fence, above that tightly tangled cluster of cold iron knots and spikes. The thought that she could fall upon it at any moment chilled her blood.

The branch she was leaning on was sturdy. It extended in an arc above the fence and continued to the other side, where she would be free. The leaves at its very end were interlaced with those of an oak on the slope of the hill.

She would have to cross the entire branch as if it were a bridge and jump down onto the other side.

There was no sound in the woods. A good time to start. Luciana pressed her entire body against the branch and put her arms around it. She began sliding along. She made progress. About halfway across it she realized that the branch was getting narrower. Would it hold her until the very end? She continued a little further with her eyes closed. And even if it supported her to the very end, could she jump off it from such a height? She reopened her eyes. The branch was holding, though she began to feel a slight swaying, a springiness that didn't seem too dangerous, that might even make jumping off easier. She looked down. She was beyond the barbed wire fence. On the other side. She was free. Now it was merely a matter of getting down. She couldn't go forward anymore, or the branch would break. She had to hold onto it with one hand and reach with her other hand for a branch a little beyond it, and get down from there. It wouldn't even matter if they broke; there was grass below and the ground looked soft and damp. Still, her heart was beating quickly. Then Luciana told herself that a mother whose little boy came back from the dead after seven years can jump down from here without getting hurt. She grasped the two branches, the one close-by and the one further out, and slowly moved away from her support. She jumped, felt herself falling and tightened her grip. The two branches bent sharply under her weight and she hung in midair. She stayed that way for a very long time, afraid to let go. One of the branches creaked under the strain, then broke but didn't separate completely. A strip of bark still held it to the trunk. A whirlwind of sun-flecked green swirled around Luciana. The bark of the shattered tree was pulling away from the trunk, becoming ever thinner. Then the second branch cracked. Luciana shut her eyes, slowly released her grip, tried to contract her body and stiffen it, and fell to earth heavily. "Here I come, Ramiro," she murmured as she struck the ground.

9 SHE STAYED PUT A LONG TIME, confused, crushed and happy. She didn't dare move for fear she'd find she was in pieces. Her confusion deepened quickly and her vision dimmed. She felt as if clouds were massed before her eyes. Yet for all the darkness, her mind was functioning, drifting comically. "The flying lady" in the circus, from one trapeze to another. Off she goes just at the moment that the music holds its breath! Ah, did the music remember to stop when Luciana was flying off her tree? She laughed to herself. Good-bye sanitarium and psychiatric care, just for women, of course. It would never occur to them that just a woman, and a psychiatric patient at that, could climb a tree and slide out on a branch. But the "snake woman" could do it. Though she really should have had on tights with iridescent scales. And as for flying through the air, that called for flesh-colored tights. If anyone saw the way I look now. As soon as I can move, we'll see how things stand. I'll put the skirt back on, though it could use an ironing. There's no electric iron in my bag, but then I couldn't have used one anyway because there's no power here. Oh, look! If that barbed wire were electrified, I could stick the iron into one of those poles. A little more and I would have been stuck on one of them. A missionary in cannibal country. The famous psychiatrist, the handsome blond, the golden blond, the honey blond must have a few gray hairs by now. What did Arianna want? Do you know I'm here, Ramiro? Why don't you come looking for me? Why did you call mamma from the street? My sweet, darling baby. Will I see you today? No, not today. Maybe not even tomorrow. Maybe no one ever gets away, has ever gotten away from here. Oh, the sun is in my eyes. I can move my head, but nothing else. If an army of ants attacks me, they'll have no trouble running all over me, planting their flag on my forehead. The ant flag? I haven't got slightest idea where I am. Outside the asylum, that's for sure and that's a lot. In Lazio, yes. North East West South. Is there a wind? maestro? sirocco? In adventure books there's always a compass. Or the north star. Or moss on tree trunks. There's also the sun, but you have to know the time of day. What time is it? If I were hungry on an ordinary day, it would be noon. But this is no ordinary day. This is an extraordinary day. No day is ordinary not even at San Felice Circeo. And when Ramiro ran into my arms—after seven years of walking where the air was cool, so cool around him. I don't feel like breaking into pieces just to get some crackers out of my miraculous bag. Robinson Crusoe's bag. No, the Swiss family Robinson's. Where was it? Oh, look out! That wasp just spotted me. Here it comes. They say you shouldn't wave them away if they're not bothering you. Is that's true? It went away. It didn't like me. Oh, get out of here, you. Go to the sanitarium. They'll get you a psychiatric cure. And if you end up in the famous psychiatrist's beard, no one will even know you're there. Oh lord! The sun is moving. How can it be that the sun keeps moving, but time doesn't pass? No one passes by here. So much the better. If anyone came by and saw me, "Look, it's the flying lady" and he'd throw me back over to the other side. If a peasant came by, he'd run away in fright. If an ox with a plow came by, he'd cut me in half. No, he'd plow me under. Luciana died being plowed under. What could be more original! Plowed under. In my eyes again? Doesn't it ever stop? When will the sun finish going around? No one knows. No one will ever know. Maybe Ramiro knows. He spent seven years out there. And maybe I have to spend seven years out there too. And this is the way, through darkness, black as night, and so much cool air all around.

The sun was no longer in Luciana's eyes when she awoke several hours later from a deep sleep. Disoriented, on wakening, she sat up quickly. Instantly, a twinge of pain in her side reminded her where she was. But fear of being found, of ruining everything because of a moment of inertia, made it seem urgent that she leave the woods immediately. Ignoring her aches and pains, she pulled herself to her feet. She leaned against a tree, undid the skirt from around her, smoothed it down with her hands and put it back on, hiding the places where it was torn. She combed her hair. On the whole, she felt able to set out on her journey. Good-bye oak tree. Forgive me the broken branch, and thank you. She walked a short way up the hill and found a path that took her to the top. The other side of the hill was bare and the sun shone along its slope and on the meadow below. Recalling the darkness of the woods, Luciana trembled. She didn't know the countryside around Rome and had no idea where the open fields below her might be. But it didn't matter. The only thing that mattered was the fact that when she looked toward the foot of the hill there was a clearly delineated ribbon of road, a narrow curved strip which, after paralleling the meadows for a bit, opened into a larger road.

She went down the hill almost at a run until she reached the narrow part, where she heard the sound of approaching wheels. From around the curve a cart appeared, and at a sign from her the driver stopped.

"Could you give me a ride? I was on horseback when my horse threw me and ran up there." She made a vague gesture toward the hill.

The driver helped her into the cart. Standing against its side, her body ached more than it had all day. But she didn't mind.

After a long ride and endless turns that left her completely disoriented, they reached a square opposite a bridge.

"The Molle Bridge, signorina," said the driver.

They crossed to the other side of the bridge.

"There's a bus that goes by here. You can wait for it there."

Luciana got down from the cart and gave the driver a few of the coins she had in her purse.

"I thank you very much," she told him, "and wish I could give you more money, but I don't have enough with me. But if you get into Rome, go to the address I'm going to write down for you, and they'll give you a lot more."

Using a pencil she wrote Mariano Parigi's via Abruzzi address on a slip of paper, then the words, "I request signora Arianna Parigi or signor Mario Parigi to reward this man who offered me the hospitality of his carriage and transported me back to Rome. Luciana." Smiling maliciously, she presented the note to the driver.

She waited for the horse-drawn bus that went to the piazza del Popolo by way of via Flaminia. On the bus she asked another passenger the time. It was five o'clock, which seemed extraordinary to her. She got off the bus outside the city gate and entered a trattoria. It was an exertion for her to eat, and even as she did so she was thinking of what to do next, where to go.

She thought: Mariano Parigi had absolutely no right to have me confined. I'd never have found a way of getting out of that place because I don't know anyone, while he with all his connections could do whatever he wanted. But now that I am out of there and don't live in his house anymore, I'm free and there's no reason for me to hide. The first thing to do is to find someone to protect me.

She asked for a Rome directory and looked up the address of a well-known attorney, a signor Massimiliano, whom she had heard Parigi mention as a past adversary in a civil suit.

She found a carriage in the piazza del Popolo and had the driver take her to Massimiliano's office.

At first glance the famous man disappointed her. She had imagined the attorney as muscular and heroic, an overwhelming orator with wind blowing through his hair, whose every gesture could shake the towers of the distant city. Massimiliano was a small dry man with a hooked nose, a few hairs smoothed over an oblong cranium, eyes like two tiny black pinheads and long, bony hands constantly clawing at the air.

His curiosity was aroused when he heard Luciana Veracina's name, and he fairly burst with enthusiasm on learning of her latest experience. His face filled with heated animation and his spare little body produced gestures and movements of unexpected energy.

"Wonderful, signora, stupendous," he shouted. "A first rate case."

His southern style of speech, which Luciana first found laden with skepticism and indifference, now overflowed with professional exuberance.

"You are very fortunate to have come to me. You're talking about the unlawful imprisonment of an individual—clearly and evidently present here—a case which can be won in five minutes. A child could do it. But for us this is a giant trampoline, a jumping off point, the base from which we take flight. The unlawful imprisonment of an individual, of signora Luciana Veracina. Absolutely the easiest thing to win. But we will graft a much more brilliant case upon it, a more exciting, extraordinary one, a colossal case, the only such case in the entire world. You don't understand? Ah, we will issue a summons to signor Mariano Parigi. We will call him into the halls of justice. Do you know why? Because he is keeping, detaining, holding your child for himself, in fact, sequestering him within his own home. Your unlawful imprisonment in a sanitarium and the sequestering of the boy, your son. We will petition the courts to resolve the issue of whether the child is his or yours, and who has the rights in the case. We will have to show that the Parigis haven't the slightest claim in this matter."

"Oh, yes. Will that be easy to do?"

"Easy? It will be extremely difficult. A superhuman undertaking. It takes a strong stomach to undertake such a case. The stomach of a Massimiliano is what it takes, my lovely lady. How clever you were to come to me. And what a stomach that is! This will be an historic case. It will be included in every book on famous cases. To think, there was so much talk about 'the Parigi Case' that I was reading every newspaper every day, following each and every turn in it, point by point. I'll have the whole thing at my fingertips with just one night of study. Of course, you'll fill me in on all the details. And we'll whip things up. We'll whip them up. Do you realize that everyone in Trastevere believes in this miracle and will be on our side? You didn't even consider Trastevere. I won't even have to raise my little finger to turn this into a political issue."

Massimiliano was an ambitious young man. His dream was to become a member of parliament, then a cabinet minister.

"But tell me, can I go see Ramiro now? Tomorrow, at least?"

"Ramiro? Ah, the child. That remains to be seen. I will file your suit, get it moving. I will control it, stir it up, nurture it and shape it anyway I want. And I will win it. Resoundingly! That is my responsibility. Magnificent. But as to when you can see the child, that is not in my hands. That is in the hands of a magistrate who will decide; although he will, of course, be influenced by the suit. In this way, I will impose the decision upon him, but still, my dear girl, it has to come from him. And it will be a long, difficult case; otherwise, what kind of a case is it?"

Fatigue finally overcame Luciana.

"You ought to rest now," Massimiliano told her. "Get some

sleep. For today, at least, it would be better if you didn't go home. A hotel would be best. Some inconspicuous hotel. In fact, I'll take you to one and introduce you. They won't give you any trouble. Get a good night's sleep. Tomorrow morning get yourself and your clothes fixed up, and be back here at my office at exactly two. Obviously, you don't have any money with you. Allow me. You can repay me later, when you return home."

"When will that be?"

"Tomorrow, I think, two days at the most. Don't worry about it."

He took her to a hotel and introduced her as he had promised. As soon as they parted, Luciana began thinking of ways she might get to see Ramiro immediately. The famous attorney began thinking of the reverberations of his celebrated and historic case—the case which in his hands would become a political issue and throw all of Trastevere into an uproar.

The next morning, following Massimiliano's advice, Luciana spent some time getting her wardrobe in order. But she didn't arrive at his office at precisely two. She was unable to resist the temptation to see Ramiro, just to look at him, even if only for a moment and from a distance.

A little after one o'clock she posted herself along the Belisario Wall at the place where one can look down the entire length of via Abruzzi. She was in a closed carriage with her face veiled as if she were guilty of a crime. She waited a long time and, feeling disappointed and anxious, was about to leave when the boy suddenly sprang into the sunlit street followed by Arianna. They began walking toward the carriage. At every step the boy's features became more distinct. Luciana could see his face clearly. Is he a little pale? Arianna took his hand. She seems deep in thought. Now she's leaning over him. What is she saying to him? Ramiro looked up at her and answered with a laugh. Luciana was gripped by a jealous fury almost impossible to control. Now the woman and child were no longer speaking to each other and were getting closer to her. When they reached the corner of via Campania—ten steps, just ten steps from your mother—they turned, apparently without noticing the stopped carriage, and walked past it. Good-bye. Good-bye. Now Luciana could only see their backs. Ramiro's shoulders have always been somewhat narrow. I must get him down to the seashore quickly, within the next two weeks. But why are they slowing down? Look, the child has stopped and made Arianna stop too.

Ramiro had turned and was looking around, as if he'd heard his name called.

But Arianna hadn't heard anything and just watched as the boy, who had moved away from her, continued to look in every direction. She is letting him, so he'll see that he's mistaken. Ramiro shook his head and put his hand in Arianna's again. They resumed their walk and disappeared into the distance.

Impetuously, Luciana decided to rush after them and grasped the door handle. She felt sure Arianna would not give her away. But in a moment she knew it would be a mistake. Ramiro would never understand why his mother would have to leave him again. And he'd talk about it at home in front of Mariano, only complicating matters. No, the first thing she had to do was to see the lawyer. But more than anything else, deep within herself Luciana felt, without being fully aware of it, that to reveal her presence now, to ask for, to plead for a greeting or a kiss and then go off again, would imply she was retreating. She, his mother, who in Arianna's presence had never, not even for a moment, indicated the slightest doubt about her right to him since the evening of that miraculous embrace twenty-three days ago—such a long time ago, such a distant evening—she, who with self-assurance alone had always dominated her rival.

And now her rival is crossing down there, disappearing from view, taking her darling child away. Luciana leaned out of the carriage window in anguish. She could no longer see him. She could no longer see anything, neither the trees nor the street. She threw herself back against the seat cushions, gathered all her resolve and gave the coachman Massimiliano's address.

The lawyer's confidence and eloquence did little to improve her state of mind. She listened to him quietly. She promised him —as well as herself—that she would follow his advice faithfully. He advised her to do nothing rash, but assured her that she could now return to her own home without fear of repercussion. She waited until evening. It was nearly nine o'clock when she arrived at via Gustavo Modena, where Angelica, who knew nothing of her three-day confinement, greeted her without ceremony.

"There's a letter for you. A maid brought it late this afternoon and said to keep it for you until you got here."

Luciana took the letter, ordered Angelica not to tell anyone that she was back, and went into her room. The letter was from Arianna. It had been written not more than two or three hours earlier.

"Dear Luciana, we know that you managed to escape from there just the day I came to see you. No one else thinks so, but I'm convinced you'll stop by at your house. The first day you were gone I went there to bring the baby's bear back to him. I told him that you had sent it. That calmed him down a little. I told him you had to go to San Felice Circeo. He's been quieter, but today after our regular outing to Villa Borghese he became restless again and started asking for you, so I promised him I'd write to you. Please, I beg you, for his peace of mind, write him a letter confirming what I told him, that you're at San Felice and that for now you've been detained there. It will keep him calm. He'll trust me and meanwhile time will pass. Send me a letter and I'll give it to him. I feel certain that God will direct your steps home and that you will receive this letter. If not, I don't know how I'll manage with the child. I'm so tired and so worried. Affectionately, Arianna."

◆ ◆ ◆ ◆ ◆

INSTANTLY, LUCIANA DECIDED TO GO TO San Felice Circeo. Not wanting to lie to Ramiro, she would write and post her letter from there. Early the following morning she went to see the lawyer, who assured her that her presence would not be required for several days. If it did become necessary, he said, he would wire her to return. She left at once and arrived at San Felice early in the afternoon. In town she understood that these simple people, essentially isolated from the rest of the world, hadn't heard anything about her miraculous case. Not one of them had any notion that for several days San Felice had been the object of half of Europe's curiosity. Circeans at that moment were rushing down to see the Sea Gypsies, who had come ashore a few days earlier and were camped on the beach just south of the Astura tower. Luciana went to her room and immediately began writing her letter.

"Ramiro, my darling son, forgive your mamma, who had to leave you so suddenly. I swear that I am not to blame for it, and that I am doing everything possible to return to you as soon as I can, and when I do I'll never ever leave you again. I am at San Felice Circeo, the town I was in when you summoned me and from which I returned immediately. When I can come and get you again, I'll take you back here with me and you'll see how beautiful the sea is and I'll tell you many things. We'll take walks along the beach and go out in sail boats. And if you like it here, we can stay forever and you can learn to be a sailor. Then when you grow up you can take me on a really long trip in a big ship with lots of white sails all filled with wind. I hope that you are feeling well and are getting along with the people caring for you. Now sit down and write a nice long letter to your mamma, who thinks of you night and day, and who kisses you and hugs you as tightly as she did on the day we found each other. Good-bye until we see each other again. Very, very soon, my darling treasure. Your mother."

She posted the letter and went out for a walk along the beach beyond the Astura tower and Giorgio's rock to see the Sea Gypsies for herself. There were about twenty of them: men, women and children. They were of the same stock as the gypsies who occasionally turn up in our countryside, though this type is far more rare; in fact, the strain, which appears to be descended from a Finnish branch of the great family, is almost extinct. They are rather taller than other gypsies and much less ragged looking, just as all seafaring people, even when as poor as country folk, seem less ragged than they do. Their countenances fall somewhere between devious and dreamy. They follow the sea along the Mediterranean coast in small sailing ships, come to shore in canoe-like boats, and camp in sea towns along the coast to tell fortunes, put on shows and sing the strange songs that enchant the fishermen and peasants along the seacoast. Then one fine morning before dawn they suddenly sail off. Sea Gypsies are very rarely seen on Italian shores.

Groups of astonished Circeans were staring at them curiously and suspiciously from a safe distance. Others had already formed friendships with some. The previous day the oldest of the gypsy women had cured a boy of a deep wound in his foot using medication made of broom roots gathered along that very shore, which she applied while uttering incomprehensible words. And two of the youngest of the Gypsies had known how to patch up and relaunch a large boat forced up on the rocks by a storm several months earlier, which the local fishermen had decided was irreparable and were about to cut up for firewood.

Luciana stopped near Giorgio's rock. From there she could see the encampment in the distance. She stood looking at it. The villagers were beginning to return home. Down on the shore a great campfire was being lit, a gigantic circle of flame surrounded by three tents—a large square one and two smaller cone-shaped ones, which together filled the narrow sandy strip between the pounding waves and the fore edge of the vegetation. The day was dying, and from the depths of the violet horizon, the last of the sun's rays skimmed along the wide surface of the sea, struck bright flames upon the tents, and in an instant died away. Already, heaven and earth were streaming with shadows hurrying to close around every shape. Then the great campfire flared. Outlines of human forms intermingled with restless shadows that stretched and wavered along the sloping sides of the tents, bounded to the ground and slithered high and low along the uneven surface of the sand. Voices resounded, shadowy figures hurried back and forth, children's cries pierced the air. Smoke issued from the center of the flames, rose straight up, and was swallowed by the night. At the two far ends of the encampment pale lights appeared. Then the movements and voices quieted down. Luciana noticed that the gypsies were now seated in groups, some on stools, some on the ground. Their dinner was being distributed. A hurried, muffled murmur, no doubt a propitiatory prayer rose from their midst. Then there was silence and all one could hear was the infinite breathing of the sea. The central fire burned lower and lower. When it was completely out, the torch lights swinging at the extreme ends of the camp burned darker red and a few stars broke the black surface of the sky. Once more voices sprang up and mingled with each other, while shadows wound tortuously about, before disappearing under the tents. Then the torches were extinguished and there was nothing but darkness and silence.

All Luciana could see now was a mass blacker than the black night in which it stood. And beyond it, out at sea, blacker still than anything else, the shape of the anchored vessel rocking back and forth. She turned and retraced her steps. Now every one of the sea's sighs ended in a moan and the moans accompanied her along her entire way beneath a sky filled with cold stars. That night she dreamed of Giorgio and of the mad woman who'd sat under the laurel tree with her the morning of her escape. It was the woman who pointed Giorgio out to her. He was seated high up on the branch of a tree with his legs hanging over, and the sight didn't seem the least bit strange. She awakened very early the next morning and couldn't stay in bed. She went out and started walking in the still pale, unbroken dawn. Off in the distance she perceived a figure at the crest of Giorgio's rock. A man was sitting with his legs hanging over the sea side, gazing out at the ashy expanse dappled with foam to the very edge of the sky....

LUCIANA STOPPED IN TERROR AND PRESSED her hands against her chest. For a moment her heart stopped beating as well, for the human heart never becomes accustomed to miracles. However, she recovered quickly and the crazy thought that had crossed her mind vanished. If it had lasted, she would surely have died right then and there. She hurried on. Her momentary panic gave way to an outburst of fury against the desecrator.

She had never again since then, since that first time, climbed to the top of the cliff. She had never seen anyone else climb it. She had never imagined that anyone could climb it.

When she got closer she saw it was one of the Sea Gypsies. Slowly she made her way to the base of the rock. Moment by moment the dawn brightened, tingeing the sky with patches of pink. The gypsy was wearing gray cloth pants and a faded blue jersey strangely decorated by the effects of salt erosion. His arms and feet were bare. He was immersed in thought and unaware of Luciana, who, having made up her mind on the spur of the moment, climbed the steep rock steps to the very top. Only then did the Gypsy hear her and turn to look. He was speechless before the apparition that seemed to him to have sprung from the stone, or fallen from the sky, or to have been formed spontaneously at his side by the pale sunbeams in the air.

Then he recovered and said, "I see. You're the lady of the rock."

Luciana stared at him in wonder.

He went on, "Yes, the woman for whom a man jumped from here a very long time ago."

He was pointing to the sea, and his gesture struck Luciana like a blow, causing her suddenly to recall images of the most enormous event of her life. Her face flamed with anger and shame.

She sought vainly to reply. Eventually, she became calmer and sat down beside the Gypsy. His arm was tattooed with strange letters and with stars.

"What is your name?" she asked him.

"Solwanah."

He pointed to the large ship at anchor with its sails furled. "The ship's name is Vieghliah, for my father's mother."

He'd stopped looking at Luciana when he began speaking.

So darkly was the Vieghliah's worn planking reflecting the water's surface that the ship seemed to be made of metal.

Solwanah turned toward the encampment.

"They're all still asleep. At sea they rise up before the first light of dawn. As soon as they get on land they get very sleepy. Our encampment is called Zalna."

The large tent was now as red as blood. The tips of the two small conical tents were blazing in the sun light.

To point out the encampment the gypsy had turned to face Luciana, who studied him. His eyes were light colored, bright as cold metal. He lowered his eyelids and spoke huskily.

"I'm the only one who couldn't sleep this morning, so I got up, left camp and climbed up here without thinking. I'm sorry, I meant no harm."

"Were you ever in Rome?" Luciana asked him.

"Never. Once we sailed past the mouth of the river, but we

stayed out to sea. Vieghliah may look flimsy, but she sails anywhere."

Solwanah stirred as though to get up and asked meekly, "Would you like me to leave?"

"No. Tell me about your life."

The gypsy racked his brain a moment. "There's nothing to tell," he replied. "Haven't you ever seen gypsies?"

"Only the ones who go around the countryside in big wagons."

"It's the same thing, except ships are much nicer."

Luciana was silent, then staring at her knees and twisting one hand against the sharp stone, she whispered, "One of the things they say about land gypsies is that sometimes they steal children."

Solwanah didn't answer.

She persisted. "Out in the country when a child disappears, right away the people think the gypsies took him."

"What for?" the gypsy asked innocently, and pointed toward the encampment. "We treat children very well."

Luciana looked at the now gleaming ship and asked, "Where did you come from? Where are you going?"

"We never know the names of places."

Solwanah felt somewhat embarrassed. Searching his memory, he pointed into the distance and whispered, "Africa."

Then seeking something else to say, he pointed to the two dugouts pulled up on the pebbled shore between the tents and the sea. "Those canoes can go pretty fast. Sometimes I leave the ship and go different places by myself. I take a canoe along the coast or out to sea. Meanwhile, Vieghliah goes on its way and later I catch up with it."

He continued in a confidential tone, "I'm good at fishing."

"Sometimes I do it with dynamite," he added confidentially, "but it's illegal."

He reached into his pocket and, smiling, showed her three or four sticks of the explosive.

Luciana looked at them curiously. "They'd make a big explosion?"

"Enormous."

"Could it blow up a cliff like this?"

"Sure. You'd have to make a lot of holes and put fuses in them."

Luciana felt almost intoxicated. She stared into his eyes, which under her gaze became still lighter and filled with uncertainty, while his face turned red as if he were a child.

"Solwanah," Luciana told him, "it was wrong of you to climb up to this rock. No one must ever come here again. And no one ever will. You will blow it up."

"All right."

"You promise?"

"I swear, signora. I won't leave this beach. I won't board Vieghliah again until I've blown up this rock."

"When?"

"I don't know. Just before we leave, because otherwise they'll catch me and put me in jail."

"That's fine. When are you leaving?"

"I don't know. We never know before."

Luciana sat silently for a long time. The sea was sparkling and the horizon filled with sails. She stood up. "Good-bye," she said.

"Do you want me to help you down?"

"No."

She descended the cliff and without looking back walked off.

Solwanah watched her for a long time, then stood up on the rock to keep her in view. When she disappeared, he went on looking at the deserted path she had followed. Slowly, he repeated the words they had exchanged.

Luciana spent the rest of the day in her room. When she looked out the window the next morning, the ship that had been at anchor was gone. She walked down to the beach and all the way to the place between the tower and the cliff where the encampment had been. It too was gone.

That's the way it is with Sea Gypsies. One fine day before dawn without warning they sail off. And Giorgio's rock was intact. Luciana thought bitterly of Solwanah, who had broken his promise. The thought gave her a strange uneasiness she couldn't shake.

Returning along the shore on the path between the bushes and the low lying vines, she paused.

From behind the twisted trunk of a fig tree, she thought she had seen the sudden flash of eyes as clear and cold as metal.

She waited a moment, then shrugged. She returned to her room and remained there for the entire day, feeling restless and drained. She couldn't read. Distracted, her mind wandered from one incongruous thought to another, incapable of fixing on anything. Time moved slowly and laboriously, as though it were a rusty machine. Waltz tunes tormented her like stubborn flies. Fragmented images rained down upon her. She moved agitatedly about her room, unable to stop that unceasing flow which was making her sick to her stomach. From time to time she would suddenly see Solwanah's eyes, the only distinct image in all that confusion. But she hurriedly repelled the vision, for that, too, upset her. The following day she received a note from Ramiro, which she clasped to her breast, and a telegram from the attorney that read, "Come see me either tomorrow or the next day." She left immediately.

The soft joltings of the carriage along the strip of road that runs from the headland to Terracina shook the anxieties from her mind. She felt she was heading into a daring battle.

But when the carriage was about to enter Terracina, Luciana

was startled a second time. Again she saw that glance, not merely in her mind but with her eyes. It had flashed from under an arch of the city's watch tower. The carriage entered and passed through the archway. The source of the glance had vanished as if it had instantly retreated to the other side of the tower. On the train, Luciana fell into a troubled half sleep. Every so often she would open her eyes and think, "I never thought he'd go off like that without keeping his promise." Then she'd close them slowly, saying, "I bet I see those eyes again before I get to Rome." In fact, when she got off the train and was walking behind the porter on the narrow sidewalk amid hurrying travelers, there they were. This time she saw not only eyes, but in a flash briefer than lightning, a figure as well, a tall, slim figure. Then both glance and figure disappeared behind the corner of a large coach right at the moment that a passenger turned to Luciana to say, "I beg your pardon," after having bumped her with his suitcase.

The next morning, the fourth of June, Luciana was at Massimiliano's office.

10

"WE'RE DOING THIS IN THE GRAND manner," Massimiliano said loudly and with fearful velocity, as soon as he saw her. "Look at what's happened already. The morning of May thirtieth you were still behind bars. Since yesterday, the third of June, it's your persecutor who's got his feet to the fire. He's received notification of our claims and intentions, and on the ninth the fun begins. We've accused signor Mariano Parigi summarily, and along with him that crack-brained psychiatrist, just to get a good laugh out of it, of imprisonment, of having locked your charming self up. And that's nothing. We have at the same time accused, do you understand, accused, not merely summoned, the same signor Parigi to answer for a second charge of imprisonment. Do I have to explain myself? No? You are not mistaken. No one would have expected a nervy move like that. The denunciation of the aforesaid Mariano Parigi to the Royal prosecutor for detaining a child not his own and for forcing the child to live with him against its will. Is it, or is it not true that the child is living in the Parigi household instead of yours? Is it, or is it not true that he is living there because Parigi and his wife, his accomplice in this affair, want him there against his mother's, that is, your own, wishes? This is not a case of physical restriction, as it was in confining you to the sanitarium, but a case of moral, emotional restriction. What reason would you have to live with the Parigis on via degli Abruzzi from"—and here the attorney looked down at his notes—"from the ninth of

146

May to the twenty-seventh? And the child as well, from an even earlier date and against his will, as expressed clearly and violently on the seventh of May just passed. Your abduction and confinement were offenses committed in order to enable them to continue to enjoy their previous crime without interference. I know that there is a difficult, thorny issue to resolve here, one that will be as hard to cut through as a diamond. Their side will say that the child is not yours. On this issue, however, the civil law takes over from the penal. Here our case grows, swells, becomes multifaceted, superhuman, the most unique case the world has ever seen. But during the penal trial you will also be preparing the ground for the civil trial. Now, sign here. You will be questioned. For witnesses, I've summoned signora Arianna, not as an accessory, but as a witness, our witness, do you understand? Also, the grocer, your housekeeper, and the carriage driver from the now famous stall at number 115. Remember that all of Trastevere will be on our side. And then of course the boy will also have to testify."

"Ramiro testify? In a courtroom? In front of all those people?"

"Absolutely! It will make for the best scene of all, move everyone to tears. It is where the trial becomes pure poetry. Arguments begin before the Penal Court of Rome on Saturday morning, the ninth of June. What do you say to that? And all within six days and without any preliminaries or hearings, which would have cost us time and trouble! Oh, how I would have liked to see dear signor Mariano's face yesterday when he received the news of our accusation from the illustrious Crown prosecutor."

And, in fact, upon receiving the papers demanding his appearance at a summary procedure, Mariano Parigi thought he was dreaming. At first he considered the order so completely insane that he had nothing to fear from it. But very quickly he realized that the issue of Luciana's confinement was not something to have been taken lightly and he became furious with those who had advised the course. He went with his attorney, Remo Caronte, of Rome, to the office of the Penal Court (which in those days was housed in the old Filippini monastery, where the Chiesa Nuova stands today) to read the documents. The audacity of the plaintiffs terrified him. They had gone so far as to call his wife, Mario's mother, as a witness for their side. During the last few days before the trial, he and his attorney tried to explain the circumstances to Arianna and to suggest the responses that would best serve their defense. But they saw how trying it would be for her merely to state simply and sincerely what she had seen and heard. Poor Anna was depleted, exhausted, and in torment over Mario's behavior. The child was calm, but withdrawn. He didn't ask about Luciana or speak about his other home. He seemed preoccupied and passive, and would spend hours in quiet indolence, a kind of dulcet boredom, which certainly wasn't forgetfulness, but which might have been covering a secret and ardent anticipation. He was on good terms with Arianna, though not affectionate. He treated her with indulgence almost tinged with sympathy. Mariano Parigi had lost his self assurance and his ability to act decisively in regard to the boy. The child's mysterious presence confused and incapacitated him. He avoided speaking to him and finally even seeing him. It was an inhuman and inhumane situation filled with immeasurable anguish, and without any possible solution.

Arianna awaited the day of the trial with mounting terror. She suffered endlessly during sleepless nights trying to imagine what it would be like, but never succeeded in doing so. All she could visualize was a deeply dark, high shadowy place that she would have to enter. She would be a tiny figure, holding Mario's hand and walking forward in the darkness, through strange terrors. They'll ask me a lot of questions, and I'll have to answer with so many people around, all staring at me. How I can describe what happened? No one in the world could describe what

I've been through. I'll die right there without ever saying a word. Well, so what if God takes me tomorrow? But no, what would Mario do? They're going to ask him questions too, and he'll get sick again. He'll get all mixed up and his fever will come back. If only I knew how to escape, to take him with me and get out of here. Luciana escaped. She would know how to do it. Ah, to run right now, holding Mario close to me, close in my arms. To get on a train with him and go someplace far away. Like the time we went to Rome. Why did we ever come to Rome? To this cursed city, where all this suffering was awaiting me. But who could have known it? And then? Then afterward? Will it be still worse? If at least I knew what was ahead for me? But I can't even imagine it. I can't think of what to do. Any other mother would run off with her child, would instantly take him away with her. Why can't I do it? No one ever taught me how to do these things. There's no one who can help me. Mario still doesn't know that in two days we'll take him to that terrifying place. It must be a huge room and very high. I have to tell Mario that we're going there, prepare him so that he won't be frightened.

It never became clear to Arianna how to explain the matter to Mario. She decided to put the problem to her husband, who was no more lucid on the subject than she. They put it off. Parigi tried in vain through mutual acquaintances to get his adversary, in the name of human decency, to relinquish any public interrogation of the boy. It was like trying to get a tenor to relinquish his great second act aria.

The morning of the ninth dawned, and Mariano and Arianna had still said nothing to the boy.

Caronte arrived. He and Mario left immediately to be present at the opening arguments. Arianna and the child were to be there an hour later.

And in the carriage an hour later Arianna finally managed to speak. "Darling," she began, "do you know where we are going?"

Mario seemed not the slightest bit curious. "No," he said.

"We're one our way to do something very disagreeable, but let's hope it won't last long. And, if you'd like, tomorrow or the day after, I'll take you to the country."

"To the seashore? To see mamma? Oh, to San Felice Circeo where I wrote to her?"

"Maybe."

"Then let's do the disagreeable thing right away. What is it?"

"We're going to a big, ugly, closed up room. There'll be a lot of people in it. And there'll be a judge too, who asks everybody what they do, and what they've done. And you'll have to answer everything. They'll ask you about...."

"Oh, like in the story about Gocciastella, where the king questions everyone who comes into the big hall? Do you remember?"

"Yes, yes, just like that," Arianna answered. But after this momentary reaction during which he recalled the fairy tale, Mario sank back into apathy and appeared not at all curious or concerned about the questions that would be put to him. As a result Arianna's task was easily accomplished. When their carriage arrived at the square near the Filippini, it stopped. There were knots of people standing in place, groups of people milling about. Caronte's assistant met them. He helped them down from the carriage, led them through the labyrinthine corridors, and left them to wait in a large, extremely high-ceilinged room almost devoid of furniture. Every one of their movements produced a sound, and every sound an echo which spun upward to that high, gray ceiling before dying away against dirty glass windows. They waited a long time. Every so often they'd hear distant voices that soon faded away. No doubt these were arguments in the proceedings taking place just beyond their room.

The Boy with Two Mothers

◆ ◆ ◆ ◆ ◆

THE FIRST PART OF THE TRIAL PROCEEDED quickly and smoothly. There could be no substantial dispute about Luciana's confinement, but Massimiliano had no intention of lingering over that charge and had skillfully steered the proceedings, in fact had even hastened them toward the burning, the extraordinary, the insoluble issue. Already, harbingers of future battles had become evident during Luciana's interrogation.

Luciana had told the story of her life with simplicity. Sitting erectly and essentially motionless with her gaze focused unwaveringly on some distant point and speaking in a flat voice as though reciting a litany, she enthralled her listeners.

No one had dared even the slightest whisper when she described the boy's return from the dead.

Presently, she was telling of her stay at the Parigi home before her abduction, and every time she innocently referred to the boy as "my son" Caronte would let loose a stream of impatient, ironical and audible mutterings. At one point he seemed about to leap up in rage, but a gesture from the president of the tribunal stopped him. Massimiliano was on his guard. He had managed to bring the issue to the public's attention, but was reluctant to have it discussed too deeply, foreseeing that the problems it presented would interfere with the present penal trial.

Luciana's recitation kept the onlookers rapt in anxious admiration. A substantial block of Trasteverites occupied most of the seats available to the public. Massimiliano kept watch over them as over a precious resource. The reserved seats, notwithstanding the heat of the season, were occupied by the most elegant citizens of the eternal city.

When Luciana had concluded her testimony the president agreed to have Arianna and the boy appear together. "Parigi, Arianna and Parigi, Mario" the bailiff called toward their room.

"The case is decided," Caronte shouted.

Massimiliano jumped up, "Quiet."

"But it is," Caronte insisted. "The moment our most illustrious President had them call for Mario Parigi, and not for Ramiro Stirner, the decision became clear."

A hostile murmur arose from the Trasteverites. The President of the Court glared down at them and threatened to clear the courtroom. Massimiliano was about to say something to relieve the tension when agitated whisperings of "they're here, they're coming in" from the reserved seats restored silence to the room more quickly, and efficaciously, than any threat could have done. Spectators rose to their feet, and a palpable tremor ran though the courtroom as Arianna, holding Mario by the hand, entered.

Arianna's face was filled with infinite sorrow.

Her eyes were swollen and brimming with tears for she was terrified of not being able to say what she had to. The long wait had left her mind a blank.

She was sworn in, and, at the request of the President, turned to him to begin recounting the events at the Villa Borghese the day Mario's first symptoms appeared. At that moment, the child, seated at her side, who had been looking boldly and somewhat curiously around the room, suddenly noticed Luciana sitting below him and staring at him with burning eyes, as if to absorb him. He leaped up wildly, raised his arms toward her and called out, "Mamma!"

Luciana ran to him, bent toward him and stood still. As she enfolded him in her arms, a groan of unrestrainable emotion burst from the crowd.

Instantly, Massimiliano was on his feet. "Look at them," he exclaimed, and suddenly he appeared to be tall and handsome.

At the sound of his voice, Luciana and Ramiro turned and raised their faces toward him. Luciana was on her knees with her arm around the boy's waist, so that her face was level with his. Massimiliano stared at them as if his eyes were emitting powerful rays of light. Indeed, their two faces were luminous. For, heedless of all around them and glowing in the delight of being in each other's arms after having been apart for so many days, Luciana and Ramiro composed an innocent picture of love and happiness.

"Look at them," the orator proclaimed again, adding a note of sympathetic protection to his voice. "Who could say that they are not mother and child? There you have it! The questions that theologians, theosophists, physiologists and jurists will never be able to answer. There it is, honored judges, resolved by that sweet, sublime sight. It is not enough to say that these two faces resemble each other. One is compelled to say that they are one face in two incarnations, one angel in two, the woman angel and the child angel. It is only one same smile of joy and laughter that illuminates both their faces. Just look at them!"

And in fact, in joy their two faces had assumed an extraordinary resemblance.

Everyone in the courtroom was transfixed. No one dared utter a sound. Perhaps the President of the tribunal would also have remained silent, awaiting who knows what supernatural intervention, had he too been overwhelmed with the enchanting sight. But from his position high on the bench, he could see neither the woman's face nor the child's, which, of course, made it possible for him to escape their spell and to recall the cold duties of his office.

"I request the complainant, Signora Stirner, to return to her seat, " he said, "and the witness, Signora Parigi, to reply to the questions I put to her."

Luciana kissed Ramiro on the top of his head, released him and returned to her seat. The child sat down, but as he watched her walk away his face became sullen and his lips trembled. Arianna, who had sat rigidly during the entire episode to keep from bursting into tears, now began speaking in a tremulous voice.

From the defense table Caronte, surprised and stung by his adversary's triumph, watched her carefully, hoping to spring a trap of his own.

Though the spectators could not hear every word Arianna spoke, they were moved by her emotion and bewilderment.

"I began walking behind him very quietly," she said. "I put my hands over his eyes."

She had thought about that horrid scene over and over during her long months of suffering. But never before had she experienced it in all its strange, frightening detail as now, when shy as she was, she was forced to describe it in its entirety, and out loud to an audience.

Caronte looked at her as if he wanted to transfix her. Then he looked at the agitated, resentful child at her side. Instantly, an idea formed in the attorney's mind.

Arianna's voice went on, "and your Honor, afterward he said …he said," she hesitated, not wanting to cry again. And now Mario, looking anxious and troubled, turned his face to hers.

Caronte was watching attentively.

"And when he said, 'I want my mother,' I said, 'darling, I'm your mother.' But he answered, 'No, no you're not.'"

Arianna couldn't go on. She burst into tears and remained standing there, motionless, weeping so that her body heaved, so that deep sobs rose to her lips, and long tears streamed down her face and slid to the floor, for she hadn't the strength to wipe them away.

Now Caronte rose and took a step, almost a leap forward. He pointed his arm at the boy, stared at him angrily and shouted, "Mario. Why did you make your mother cry like that? You're a bad boy."

The child, terrified by the lawyer's apparent fury, shrieked, grabbed Arianna's skirt and burst into heartbreaking tears.

Arianna bent toward him. Through her own tears she moaned, "No, no," and took him in her arms and picked him up so that his face was close to hers. Their two countenances were as one in their mingled, comfortless weeping.

"Look," shouted Caronte. "Just look. If it is blood that makes for resemblance, who could deny that these two are mother and son? What child has ever resembled his mother more?"

It was true. The two faces close together beneath that storm of tears seemed mirror images of each other.

A tide of madness flowed over the spectators. They were no longer for or against either side. All were overcome by the same sense of wonder at the boy who looked like one mother when he was crying and another when he was smiling. And, in each case, with such a perfect resemblance that it defied imagination.

THE NEXT TWO MINUTES SEEMED AN ETERNITY.

Then the Minister of Public Affairs and the President of the Court whispered together briefly.

Finally the President spoke. "The Minister of Public Affairs has raised an exception in this case and has asked the court to remand it to a civil tribunal for resolution of the issue of the child's maternity and paternity, which is essential to the decision that this penal court must render."

Thereafter the spectators were dismissed.

The public filed out in silence, still exhilarated and confused. Mariano motioned to Arianna from a doorway. She was holding Mario by the hand when she joined him, but could not lift her head. Mario was once again apathetic.

Luciana watched from a distance, uncertain whether to approach them. Turning away to look at the departing crowd, she felt as if she were suspended in midair, and saw strange shadows hovering above their heads. Suddenly she saw one of those shadows shape itself to the outline of Giorgio's rock and vanish.

Then the gypsy's clear-eyed glance flashed before her, taking much longer to fade away. The sound of Massimiliano's voice dispersed her phantoms. The attorney ushered her into an adjacent room to discuss preparations for the civil case.

When his wife and child reached him, Mariano Parigi spoke quickly. "I'm staying here to go over the case with Caronte, Anna. I'll be home within an hour. Wait for the crowd to thin out before you leave."

After the spectators had dispersed, Arianna and the child walked down the large staircase and through the entrance hall. The street, however, was still jammed with people. Some of the Trasteverites saw Ramiro and stopped to look at him. Frightened, Arianna stepped back to lean against the high doorposts.

Beyond the crowd she saw an empty carriage approaching. She motioned to it with one hand, but it continued slowly on its way. She dropped the child's hand for a moment, took two steps forward, and waved at the carriage again. This time the driver saw her and turned. Arianna moved back again. Just at that moment a soldier, who was walking behind her, bumped into her. She stumbled briefly and the soldier apologized. "I'm sorry," he said.

The entire sequence had taken less than a minute.

"It's nothing," Arianna stammered regaining her balance, and turned to reach for Mario's hand.

The child was no longer there.

Arianna looked toward the back of the entrance hall, but he wasn't there either. She turned toward the street again. Anxiously she questioned people standing near her. No one had seen him. The carriage arrived. The uproar grew. Someone screamed. Arianna was frantic. People crowded around her. Breathlessly, she described Mario's appearance, and groups of them began running here and there asking questions, searching for him. The news spread. It entered the high doorway and traveled the stairways of the Hall of Justice. It reached officials who asked Arianna still more questions and who, with crowds of people in front and in back of her, led her back upstairs. There they resumed asking questions. They consulted, issued orders, shouted, telephoned. Arianna half-swooned. Marianno arrived in a panic and almost immediately thereafter Luciana threw herself into Arianna's arms screaming, "No, no, no."

Later, when Arianna, Luciana, Mariano, and the two attorneys finally left the building, they could barely get through the mob of Trasteverites creating a commotion in the streets.

The Trasteverites devoted the rest of that day to running from one place to another, covering the city of Rome with their inquiries. The police, too, mobilized all their resources. But one, two, three days passed and not the slightest trace of Mario or Ramiro was found, not one shred of evidence that might offer the pretext of hope, not even one clue on which to base further searches. In those two or three days Mariano, Arianna, Luciana, and their friends exhausted every possibility. They no longer knew what to do, where to turn, yet they lacked the heart to admit that further inquiries were useless or that the time had come to abandon even the faintest hope. During those three days Mariano Parigi deteriorated. His hair turned white and he languished as though his life had been thirty years of suffering. Arianna sank into a bitter stupor. She didn't speak and seemed not to think. Completely withdrawn, she reproached herself unrelentingly and relived the scene a thousand times: the carriage that didn't come right over, the two steps she'd taken, and the soldier's push. Then she'd start all over again.

Mariano and Arianna spent all of the fourth and fifth days apart, he in his study, she in the bedroom. They no longer had the strength to be together, to see each other. On the evening of the fifth day Luciana appeared. She was pale and seemed to be filled with a strange bright light, which made her appear distant. Upon seeing her, Arianna burst into tears and suddenly felt relieved. Luciana sat down at her feet. Mariano Parigi, his back bent, entered the room. He looked at the two women without interest, walked around the edge of a table as if he were doing an exercise, and left by the other door with his hands behind his back, his head down and his eyes fixed on the floor.

A LITTLE WHILE LATER LUCIANA LOOKED UP at Ariana with ever widening eyes and said, "Do you want to go looking for him?"

Arianna seemed confused. She opened her mouth, but could not reply.

Luciana went on. "They can't find him," she said, pronouncing "they" so that it was a sweeping gesture of condemnation of the entire world. "But you and I can. Only a mother can find him. Let's go to look for him, just the two of us."

Through the haze, Arianna saw a light, a pale, warm light. Luciana was a miracle. "Really," she asked her. "We can do it?"

"Yes, Arianna. Let's go."

"But where?"

"Everywhere, anywhere in the world. Every day we'll follow a sign, a voice. We can' t go wrong that way."

But Arianna lacked imagination. At the sound of those words a mist descended about her and she shuddered. It fell upon everything in the room, on Luciana's head, on her words and on the meager light of hope, for hope is made of imagination.

After a long silence Luciana rose, took Arianna's hands in hers, looked into her face and asked, "When do you want to leave?"

Arianna's eyes were large and she stood up too. "You really meant it?"

"Of course."

Arianna looked about in confusion. There was no reason to object, no reason to believe.

Luciana spoke again. "We'll take one suitcase each, nothing

else. Mine's already packed. It's at home. I'll help you get yours ready."

"But what about…" Arianna lowered her voice and her eyes. "What about Mariano?"

Luciana walked to the door, opened it cautiously and looked into the next room. Parigi was in there with his forehead against a window pane. One of his hands was set upon its handle, though he was unresolved as to whether to open it.

Luciana approached him. "Signor Mariano."

He remained in the same position. "Just a minute," he said. "I have to open the window first."

He withdrew his head from the pane and slowly completed the task. Finally, he turned to her and spoke. "Did you understand?"

"Signor Mariano, unless you have some objections, Arianna and I are leaving now."

"Let's see," Mariano answered.

Arianna was listening from the doorway. She hadn't yet made up her mind. Luciana put her hand on the man's shoulder, looked directly into his eyes and said in a low voice, "We're going to look for him."

"Ah yes, quite so," Parigi replied. "Now let me close the window properly."

And once more he turned and leaned his forehead against the pane of glass. Luciana pulled Arianna back into the room and helped her with her suitcase.

The suitcase was packed, but Arianna still wasn't prepared to leave. "What about him?" she murmured. "I don't think he really understood."

Just at that moment Parigi entered the room quietly and stopped before the two women. "Will you be gone very long?" he asked.

Arianna felt relieved and released. Luciana answered him.

"Who can tell? We'll write every day." Arianna put her arms around Mariano, leaned her head on his shoulder and wept silently. Mariano Parigi abided her embrace and patted her affection-ately on the back. As Arianna continued crying, Mariano's pats took on a rhythm which he became intently interested in per-fecting. In the meantime, Luciana arranged for their departure. She called a carriage and had the luggage taken downstairs.

"You don't have to change your clothes," she told Arianna. "Just take a coat. It's almost dark."

At the sound of those words, Arianna raised her head from Mariano's shoulder and dried her tears. Mariano stood still for a moment before beginning to pace the room, trying to make his steps reproduce the rhythm of those interrupted pats.

AT HER HOUSE LUCIANA ANNOUNCED, "We'll sleep here tonight and leave tomorrow morning."

"For where?" Arianna asked.

"We'll decide when we're ready to leave. Trust me."

But Arianna could sustain no faith. Everything she saw tore at her heart, the terrace windows, the divan on which she'd spent that incredibly painful night while Mario on the other side of the door slept in another woman's arms.

"Do you want to go to sleep right away?" Luciana asked her.
"Yes."

"Or would you like to go out on the terrace with me for a while?" Her answer was the same. "Yes."

"We'll ask the stars," Luciana went on.

She pulled an armchair onto the terrace, explaining, "Angelica's in bed already." Then she helped Arianna lie back in the chair. It was in a corner of the terrace, the corner in which Mario had ridden his horse.

The small patch of sky above their heads was filled with stars. Between the stars the soft blackness was breathing as though it were alive. Settled back in the chair, Arianna looked directly into the starlight.

Standing beside her, Luciana pointed to the heavens and said, "I don't believe in the old constellations, Arianna. I know the real ones. Look at the those two clear stars close together, beating as if they were two hearts. They're talking to each other, trying desperately to reach each other. They're the Parted Lovers. See those eight stars, the first one is just above the chimney top, then two curve to the right, three to the left and two more higher up making a cross? That's the Ship of Love. See the outline of the sail? It's going to heaven with all the lovers who disdained worldliness and spurned the opinions of others. Now, turn your head a little. Look along my arm, like that, far left of the ship. There's a group of four or five stars nearly crushed together with pale dustiness all around them. That's the Island. It's where people who knew how to live in solitude go. From here you can't see any other constellations, but some night, someplace more open, I'll show you a lot more. And there are single stars. There's one you can't see from here that's right at the edge of the Milky Way. It's my father. My father died eighteen years ago and I'm positive that star wasn't there before then. For the past fifteen years Giorgio's been a star too, a faint one that comes and goes like a firefly. What's the matter, Arianna?"

"Nothing."

"You're shivering. Here, take this."

Luciana removed her coat and put it around Arianna, who was so dazed she felt nothing. "We'll find him," Luciana went on, "by following the signs in the stars. I understand them all. Look at them. Maybe there are some up there you'll recognize, too. What is it?"

"Nothing. I don't see anything. I don't understand anything. I can't even see the sky any more. The only thing I see is a mist. Forgive me."

"Let me take your hand. Why are you trembling? Come, don't give up, Arianna. We have to find him. But it takes real faith. If you doubt, we won't find him."

Arianna's head fell forward. Luciana put her hand to her friend's face to caress her and felt it was wet.

"You're crying?"

And beneath the tears Arianna's face was burning.

"What's the matter?"

"Nothing. Except that I don't know how to understand. I don't know how to find. I'll never find him. All I knew how to do was to lose him. Twice, I lost him. Ah..."

"What is it?"

"Nothing. I feel as if I can't breathe anymore. What's that? The stars are falling toward me. They're all tumbling. Cover my eyes, Luciana."

"Let's s go back inside, Arianna."

"What did you say?"

Half pulling and half pushing, Luciana helped Arianna to her feet. By now Arianna's eyes were closed.

She opened them again when she was beside the bed and felt Luciana trying to lift her into it. Struggling, she managed to get herself onto the bed. It was the bed in which Mario had slept in Luciana's embrace. Luciana was trying to undress her now.

"No, wait. I'm exhausted."

Her breathing was increasingly labored. Luciana became frightened.

"Just a minute," she said. "Just one minute. I'm going to wake...."

"No," Arianna managed to shout. "I don't want...anyone...to see me."

Arianna's terror stopped the other woman.

"Look at me, Arianna. It's me. It's Luciana. Why don't you look at me?"

"I can't. My eyes are tired. And I don't know how to look. Forgive me. You must forgive me for everything. He wanted to go to San Felice Circeo. Shall we go look for him there?"

"Wherever you want. But don't talk. Rest now."

Arianna's breathing was extremely shallow.

"Sleep, if you can."

"Yes. Maybe I'm going to become a star too, one more star. And who knows? Maybe he's up there, Mario, Ramiro...."

Arianna seemed to have fallen asleep. Luciana tried to move Arianna's head to place it more comfortably on the pillow. It fell to one side. Luciana bent over Arianna's mouth. There was no breath. She opened her blouse and felt for a heartbeat. There was none.

11

ARIANNA DIED FOR LACK OF IMAGI-
nation when only imagination could
have saved her. Mariano Parigi, who
had been summoned immediately, spent an entire day and night
in that unfamiliar house sitting on the unopened suitcase that
had belonged to Arianna—Arianna, who had left home to search
for Mario. After Arianna's funeral Luciana was no longer certain
that she ought to venture into the world following signs, stars
and voices in search of Ramiro. Then she remembered that before dying Arianna had spoken of San Felice Circeo. As though
in a trance she left immediately for the shore, for San Felice—
to recover and reaffirm the faith and imagination that were wa-
vering in her soul and fading from her eyes—so that she would
not die like Arianna, founder like Mariano, or disappear like
Ramiro.

Early that evening she left the inn for a walk as she had
done every evening during her seven years of heroic waiting for
the day of the wasted miracle.

From the distance she saw the peak of Giorgio's desecrated
rock and felt a surge of anger at the perfidious gypsy who hadn't
blown it up. As she proceeded along the gravel path which ran
between it and the sea, the cliff stood before her in all its great
height. It stood so straight and its chipped surface sparkled so
in the setting sun that it seemed about to hurl itself into the air
or dissolve into the light. Luciana walked past it to the point
where the bushes began.

Suddenly she stopped and screamed.

Someone had leaped out from the bushes to block her path. The sea gypsy.

Luciana pressed her hands against her chest in fright, but in a moment recovered.

The gypsy's clear glance was filled with humility, and Luciana understood that he was waiting for her to speak first.

"It's you, Solwanah?"

The gypsy's face reddened to the edge of his hair.

"Why are you blushing?"

"Because you remembered my name right away."

Luciana studied his blue shirt with its salt-worn design.

"I thought you'd left a long time ago."

Solwanah looked up in surprise. Unable to think how to reply, he turned instead and pointed to the top of Giorgio's rock and said almost reprovingly, "You know I have to blow up the rock first."

"That's true, Solwanah."

Together they looked at it. The sun suddenly went down. The rock was outlined against violet shadows.

Then Solwanah turned back to her. Once again he struggled for words. "I took him," he finally said.

Luciana felt the blood rush from her head and felt as if she were going to faint. She ordered herself to remain standing. A surge of intense heat rose to her head, then like a whirlwind fell into her heart, which began beating frantically. When the beating subsided, it occurred to her she had misunderstood.

Solwanah hastened to reassure her.

"Don't worry. We take very good care of little ones."

"Where is he?" Luciana asked.

"On the ship."

"The Viegliah."

He laughed with pleasure.

"And where is the Viegliah?"

"Out there."

Solwanah made a vague gesture toward the now dark, still sea.

"We've been forbidden to come back to Italy. But I can get you out there. I have a canoe. It has a sail we'll hoist at sea. It will be a very long trip, hours and hours. Does it scare you?"

"No. Can we go right now?"

"A little later. I hid the canoe under some branches on the other side."

He pointed to a promontory behind the inn from which Luciana had just come.

"When the rock blows up you'll hear it even in the hotel. When you come out the door, walk around there and you'll find me with the boat. Everyone else will be running the other way to see the rock, so there won't be anyone where we are. The headland will hide us. We'll be gone before anyone knows it. There's a good sea."

Solwanah's manner was that of an efficient and obsessive servant reporting on an order he had been given.

He looked behind him.

"There's no one here. Don't go any further. Go back to the hotel. I'll do it within the hour. I've already made holes wherever I need them and the fuses are in too."

He paused thoughtfully for a moment, then went on. "Don't come down right away. As soon as the rock blows up, I'll run back and hide in the bushes. When everyone else begins running toward the rock, I'll come out and walk along the shore in the water. You'll see me when I get to the stones below the house. The water comes up to here on me there." His hand pointed to his waist. "That's when you come down."

"All right."

Solwanah seemed to be waiting for something, an addition

to his orders, some parting words. He sensed there was something Luciana wanted to say. And she did finally speak. "Were you waiting for me?" she asked him.

"Yes."

"And if I hadn't come back. If I'd stayed in Rome?"

Solwanah answer was simple. "There was no question you were coming back."

After another moment of silence, as though he'd decided to put an end to further delay, the gypsy stood up and took his leave. Then he bent over and vanished as though swallowed whole by the bushes.

Luciana felt dazed, uncertain whether she'd heard or imagined, seen or dreamed.

She looked up again at Giorgio's rock, which was just about to fade into the engulfing gloom. She turned away from it and hurried back to the inn. There in her room she went to look out her window, and it seemed to her that as soon as she appeared there the sea softened its moans. It was vaster than ever before, very strange and black beneath the rapidly falling night.

THE HOUR TOOK FOREVER TO PASS. Luciana could no longer make out the sea or the sky. She thought of the moment when Ramiro—the innocent instrument of treachery—had called her from the street. Perhaps, right now, he's calling me again. She listened carefully, wondering whether the sea, the sky, or some distant land beyond both would bring her his tiny voice asking *Where are you?* Solwanah said, "Out there." Out there is so, so big. But afterward we'll be together forever, for all our lives and then in that other life too.

She was seized with impatience. She would have to wait. Wait for what? Oh yes, for the rock to be blown up. But why? What's so important about the rock? She no longer felt the exhilaration that had made her order that dramatic spectacle. She no longer understood why she'd wanted to have the rock blown up. There was something more important, much more urgent to do now. Ramiro is out there. I can't keep him waiting. Why didn't I think of it right away? Why did I let that gypsy go on and agree to it? Now there's a chance he'll be caught, held for questioning, maybe even imprisoned, and we won't be able to get to the ship at all. Maybe they won't even let me talk to him and he's the only one who knows where Ramiro is.

Her impatience became a torment. She had no idea how long she'd been waiting.

I've got to go out right now. Get to the rock. I've got to find Solwanah, tell him not to do this. We have to set out to sea immediately. Ramiro is waiting for me. Calling me. Calling loudly.

She hurried down the steps and began walking along the path, but the darkness slowed her pace.

Everything about her was silent. Even the sea held its breath. Giorgio's rock stood high and very dark.

Luciana had almost reached the spot where the brush began when suddenly there was a blast followed by a roar. Through the shadows, she saw a mass of black explode from the top of the cliff, then fall back. It splashed heavily into the sea. And immediately after that a little lower down, a flash of light, another roar, another splash. Luciana had stopped to watch, waiting for the blasts with her eyes tightly shut. Ten or twelve other explosions followed, one upon the other. The rock was surrounded with black dust, which dispersed to reveal that the top half of the rock was gone. Still more detonations followed. A strange icy terror came over Luciana. People had begun running along the path. Others were coming from the inn. Luciana looked about her. In the village above, torches had been lit and were moving this way and that. Then the torches came bouncing down the slope. There was shouting near and far. She hadn't moved from where she'd stopped. She watched for Solwanah's shadowy figure to pass along the gravel path or in the waist-deep water. The crowd was growing. People had already climbed the rock to the site of the explosions. She could see their shapes moving up there amid an array of lights that were bobbing crazily in their hands. Then she heard strange cries and shouts.

Solwanah did not pass. Luciana considered turning back to where the boat was hidden and to wait for him there. Because Ramiro was calling her. Calling loudly.

While she hesitated, some of the townspeople who had been at the rock came running back. Their exclamations flew against the questions of those just arriving. "A mad man," someone shouted. "Who saw him?" someone else asked.

"Can't recognize him."

"Hurry up with the matting."

Luciana neither understood nor had the courage to ask what had happened. Someone recognized her and warned, "Don't go, don't go." Staggering sentences poured in on her from all sides. There was a veritable competition to convey the news.

"While he was lighting the last fuse, the first one must have exploded."

"He didn't have time to get out of the way."

"They couldn't find even half of him."

"His head is blown to pieces, but you can tell he's not from around here."

"Why did he do it?"

"A maniac."

"They found his arm six meters away."

"And a big piece of blue shirt."

"One of his feet was hanging to his leg by a single nerve."

"They'll have to leave everything down there, on that covered stretcher. Don't go. Don't go."

She didn't go. She didn't speak. She didn't move. She waited till all the activity and commotion died down. Only a small group of people remained on the beach to watch over the stretcher with the covered remains. All the others had returned home. After a few hours everything was once more silent and dark.

Now Luciana sat down on the pebbles at the edge of the sea. The sea had resumed its rhythmical breathing. A light foam reached her feet, wetting them, but she didn't move. The constellations were making their rounds above her head in the soft black sky, the old ones and the new ones. The Parted Lovers passed, the Ship of Love passed, the Island passed and all the other constellations that Arianna hadn't seen. One by one, quietly, they descended the arc of heaven to take their rest in the dark bed of the horizon. Slowly, very slowly, waves began lapping at Luciana's legs, then pulling back. Luciana stared into the distance and felt nothing. Now the constellations were vanishing into the fading night. At dawn the sea was a flat, gleaming expanse, white as milk, all the way to the furthest curve which encloses and seals it to the heavens.

the life and
death of adria
and her children

contents

adria I

———◆◆✕◆◆———

1 "FREE ALL" IS THE BEST GAME IN THE WORLD. It's not just hide-and-seek, not just tag, but a complicated game that covers a lot of territory. It goes like this. There's a starting place called home base. The seeker, *it*, who's chosen by lot and blindfolded, leans his face against the base, which may be a tree, the corner of a hedge, the end of a wall. The others run off on tiptoe to hide while *it* counts out loud—all the way to 31 at a slow rhythmic pace long-established by custom. Before he finishes, everyone will have found a hiding place and he will no longer hear the sounds of breathing or cracking twigs. He calls out "thirty-one," raises his head, pulls the blindfold from his eyes, and turns to look around—trees, hedges, lawns, meadows, walls, flower beds, but not a living soul. It's as if he's the only person in the world. He peers through space like a vulture, sniffs like a leopard, slithers like a snake, then pounces. Already he knows where some of his prey is hidden—the intuition children have for this is extraordinary. But discovering a hare in its hiding place is not enough. This is where the game gets complicated. While searching, the hunter has had to leave home base, make a number of turns, and can no longer get directly back to the base, or even see it clearly. Now the discovered hare jumps up and runs, and if he beats the hunter to the base, the hunter loses and the hare wins and can free anyone he wants to, even everyone. "Free All!" Therefore, once a hare is flushed the hunter has to chase and catch him right off. Meanwhile, others

pop out, one here, one there. They had sunk into the ground, become part of trees, dissolved in air. Right before the hunter's eyes they take shape again, reappear. He turns around, manages to catch two of them, one in each hand—quite an accomplishment—and hears a third calling from the base, "Free All."

A great game, a game for army generals. Children between the ages of seven and thirteen are best at it. Past the age of thirteen, the traits it requires—ruthless cunning and animal agility—fall away. Boys turn to more violent and less imaginative games. Girls become interested in the world around them. Up to that age boys and girls do equally well. It's best when there are several players—at least four, not more than six. But young children are imaginative and can do with less of everything, even players. More than once I've seen a child playing Hearts alone. It wouldn't surprise me to come across one who's invented a way to play hide-and-seek, tag, and Free All! alone. I can't think how. I can only think up stories. That's because I'm over thirteen, and past that age the imagination loses its ability to completely replace reality.

After Tullia and Remo's friends left—their governess having come to fetch them home for dinner—the two continued playing Free All!

Tullia is eight years old. Remo is six. He may be a little young for the game, but he's a precocious child.

It's Remo's turn to hide. Tullia, with her hands over her eyes and the backs of her hands pressed against the trunk of a magnolia tree, is counting out loud, "one, two…" She counts slowly, perhaps even more slowly than tradition requires. At each number Tullia calls out, the trees cast longer shadows across the flower bed, enveloping the rose bushes and bathing them in darkness.

"Thirty-one!" When Tullia raised her head, took her hands from her face and turned, she was surprised that evening had fallen so quickly. She looked about and started to search for her brother. Beyond the meadow where there were only a few pines, a rosy glow was fading on the distant horizon. Tullia walked carefully along the curve of a flower bed, dashed off to the right and ran into a row of espaliered myrtles, where she hesitated, then turned left and started down a path that ran between two distant cypresses. Every intuition failed her. She looked up at the illuminated windows of the house. A wave of perfume rose from the earth. Tullia shook with chill and suddenly felt alone in the world. "Remo, where are you?" she called out forlornly. There was no answer. Then a sense of honor spurred her to continue the game. Teetering on tiptoe, she went down steps that circled a pile of stones through which a rushing stream of water was singing to the evening stars. Searching for her brother among the shadowy rocks, Tullia suddenly saw his back. He was crouching between two rocks and hadn't heard her.

She could have grabbed him, but didn't have the heart to take him by surprise. "Oh," she called out. Remo's startled eyes seemed to burn through the shadow. He leaped to his feet, bounded a rock, and began dashing across the flower bed. With Tullia right behind him, and both now running and shouting, Remo got to the tree, tapped it and called out "home free." A second later Tullia got there, threw herself against him and held him tightly. Just then a voice sounded through the mottled light.

"Children!"

The youngsters separated, stood up, reached for each other's hands, and looked at each other with an intense, fearful joy.

"It's time," said Remo.

"We're over here," Tullia called out. And together they ran toward the governess, who was walking toward them. All three silently crossed the graveled courtyard which extended from the garden to the entryway of the house. They mounted the steps and entered, still without a word. The eight-year-old sister and six-year-old brother continued to hold each other's hands. Passing through rooms and hurrying along hallways, every so often they would look at each other again with that smile of understanding, and squeeze each other's fingers tightly. They reached a room that was almost completely dark, in which furniture was stored. A long, high chest stood against one of the walls. Instantly, and with practiced ease, they clambered onto it while the governess stood by unconcerned.

Set in the wall over the chest at the height of their eyes were two vertical slits. Tullia looked through one, Remo through the other. Peering through the slits, they reached for each other's hands again. Then Remo turned to the governess. "Mamma isn't there yet," he said, and pressed his eye to the opening again.

They were looking into the brilliantly lit dining room. In the center of it stood a glittering table set for two. The only person in the room was a servant who, having taken a last look at the table, withdrew toward a doorway. There he waited.

The children's hearts were pounding. They scarcely breathed. The governess said, "I'm going upstairs for a moment. Then I'll come down to get you."

"Yes, yes," they answered impatiently and, when she left, plunged back to their feverish watch. Minutes went by.

They didn't move. They didn't dare take their eyes from the slits again. Tullia heard an insect gnawing. They were afraid of missing the moment of the appearance.

"The other day I didn't see her till after she came in," Remo whispered.

"She's at least three minutes late now," Tullia answered.

There were no clocks about, but on those evenings that the appearance was delayed, the children always sensed it.

"Yesterday, by this time, she was already sitting down," Remo murmured.

"Shhh," his sister interrupted him. "She's coming."

The two pressed themselves against the wall—their entire souls were centered in their eyes. And to their eyes the light within the room seemed to glow a hundred times more splendidly as a door opened and their mother appeared and walked toward the table.

She was more brilliant than the light.

She moved forward, yet nothing of her seemed to move. It was as though space were sliding above and around her the way the sky steals away stars as it turns. Both space and sky stopped moving when she reached the table.

She placed one hand on it. Her arm, like a lily stem, was bare. Her neck too was bare, and seemed transparent. One could almost see the flow of air within it as she breathed. Every breath was a miracle.

She was wearing a pale, pearl-colored gown, a gown an angel might wear. Her eyes were as serene as mirrored lakes amid snow. Her brow was crowned with dark hair, whose long locks were fastened against the deep blue halo of a wide-brimmed hat.

Someone moved her chair and she sat down.

The gleaming whiteness and crystalline reflections that rose from the napery and glassware mingled with the silver glow that radiated from her downturned face.

Their father entered as well, and was sitting opposite her with his back toward the wall through which the children were watching.

The governess' voice startled them.

"All right, children."

"Just one more minute." Tullia begged, almost inaudibly.

"No, it's late." The governess helped them down, adding, "You know if you stay too long, your mamma won't let you come watch her anymore."

She led them into another room and prepared their supper. They ate without speaking. Finally, Remo broke the silence.

"Tullia, how many days is it till Saturday, when Guarnerio is coming to take us for a ride in his car?"

Tullia brushed the question aside.

"Quiet, let me think about mamma some more."

Then she brought her hands together and pressed them to her chest.

"Did you see? This evening she was even more beautiful."

Remo answered quietly. "She's more beautiful every time, you know that."

"No. It's impossible for her to be more beautiful than tonight."

"You say that every night."

Tullia frowned.

They were silent for a minute, then Remo looked down at the floor and murmured. "Just once, I'd like so much to hug her…to touch her."

"You can't," Tullia said fearfully. "You know it would spoil everything."

After a moment she added in a lower voice, "Not even papa ever hugs her. I happen to know that."

Remo shrugged his shoulders. "What's that got to do with anything?" he asked.

Tullia tried to think of a rejoinder, but she didn't understand any better than he. They sat there for a while feeling downcast. Then the governess came back to escort them to their rooms.

As they passed through the entry hall, they encountered Guarnerio.

Guarnerio was a friend of the family's who lived in a nearby villa; the villas were in a section in the eastern part of Rome almost uninhabited at that time. Today, new neighborhoods cover it.

The children greeted Guarnerio with great joy. He bent to hug them.

"I was passing by and came in especially to say hello, because I know that your mamma and papa are having dinner or getting ready to go out about now. In fact, I have to rush home to change to go to the theater. Did you see mamma?"

"Yes, yes, Just now."

"Was she beautiful?"

"Oh, yes, very. You know."

"So very beautiful," said Guarnerio and turned to look around him, at the air, at the very walls, with passion. Then he embraced Adria's children again and walked off as though in a trance.

The children were alone now. They looked at each other for a moment as though struck simultaneously by the same strange fear, then, sobbing, threw themselves into each others arms.

"She's so beautiful," the little boy murmured.

"Remo, Remo," Tullia cried out. "Are you thinking of how mamma will suffer when she gets old and won't be this beautiful anymore?"

Remo tried hard to think how to console his sister, to console himself. "Maybe, who knows? Maybe not everyone gets old, you know," he said.

They took each other's hands as they had done just a while before, climbed the steps and were met on the landing by the waiting governess.

As they were about to separate, Remo suddenly said, "You have to give me Genovieffa, remember?"

"That's right. Wait a minute."

Tullia ran to her room and quickly came out holding a doll. "Here."

The little boy seized it eagerly. The governess went with him to his room and helped him prepare for bed. Tullia got herself ready. She climbed into bed and shut the light quickly. All night long she dreamed of herds of horses running through a field. Little by little she found herself in the midst of the stream of quadrupeds but she didn't touch them, or feel them in pursuit, for she too was flying, caught up in a silver whirlwind.

Remo had wanted to have the doll in bed with him. He tied a handkerchief over her head as a nightcap, put her down next to him and fell asleep almost immediately. He dreamed he was on a boat.

---

2 AT EIGHT-THIRTY THAT EVENING, as on every other evening, Adria was finally free of her hairdresser who, after having arranged her hair, had placed the hat upon it with sublime art, and with the aid of invisible pins set her locks against the high dark blue brim. The remaining preparations to complete her toilette were put off for after dinner. Five years of exactly the same routine.

Five years earlier, after much long and quiet meditation before her mirror, Adria had perceived that she had attained perfect beauty and had decided it was her sacred obligation to dedicate herself to it completely. She was horrified when she thought back to the fact that she had married so young, at sixteen, and had borne two children, a daughter at seventeen and the boy when she just under twenty. An age of imprudence. At that age a woman feels covetous about her own beauty and worries about it, but doesn't have the kind of spiritual sensibility that enables her to understand the meaning of obligation and noble sacrifice. She thanked heaven for having saved her from dissipating or ruining herself forever, and closed the door to love, affection, or any other womanly interest. Her children, whom she cherished, were not allowed to visit her more than once a week (as though they were in boarding school) and then only for a brief period which was never extended. She was not afraid that their embraces would ruin her attire, but that affection would disturb her resolve to be beautiful. Beauty was her constant concern and the purpose of her every act. She considered it something outside of herself, something which God had placed in her custody. She sacrificed everything else at its altar—every feeling, concern, joy and ambition. It was not a matter of ambition, but of serving a faith. And in fact, no one censured her, no one judged her. From his place at the altar, her husband took part in the ceremonies. Her children adored her from a distance, her friends didn't ask for intimacy, women didn't compete with her, worshippers didn't fall in love. In this way her will had reshaped the world into a vast space revolving around her. Only one man had fallen in love with her, because one such was necessary to complete the poem of her surroundings. Destiny had chosen to bestow that office upon Guarnerio. Guarniero's love, like everything in that world, had never ripened. At the proper moment it had been born fully mature, with just the proper amount of passion and no more. Everyone knew about it, because in Adria's world there were no secrets. Despite the passage of months and years, her world had remained precisely as it had been conceived, and it would remain so forever. For in Adria's world time did not exist.

After leaving her hairdresser, Adria, in hat and gown, had placidly walked down to the dining room. Dinner was simple. The few words that husband and wife exchanged were, as usual, cordial and easy. Once back in her suite Adria heightened the color of her face with a light touch of makeup. Then her maids completed her attire by adding a small sash that tied lightly under her breasts to the pearl-colored gown, and by placing a lightweight blue cloak over it. Adria and her husband were then driven to the Teatro Valle.

A Nordic drama was being performed in Italy for the first time. There was an elegant first night audience. The audience applauded the play, and during the intermission studied the women in the boxes, Adria most of all.

She smiled gracious greetings toward other boxes and intuitively adjusted her smile to suit the merits of the recipient. Sometimes she nodded without smiling. When she wasn't smiling Adria's face was quite pale. Her smile cast a brief rosy glow over its whiteness. From time to time her blue eyes emitted silver rays.

Adria didn't see, nor did she try to see, how other women in the theater were dressed. Indeed, the light blue cloak and the deep blue hat with the crown of black curls set against its brim were the subject of almost everyone else's conversation. In the hallways and corridors of the theater, people discussed the play and praised Adria's beauty. Ibsen's and Adria's names flew from their lips. They told each other her uncomplicated story for the thousandth time.

At every intermission Adria had visitors. At the end of the first act there was an old man who was a business associate of her husband's; after the second act, two officials and a cheerful-looking banker. Everyone approached her with the gentle deference customarily associated with placing flowers on a country altar on Sundays. No one had favors to ask of her. Homage to Adria was a religious act accepted serenely by certain of the faithful. A handsome, white-mustached magistrate named Bellamonte, known to all by the appropriate epithet, the Judge, arrived to introduce his son, an embarrassed youth who bowed to kiss her hand, then lost the courage to complete the act. Delighted, Adria rewarded him by brushing her own two fingers over a lock of hair that had fallen onto his forehead.

Guarnerio arrived near the end of the second intermission. Everyone else left and Guarnerio sat down opposite Adria, too distracted to utter any greeting. She was very pleased by the tribute. "You look pale this evening, Guarnerio," she said. He blushed, looked down at Adria's feet, then raised his eyes and rested his gaze on her brow and hair. They were alone, Adria's husband having remained in the lobby to smoke. The theater lights went down. The curtains parted. "Do stay a while, Guarnerio," Adria said, though Guarnerio had shown no sign of leaving.

"I only have a few days to live, Adria," he replied.

He was always talking like that, and she answered him as she always did. "A lot of people say such things, but perhaps in your case it's true."

It was possible for Guarnerio to speak of only a few days to live, and for Adria to have accepted that as his fate for five years, because time in Adria's world was as motionless as it is in Heaven.

Adria sensed that people were standing in a rear row peering through the shadows to get a good look at her. After an artful pause she turned her face slightly in their direction to allow them a fuller view, and held the pose for a minute. Then she turned again to Guarnerio.

"Do you know any of them?" he asked angrily.

"No, what difference does it make? But lower your voice."

After a moment she added, "Now let's listen to the play," and she leaned her head against the back of the tall chair. Her pale face, like a glowing sea creature, illuminated the darkness around her. Her eyes were half-closed. Midway through the act her husband tiptoed back into the box. She didn't hear him. She was dozing in order to feel rested at the end of the performance.

When it was over, a group of friends was waiting in the

hallway outside her box. Someone suggested they all go out for a light supper at the fashionable club next to the theater.

Adria took a moment to think. In the process, she opened her eyes wide and turned them from one to the next of the people and objects around her. She appeared to be thinking of eternal verities, perhaps even of Paradise. After this consideration she calmly declined.

In reality, her thoughts had been quite simple. First, I have an important reception two evenings from now, so it's better not to stay out late tonight or tomorrow night. Second, the most prominent of the people who'd be at the club had all been in the theater that evening and therefore had already had the pleasure of seeing me. Consequently, there was no reason to dine there.

The disappointed group escorted her down the steps. People were still milling about in the lobby to see her. More than one stranger raised his hat in salutation when she appeared. She walked past them, leaving a diffuse and harmonious quivering in the air.

At home she undressed quickly, immersed herself briefly in a warm bath, dismissed her chambermaid, and sank between the pink silk sheets of her bed. She glanced around the room as though in greeting to the soft colors and quiet shapes that surrounded her, then reached out for a mirror on her night table—her favorite mirror, her faithful nightly companion for the past five years. She leaned on her arm, and turned a little onto her side.

It was to her own image that she smiled the last greeting of the day. It was the longest greeting and the most brilliant smile. No one else in the world knows that smile, knows her face and the expression on it at that time of day. A flicker of pink rose from the corners of her lips toward her cheeks, where it converged with the wave of tenderness descending from her fluttering eyelids. She raised herself for a moment to lean on her other elbow and held the mirror out as far as her arm would reach. She had no thought of caressing her arm. She brought the mirror closer, parted her lips slightly and smiled to see her sparkling teeth. She delighted in the sight of her mouth, of her throat, of her hair now hanging softy over her forehead. She had no desire to kiss those youthful lips smiling at her from the mirror. Her love was pure, celestial.

She put down the mirror and turned off the light. In the dark she slid beneath the sheet which embraced her shoulders and legs. With her arms along her sides, she felt as if she were immersed among rose petals and hyacinths. A light perfume emanated from the heart of the surrounding shadows and settled upon her closed eyelids. Now she slips gently beneath the perfumes which become whispers. And all the while, her fragmented thoughts are simple and encompass a small circle. The dressmaker will be here tomorrow afternoon. The fabric is ready. She wanted that lilac,lilac. Her old school teacher used to pronounce it lilàc,lilàc. I used to draw very well then, they wanted me to become a painter. Painters talk a lot. I don't. Dora's brother-in-law was offended because I looked at him without saying anything. He told Dora afterwards. That was when I was expecting Remo. Everyone was saying that it would be another girl. I think my husband should send him to boarding school. My last year in boarding school, we found ants in the refectory, walking in a long procession, like the singing friars who ring bells at funerals. Guarnerio says he will die in a few days, a few, three days, three, two.

She fell asleep and didn't dream.

3 TO HER SURPRISE, WHEN SHE AWOKE the next morning Adria found herself smiling. She was smiling at the naiveté of the people who, the previous evening, had hoped to get her to stay up late and make a show of herself at the fashionable club. She was preparing quite a different show for the following evening. It was to be the Crown Society's last reception of the season, the most important of the entire year. For the past month all of Rome has been trying to guess what Adria will be wearing for the occasion. And now two full days, today and tomorrow, are to be completely given over to this matter.

Before entering her bathroom she summoned the governess. "It's Thursday, the children's day," she said, "but it's impossible today. Tell them that I'm putting it off until Saturday just before five."

In the bath she examined her mail. There was nothing of any importance. She opened only a letter from Guarnerio, whose exact words were, "Nevertheless, signora Adria, I feel that tomorrow will truly be a definitive day. Guarnerio." That was all.

The letter surprised her somewhat. Guarnerio had never written to her before. His tragic prediction of the previous evening at the theater was a constant motif, a long habit, the first words of every conversation when he was alone with her. But he had never persisted like this. Adria had no wish to dwell on the problem. She repeated a previously given order: today and tomorrow she would see no one but her dressmaker. Absolutely no one else, no matter what. And she would eat alone in her room.

She emerged from the bathroom in undergarments and a dressing gown, and, with her maid at her side, went directly to her wardrobe room where the seamstress had been waiting for half an hour.

No stage designer ever created so simple and surprising a

theatrical scene as the view of that room from its threshold.

There were no closets. There was no furniture. Not even a chair. The huge room, illuminated by an enormous skylight, like a sculptor's studio, was traversed from one end to the other by chest-high parallel rods fixed in place by vertical supports set into the floor. These metal rods were covered in velvet; and from them Adria's clothing was hung—ten long rows of garments of every color, a bizarre vineyard. The bars terminated at both sides of the room without touching the wall, so that just as in a vineyard one could walk to the end of a row, turn and walk along the next one. Ten very long rows—perhaps three hundred outfits—for mornings, afternoons, and evenings, for indoors and outdoors, for every hour of day and of night, for every occasion of life, in every style consistent with the fashion of the times, yet all extremely simple. There was perhaps one in every shade of every color the human eye has created, but most were pale gray, or in one of the many tones of blue which Adria favored. There were also some in black and in white, several in hues of green, a number of pinks and pale violets, very few yellows and reds.

Some of those garments are renowned; her appearance in one of them in a room or on a promenade signified a date in fashion history, or perhaps left its mark in someone's life. There are some she hasn't worn yet. Perhaps she'll never wear them and after some time they'll go sadly to the same place so many others have gone after their hour of ecstasy—the ones she'd had sewn up on the spur of the moment when suddenly inspired by a fabric or a color. She needs always to have at hand a far richer choice of garments than required for the daily act of self-creation. Some that never attained the glory of enfolding her served instead as the inspiration for others that were more fortunate.

Enter the room and listen to the murmur of silk, linen,

velvet, satin, crêpe, voile and damask rustling in a hundred small and vibrant voices, like the sound of the insects one hears when walking through the countryside on a sunny morning. All those colors, all these associations before one's eyes give rise to a restlessness, a kind of intoxication and confusion, such as we feel when exposed too long to perfumes. But Adria never allowed herself to become intoxicated.

She was as secure and as sovereign in that setting—which was the restorative center, the site for meditation and for the renewal of her beauty—as she was sovereign among the people who paid her homage as performance and ceremony. She would remain clearheaded while walking along the rows, skimming her eyes over the colors, and every so often brushing her fingertips over a piece of crêpe or satin. None of those garments had come from famous ateliers, from designers who set the standards in world fashion. All of them were her own creations and had been made up under her supervision by dressmakers whose names will forever be unknown, but who, working obediently under Adria's precise and inspired instructions, managed to create miracles that stunned the age. No woman or seamstress of that era ever dared to copy a garment that Adria had created for herself. Any woman who wore a dress once seen on Adria would be destroyed by universal derision.

Adria preceded the dressmaker to the threshold of the next room. There was a large table and on it a sheet covering something. Adria did not immediately lift the sheet.

"This," she said, "is the fabric I've had made for tomorrow's dress. The pattern is ready. I cut it myself. You'll see it's really quite simple. We'll have more than enough time between today and tomorrow to get it done. Tomorrow evening you will help me get into it. From now until that time, you will not leave here. Albertina," she turned to indicate her maid, "will stay with us and help too."

This was Adria's customary way of making sure that the secret of her attire would not escape. The bed in the tiny adjoining room, where the seamstress had slept on previous occasions, was already made up. The woman was extremely curious to see the sheet lifted. Adria's ideas were almost always unpredictable.

There are many people throughout the city who are just as impatient; this includes those who will be seeing Adria, as well as those who won't be at the Crown Society's spring ball, but will hear Adria described by the elite, and will search magazines for photos of her.

They're all impatient and will have to wait two more days. But we don't have to. It is our prerogative as a writer (and we permit our readers to share in this) to skip those two days and find ourselves walking through the Society's rooms on Friday evening before midnight, just as Adria is about to appear.

The Crown Society's salons look like a beehive full of worker bees enjoying an afternoon off. In one room people are dancing, in another they're all pressing up against the refreshment tables. Every so often an invisible stick stirs the large fishpond and the multicolored creatures shift and regroup themselves, chattering like swallows in a summer sky. But here and there, in several of the smaller rooms, groups of people seated in soft armchairs next to precious little tables bearing cups of steaming tea are conversing as though at a family gathering. Foursomes in another room are gaming intently at tables whose surfaces are covered in diagrammed green baize. There are people scheming and those who are bored, and in the most hidden recesses young and old are weaving or unraveling romances. A few couples and solitary souls are pacing the large terrace and gazing up at the soft, spring stars.

Guarnerio is everywhere. Now he is hurrying across the dance floor bumping into couples one after another and excusing himself, as if he has an urgent obligation to fulfill in another room. Now he is ordering coffee at the refreshment table, but has no time to wait for it and is running off; immediately afterward he is peering over someone's shoulder, watching a card game. Then, realizing that he hasn't actually perceived anything, he walks away disconsolately. At this point, someone stops him, pins him against the frame of a large window and begins telling him the story of his life. Guarnerio, leaning against that frame, listens with infinite patience, seems to understand, agree and sympathize with everything.

In reality he is thinking about himself. Why, on this particular evening, is he recalling his entire past? He's never done so before and there's no reason to do it now. And what is that past? Nothing. Before he was thirty, he hadn't done anything. He'd learned three or four languages well and had traveled. The travels of a dilettante, the life of dilettante. At thirty, destiny had caused him to fall in love with Adria. Instantly his love had assumed the required pattern—a love of quiet desperation. And he had readily devoted every hour of his entire life to that commitment. And so, naturally, here he is now, waiting for Adria to appear.

In five years he has waited for her like this more than a thousand times. In the midst of restless crowds, he has always been the only person awaiting her calmly. He had learned to sense the precise moment Adria would appear, no matter if she were delayed, were arriving early or even unexpectedly. His waiting is like a ribbon whose length he knows. He sees it unwind more or less quickly, knows when it is close to the end. When the ribbon of his waiting is at its full length—there she is. There's nothing to go wrong. He is restless this evening, because for the first time since he has undertaken this duty he can't locate any sense within himself of the unwinding ribbon. The recollection of the note he sent Adria the previous morning is troubling him too much. He had written it and sent it off in a kind of delirium he had never before felt. "Why?" he wonders in anguish, "why did I do it?" Over and over, ten, twenty times the dreadful phrase recurs to him.

Nevertheless, signora Adria, I feel that tomorrow will truly be a definitive day. He no longer understands the meaning of his strange words. There is nothing left of the premonition that had somehow dictated them. She hadn't answered. That was only to be expected. But what had she thought? What does she think about him now? During the two days of her strict confinement he hadn't been able to see her, not even catch a distant glimpse. But this too was to be expected. Not even her shadow behind a window. He knew that she saw the children for a few minutes just before noon on Thursdays, and immediately after twelve had dashed over to find them, just to hear them speak of her. But they too had been disappointed. He'd found them wandering around disconsolately outside their mother's rooms, as if to breathe the air enveloping her. He'd reminded them of the promise he'd made to take them for a drive the following Saturday after five o'clock. Then he'd fled so as not to lose his self-control in front of them.

One part of him was still quite clearheaded and said, "This is love and it's fine." But it's not the love you had before yesterday. This one is out of bounds. It's free, disorganized, powerful, lawless, and could never bear what the other love has borne for five years. Until yesterday morning, it would never have occurred to me to write a note like that. And if it did, I would never have written it, never have sent it. So, what does all this mean? There aren't two ways of being in love. And no doubt everyone would say that this way, the way I feel now, is the real one, the only one. Therefore, it's only just now, no, it was yesterday morning that it began, when I wrote and sent that note, that I started loving her. I've loved Adria for two days. I haven't loved her at all for five years.

This notion made him truly miserable, not simply because he now loved her in a way that could become maddening, but because he had not loved her at all before, had been deceiving himself and her as well.

Consumed by this thought, Guarnerio suddenly turned his back on the prattler and ran toward a glass door that opened onto the terrace. The man didn't immediately notice. Speaking and gesturing heatedly, he had looked away for a moment, and then turning back had found Guarnerio gone. He became furious, didn't know what to do, and shuffled about uncertainly. A friend came up, slapped him on the back and said, "What are you doing here? Let's go back to the first salon. Adria's on her way in."

But the doorway of the first salon was already filled with a group of Adria's votaries, who had no intention of yielding an inch. In the center of the room a group of women was engaged in heated conversation. Every so often Adria's name sounded from one of them. The women were recalling the gowns Adria had worn at other such receptions, and by process of elimination were trying to determine what she would be wearing that night. One woman suggested pink. There was complete agreement that blue was out because she'd worn blue the other night at the theater. "But who can tell?" another woman said doubtfully. "Adria is unpredictable."

A rash young man, drawn into the conversation, put forth a daring thought: "Do you know what she might do to throw you all off? She might turn up in the precisely the same dress and hat that she wore to the theater the other night."

A howl of derision greeted the remark. The question that most occupied the women was the depth of the neckline that Adria will have chosen. That year necklines were getting lower. Bare arms and a bare neck, of that there was no doubt. But will the neckline be cut lower in front or in back? And will the front be square or heart shaped? To the cleavage or beyond? The general opinion was that the neckline would be conservative in front and more daring in back. As for the color, pale pink got most of the votes. White came in second. "I'll take your bets!" shouted the rash young man.

But a fierce murmuring overwhelmed every other voice. "She's arriving. There she is. Yes, see?" An awed hush filled the room.

Out on the terrace Guarnerio was peering through the uncertain light of the square below toward the road on the left, along which Adria's automobile was due to appear. Suddenly there it was. The car continued to a point just below him. He saw one of its doors open, but it was too close to the entryway for him to see anything else except the door closing again and the car being driven off to a parking site. He didn't rush off to watch Adria's entrance. He didn't move from where he was. He was looking across the piazza at the round, illuminated clock set high upon a public building. Then he raised his eyes upward and to the side, where the moon seemed a cartoon of that diaphanous face. A cloud passed over the moon and with it a chill settled on the piazza. Still Guarnerio didn't move.

In the first salon a deep murmur arose and intensified at succeeding announcements that Adria had reached the entrance hall, that Adria was in the cloakroom, that Adria was about to enter the room. But as soon as she appeared on the threshold, the murmuring gave way to stunned silence. Then, as she began walking calmly forward, enthusiasm burst forth. There was no applause. People were clutching at each other's hands, and saying, "Beautiful, lovely, heavenly, marvelous, brilliant." Their words spilled forth, swelled, overflowed every impediment, surged upward to the ceiling, fell back sparkling at Adria's feet. Even people who didn't know her were shouting their admiration, women as passionately as men. Adria continued into the room. In that shared enthusiasm of both men and women there was not the slightest hint of sexuality.

Adria was completely enclosed from the curve of her chin to the tips of her feet in a fluid, pearl-gray sheath made of thousands of tiny, layered feathers. From neckline to hem she was one continuous, unbroken line. The fastenings of the dress were invisible. All of her, even her arms down to her wrists, was encased in that caressing skin. It clung to her shoulders, her back and breasts as if she were a modest statue. At her waist it loosened gently into a long bell which fell to the floor just above the tips of her shoes, and extended as an oval toward the back, where it frothed in the tiniest hint of a train.

Her dark hair, parted in the center and drawn back to half cover her ears, was gathered at the nape of her neck and coiled into a tight knot that lay heavily against her neck.

She wore no jewelry, not even her wedding ring.

The delicate billowing of the feathers descending the length of her dress seemed to come from some inner source, the child-like breaths of the sleeping sea. Adria moved forward like a dark-haired angel among mortals, bringing all of heaven in her eyes.

Her luminous brow contrasted dramatically with the deep blackness of her hair; everything else was heavenly joy. There was no color around her eyes, nor on her cheeks. Even her lips were pale. Unadorned as it was, her face glowed with other-worldly purity.

She walked through every room until she reached the last one, which was her precise duty. The throngs of men and women would part as she approached, then immediately close ranks behind her. Before her there was a stunned silence, which would slowly give way to murmurs at her sides and behind her, until she was half-circled by admiring whispers. When she entered the ball room, the dancing stopped; in the next rooms the gaming stopped, and farther on the conversations around teacups. Everyone was up and rushing about. The couples in the alcoves and out on the terraces hurried in to see her, a sight which augured well for their love. Every passion, every frivolity was suspended at her appearance, and after the first stunned moment everyone's admiration turned to joy. The intoxications of dancing, wine, and bright lights generated the most unpredictable and simple-hearted homage. There were people who upon seeing her laughed with sheer delight. A young man knelt. A woman dancing alone pulled off her necklace, threw it in the air, and undid her hair like a joyous Fury. Two old men, forgetting their white hair and formal suits, threw themselves to the floor with their arms around each other like little boys in a meadow. At that point everyone began to laugh. The laughter spread from room to room, blowing like a May breeze through all the festivities, then out the doors toward the night and the moon. The laughter broke the spell, suddenly delivered everyone from the brink of madness and restored a tone of normalcy to the celebration. Adria chose a place for herself and sat down. When she was seated, the guests resumed dancing, gambling, conversing, plotting, making love, even feeling bored, but with lighter hearts, as if they'd been exposed to a purifying incense.

The corner she had chosen was in the last room. She didn't dance. Who would have had the courage to dance with Adria?

She sat in a small armchair, as though in a chalice. The skirt of her dress hung down to the carpet and, as if moved by the wind, settled in gathers before her like a mass of clouds. Seated about her in other chairs were those privileged to be in her circle. Several men stood and a few young women sat on the rug like pages in attendance.

What would a conversation between Adria and her circle have been like? That's very difficult to recreate. I had the good fortune to be present at two such gatherings (one, a year before the events which I am now recounting), and I've also heard them mentioned by others who attended them more assiduously than I. Yet none of us, once removed from Adria's circle, was much able to recall what was said. Certainly, Adria spoke very little; at times conversations flowed about her while she remained completely silent. Other times, if asked a question, she'd answer in monosyllables. But this behavior did not have the effect, as one might expect, of making her appear to be an oracle, which would have been tiresome. Indeed, I fear that what I've said so far about this incomparable woman, although scrupulously accurate and not embroidered in the slightest, nevertheless might have given a slightly false impression of her. There was nothing hieratic about Adria, nothing artificial (although everything about her, including her physical beauty, was probably born of an act of will) and nothing literary. Adria was simplicity itself. Naturalness made beautiful. And because of this, she never attracted artists. It seems strange that no painter was ever tempted to leave a portrait of her. In those conversations surrounding Adria it would eventually happen that, talking among ourselves, we would somehow forget her physical presence, while at the same time continue to feel her influence. Every subject, even the mundane, the nothings, seemed in her presence to partake of something luminous, as occasionally happens in a dream. For these reasons, too, this woman, who for several years in quiet times dominated an aspect of social life in Rome, did not become a legend. I myself don't feel the slightest temptation—which historians do, and more often biographers—to seek out singular accents and rare colors to heighten and recreate the exact reality of her passage through the world.

But let us resume the thread of our story and unfold the events of that horrendous night, the 18th of April, 1903.

In the chair next to Adria sat the young prince Vetere of Castellana, president of the Crown Society. "Here we are, all sitting around you this evening, signora Adria, bright and happy," he said to her. "The other evening at this hour we were all more or less unhappy and asleep. And we didn't wake up until the end of an act when we had to applaud. So I'm not going to ask you if you enjoyed the play."

"It was a drama," said a very precise gentleman.

"Even dozing a little," said Adria, "I enjoyed it. The women in these northern plays interest me."

A man at the outer edge of the circle shouted a judgment. "I don't like it when they do these exotic plays. Women like that set the worst examples for ours. They're always thinking and they'll end up teaching our women to think too. Roman women shouldn't be thinking."

"Oh, and what should Roman women be doing?"

"Their duty is to love." This was said with such deep conviction that everyone laughed.

The moralist didn't retreat. "Yes," he insisted. "They have to love without trying to understand everything."

"I heard," said Adria, "that at the end of the last act, the hero..."

"The poet?"

"Yes, the poet, complains about his wife..."

"Roman husbands complain about their wives too."

"And he said," Adria went on, "'we've been living together for fifty-two years and three months, and my wife still doesn't understand me.'"

"So you see, even in the north women aren't so intelligent."

Vetere was about to reply when Adria asked, "Why isn't Guarnerio here?"

Everyone looked around. And, in fact, that seemed very strange.

The boor from whom Guarnerio had shortly before fled so discourteously and who had been left talking to himself at the terrace door, was part of the circle. He hesitated a moment, then spoke through clenched teeth. "I was just speaking to him."

"Who's going to find him?" asked Adria

There was a moment of uncertainty. Then another voice spoke up. "I'll go. I'll bring him back dead or alive."

"Alive, alive."

The man who went to look for Guarnerio was the handsome magistrate with the white mustache, Bellamonte, known as "the Judge," whom we saw greet Adria in her box.

He looked through all the rooms, then went out on the terrace where he discovered Guarnerio pacing in a strange way.

"What are you doing out here?"

Guarnerio stopped, stared at him for a moment as if he had difficulty remembering him, then said, "I know you very well. You're the Judge. Or as they say in court, 'your Honor.' But here you are a man. Well, your Honor, speaking as a man, I am going to tell you the truth, the whole truth. I am looking down here in the terrace pavement for the reflection of the seven stars in Ursa Major."

And he pointed to the constellation in the sky, where the moon was setting and the stars appeared brighter.

The judge looked up to the heavens, then down to the ground and stared hard at Guarnerio, who appeared to be in earnest. He suspected he might be drunk, but couldn't quite believe it.

"Let's go in," he said. "Signora Adria was asking for you."

Guarnerio followed him meekly all the way to the last room without uttering another sound. When he stood before Adria, he bowed.

"Why weren't you here, Guarnerio?"

A malicious smile spread across Guarnerio's face. Staring at the feathers cascading from the curve of her knees, he murmured. "Mysteries. Heavenly mysteries." And a blank look filled his eyes.

Everyone was stunned. No one had ever seen Guarnerio in such a state. Even Adria fluttered her eyelids for a moment, then turned to an officer seated two chairs away from her and said, "My husband wants to buy me a horse. I'd like your advice."

Everyone sighed with relief at this distraction. The officer blushed, shrugged his shoulders and, looking pleased with himself, promised his best advice.

Guarnerio stood up and, glancing around at the group, announced, "My presence is not necessary. Just remember that I'm an astronomer. Ah, signora Adria, signora Adria, so many faded stars in heaven…"

He had spoken these mindless words in one breath without any expression while staring at the hairline of Adria's forehead. Then he made a careful turn and walked off with his head bent as though he thought he were making himself invisible.

Someone said, "What's the matter with him? It looks like he's…"

But the person next to him elbowed him to keep quiet, sensing that Adria would not want to discuss the distressing situation. Indeed, she had already turned to the person on her right, the aforementioned Prince Vetere di Castellana, asking, "Who is that very tall, blonde, young woman I saw passing through the ballroom. She looks like an American."

"She is indeed American. She arrived in Rome just two days ago. But that reminds me of my presidential duties. I beg your leave. I'll return shortly."

He rose and walked off casually, but as soon as he out of the group's sight he hurried his steps and caught up with Guarnerio. Slipping his own arm under his, he spoke with ease.

"Come along with me for a moment to see what's going on in the ballroom. And don't leave me alone, Guarnerio, otherwise

I'll run into a pack of boors who'll intercept me. You be my shield."

Guarnerio let himself be led like a child. After only a few steps Vetere was convinced he wasn't drunk. They walked into a flutter of multicolored confetti and were greeted by wild shouts. Vetere ducked into a deserted hallway. Streamers hit them, a red one hung around Guarnerio's neck like a sash of honor. Vetere drew him into a corner near a window. Looking intently into his eye, he spoke with great kindness.

"What's the matter with you, Guarnerio?"

The other exploded.

"Nothing. Nothing's the matter. The same with the Judge. You're the president of the Society. And let's say I'm an astronomer. I told him. I am telling you, but I can't go around repeating it to all of Rome. I am studying the reflection of the stars in Ursa Major. All right? On the Society's terrace here. And so what? The terrace is yours, okay. But the reflection of the stars is mine. Do you understand? Mine, mine. And do you know for how long? For five years."

His voice was rising. Vetere stared at him severely, and suddenly Guarnerio fell silent. Now Vetere spoke more accommodatingly.

"That's fine. Who's arguing with you?"

Guarnerio hesitated. "Actually, you're right. No one," he stammered. "But believe me, Prince, you can never take too many precautions."

After a moment of silence Vetere said, "It's late."

Guarnerio answered, "I don't know."

Vetere was hoping to get him home and was trying to think of whom he could ask to accompany him. He made a try at it himself.

"It's late for me. I want to go to sleep. If you're leaving too, we can go part of the way together."

Guarnerio responded quickly.

"No, no. I'm staying. You go. Go. And I'll look out for things here. You can rely on me. I'll represent you. You're so kind to me that I'll be happy to help you. So go on. What are you waiting for, for godsakes?"

Vetere looked around. No one was near them. They were in a kind of corridor on whose white walls were hung a row of small lithographs, hunting scenes, in black and white.

"Now I understand," said Guarnerio. "You're scared. Scared. About the terrace. About your terrace. You make me laugh. Do whatever you want." His voice had become sharp, insolent.

Then suddenly he sounded piteous. "I'm going to get some coffee."

"Good idea. I'll go with you."

Guarnerio's mood seemed about to change again. "Oh? where?"

"Back inside, to the buffet."

Guarnerio laughed harshly. "Yes, of course. Of course. There's no coffee without a buffet and there's no buffet without going back inside. Therefore let's go. Let's go."

It's not hard to imagine what was going through Vetere's mind. Reaching the buffet counter, he got Guarnerio, who was once again quite docile, to sit down on one of the stools, and behind his back motioned to the waiter to keep an eye on him. Running out of the room, he bumped into the Judge who, concerned about his long absence, had come in search of him.

Vetere spoke quickly and quietly. "Guarnerio's lost his mind. He's raving. I'm sure he's going to explode any minute. You've got to help me get him out of here before he does. We'll have to get him home and get him a doctor. He's at the buffet. Run over there and don't leave him alone, not even for a minute, until I get back."

The judge went off immediately. Vetere found Adria's husband in the gaming room, where he was watching others play. Vetere took him aside and described the situation.

"I'll go back to where Adria is," the husband said. "I'll work it out so I can stand watch at the door. Nothing of this must get back there."

He entered the last salon where he was greeted enthusiastically by Adria's friends. One after another, they offered him their seats, but he refused and remained standing. He positioned himself in the doorway where he could engage in conversation and at the same time keep watch on the other rooms.

Everyone in the room was greatly disconcerted. They recalled Guarnerio's mysterious words and his elusive withdrawal. They had seen Vetere go off and not return, and then the Judge disappear as well, and now here was Adria's husband trying to appear relaxed and not succeeding.

Only Adria remained at ease.

A man from another room came cautiously up to the doorway and whispered to the husband. Immediately after, Adria thought she heard a different kind of rumbling in the confused din reaching her from the distant rooms. At that moment, her husband, feigning the utmost casualness, brought the two panels of the door together, leaving them open only a crack. Adria tried to keep the conversation going among her frightened friends.

Still another messenger arrived and spoke to her husband from the other side of the door. Instantly, the latter shut the doors so that even the crack was gone, but not so quickly that for a second one couldn't hear a great roar overwhelm every other sound of the party.

A gentleman sitting near Adria rushed toward the door, but Adria restrained him, asking in a surprised voice, "What are you doing? Oh, perhaps it is very late."

"It's two-thirty."

"In that case it is time to go."

The door opened abruptly, but the husband rushed through

it and closed it from the other side, once again choking off the strange clamor.

Adria stood up and the others did, too. Now they were more distraught than ever, fearing to allow her to confront the mystery of what was happening beyond the door. But she extricated them from the dilemma by saying, "Let's go out on the terrace. I need some fresh air right now."

The captain hurried ahead to open the glass doors, and everyone followed. Adria addressed him, "I'd appreciate it if you went back through the rooms and told my husband to meet us in the lobby."

The terrace circled the entire building, so that they reached the lobby without having to reenter the building. The lobby was empty, the attendants having rushed into the main rooms. Adria's husband arrived and retrieved her coat himself. She bade farewell to her followers with a quick wave and a heavenly smile.

In the piazza a group of chauffeurs and coachmen were talking animatedly and looking up at the windows of the Crown Society. Adria's chauffeur hurried off to get her car and bring it to the doorway. While her husband was helping Adria into the car, a friend of his came rushing out of the building bareheaded. The husband ran up to the man and spoke quickly. "Call me at home in a half hour. I'll be back." Then he entered the car, sat down beside Adria, and began speaking. "I have to tell you what's going on."

She interrupted him.

"Whatever may have happened, I don't want you to tell me about it until tomorrow evening. I'll be resting all day tomorrow. I'm very tired."

He didn't persist, for which she thanked him with an affectionate smile. When they reached the house, he ordered the chauffeur to wait for him and accompanied Adria to the door of her suite, where he left her after kissing her hand. Then he hurried to his own room where the telephone was ringing. From someone at the Crown Society he learned how the tragedy had ended. At the buffet Guarnerio began railing against the Judge and Vetere. As they'd reached for his arms to calm him, he had leaped up onto the counter and, while a waiter caught at his feet, he had fired two shots from a revolver, killing both Vetere and the Judge instantly. Then he had thrown himself down headfirst, and with his head split, in the middle of all that blood on the floor, he had struggled as though possessed. It had taken six men to restrain him.

Adria's husband had his driver rush him back to the Crown Society. An ambulance had already arrived with two doctors and several attendants, who had gotten Guarnerio into a straitjacket and were about to take him off to an asylum.

---

4 THE NEXT DAY AT VILLA ADRIA was completely disorganized. Adria's husband arrived home early in the morning, unnerved by the dreadful night he'd spent in the asylum waiting room. The governess gave him a brief report. "Signora Adria left orders last night that she was not to be awakened before two in the afternoon and said she doesn't want to see anyone all day. She had the telephone in her room disconnected and doesn't want anyone to speak to her about anything but household matters. She's taking her meals in her room and told me to tell you, sir, that she wants to go out for a long drive tomorrow morning at eleven and therefore asks, sir, that you leave her the use of the automobile. She'll be going to Fregene or Castelli alone and won't be back until evening. She had a lot of books brought up to her room for this afternoon and evening."

The Life and Death of Adria and Her Children

Adria's husband slept badly for an hour, changed his clothes, and left orders of his own for the governess before returning to the asylum. "Telephone the children's teachers not to come today and give the children the day off from lessons. At about eleven take them to the Mayers'. I'll telephone the Mayers beforehand. They can spend the day, have lunch and supper there, and if I'm not back before eight-thirty, go get them then. The driver is coming with me. But no matter what, the car will be at my wife's disposal tomorrow at eleven. When the children get up tell them that I will be out all day and that before leaving I stopped into their rooms to see them." And, indeed, he went into each of the two little bedrooms where the children were sleeping quietly, kissed them gently on the forehead, and left.

The Mayer house was almost at the end of via Nomentana, but set very far back along a lane that crosses the street from the left, just before it gets to the great gorge at Aniene. The Mayer children were friends of Tullia and Remo. The father had chosen the Mayers to visit rather than other friends because they were foreigners and isolated, making it less likely that news of the tragedy would have reached them yet. He hoped to put off the children's knowledge of it as long as possible. He wanted to prepare them carefully.

The children were delighted when they awoke and heard that they weren't going to have lessons but were going to Villa Mayer instead.

"And papa?"

"He had to leave very early so he stopped by and kissed you both an hour ago, though you didn't feel anything."

"That's too bad."

Since their father was using the automobile, the governess and the children had to take the streetcar, and as they did this very rarely, this too was enormously entertaining. The governess left them at the entrance gate of the lane while the Mayer children, having seen their approach from a window, came rushing out to greet them.

They played a number of games in the garden. Tullia and Remo had fun with their friends' mispronunciations. At lunch they were praised by Mrs. Mayer for their exemplary manners.

(None of their hosts noticed that every so often Reno and Tullia looked at each other as though waiting to exchange a secret.)

After lunch they all went out again to the garden. The house was situated on a kind of elevated plateau in the middle of the countryside where the land slopes off to the east into the most gentle of the hills surrounding Rome. On every other side the hills are sharp and peaked. From a lookout facing north, Tullia noticed a double row of tall plane trees leading all the way into the city. She pointed it out to one of the children. "That's via Salaria," he answered. Then Tullia remembered that once they had driven to the Mayers along that road instead of taking via Nomentana, and that the road turned to the left from there, at about the elevation of the Royal villa, and opened into an area of low land contiguous to the garden of Villa Adria. She said nothing, however, but kept to herself, as though it were something precious, the knowledge that the large road ran almost directly to her house.

Continuing her walk through the garden, Tullia quickly pulled her brother aside and told him, "We mustn't forget."

"I know, I know," he interrupted.

"What do you know?"

"That at five today we have to go see mamma because we couldn't on Thursday."

"Maybe the governess doesn't know it, but I didn't say anything to her, because we don't usually have to. But now she's not coming to get us until evening."

"Then we have to go right away."

"I know the way, but we have to tell Signora Mayer that we're leaving."

"So we'll tell her."

"No, she won't let us go, because she knows someone's coming to get us at eight-thirty."

Remo became so upset he was on the verge of tears. "But I want to see mamma."

"Don't worry. I'm thinking about it."

The other children caught up to them and suggested they all go back in the house and play cards.

"How about billiards," Tullia said.

The idea was greeted with delight.

"Let's go, let's go," said Remo.

Tullia stopped him with a sharp look, then said to the others, "You go on in, and get everything ready. Remo and I are going to wash our hands." She thrust out her own hands, which were completely covered with dirt.

The billiard table was upstairs in a second floor room.

So Tullia and Remo were left alone. Then Tullia, behaving mysteriously, took Remo's hand. "Come on," she said.

Running, she led him to a corner of the belvedere where a narrow, stone staircase descended all the way to level ground. She sat him down on the first step and said, "Will you be all right waiting for me here?"

"A long time?"

"Not too long. You're not a little boy any more. You're past six, so you mustn't get scared. If you do, we won't see mamma at all today."

"Come back fast," Remo said, and Tullia flew off, her heart bursting at the thought of the complex adventure into which she was rushing.

She ran back to the house, but instead of going upstairs went into the ground floor room where signora Mayer had begun dozing over some illustrated magazines.

"Signora," Tullia called out to her. "Our governess has come for us. Papa is home now."

"Oh, I'm so sorry. Where's Remo?"

"He's waiting for me outside at the gate. We have to leave right away. We both thank you so much."

Signora Mayer's head and eyelids were already falling forward, but she managed to reopen her eyes. "Oh, I'll walk out with you. And where are the others?"

"They're upstairs. Please don't trouble yourself. It's really not necessary."

The woman slowly stretched her arm towards the girl. Tullia leaned forward to be kissed, and by the time she began moving away, signora Mayer was once more drifting into the world of afternoon dreams.

Tullia ran from the house as if possessed. She was careful when crossing the garden to keep low behind the hedge in case any of the children were looking out from the second floor. By the time she reached Remo, he was frightened.

"See how fast I was? Let's go. Hurry up. We have to get to those trees down there."

They went down the steps. At the bottom there was a narrow path that led through meadows and fields to the highway. An April breeze and the importance of their mission spurred them on. This first part of their flight was easy. The path ended at a kind of dry gully, where they would have to climb up a short escarpment.

"It's like in that book, *Trottolone on Firefly Island*."

"That's right."

Sweating from exertion and flushed with joy, they clambered up like two little savages and found themselves on the road lined with plane trees.

They felt as if they were halfway home.

"From here, all we have to do is go straight. That's Rome."

For a while they walked effortlessly. They kept to the right shoulder of the road along the plane trees. They saw no other people, though a few carts passed them. In the quiet warmth they were unafraid. They walked intently without looking about. All they saw was the strip of road on which they were traveling, which always stretched the same distance ahead of them, a road without end. The huge tree trunks that followed each other along the road seemed to be keeping them company. But as they walked onward, the plane trees never ended, never reached Rome and the house where their mother had said she would see them on Saturday just before five. Today is Saturday, but who knows when it will be five? The road doesn't ever stop. As they walked, every so often the light around them seemed to waver. By now Tullia had taken Remo's hand, and after a few minutes realized he was lagging behind and that she had to tug at him.

"Are you tired?" she asked.

"A lot."

"Do you want to take a rest?"

They sat down at the base of a tree, and he leaned against his young sister, who seemed so grown-up to him. Now they both shivered with cold. Remo dozed for a few minutes, then woke. "Will it be night soon?"

"Silly, can't you see how light it is? But it's better to go on."

They rose. As before, the road was flat and straight and lined with enormous plane trees, even larger than those they had passed. But now walking on it was difficult; it was burning their feet.

In the distance they heard the sound of a wagon. Gradually it reached them. "I want to go in the wagon," Remo wailed. But the prospect frightened Tullia.

"Quiet," she said and they hid behind a tree for fear that

the wagoner would see them. Actually, he was asleep under the hood of his multicolor canvas while the horse proceeded on its own, shaking its head as though singing to itself: "Look at what those children are doing."

Now Remo was really dragging his feet, and Tullia feared she too was getting tired. They stopped walking. Down in the plain they saw a few small houses—all of them closed up and apparently empty. The entire world seemed empty to the two children walking toward Rome.

Just at that moment, a cyclist sounds his bell frantically behind them. It frightens them out of the fatigue overcoming them as they stand alongside the plane trees. They shriek at the sound but don't move. The cyclist, who could have broken his neck at their side of the road, has to turn sharply toward the center, skids, almost hits a tree full on, and lets loose a torrent of curses at the children, which blend into the cloud of dust that follows behind him and eventually disappears. Now Remo breaks into tears, Tullia puts her arms around him and cries silently, and they sink to the ground. A gust of wind blows through the trees and sounds to them like a hurricane. The shadow of a cloud drops over them, engulfs them, and seems about to carry them off in a whirlwind. But there they sit, motionless on the ground, faint with fear and fatigue, like two pieces of fruit fallen betimes from a tree—the plane tree—decaying before they can ripen.

There's no telling how long they lay there before a cart proceeding quietly down the middle of the road reached them. The young man who was driving it saw them and stopped instantly. He hurried to their side and carried them bodily into the carriage. Tullia woke immediately but didn't know where she was. Remo wakes too and looks around wide-eyed. Now the plane trees cast long shadows on the road, on the seat cushions, and on the face of the smiling youth, who, having given the children something to drink, brushes the dust off them and tries to get them to speak. Who was he? We'll never know. Perhaps he was an angel, the Guardian Angel who rescues courageous souls, even if they're very little eight-year-old and six-year-old souls like Tullia and Remo.

The children revive almost instantly and, standing up, look around as one does when one wakes in a strange room. The young man's appearance was so friendly that Remo laughed and Tullia spoke to him.

"It's our mother," she exclaimed. "We have to go see our mother. She's waiting for us."

"Where?"

"Down there."

"Then sit down, I'll take you to your mamma."

The youth, that is, the Angel, sat the children down close to each other at his side and, whipping up the horse, started on the way. Every once in a while he would smile at them.

"You'll tell me the street where I have to turn?"

"Yes, It's near here. What's that over there?"

"That's Villa Ada, the King's villa."

"Oh, it's before that. Wait, go slow. Here, here, turn here." Tullia pointed to the left. They turned. Then, recognizing where they were, she clapped her hands and leaped to her feet.

"Down there. There. See that tree? It's right there. And there's the gate. Our gate."

The Guardian Angel, still smiling, stopped the horse and set the two children down in front of the gate. He saw that a gardener on the other side of the fence had recognized them and was rushing over to open it. At this, he quickly took up the reins, raised his whip high and, shouting "good-bye, good-bye," disappeared without even giving them time to say thank you. That's how Guardian Angels do things.

"What time is it?" Tullia asked the gardener anxiously.

"A quarter past five," he answered somewhat surprised.

"Come on, come on," Tullia shouted to her brother. They ran across the short driveway, up the steps and into the hallway.

They were stunned not to find anyone about in the house. One of the two maid servants was out, the other was in Adria's room. The manservant was with their father, and the governess, having nothing to do until 8:30, had taken a walk. The children went up to the landing outside their mother's suite. Two palms in great pots stood at each side of it.

Her door was closed. There was a strange silence.

Long shadows rose from the well of the staircase, as though the shadows of the plane trees had reached this far. They stood outside and waited. Their mother had left word the other day "toward five." It was after five now. Had she gone out?

They listened closely, but there was only silence.

No matter. Tullia and Remo felt that their mother was there, on the other side of the door—two or three rooms beyond that door—but there. That much was certain. The air is different when she is not within. Can't you see it? It's nearly dark, but that door, the very wood of the door, is giving off a pale light, flickering faintly like the Milky Way. That means their mother is home. They stood and waited some more. They were tired and sad, much more tired and much sadder than they had been at the side of via Salaria.

Suddenly they both knew that there was no reason to wait any longer. They felt it and turned away at almost the same instant. They descended the staircase on their toes, without looking at each other, like a pair of criminals.

Downstairs, Remo said, "Guarnerio will be here at any minute to take us out in his car, remember?"

"Yes, and he'll tell us what's going on. Are you tired, Remo?"

"I'm awfully hungry."

"Me too. Wait, come on."

She led him into the pantry and turned on the light. There was no one there either, but by now they no longer found it strange. Their rummaging distracted them somewhat. They found biscuits, butter and jam, stuffed themselves, and wiped their greasy faces.

"It's time for Guarnerio to come," Tullia said. "When he gets here, he'll come upstairs to look for us."

So they went upstairs and threw themselves on the bed in Tullia's little room, and fell asleep for a short while with the light on.

Tullia awoke first. Something inside her told her to awaken. She called out, "Remo, Remo."

He roused instantly and asked, "Is Guarnerio here?"

"No, but it must be late."

"What time is it?"

"I don't know."

"Let's go ask the gardener."

"No. Let's look at the big clock. I can tell time."

They went downstairs and stood before the tall pendulum clock in the hall. Studying the numbers, Tullia looked at it a while and spoke confidently. "You know? It's a lot after seven."

"What about Guarnerio?"

"Who knows?"

"Is it after seven-thirty yet?"

And so a new hope rekindled a light in the two small unhappy faces.

"Not yet seven-thirty," Tullia answered, "but nearly."

"Then any minute now."

"That's right."

They both laughed.

Once more they climbed the stairs, feeling no longer tired. Slowly they walked through rooms, then crossed that particular hallway and reached that particular room, the dark room where the furniture was stored. There was no light to turn on.

The only light that room received came from the hallway. But they hadn't even turned the hall light on. In that part of the house they don't need light. They know it too well. They crossed the dark room without a moment's hesitation, reached the high chest, climbed onto it, found the slits and looked through them.

On the other side, though, everything was dark, even darker. They waited and nothing happened. They were waiting for the lights to go on, for their mother to appear as she did every evening. Instead, it grew still darker. Perhaps the room with the dining table no longer existed, the entire world no longer existed, but was a great black mass filled with fear and cold.

They stood there a long time with their eyes pressed to those slits. Perhaps she no longer existed as well. Slowly they sank down into the endless shadows on the hard-surfaced chest, their faces wet with quiet tears. Alone, exhausted and in despair, they fell asleep one atop the other, like dolls in an abandoned shop window.

adria II

————◆►◄◆◄◆————

1 ADRIA DOESN'T GO INTO THE WATER. Her style at the seashore is to settle herself on the sand in her swimsuit under an enormous gaily-colored umbrella that shoots bright flames to every horizon. People come hurrying from every direction to see Adria sitting on the sand in her emerald swimming suit. Perhaps even the sail boats far out to sea momentarily slacken their leisurely pace across the curved horizon. The sun strikes them from the sky, the colors of Adria's umbrella from the shore. Out on the blue sea they sail off dazzled with light.

Adria doesn't go into the water. From her island of shade her pale blue eyes roam the glistening sea. She listens to tender words, idiotic words, words as frivolous as flies. And like swarms of flies, men and women cross the sands, buzzing as they flit to the edge of the sea, holding hands in a line like strings of paper dolls.

When the sun begins to set, Adria retires to her cabin to change. When she emerges she is dressed completely in white, pale as snow, and wearing a large soft hat whose brim rests on her shoulders. Adria bids farewell to her entourage and walks alone through a pine grove scented with resin. It ends at a white hot street, which she crosses, raising only the barest puffs of dust with her light step. She has come to a fence, follows the curve of a wide street and enters her hotel. The bellman approaches her in the lobby. "A gentleman has come to see you. He is waiting in the lounge," he says, pointing to a corner on the left at the far side of the lobby.

"His name?"

"He didn't say. He said he would just rather wait." The bellman's face betrayed a hint of mockery for the gentleman's naiveté.

And, indeed, Adria shrugs her shoulders slightly. It isn't necessary for her to tell him what to do. The bellman withdraws. By the time he will be disappointing the poor gentleman, Adria will be out of sight.

But instead of going up to her apartment Adria has decided to have tea in the garden. Thus, with her cloud-light step she walks the entire length of the lobby. But when she reaches the back of it, instead of stepping through the open glass doors on her left, she enters the corner lounge.

Hardly had she set foot on the threshold, than she realized the foolishness of her action. And because the first thought lasted only an instant, she even had time to wonder at what she'd done.

A very young man stepped from the shadow of heavy drapes and walked halfway across the room, where he stopped.

"Signora," he said, but didn't go on.

"Who are you?" Adria asked in a voice which contained neither condescension nor reproof.

The man was now forced to respond. "Forgive me for not having given my name, even though I risked not seeing you thereby."

"Precisely."

"Indeed, it's quite strange that you did come. I can't believe it's true."

"And even now you can't tell me your name?"

"Yes, of course. I didn't have the courage to have it presented to you because I was afraid that in some way...I understand that you..."

He'd become enormously confused. He looked down at his feet, didn't know what to do with his hands, as though he were on stage for the first time in his life. But in the silence that followed he found the courage to look up at Adria. Seeing her, still on the threshold, quite calm, filled with otherworldly radiance, he was suddenly ashamed for having come to see her and almost afraid that he was committing a strange crime.

Adria took a few steps toward him, and he withdrew as though in terror, as though awed by a miracle.

Finally, he began speaking rapidly. "Signora, I've already met you. But of course, you do not recognize me. Perhaps because I was just a boy then and now I'm grown, almost five years older. I'm twenty-one. I wasn't much more than sixteen then. I only saw you once. I was introduced to you by my father, my poor father. It was in Rome, one evening when you were dressed completely in pale blue in a box at the Teatro Valle. You won't remember because who knows how many times you wore pale blue and sat in a box. But I..."

Adria felt a kind of anxiety rise within her, felt her memory spring up, begin groping in the past. She had the vague feeling that she was about to face some unpleasant recollection. But now the youth, after his abrupt pause, was speaking again, more quickly than before.

"...I never saw you in anything else, nothing. And then, immediately after that there was that terrible tragedy. That, you must remember. Then I went on a trip around the world. Anyway, my name is...my name is Giovanni, but that doesn't mean anything, Then there's my last name, which is, which is Bellamonte. Yes, Bellamonte, the son, of course."

Adria felt an enormous upheaval throughout her being. Instantly she felt distressed. She refused to permit herself to dwell on it or ask its reason, but willed herself to remain as controlled within as she appeared calm and courteous without.

"I remember," she said. You say it was five years ago? You're probably right. I remember that you bowed to kiss my hand and stopped in the middle."

Giovanni Bellamonte turned fiery red. He wished the earth to open and swallow him. And Adria now regretted her words. After a moment of silence, Giovanni spoke impetuously again. "And now I didn't even begin to kiss your hand."

Adria looked into his eyes. They were clear. She couldn't have borne it, if in the far reaches of those eyes there had been an accusation. In a moment she felt reassured. "But why an accusation?" she wondered.

Acting impulsively as well, she extended her hand to him. He kissed it as though he were being allowed to kiss the edge of a cherub's wings. Once again Adria was filled with regret.

She was struck with shame at the turmoil in her soul. No shadow of it crossed her face. Quickly, she matched her words to the calm of her features, set herself to the polite inquiry one is obliged to make of one's guests. "And what are you doing now?"

"Right after that, I began traveling with my uncle, who's a sea captain. I've never been back to Rome. In eight days I'm sailing out again for southern seas. I came here for a week's vacation with a friend of mine. Two hours ago, I heard someone mention your name and say that you were staying at this hotel, so I came to see you, but I don't know why. As soon as they sent me into this room, I was sorry for the whole idea. I suddenly realized what I'd done. I wanted to leave, but I was too embarrassed in front of the bellman. What just happened here is the strangest thing in my life. I don't think anything stranger will ever happen to me."

Adria offered no response to this candid confession.

"I'm also about to take a trip. I'm going to spend this winter in Cairo," she said instead.

The fact is, until that moment Adria hadn't given the slightest thought to being in Cairo. She didn't like traveling. Nevertheless, at that moment, she wasn't lying. She had an instantaneous desire to spend the winter in Cairo, had settled it in her mind, and with that sudden resolution made her announcement to Giovanni Bellamonte.

"Cairo," was all he said, and felt as if he were completely obtuse.

It occurred to Adria that she might like to take a trip around the world. She had no idea of the import of this new fantasy.

She extended her hand to Giovanni and said, "I thank you for having remembered me and wish you a wonderful trip and good luck."

It took a minute for Giovanni to realize that he was standing alone in the middle of the room, which had become dreary and cold.

Adria went out into the garden where she met her husband. She had tea with him and two other gentlemen. Other people joined them, then it was time to go upstairs and change for dinner. She seemed to have completely forgotten the unusual reactions that had pervaded her.

Ascending to her room, she found herself thinking, "That's the way it could end." For a while she couldn't understand to what her thought had referred. Then suddenly she grasped the part of it that had escaped her. The complete thought was: "A trip around the world might be a very nice ending." She recalled having thought about a trip around the world the moment before taking leave of Giovanni Bellamonte. But what was ending? Her chamber maid arrived to help her dress. Adria postponed examining the tangle of thoughts—something she had no experience dealing with—until later. After dinner, as she was taking part in the usual conversations and smiling a little at everyone, she was suddenly seized by a great impatience to be alone. She cut the evening short. As soon as she reached her room she sent her maid off, almost in anger.

She sat down, but instantly rose again and began to pace the room. Something akin to fear filled her. She managed to overcome it, then to recall one by one the new and rash impulses that had surprised her so much in the few minutes she was alone with Giovanni Bellamonte. I decided to spend the winter in Cairo. Why? I even wanted to take a long trip around the world. Why was I so kind to that boy? But before that. I have to think of before that. Because for a moment I felt awkward with him. Did I want to be sure he wasn't feeling reproachful toward me? Reproachful for what? How can it be my fault if a mad man killed his father? He said five years. Then Guarnerio has been in an asylum for five years? What's five years? And now her anxiety, and the misgivings it had raised, dissolved into a diffuse melancholy. Under this heavy cloud she undressed herself slowly and got into bed. But she did not lie down.

She tried repeating "five years" to herself. She wanted to understand its full significance. But each time she repeated the words, just those two words, they lost their meaning, became merely dull and empty sounds.

With the practiced motion performed every evening at that time, Adria extended her arm toward the mirror on her night table.

Upon seeing her reflection she had the strange sensation of not recognizing herself, but recovered immediately. Yet, there really was something new in her face, which had always looked exactly the same to her. The passing days had never wrought a single change. From the time when, ten years ago (though she still has no idea what ten years means) she had fixed upon dedicating her entire being to the worship of her own beauty—from that time, by imposing an unalterable equanimity upon her soul no matter the vicissitudes, by banishing that event from her life, she had kept her face unaltered as well.

But this evening Adria is more beautiful.

She sees that she is more beautiful and this is what frightens her.

Her intuition is quite right on this subject. She must not be more beautiful. Even though at first she doesn't clearly understand the reasons for it, her fear is legitimate.

Becoming more beautiful comes from a deed, from something that stirs the soul. Look at her, the same features she had yesterday, the same as always. She is more beautiful because of a new expression, because tenderness and apprehension have settled in among those other features, where until yesterday there was only heavenly and cloudless light. Perhaps passion is more beautiful than Paradise. But passion leads to decay.

Adria didn't laugh at her image as she usually did. She smiled weakly and the smile left a trail of anxiety along the shadows in her face. Still looking into the mirror, her eyes were no longer focused on her image, but had moved insensibly into a void, a distant region filled with danger. The region of recollections, of regrets perhaps, of measuring and weighing. There is a confused din from there, from the room in which Guarnerio went mad. "Five years," said young Giovanni, son of the man killed by someone who had gone mad for love of her. More clearly than any other memory, Adria recalled the morning she had opened Guarnerio's prophetic note. She hadn't ever thought of it again, yet now the words sprang forth from a distant region and sounded one by one. *"Nevertheless, signora Adria, I truly feel that tomorrow will be a definitive day."*

She tried to dismiss these intrusive thoughts. She set the mirror down precipitously, turned out the light and slid down beneath the sheet. A murmuring arose from the shadows, strains of distant music, the rhythmical breathing of the sea. Outside, the night must truly be filled with stars. Adria shut her eyes, pressed her cheek against the pillow, curled her body tightly, and fell asleep.

But now, for the first time, after all these years, she dreamed. Inchoate faces and voices crowded about her, then silently disappeared. Her sleep was filled with blue landscapes that receded into a series of crystalline grottoes, and beyond them, far in the background, a streaming river sparkled like diamonds and disappeared into the distance. The murmuring of bees enveloped her, as it had once done in the country many years ago when she was a child. She saw the faces of people whom she had never known. They vanished, returned, and then the air was filled with a fixed dazzle such as one sees when one's eyes are focussed on a bright light. Just like that, in the middle of this light, a large, hard-surfaced building appeared, with a square whitewashed façade. There was only one small door, barred and guarded by an enormous man holding a huge stick in his hand. Adria looked up and saw that all the windows of the house were enclosed by thick iron bars. Shouts were coming from them, but her husband closed a door and the shouts could no longer be heard. The seascape returned and with it a swarm of people, fat as frogs lined along the edge of a ditch. Every so often one of them would leap belly first into the water, sending it splashing up to the ceiling. But there was one who didn't jump like the others, who remained apart from them and turned toward her, and who became larger as he drew closer to her with his dark face and two enormous eyes filled with fear. It was Giovanni Bellamonte. Instantly she said "good luck" to him, as one does to people one will never see again, but in a whisper because they were at the theater and the curtain was up. She extended her hand to him, but dreamed another hand clearly, very clearly. Giovanni's hand, which was reaching out to hers. Giovanni's brow grew larger. He was bending forward with infinite slowness, and was about to place his lips upon her hand. Now she knows that she is about to dream even his mouth clearly, very clearly, and it was making her blood run cold because she didn't want to see it. She cried out desperately to stop herself from dreaming the mouth, to stop dreaming altogether, and tore herself from sleep, but not quickly enough to avoid feeling the soft warmth of those lips on her wrist. She awoke in the dark, her face suffused with heat.

Through a window a gleam of white was already piercing the darkness.

Upon this depressing reawakening, yesterday's anxiety has become almost horror, a horror of herself. Adria is terrified of no longer being as she has always been, mistress of herself, mistress of her will, of her wakefulness and sleep. She had thought always that she was completely exposing her soul as a smooth surface which, happily, reflected the rays of her beauty. But there were wrinkles in her soul, tiny treacherous wrinkles. Now the dreadful dream, completing the work begun by last evening's anxieties, had revealed those wrinkles to her. Perhaps there are others as well, if one could no longer rely even on oneself.

She got out of bed and opened a shutter. Dawn was trembling beneath the heavens like a little girl constrained to beg. Adria walked slowly back toward her bed. In that dreadful light she felt as if she were walking through deep water. She lit a bedside lamp. The two lights mixed in a sickening glow. Adria sat down at the edge of the bed.

She looked at her night table. Then she put out her hand and pushed away the mirror, which seemed to be thrusting itself at her.

It was the faithful mirror, the one in which, for so many years, Adria had greeted herself every evening, the one she'd taken everywhere with her. The very one in which, seeing herself one day so long ago, she had decided to live for beauty's sake. All that was ten years ago. Now she knows. Five years, someone said yesterday, referring to Guarnerio. Ten years, Adria says, thinking of herself. Two times five. Then Guarnerio's madness divides her life of beauty precisely in half?

She rebelled against that conclusion. And why "in half"? What kind of arithmetic was that? Is her beauty perhaps declining, ending? That's where the trip around the world fits in—a voyage as the conclusion. To show herself to the entire world before the end. But who has declared that it is over? It's not true. In fact, she was even more beautiful last night. Ah, that's the snare. Adria's beauty will fade if she cannot maintain her peace of mind. If she is more beautiful one day than another, if she wants to travel, if she goes into a lounge without knowing what's she's doing, and if she dreams then wakens in a fever, what does it all mean? She has let the reins fall from her hands. Yes, the reins with which she has been restraining time, heavy on earth as bronze. "Ten years." Yes, a few months more or less didn't matter. Ten from the day she'd first made that resolution after having had her second child. She was barely twenty then.

Twenty. And now? Arithmetic is even more inexorable than dreams.

Now, finally and unexpectedly, the way a mound of stones may suddenly appear at a bend in a road, she has understood. She took pleasure in honing the arithmetic, turning it in her mind to a sharp point. She has understood. And since we are dealing with arithmetic, let us say that this is the end of August, that she was born at the end of September. She has understood, therefore, that in less than a month she will be thirty years old.

The thought left her breathless. She began to laugh, but stopped immediately because the sound of her laughter disturbed her. It was too different from the joyous laughter she was accustomed to hearing at the sight reflected in the mirror of her mouth and gleaming teeth. Nevertheless, the idea really deserved to be mocked. It was so ordinary, common. Every woman who reached thirty was filled with fear. Adria must not be like other women. The others stop worrying and go on with their lives, then at forty become fearful again. But she, Adria, will not. She must not do what every other woman does. And she thanks Heaven for having sent her the warning.

Thank Heaven for having sent Giovanni, for having sent Cairo, sent the dream to caution her, forewarn her, not so much that she is thirty years old, because that is not the important issue, but because the wrinkles in her soul are filled with shadows. They are warning her—she would be deceiving herself to think otherwise. Everything is about to change and therefore everything will have been useless unless she prepares herself. In a moment of distraction she had fallen into the stream of time, into a dusty road, into the capacity to feel something from here or there, something about the sanctity of her beauty. As a result, a spring in the complicated mechanism of her will has broken. She will no longer have the will she needs at every hour, the will she had every morning upon awakening, and the will she had every night, to sleep without dreaming. It is necessary to take steps for her entire sacrifice not to have been in vain. She must gather her will all at once and into a single act. Something other than wintering in Cairo.

The resolution, decisive though unformed, calmed her. She fell into a peaceful sleep and awoke at her usual time. No one who saw her during the day was aware that she had gone through a tremendous experience. At dinner that evening she told her husband that she wanted to return to Rome immediately, and they left the following morning.

2 DURING THAT SECOND NIGHT, ADRIA had become clearer about her decision. She had considered the matter calmly, and had remained awake for a half hour, which was sufficient for her to plan the first steps she was going to take. She no longer felt even a trace of the anxiety that had so troubled her the previous night. Her decision was made with the clarity and will power which for ten years had sustained her in the religious construction of her everyday life. The image of Giovanni had completely disappeared. Perhaps because by his appearance in that hotel lounge Giovanni had fulfilled his function in the world. He might even have vanished from it, as he is now vanishing from our story.

After that half hour of decisive deliberation, Adria had slept in untroubled peace, and in the morning, as we already mentioned, she and her husband left.

During the trip, knowing that she would find in him an intelligent friend, she told him of her plans.

In the reserved compartment in which they spent a few hours, she spoke with great simplicity.

"I've decided something quite important. Within the next two months I want to withdraw completely."

"Withdraw from what?"

"From society," she answered, smiling. "Indeed, from the world. I plan not to let anyone see me anymore. No one in the whole world. Not you, not the children, not any friends, not people I don't care about, not even strangers. No one must be witness to my—how to say it?—to my decline."

Now it was his turn, though aghast, to smile and reply chivalrously.

"That does not seem imminent."

"It makes no difference. It will begin tomorrow, or in a year or five or ten. The important thing is that I not be waiting to discover when it begins. Please don't oppose this or try to dissuade me."

"I won't."

"In another age, I would have gone into a convent, I would have had an aunt who was an abbess in a cloistered convent. I'll be in a cloister anyway, but it will be private, rather than communal, that's all. Outside of Rome, of course. But not in the country, the thought of a great void about me would be depressing. In a city, a large city outside Italy where no one is likely to have known me. A large city is a place in which I can be anonymous."

Her husband had been staring down at her hands while she spoke. When she finished, he raised his eyes to her face. But he couldn't endure the sight of those quiet blue eyes which he loved so much, and which were now gazing out beyond the world.

Adria felt she must speak again.

"As for the details," she said, "I'll tell you about them later. I'm still not sure of everything myself."

He rose, took a few steps in the little space around them, moved a suitcase that was protruding from a rack, then sat down opposite her.

"And the children?" he whispered.

"I want to see them before I go," Adria answered. "I'll leave in a week. Paris is the best place. It will take me a few days there to prepare a house—my cloister." She was smiling as she spoke, as though to veil those cruelest of words with charm.

Her husband was now looking away through the windows. The sea and sky were pale and empty.

Still staring at the horizon, he began, "As for me..."

"You," Adria interrupted him sweetly, "you'll stay in Rome

in the house. Of course," she added, "for now, neither you nor
I will speak to anyone about this."

Once in Rome, Adria immediately began packing trunks
and cases.

There was nothing hurried about the work. She had arranged for letters describing her needs to be sent to people in
Paris, so that a search might begin.

Tullia was visiting with a paternal uncle at a country villa
near Viterbo. She was just past her twelfth birthday. Remo had,
for a few years now, shown himself to be gifted in music.
Sgambati, the composer, had seen several of the boy's pieces—
composed intuitively at the keyboard at the age of eight before
he'd had any instruction in music—and had entrusted Remo's
studies to the care of a student. Every once in a while the old
maestro checked his progress. During the time that Adria spent
at the shore, Remo, whose nervous system could not tolerate
sea air, had been traveling through Germany with his young
tutor, and was, in fact, due back at the beginning of September. The father wrote to Tullia's hosts asking that she be sent
back to Rome immediately. The brother arrived from Germany
and the sister from Viterbo on the same day. It was the eve of
Adria's departure.

We left the two children, exhausted and asleep on a high
chest in the dark on an April evening almost five years ago. We
return to them now on the afternoon of September 7, 1907, a
day they will remember forever as the most important of their
lives.

They are in a parlor with their father.

Remo has grown a great deal. He is as tall as his sister. He
is pale and his eyes are large. But it is not easy to look into
them because they flit here and there and most often are fixed
downward at the ground.

His father is questioning him gently about the things he

has seen in his travels, and about the music he has heard, but the boy's responses are short, as though he feels uncomfortable and doesn't want to talk about himself. Tullia is restless. She keeps looking at the door, and every so often runs over to it without reason, then she comes back and stands close to her father, who is seated in an armchair

"And now, I have something to tell you both, something important. Mother has to go away on a trip. Yes, she has to go to Paris."

"Paris!" says Tullia.

Remo is silent. He seems to be completely absorbed in the task of pressing the collar of his sailor suit against his chest with two fingers.

"Paris. And she'll be there a long time."

"How long, papa?"

"We're not sure yet. Quite a while. She's leaving tomorrow."

"Tomorrow?"

"Yes, and now—any minute now, she'll be here because she wants to kiss you both good-bye before she leaves."

Tullia shouted, Remo leaped in the air. Then he looked down at the floor, and his face reddened and paled remarkably. Tullia broke into a joyful, nervous laugh and instantly she too stopped herself, suddenly overcome by timidity. The father did not know what else to say. And so those three beings—Remo, with his closed and precocious soul; Tullia, whose soul was filled with passion; and Adria's anguished husband, whose heart was overflowing—trembled and waited. Silence bound them together. Their eyes were clear, but the air in that room was heavy with hidden sorrow.

Then music descended from heaven, and in the midst of it Adria appeared.

Her husband stood up. The children, one at each side, clung to him. Adria stopped for a moment on the threshold, happily allowing herself to look at them. Then she moved slowly forward with that walk that was the most beautiful thing about her. When she was close to them, the two children stepped back, overcome with awe.

The father pushed them gently forward. They felt themselves surrounded by a wave of perfume, sank into the softness of her clothes. Their mother placed a hand on each of their heads.

"Darlings."

As she did so, the father, silently, drew back a step.

She spoke again. "Darlings."

It was her turn to be overcome by uncertainty. She wanted to take them in her arms, but seemed not to know how to embrace her own children. Her hands descended from their heads to their cheeks, their necks. The two children were pressed against her dress, Tullia sobbing, Remo trembling. Adria bent to kiss them one after the other, almost fitfully, but softly on their foreheads, on their chins, while her arms encircled their shoulders. The moment was perhaps an eternity. Then Adria drew herself up again. The children withdrew, as if from the edge of an altar.

Adria knew, knew as clearly as if she were seeing herself in the mirror, that at that moment she had become more beautiful, as beautiful as she had appeared to herself in the mirror several nights earlier. Tullia saw it, and Remo, too, who through superhuman strength had raised his face. Even the father, who had remained a step behind the children, saw that suffering and sorrow had brought new beauty to her face. A breath of madness swept over them in their silence.

Then Adria recovered herself, and once more seemed to belong to a distant heaven. Still she could not speak.

Shortly thereafter, Tullia and Remo left the room together. Tullia had not seen her brother for two months, not since he had left the country. He seemed much changed to her. He seemed to have become very strange. She felt almost uneasy in his presence. She tapped his shoulder and asked. "What are you thinking, Remo?"

He withdrew as though he'd been struck, and answered almost angrily.

"Nothing. What do you care what I think? What's it to you?"

Tullia couldn't breathe. A sharp pain pierced her heart.

⧫━━◆⧓◆━━

3 ADRIA WAS DUE TO LEAVE AT THREE in the afternoon. That morning at eleven she went out alone for a walk. She took a carriage to the square in front of the Villa Borghese where the road separates, one fork leading into the densest area of the park, the other directly into the city. She got out of the carriage and walked slowly toward the Pincian Gate. It was a tender Roman September day filled with warm caresses and perfumed breezes. Carriages were passing in every direction, men and women were strolling and every one of them looked at her. She was wearing the same white dress in which she had gone to meet Giovanni Bellamonte, but this time she was wearing a very pale green felt hat with a brim that shadowed her forehead. Her neck, which the dress exposed, was circled with a garland of jasmine which she had wound for herself that morning. The blossoms, set against the white of her neck, seemed tiny droplets of light. She passed through the arch of the Pincian Gate, entering via Veneto. From the willow chairs of the cafés along the way, her subjects leaned forward and turned to look at their chosen queen. Beneath the foliage of the plane trees a soft coolness was tempering the heat which summer had burned into the earth. Adria's passage opened a path of joy. No one knew they would never see their

queen again. She completed the great curve of the street just as bells began to sound. Her carriage was awaiting her at Piazza Barberini and took her home. She left Villa Adria with Albertina, her chambermaid, at three o'clock that afternoon, and twenty-four hours later was in Paris. The dull day and heavy sky were of no consequence to her. She had no desire to see anything of Paris, a city she didn't know. She spent about ten days in a hotel, leaving it mornings only to supervise the work being done in the house which her friends had chosen for her, and which she had summarily approved. The work was going quickly.

The house in which Adria was to seal away youth and hide death, was in the southernmost part of Paris among a maze of small streets which no longer exist, having been demolished to create the half-moon neighborhood whose bow is the new Avenue Junot and whose string is the first of the slopes of the rue du Mont-Cenis, beyond the rise where Saint Denys was martyred. The street was short, stony and steep, and had a barren look which in some way excited Adria. In her daily journeys the carriage took a long curved route to minimize the ascent. Adria would see the city change in the most unpredictable ways before her eyes. She would speed past busy streets filled with traffic and life to a wild, deserted area—from the loud hectic confusion of rhythmical motors and voices, to stony silence broken every so often by sudden calls or clangings instantly cut short as though the street were hiccuping. She liked her new street—stretches of unadorned, slanted walls without any aperture, resembling the sides of a fortress, then rows of low houses of various shapes. Some were not much more than shacks, others were one or two stories at the highest. Some had additions constructed at various times for various purposes in a most disordered fashion—turrets, rooms set into roofs, fragments that seemed forgotten up there. They looked like child-drawn scenes with sad, whimsical odds and ends and lots of chimney pots.

The roadbed was stony and there were no sidewalks. Two thin streams of muddy water ran along each side of it. Every now and then rusty pipes descending from gutters disgorged spurts of filthy liquid. The middle of the road was spotted with reddish splotches of uncertain origin, and with dried animal dung left who knows when. Outside one front door there's a tin pan filled with scraps; a wretched mutt pauses there, another prefers the lamp post at the end of the street: the lamp post has had a stroke—it's dangling to one side. Adria would see groups of half-frozen children running down the hill, then the street once again resumed its contorted, fossilized aspect.

By contrast, the interior of her house, in accord with her instructions, hourly was becoming more light, simple and airy. The furnishings and finishes rivaled each other in elegance.

She had shutters and blinds added to every window. She allotted the ground floor to her servants (a second maid had joined her from Rome, the others were hired in Paris). She would live on the upper floor: two sitting rooms, a bedroom and a bathroom. Above it was an unused attic with a dormer window.

Two weeks after leaving Rome she moved into her new residence, certain that she would never ever leave it.

Adria crossed the threshold without looking back. Her staff knew nothing. She felt calm, resolute, as self-possessed as a zealot, and immensely proud of herself.

Her entry into her last home took place on the twenty-second day of September, which turned out unusually sunny and warm. The days preceding it had been windy and gray. Perhaps that morning, to bid Adria farewell, or to try to tempt her back, Rome had sent her a little of its own light. But Adria, passing under the low, black archway, hadn't turned to look back at the sun.

4 No one at Villa Adria spoke about the mother's absence.

Adria's husband's burning desire now was to devote himself completely to the task of bringing up his children. That first evening, the three of them sat in the dining room feeling as if they'd just returned from a long voyage to a house that had been closed for many years. In the eyes of the children, the room that they had looked upon from their slits in the wall as an unattainable Paradise had hardened in every aspect, even its light had become metallic. To the father, however, every object Adria had ever touched, every glass, every piece of cutlery had become as weightless as a shadow, as if it were about to disappear from his hands.

No one sat in Adria's seat. Opposite it, as before, was their father; on either side of him, Tullia and Remo.

Tullia's eyes were searching for the spot behind which their observation post was located. She couldn't find it and was overcome by an irrational fear that her father could follow her glance and understand its purpose. Remo, on the other hand, stared continuously down at his plate. The father tried vainly to find a subject they could talk about. They might have been three travelers awaiting separate trains at a railway station. After dinner the young musician who had accompanied Remo to Germany arrived, as well as an older woman, a longtime family friend. The father had invited them because he'd feared being alone with the children for the entire evening. The guests' presence did nothing to animate the conversation. All five were overcome with embarrassment. The governess entered to take the children upstairs, but the father wanted to escort them to their rooms himself. Remo stopped on the landing, allowed himself to be embraced, and said "good-night" in a disembodied voice.

In Tullia's room the little girl threw her arms around her father's neck and began sobbing violently. Then, noticing that he was crying quietly too, she raised her head and despite her tears smiled at him.

The father thought he was seeing Adria smile. No one else would have seen the resemblance, which had sprung to his mind from some strange source. Because Tullia was not beautiful. Though her eyes were. They were dark and filled with energy and much gentleness. Seeing her father in that state, she chided him, "Papa, a man mustn't cry, it's not right," and, taking his handkerchief from his pocket, she dried his eyes. "Now go back, go downstairs. You can't leave guests alone."

She put the handkerchief back in his breast pocket and adjusted it properly. The father returned downstairs. The two guests were already on their feet, waiting to say good-bye and to leave.

The father planned to follow his children's education closely. Tullia was entering the third year of high school and within a few days resumed her classes. Remo continued his studies with his young teacher. Music was his principal field of study— another tutor came on alternate days to teach him general subjects. Remo wouldn't talk about himself under any circumstances. One day when he was practicing the piano and thought himself alone, he turned suddenly and saw that his father had been standing and listening to him for a few moments. He flew into a wild, almost hysterical rage. The father rushed to embrace him, but he wrenched himself away violently and began screaming, "Leave me alone. Leave me alone." Because the father was heedful of not forcing himself on the boy, he quieted down. Nevertheless, for two or three days after that, Remo didn't go near the piano, but would spend hours alone in his room, emerging from it grim-faced. The father had the piano moved to the most remote room of the house on the upper floor. Remo resumed practicing without their exchanging another word on the subject.

There were days when other children came to play with him in the garden or got him to go out for walks or to play tennis. He was much livelier with them, especially away from Villa Adria. For a few hours he was cheerful and intensely active, before falling back into silence and surliness.

Tullia still was, and would always be, affected by the painful way her brother had responded to her when they'd left their mother after bidding her good-bye on the eve of her departure. Filled with emotion, she would recall Remo as a child, the Remo of five years ago, and the games they'd played together. Nights, she found it hard to fall asleep when she relived that time. The flight from the Villa Mayer and the desolate night that followed would reappear to her like a tale reaching her from distant regions to a musical accompaniment. She wanted so much to speak to him about those things, but spirited though she was, she lacked the courage.

Adria wrote to her husband every two or three weeks. Her letters were short, simple and affectionate. The father read them aloud to the children. Tullia would always say, "again," and he would re-read them, occasionally two or three times, more slowly each time. Remo never said anything, but would absorb every word. Neither child ever asked the father when the mother would return, nor why she had left. One day, after such a reading, blushing and stammering, he tried to explain. The children said nothing and he never knew whether they had understood. They never spoke of it again.

The father, disheartened at not being able to reach Remo— who remained withdrawn in his private griefs—now tried devoting all his attention to his daughter, and for a while deluded himself into thinking he had succeeded with her. Before long, however, he discovered his error. Tullia was compliant, gentle, often impetuous and effusive in her replies. But he soon realized that she was being compliant out of kindness, answering his questions and telling him about herself out of loving condescension, so as not to hurt his feelings. In reality, though clearly not aware of it herself, she had no genuine interest in talking to him.

They continued this way, spending long days and disconcerting nights sitting beside each other, each locked in dull solitude. Then came the last week of the year.

They were invited to spend Christmas day at Villa Mayer. The house was crowded with children of every age. The father joined them there in the afternoon and found Remo animated, Tullia happy. They returned home late. As soon as Remo got in the car he became silent and withdrawn. Tullia spoke incessantly. She described every game she'd played, and told how she'd made new girlfriends and had invited them to Villa Adria.

From the following day onward, there wasn't one afternoon that little girls, some younger, some older than she, didn't come by in twos, threes or in droves. The father saw his children only at the dinner table, where Tullia admiringly described her friends' virtues and everything else about them that she knew.

It now occurred to the father, who correctly considered his children very intelligent, to forsake his supervision of their education, and to try to engage their interest by discussing business matters with them, and thus treating them as grown-ups.

One evening he said, "I need your advice. My brother wants to sell the woods in Viterbo that he and I own jointly. He wants to use the money to invest in the stock of a large bank that's being established with mostly American capital. What do you think?"

Tullia opened her eyes wide and stared at him in astonishment. But he appeared even more astonished than she upon hearing Remo's sober inquiry, "How much can you get for the Viterbo woods?"

"We'll each get about seven hundred thousand lire."

Remo shook his head. "I'd wait. You can't rely on anything when it comes to banks."

The amazed father thought, "At the age of ten I didn't even know what a bank was."

In a moment Remo went on. "If there's a war, do you have any idea how much the value of those woods might go up?"

"A war? That's crazy. No one goes to war anymore."

"Who knows?" Remo said.

Tullia interrupted them.

"Papa, papa, tomorrow some of the girls who board at the English Women's School are coming over. They still have two days of vacation before they have to go back. Do you mind if they stay over those two days? We could put them in the red bedroom."

The two days became four, and in those four days Tullia's houseguests and all her old and new girlfriends, who descended on Villa Adria, were so combative at their games that the house seemed a barracks in constant mutiny. Remo did nothing to hide his irritation. However, when on occasion the din abruptly increased, he'd utter a tolerant, "These women," to his father.

Then the uncle from Viterbo arrived. He'd been surprised by his brother's decision in regard to the sale and wanted to know his reasons. The father didn't dare tell him that he'd taken the advice of a child, and though his brother was insisting on the sale, he didn't have the courage to go back on his decision because of what Remo would say.

The uncle stayed three days. He made no secret of his complete disapproval of the way in which his brother was raising his children. Nevertheless, the children didn't consider his presence intrusive. On the contrary, the evening before his departure Tullia told him, "You ought to come stay here at Villa Adria too. There are so many rooms."

The father repeated the invitation. The uncle laughed and left without saying yes or no. The father hadn't uttered a word about Adria to his brother, who had hardly known her, and had probably always disapproved of her way of life.

Thinking about that silence on the subject of Adria after his brother's departure, the husband came to extraordinary conclusions, which had never occurred to him before.

"No one," he thought, "has ever said a word to me about Adria. All her friends have disappeared. That's to be expected of ordinary admirers of a woman who has gone off. But to them, Adria wasn't a woman. They were, rather we all were, with our varied status, a religious sect. We've lost our visible goddess. And the sect has dispersed."

It had been easy getting to this point. But now his perception went further and he saw something else, something terrible for him to face. Suddenly and clearly he understood that even the two children were in that same strange, sad position. Adria wasn't a mother to them. They weren't children whose mother has gone away and who can find shelter in their father's arms. It was that infuriating veneration alone that had held them enthralled within the circle of Adria's life. Those two babies were the devotees closest to the Goddess they believed in, and therefore, at the same time, the most oppressed by sacred awe in her presence. This seemed staggering and monstrous to him. Now there was nothing to tie them to the house in which they'd suffered their pangs of adoration. There was nothing to hold them close to each other, or to him, who alone not only worshipped her, but loved her. Villa Adria is an altar without a Cross—desecrated remains. He sensed, without any hope of being wrong, that the children were about to escape him in body as well, and that he lacked the power to restrain them.

The circumstance he had foreseen suddenly came to pass.

One afternoon, approaching the house, he heard a commotion behind it, where the automobile was kept. He hurried over and came upon a sickening scene. Remo, disheveled and pale with fury, was kicking the chauffeur with unbelievable violence, while the latter, up against the car, was trying to shield himself. Still worse, in his fury the boy was spewing the most dreadful insults upon the man, horrible words that no one would have thought he knew. The father, overcome with shame, ran up behind Remo and closed his arms around the boy, who upon being touched fell in a half faint. The father carried him to the house, set him on a bed, and waited until he saw him fall into a natural sleep. Shortly thereafter the young music teacher arrived for a lesson.

The father opened his heart to the young man, told him of his anguish and asked humbly for advice.

"None of this surprises me," the teacher said. "Remo is far too brilliant for his age. He has certain very strange musical intuitions. I've watched him closely all summer long in Germany. If you want my objective opinion, I'd say send him back there. It would be wonderful for his studies and for his life, too. It's stimulating and exciting there. He'd have many ways of releasing that intense sensibility of his without resorting to violence."

He concluded by offering to return to Germany with Remo and to spend the entire winter there with him. He'd already given this some thought and had an itinerary ready. First Ratisbon, then Lipsia, then Monaco. Remo's father understood full well that this was not disinterested advice, but he saw, too, that it was the best course.

"And Remo would like it?"

"Like it? He'd love it. He's been yearning for those places, for that kind of music."

The father now felt a morbid desire to conclude the matter quickly, to see it actuated in the shortest possible time.

Fate often creates harsh juxtapositions of events. The father had not yet said anything of his plans to Tullia (though he had immediately written to Adria of them), and had not yet mentioned them to Remo (though he, no doubt, had already heard of them from his teacher), when one morning Tullia threw herself into his arms.

"Papa, papa, you have to do something for me."

"What is it, darling?"

"Do you remember when we asked Uncle to come stay here at Villa Adria? Ask him again. Try to make him do it."

"Yes, of course, but why?"

"Why? Oh papa, forgive me, I want so much to…"

"To what, Tullia?" His heart was pounding as he stroked her hair.

"To go to boarding school—the English Women's School. I'd be so happy there, papa. And you could come see me often, right? Even two or three times a week. I found out all about that already. My best friends go there. It's a very good school. So I thought that it would be better if Uncle were here, to keep you company. I won't go if you don't make Uncle come. You really won't be unhappy if I go to live at the English Women's School?"

Within a week—it was the end of January, four months since Adria had left—the father, having rushed to complete the necessary arrangements, was writing to his brother: "This morning I went to the railroad station with Remo, who left for Ratisbon with his teacher, as I'd told you he would. And Wednesday afternoon I'm taking Tullia up to the boarding school. It would be good if you came to see me here at Villa Adria on Thursday morning."

Wednesday evening, upon his return from the school, Adria's husband mounted the staircase slowly, and stopped on the landing outside her suite, where the two palms in huge vases flanked its door. A shadow rose from the well of the staircase. He didn't enter her rooms, but walked back and forth through the house for a while. He didn't know what to do with himself and decided he was bored. Tullia's right. Tomorrow I'll ask my brother to come live with me here at Villa Adria. It would have been better to have asked him to come tonight. It's the worst night. He could have kept me company. I would have told him to sell the woods. We'll arrange it all tomorrow morning. We'll have to get advice from the bank's officers. What's the name of the bank going to be? Who can remember anymore? They always pick stupid names. Who knows what they thought up. It makes no difference. All right then, Sunday at two, I told Tullia. I have to go see her on Sunday. Today is Wednesday, so one, two, three, three-and-a-half days yet. I won't count today, but this evening is going to be long.

He kept pacing slowly without pause, back and forth, up and down, musing in this way. A long evening. Perhaps it will never end. We don't know, we can't know anything. The sun hides every night, and after a few hours, reappears. Well, at least until now, for as long as anyone can remember, it's always happened. But who can say it's an eternal law? It could be a limited cycle. It's possible that one of these nights it will get dark and just stay dark forever. If people would only stop and think every evening that each day might be the last of sunlight, they'd put much less value on a lot things. Up to a certain point they'd adapt their lives to the new condition. The world in total darkness. A lot of things would change. Others wouldn't. The Lazio-America bank—there, that's its name, Lazio-America —will be established just the same. Then it will get bigger. It will have a lot of branches, one in Paris, maybe one in Ratisbon? What does Ratisbon have to do with this? Anyway, it's important always to be aware of the direction in which the sun sets.

From this room, for example, one has to look…but where am I?

He realized that he had climbed up to the top floor and that he was in the furthest room, the most secluded room, the one to which he'd had Remo's piano removed so that he could practice without distraction.

It's dark, but there's the piano. You can see the white keyboard. He'd left it open. So on the other side there's the window which from here must face, yes, exactly, west, toward Rome. He went to the window and opened it. The air was cold.

He turned up the collar of his jacket. Those houses down there are at the very edge of Rome. There's still a lot of open land around. I bet in ten years it will all be built up. The Lazio-America bank could buy it. To hell with the bank, I don't want to think about it any more. And the sun? It set a while ago. Why are the city's lights so faint tonight? It looks like they're fading. Maybe there's some mist. That's unusual for Rome. I'd better close the piano or it will get out of tune.

He moved back without remembering to close the window. Even the white keyboard, like the lights of Rome, was now wrapped in mist. Perhaps my eyes are a little tired. Walking unsteadily, he crossed the room holding onto the wall with one hand. He felt an aversion to turning on the lights. He stopped and stood in front of the menacing mass of the piano. There's the back of the piano seat. He groped with his hands for the music stand. A half sheet of coarse paper was on it. Remo's composition. He folded it carelessly and put it in his pocket. Why have I suddenly lost faith in Remo's music? What a lot of difficult things. The wall is most certainly there, right behind the end of the piano. Then why does it seem so far away? Even over there, there's mist and fading lights.

The cold entering through the window permeated the room. An intense chill seized him from head to foot. A rush of icy air whipped against his legs and they gave way. He fell heavily onto the piano seat, the flat of his hand struck the keyboard which sent out a sudden burst of sound. He twitched with fear at that deep rumbling in the dark, and his heart thumped in consternation two or three times, then quieted down. But his hand felt heavy and remained pressed against the keys. The wave of sound continued on, like a rumble of thunder, and his exhausted body fell forward against the music stand. It dug into his arm, causing a sharp pain, but he couldn't move, so the wave of slowly fading sound circled his face, which kept sliding ever lower. Thus, as the sound vanished, Adria's husband, sitting at the piano with his coat collar turned up, died a bitter death.

---

5 I'VE NEVER BEEN ABLE TO FORM an opinion about Adria, and recalling her life fills me with fear. The three rooms in which Adria was living on the second floor of the little house near Sacre-Coeur were painted a gleaming white, and were illuminated by light that entered from the south and the east. There was a variety of fabrics and small tables throughout, with rows of books on single shelves mounted here and there, and comfortable-looking chairs, cushions and lamp shades, all in light colors. The last room was very large, and most of it was filled with rows of clothing hung from horizontal poles in accordance with Adria's system. In the back of the room was an open alcove with a bed covered in pale gray silk, which was the dominant color in each of the three rooms. From the very large bathroom, with its wide tub set into the floor, there was a spiral staircase that descended directly into Albertina's room on the floor below.

Alberta and the other servants received their basic instructions immediately. Adria had a deeply habitual temperament, and in a very short time her life took on a daily routine which would never again change.

The basic rule that governed Adria's new life had its roots in the motive for the extraordinary resolution which had led her to cloister herself in that house for decades awaiting death. The rule was that no one in the entire world must ever again see her.

Thus, of greatest importance, she would never leave the house. The ground floor door which opened to the landing of the staircase was walled up and disappeared behind a huge set of shelves filled with crystal.

Second, not only was no one to come visit her, but also no one on her staff, except Albertina, was permitted to come upstairs to her rooms. And when the latter needed to speak to Adria about domestic matters, the rooms were all in semidarkness. Adria would remain in the alcove which was totally dark, and speak from behind the protection of a voile curtain. However, most of her orders were given by the telephone she'd had installed, which communicated within the house as well as with the rest of the city. She dressed and undressed by herself. At prescribed hours Albertina brought up prepared meals, set them on a small table in the first room, then withdrew. Adria would serve herself, take her own coffee or tea.

With the will that was the source of every act of her life (perhaps of her beauty as well from the very beginning), the same will which had enabled her to sleep without dreaming for so many years (until the dream that had driven her to her present situation), she now willed herself never to fall ill, so that she would not be forced to expose herself. In this she succeeded until the very end. As the days and months passed, she became ever more fearful of that danger. She decided that if anyone ever managed to come close enough to see her, she would either have him killed (she felt capable doing this), or would herself die.

Mirrors were banned from her rooms.

She was particularly scrupulous and wary on this issue. The furniture had an opaque finish. The window panes were fitted with white curtains, hung in such a way that when a window was opened, it would not unexpectedly violate the ban and become a reflective surface.

But on the day she entered the house she withdrew her mirror from its case, the very same mirror in which she had bid herself good-night every evening for ten years. That day, looking into it, she said good-night for the last time. She studied her image avidly, cruelly, for perhaps an hour. Then she put the mirror in a box, set it down slowly, and looked as if she were about to toss a handful of earth into it. She closed the box, tied it, and sealed it. The wax hardened and cooled quickly. Adria wrapped the case in additional fabric and buried it at the bottom of a large chest.

She spent her days reading, designing clothes (some of which she sewed herself) and completing the decoration of her home. Often she did nothing, but never felt bored. She had arranged to receive books of every kind, had subscribed to a number of magazines and newspapers, and was far more informed about world affairs than when she had been in society and conversing with so many people. I've heard it said that from the first day she'd begun writing about her experiences and all the people she'd known. I don't believe it. Beyond the fact that there is no trace of anything (but this would be natural, considering how it all ended), no one with whom Adria was in touch, by mail or phone until the very last days of her life, knew anything about it. Nor could I ever ascertain how and where this rumor originated.

She was always surrounded by the brightest light. On a clear day sunshine filled the three rooms. As soon as the day began to fade she'd turn on every lamp. Light flowed from one room to the other, as if it were air. When I visualize that woman moving about completely alone in the midst of all that brightness, without a mirror in which to see herself, it gives me the feeling of living in a terrifying dream. She hadn't kept even one picture of herself. Since this seclusion lasted many years (as we will see), I believe that after some time Adria would have stopped thinking of her own face, and the changes in it, which was precisely her intention. It is not this astonishing situation, her enormous constancy—in a life which was not at all the life of someone shipwrecked on a desert island, since that is a life of continual expectation, where every minute is an event— which upsets me, but the fact that Adria had completely banished events and expectations.

The news of such a strange resident didn't spread very widely through Paris, although a few people heard of her. Some wrote to her and received replies. Friends came from Rome, spoke to her on the telephone and were able to introduce other people to her. Thus, Adria's life became filled with friendships with people whom she never saw, telephone friendships, some of which lasted for years and were in no small way responsible for the rapid development of qualities in her, which prior to her retirement had been completely unknown to everyone, including herself. One day, about three months after her arrival, a woman telephoned without any prior introduction, spoke to her, and instantly seemed quite likable. The woman told her that she knew almost everything about her situation, and that she understood it quite well.

"I doubt it," Adria replied. "Will you tell me your name?"

"I want to have a name especially for you. You can call me Atena. Is that all right?"

"Are you that wise?"

"Not really. I hadn't thought about it that way. I said the first name that came into my head."

"Then it's certainly the most appropriate. Let's use it. Tell me what you're like."

"What do you mean?"

"Tall and thin, short and dark, twenty years old, fifty?"

"My distinguishing features? Do you want me to send you my passport? I never expected that from you."

"You're right. I'm ashamed. I can feel myself blushing for having asked such a question. Atena, that's enough. If you tell me anything else about yourself, we will never have another conversation."

"And if I don't?"

"Then I think that we'll speak frequently."

Atena phoned again the following day and after that they spoke almost every day. They conversed on literary and general topics. Atena would tell her about walks she'd taken outside of the city, or about evenings at the theater. Adria skipped from one subject to another without connection. She began a conversation like this: "Could you tell me why a completely blue cloudless sky is more frightening than a cloud-filled sky when it is about to storm?" Atena always answered to the point, and never expressed surprise about anything. Their conversations grew longer. Atena sent her several books, among them Plato's *Phaedo*. Adria had never read anything of that nature. It made her feel inferior, and she complained about it. She telephoned her friend.

"I don't want to finish it. When those two demonstrate to Socrates that the soul is not immortal, I got completely lost like everyone else in the dialogue."

"But further on, when Socrates speaks, you'll be convinced that the soul is immortal. You can't avoid that."

"But I don't have the slightest desire to believe that the soul is immortal."

Atena never asked Adria a single question about herself, nor did she manifest any desire to get closer to her. As time passed, it would have seemed dreadful to both of them. Nor did she ask anything about her family, until the day on which Adria said, "It's curious, speaking to you,"—they were by now on familiar terms—"I feel as if I'm speaking with an adult Tullia, a Tullia who's gotten to be twenty-eight or thirty."

"Who's Tullia?"

"My daughter. She's not even thirteen yet."

Later that day, Adria received, one after the other, two letters from her husband. The first told of Remo's planned departure for Germany, the other of Tullia's imminent admission to the boarding school. She hadn't answered immediately and the following day there was a disorganized, detailed and terrified letter from her brother-in-law. It told of the dreadful Thursday morning when he arrived at Villa Adria in response to his brother's invitation, only to find the servants in a panic, having just discovered the master's body. The doctor had said that death must have occurred more than twelve hours earlier. "I didn't send you a telegram to avoid the shock of such harsh news without being able to give you the details." He had already been to see Tullia, whom he had left "distraught, but surrounded with much warmth." At this point he added ingenuously, "Although I expect you will want to return to Rome for Tullia's sake and to attend to business matters, and then perhaps to remain here or take Tullia away with you (as for Remo, my advice is to leave him where he is, for now), I will nevertheless be in Paris the day after you receive this letter—that's Sunday afternoon—to discuss all of this with you as is my duty, and to place myself at your disposal and escort you back to Rome. It's not necessary that you reply. "

As soon as he arrived at his hotel that Sunday, the brother-in-law telephoned.

"I'm in Paris, Adria. I'm coming right over to see you."

"Don't come."

"Didn't you get my...?"

"I received it yesterday. Let's not talk about how I felt then and how I feel now. You can imagine. But I cannot go to Rome, not now or ever. I cannot ever leave here. I cannot change. I assure you that I wouldn't be of any use to anyone."

"This is difficult on the telephone, Adria. I think it's essential that I come there and speak to you in person."

"No. I entrust the care of all of my affairs and those of my children to you with absolute and complete faith. I will write this out for you. Or better still, send me the proper papers—whatever I have to sign."

The unhappy man heard her words, knew their meanings, yet felt as if he understood nothing. Unable to accept the situation, he kept trying to argue his point. Adria knew he was completely lost. "I see, my dear, that you can't understand all this. Think of me as a nun in a convent."

The following days were filled with depressing rain. The Parisian air was the dirty gray color of lead. Adria kept the lights on all day long. Atena had left that morning and would be away for an extended period. But Adria finished reading *Phaedo*, then immediately read it a second time. She conceived a gold dress with a green sash. The next morning she awoke with a strong desire to write a long letter to Tullia.

She had never written one. Her style was telegraphic. The desire tormented her all day long. She couldn't get herself to begin and hadn't the least idea what she wanted to say. She wrote "Tullia" and was immediately afraid of the words that might follow it. And what will Tullia say when she gets a letter like that? A letter like what? And while questioning herself, she began writing, as follows. *Tullia, I don't know whether you are big or little and I don't know whether you are my daughter, as we are all daughters, or whether you are perhaps my soul. The souls that belong to each of us are not always within us. Some people's souls must be outside them, perhaps in another person, perhaps in heaven, or even in a plant, as though it were nurtured there, and when you find it, you can call it and it will come, because until then, it doesn't even know that it's yours. One day or another, and one at a time, everyone whose soul is external finds out about it. But there aren't many like that, most of them are in place at the very beginning, so there's nothing to worry about. I don't know, Tullia, if you understand these things. I'm writing them and hardly understand them myself, and it's possible they don't mean anything so there isn't anything to understand. I think that for those who don't yet have their souls within them, they may not be easily available in another being, but may be in several others and somewhat dispersed here and there, for example, in the colors of things, or in certain lines that one perceives walking where there are lots of trees. Also in flowers when they're blown by the wind. I, for example, think that I was one of those. I would gather them from here and there. You can't ever know these things except when you die, but surely then, everything is far grander, and it no longer makes any difference to you. Therefore, it is possible that the one I was gathering was someone else's and that you are mine. The thought that you are mine occurred to me two days ago, just an hour before I received the news that has brought us both such sorrow. And Remo too, who is far away. But one must be brave. And so I know that you will do something wonderful in life, Tullia.*

Tullia generally told her closest friends every detail of her daily life, everything she saw, or thought about. But she said nothing of this letter, even to them, and kept it a secret completely her own.

tullia

—◆◆◇◆◆—

1 THE DEAD ARE MOTIONLESS. Time passing surrounds them, yet does not draw them along, press on them, or even graze them with its infinite flow. But time flows quickly for the living, not around them, but within their beings. For in the veins of the living, time constitutes blood. And that coursing of time within their veins makes up their mortal lives. Only death conquers time completely. Sometimes people create or are destined to experience simulations of immobility and death which produce false victories over time. Such is intoxication, though too short-lived. Such, too, are habit and rapture, which may endure and delude for longer periods. Adria had defeated the enemy once, with a life shaped by both habit and rapture. When she perceived that it had insidiously breached the first high walls of her fortress, she took refuge in those other proven simulations of death, imprisonment and withdrawal. Thus, in her new existence, the passage of years could allow her the illusion of having regained the upper hand.

But time does not pass around Tullia. Time enters and transmutes her, as a being in the full power of life. Those same years coursing through her veins have altered the deepest substance of her being. We left her first as a stricken child, then as an impetuous and disconsolate adolescent. We rejoin her now, an intelligent, passionate young woman.

Eight years have passed in Paris and have wrought no change to the three dazzling rooms on the street near Sacre-

Coeur. Perhaps there were no changes, either, in Adria's face, which no one, not even she, has seen again. Eight years have passed in Rome and everything about Villa Adria has become brighter, even its mood. That style of effete strangeness which prevailed in all its rooms has given way to sensuous shapes and brilliant colors. It is the spring of 1915. At twenty, Tullia is the mistress of Villa Adria, where her uncle is also living. Remo seems ever more distraught when he turns up there, as though he is unable to live or breathe except in the dreary North amid far-off people. In Tullia's heart, Remo is still the little boy of the flight from Villa Mayer, and of ecstatic moments waiting on the discarded chest to look upon Paradise.

After her husband's death Adria had written Tullia other letters—though not very many—similar to the one she had just received, arising from who knows what source. Generally, her letters to her daughter were short, a quiet sign of life and a greeting. But every once in a while, at unpredictable intervals, there would be a more profound letter, laden with mystery and truth, revelations which troubled Tullia, and flashed sudden light on transcendent matters. Tullia always knew, the moment she received a letter, whether it was one of those. If she didn't immediately have time to be alone, she would wait to open it, sometimes even for an entire day. The observations in those letters agitated and nourished her. Rarely did she look at her mother's portrait, which she had stored away. Rather, she read those letters endlessly, scoured their deepest recesses, and found within them strange sources and insights which Adria never suspected. Between her father's death and the spring of 1915, the days on which these letters arrived were the most important in Tullia's life. No one else in the world knew of them.

Everything about Tullia's life had changed. Without being fully aware of doing so, she altered many things in the house. None of the people who were once house guests still visited it.

No mementos or memories of Adria seemed to be left in it.

Tullia was in her second year of medical school, and the young men and women who now visited the house were generally her classmates. She would spend most of her days at lectures, or in the anatomy room, and often entertained her friends in the evening. Her uncle didn't take part in these gatherings.

To tell the truth, most of Tullia's friends weren't very interesting.

One April evening an argument broke out.

"War is murder, nothing else!" shouted a plump, rosy-cheeked young man with blond hair. "Christianity has taught mankind nothing. It hasn't spared us one war, one revolution. Man needs to kill. As soon as he has some pretext tinged with public necessity, he throws himself into it with gusto. Not until I see every single person in a country renounce warfare will I believe in Christ."

"And defensive wars?"

"Every war is a defensive war," said a Polish student. "If a nation takes up arms first, it's to protect itself against more insidious wars, trade wars, wars of attrition that other countries start against it. Germany knew very well that England was preparing to starve her out."

"If Italy doesn't enter the war," someone else shouted, "I'll become French, German, Russian, it makes no difference. But I'd be ashamed to remain an Italian."

A sensitive-looking young man suddenly became red-faced, pulled a newspaper from his pocket and, interrupting the discussion, began reading aloud.

"Listen, to this. It's by Fauro. 'Errant Italy is bearing her misery and anger against her step-motherland for all the world to see. Tomorrow, after the war, it will be a nation and will demonstrate to the world its will to dominate, its victorious power, and lastly its status; Italy as a people and as a state.'"

"Italy will enter the war," Tullia said.

The blond anarchist looked as if he were about to explode, then checked himself.

"Italy acted with honor in withholding its support from the Empire. It will act honorably and withhold it from the Allies as well."

Everywhere in the room voices were raised in protest.

"But it has to negotiate, even its neutrality. Politics is nothing but negotiation."

"And at the end of a war the victor, whoever that may be, will destroy it."

"Not on your life," the anarchist shouted. "At the end the winners will be as exhausted as the losers. That's when the people will strike the final blow against the rotten bourgeoisie, who are betting on the slaughter of the working classes as their last possibility of survival. It will be the Italian populace who will inaugurate a new era on earth."

Tullia spoke again.

"There's something I can't understand. I'm completely devastated when I read the French or German death lists. I never could stand the idea of death. Every time I hear that someone's died, every time they bring some wretched corpse into the anatomy room, I hate Nature that obliges us all to die. Yet when Valoria got restless and went to fight in France, I was overwhelmed by admiration for him. I felt he was a far better person than those of us just sitting around here, waiting and talking."

Valoria was a classmate who had enlisted to fight in the Argonne.

A silence fell upon the room. The young man who had read Fauro's piece had been looking at Tullia more intensely than anyone else while she'd been speaking. Now, he walked over to her, but said nothing.

Seeing him, Tullia smiled. "No place to sit, poor Ràmy?

Come on, I'll give you half of my seat. We'll fit fine together."

When she made room for him, the conversation among the others resumed. But it was soon interrupted by the entry of a maid carrying the tea tray. Tullia hurried to help her. The circle broke into small groups that carried on separate discussions in various parts of the room.

While the others were taking their tea, Tullia and Ràmy stood near a window at some distance from the others.

"Are you in love with Valoria?" Ràmy suddenly asked her.

"Not in the least," Tullia answered

Ràmy felt her reply was sincere. In a moment he spoke again.

"Look, Italy is going to be in this war. I'm as sure as you are. Maybe in a month, maybe sooner. I'm enlisting. Right away."

Tullia's eyes on him were large and clear. In the pocket of her dress one of her hands was resting on a letter from Adria. She'd found it upon returning home, and had sensed that it was one of those letters, the kind she hadn't received for several months now. She hadn't opened it, knowing that she wouldn't have time enough to read it in the way she wished to, between dinner and the time her guests were due. She was saving it to read later, alone in her room.

Ràmy was speaking again.

"Tullia, you know how I feel about you."

Tullia was no longer looking at him. "Yes," she whispered.

"Can you love me too? When I come back from the army will you marry me?"

Her reply was slow in coming.

"Ràmy, if I loved anyone, it would be you. But I can't love anyone. Don't ask me why. It's my secret."

Tullia's words frightened him.

"Why does that scare you?" she asked, seeing his distraught look. "There's nothing really wrong about it. Nothing bad. And don't worry, it's not a love secret." She smiled at him, "It's about the most precious thing in my life. Something I can't give up."

"But I'll never ask you the secret. Tullia. I'll respect it. Always. Do you want me to swear?"

"No, it's I who wouldn't be able to hide anything from the person I love. I'd have to tell you about it. I'd feel it as an obligation of my love. And then the only thing in the world that I cannot share with people, with anyone, would no longer be my secret."

Ràmy perceived a flash of madness in Tullia's dark eyes which doomed his love forever, and understood that it would be useless and unkind to persist.

Later, alone in her room, Tullia thought of how much she loved Ràmy and felt happy and quickened by the great sacrifice she was making.

Seated on the edge of her bed she read Adria's letter.

Tullia, haven't you ever thought that the world is nothing? I now dream every night (once I didn't want to). I dream of certain wonderful places filled with ice and sun, or with waterfalls that run into streams that flow under marble arches and through long underground passages like rivers of precious stones which give off strange lights in all kinds of colors. I also dream about new people, people I've never met, and about the things that happen between me and these people. Nothing I dream is misty, clouded, unclear, but as precise as the things that I can see and feel and touch right now. And I'm sure that I could feel and touch the things I was dreaming, too. Even the people are as clear in every respect as the people I knew in real life. This is where something terrible happens. I dream these new people as if I knew them for a long time, as if we had a past together. Then, when I awaken, it's hard to know the difference between the people I really knew and those I've only dreamed of that night. So, I can't figure out how it is that while a dream lasts only a moment, yet in that moment I think of the new person I'm dreaming of as someone I've known for years. The point is, the only thing that would distinguish a dream from reality would be the time the dream lasts. But if we can dream the passage of time and years, then there's no longer any way to be certain of anything. That's why I say it's a terrible thing. I didn't know that one could dream the passage of so many years. Besides, even dreaming, sometimes you think, 'I was dreaming that.' I mean, you can even dream of dreaming. So how can I know, for example, whether this room I'm in, and all this light and that row of books over there, are really around me, and have been for several years, or whether I've been inventing them in a dream for the past few minutes, and that when I finish dreaming they'll all disappear? And I can say the same about this letter, and even, for example, about you, Tullia, who'll receive it. If it is really true that everything is a dream, then I'm in it too. I'm even dreaming of myself. I need to be certain. Think of it, I would be immeasurably alone, and everything else nothing. Then the world becomes ice without end, too brilliant, and filled with nothing but empty light. But if one could be sure of this in life, one wouldn't have to take so many precautions.

At first this letter agitated Tullia more than any of the others she'd received previously. Not merely because she was drawn into the whirlpool of those fears, but because she began thinking about her mother. With her mystical faith in everything that had to do with Adria, she had never had the slightest fear for her life, even while reading the news of the terrors threatening Paris. But now, all night long her sleep was tormented by images of the supernatural solitude in which Adria felt herself immersed in the center of an empty universe. Dressing the next morning to leave for the hospital, Tullia kept asking herself, "What can I do to convince my mother that I really exist? That's the first step. And if I succeed, perhaps freed of that thought, suddenly forced to believe in a completely different reality, her spirit might be driven to simpler, happier conclusions and who knows…?"

Tullia visualized her mother leaving that dreadful life and joining her, and from that moment saw herself leading her mother onward by the hand into a life of pure and simple peace which she could never have known before. Tullia was fired with this vision of filial duty.

In front of Porta Pia and on the avenue leading to the hospital she passed noisy crowds advancing toward the center of Rome. The city was brimming with spirit and song. Every day its mood became brighter as the turbulence of events, so close around it, erupted into its streets and squares. During the following days and weeks the rush of public affairs distracted Tullia from pursuing her thoughts and forming any plans. Demonstrations clamoring for war broke out in every quarter of the city at every hour of the day. A cheerful god, invisible behind golden clouds and light-tossed air, began his descent from heaven.

Most of the demonstrators were university students who, it seems, deserted their classrooms daily for empty streets, where they strewed gun powder, then set it afire. Tullia and her boldest friends threw themselves headlong into rallies calling for intervention. Every day was filled with actions. They blew windows to smithereens—those of the Austrian Embassy, those of slow-acting ministers, and those of Villa Malta, behind which the Prussian ambassador was hurriedly tossing his last illusions into leather suitcases. Tullia learned how to throw stones, and how, by holding hands in a chain, to break through police cordons. She'd even spent a night in jail singing *Brothers of Italy*.

Tullia gave no thought to what she would do once war was declared and her closest friends were gone. She was living from day-to-day in a state of excitement which had intensified her life and filled her eyes with fire.

She worried a great deal about what might happen to Remo.

For many years he'd been living with a family in Berlin. In his infrequent letters he'd told her that he was doing well and that by now he considered that city and that home to be his own. But the looming war made his status uncertain. Tullia tried to persuade him to return, and enlisted her uncle's and even her friends' solicitations. Finally there was a letter from Remo. "Don't worry about me. If Italy is stupid enough to declare war against the Empire, they'll intern me here and I'll get along fine, much better than if I returned to Italy, where pretty soon you're going to have a heavy price to pay." Remo was eighteen, exactly Valoria's age, and just a little younger than Ràmy. Tullia cried with shame at the letter, tore it into shreds and burned it, then spent the entire evening feeling agitated and depressed. The gun powder in Rome's streets exploded ever more frequently and flamed ever higher. The blarings and rumblings from heaven drew ever closer to earth, and one morning the golden clouds tore asunder and the god appeared amid rays of sunshine. On the twenty-fourth of May the first shots were fired at the frontiers, and the Roman sun shattered into pieces which plummeted to earth and danced along with men and women everywhere within the circle of Rome's seven hills.

2 TULLIA'S LIFE THOSE FIRST DAYS was filled with joy and loss. Her closest friends left Rome. Ràmy got himself assigned immediately to an accelerated course at the front for young officers. He'd made no further attempt to speak of love, and had avoided being alone with her. Other friends went off in various directions. Soon the fervor and clamor of the early days was succeeded throughout the city by a tension so

deep it was painful. Still, everyone thought that the war would be over in a few weeks. Classes at the University ended early. Tullia suddenly lost all interest in studying. Studying for exams seemed much ado about very little.

She spent hours wandering through the rooms of Villa Adria or walking through the countryside east of it. She didn't follow streets or paths, but preferred to roam the living land where the exuberant growth of vegetation exploded in a thousand forms. There, amid a whirlwind of greens and yellows, she felt herself as rich as the very earth and hungered to expand her being to fill the space between the heaven and earth. She prayed for something to happen that would sweep her away, some overwhelming occurrence that would engage the powerful energy ready in her heart. Tortured by this desire and her inactivity, she reread her mother's letters.

This time they seemed far different to her than they had previously. They were filled with sudden transports to overly enchanted lands, with appalling silences or frightening words, with pressures as heavy as ocean depths, or as rarefied as ether too high above heaven.

Every so often her uncle would suggest they take a trip to the shore. The thought aroused an irrational fear in Tullia. She would put him off without knowing why. Occasionally, she would suddenly think of Ràmy, sometimes with a rush of love, sometimes with quiet affection.

Summer had already parted wide its rosy curtains over Rome, when Tullia received a letter from her mother, which she opened distractedly, thinking it one of her usual hurried greetings. Instead, this was a letter in which Adria in her childish and preternatural way spoke about the war. *Tullia, I think of myself as being everywhere there is war, and in every person who dies, and in those who survive, and in every blade of grass on which blood is falling. Then I think that everything human be-*

ings do is enormously wonderful and nothing in the world is really horrible, even if they are petty and want to do mean things and don't understand. Whatever people do, when, for example, a mother gives birth, or when someone kills someone else, or when lovers kiss, or when a shepherd leads his flock of sheep from a mountain pasture, and even if someone is only leaning out a window, just looking around and thinking, any of these things a person does becomes an action that circles the entire universe. I'm talking about the smallest and most ordinary things that we do without thinking. So even when a man says "get out of here," to an annoying dog, his action moves something almost to the stars. This is the reason life becomes something magnificent. And now, because of this great war, I'm certain when I look out the window at night at my piece of sky, that I see more stars there every night. And I think there must be many, many more over Rome. I think, too, that the great sorrow for all the dead produces a brimming soul even in the most hardened people, and that fear is as great as courage. And standing on grass soaked in red, I see that the dead battle more than even the living to preserve a place for themselves. That's why the fact remains there's no hate in killing, which would be the only evil thing in the world. The human soul can never hate even if it thinks it does. And war is as if everyone agrees at the same time that the earth wants to provoke the heavens, become higher and greater, burn completely like metal, then float upward like a yellow cloud. But since there is a war, there is no longer any solitude in the world. And I think of how wonderful it would be to be clasped together mother and daughter, waiting for all this to be over.

The letter put Tullia in a state of extraordinary exhilaration. She reread it perhaps twenty times. And each time as she approached the end, she read ever more slowly to enjoy the surprise of the last sentence, as an adored woman awaits a kiss on the nape of her neck. That sentence stood alone in her heart.

I think of how wonderful it would be to be clasped together, mother and daughter, waiting for all this to be over. Then something even about these words felt depressing, as if it were all hopeless. And with the letter limp on her lap and her gaze off into the distance, Tullia murmured to herself. *I think of how wonderful it would be to be clasped together, mother and daughter, waiting for all this to be over.* All night long she dreamed that sentence as if it were something gentle perched against her neck.

The next morning she ran in search of her uncle. "Don't say no to me," she told him. "I want to go to Paris. No, don't say anything. I'll just be a few days. I have to see my mother. "

She didn't allow him to raise any objections, she overpowered him. As she couldn't tell him the real reason for wanting to go, she lied. She invented an inane lie.

"I dreamt she was sick, that she was dying. No, I don't want to send her a telegram. They're useless. No, I know it can't be true, but I want to go. I want to see her right away."

She forbade him to accompany her and made him swear not to tell anyone where she had gone.

She didn't answer Adria's letter. She managed to get a passport within a few days, days spent in a fever. She left in the evening. The train was a furnace. She traveled for a night, a day, and then another night without any sleep. Every station on both sides of the frontier was filled with soldiers and singing. She arrived at dawn when the light was still thick and gray. She knew it was too early to go see her mother, so arranged to be taken to a hotel in the center of the city. Even there she couldn't sleep. She tried to undress, but couldn't. Her hands refused to behave normally. Unable to sit, she walked back and forth in the room. She leaned against a doorpost and stood there for a long time, eyes wide open. *To be clasped together, mother and daughter.* Then a mist formed before her eyes, and she felt them brimming with tears.

It occurred to her that hours must have passed. Her watch had stopped. She was reluctant to ask anyone the time. Certainly, the light outside was much brighter. She almost flew out of the hotel, and in a very slow carriage was driven to Adria's address.

"Is this really the street?"

"This is it. Can't you see?"

The raw look of the street surprised her. A dry sun was beating down on the stones, cutting across bare walls. The chimney pots and towers seemed to be gasping.

"Here, for eight years?" The street was deserted.

She stared for a moment at the small door set into a black arch. Then she stepped back a few strides to look further up. The windows of the round floor were half-open, those on the second were hidden behind a series of closed green shutters.

"Eight years."

She was overcome with fear that one of those shutters would open and that Adria would appear.

She hurried to the door and rang the bell. Steps approached and the door opened. A young chambermaid stood before her.

"Is the signora at home?"

"She's sleeping. Who are you?"

Tullia felt herself blushing. She paused for a moment, then asked, "Is Albertina here?"

The maid turned toward the house and called upstairs. "Albertina, come down."

In doing so she had moved aside and Tullia entered a small hallway that led to the staircase.

Albertina came down, looked at the girl for a moment, hesitated and seemed at a loss.

Finally the girl said, "You don't recognize me. Eight years ago I was a little girl. I'm Tullia."

Albertina threw her arms in the air, shouted in surprise,

then suddenly stifled her reaction. By then the surprise on her face had given way to a look of dismay.

Tullia spoke. "I know, I'm too early. Mamma is still sleeping. But when she gets up, I want to see her."

"See the mistress? Oh, Miss Tullia!"

It sounded as if she were speaking of a sacrilege.

But Tullia wasn't disheartened. She smiled. "I know that no one can, that no one could. But this time you'll see. She'll say yes."

Albertina looked at her with pity

Tullia lowered her voice, "I'm saying it because I know." In a still softer voice, she added, "She wrote to me."

Albertina undoubtedly thought the girl had lost her senses. She smiled lovingly at her and asked. "Is there something you need?"

"Nothing, Albertina. The main thing is that I have to see my mother."

There was silence.

After some thought, Albertina spoke again. "Well, anyway, she'll sleep until eleven, as usual."

"What time is it now?"

"It's not even eight yet."

"That's all?"

"Yes, I'm not sure where to put you, Miss Tullia," Albertina said, looking around her and toward the staircase in such consternation that Tullia smiled again.

"Don't worry about me, Albertina. All I need is a chair."

"You're tired. When did you get here?"

"Three hours ago. I went to a hotel. I didn't know what time it was. I thought it was much later."

"My Lord! Anyone can see how tired you are. Listen to what I'm going to tell you. Go back to the hotel now. If you'd like, I'll walk out with you and help you find a carriage. Go back and have a good rest. As soon as the mistress wakes up, I'll tell her, then I'll telephone you at the hotel right away."

Tullia didn't like the idea.

"Do as I say, Miss Tullia. Come on, come along with me."

Albertina set off toward the street and Tullia had no recourse but to follow unwillingly, though she knew that Albertina was right.

The moment they were in the street Tullia tapped Albertina on the shoulder. Almost whispering she asked, "Show me which is mamma's room."

Without answering, Albertina led her around the corner of the house and with a reverential gesture pointed to the first window on the second floor, set behind shutters like those at the front.

"That's her bedroom window. The ones in front are the sitting rooms."

Now they climbed the stone-filled street to a small square with a fountain at its center surrounded by chestnut trees. Tullia was gasping with effort. In the shade of the chestnut trees stood a carriage with a weary-looking horse.

Albertina helped the young woman enter the carriage and gave the driver the name of her hotel. Tullia felt exhausted. The trip seemed endless to her. The carriage bounced dreadfully on the descent along cobblestone streets, then reached a level, well-traveled road where the going was smoother. Stores were opening and people were beginning to appear in the streets. Tullia heard confused sounds but saw nothing. In her room at the hotel even removing her hat was an effort. She dropped fully dressed onto the bed and, with a heavy heart and shadows before her eyes, fell into a deep sleep .

When she awoke she sat up in fright, with no idea of where she was. Her memory returned, and with it alarming thoughts. "Albertina phoned. Maybe they rang my room and I didn't hear.

Or maybe mamma wanted to speak to me and they told her I
was sleeping and she didn't want them to wake me. What time
is it? It must be late. No, hours ago it seemed late to me, too.
Maybe I only slept an hour."

This time she rang for someone, and when the chambermaid appeared, asked her the time.

"Four o'clock, mademoiselle."

"Oh my God. Did I get a telephone call?"

"I'll go find out, mademoiselle."

Waiting, she felt wretched, hating herself for having slept
so long.

The chambermaid returned. "No one telephoned," she said.
"But there's a letter for you."

Tullia snatched it from the woman's hands.

"Who brought it?"

"A servant. She said to let you sleep and to give it to you
when you woke up because it wasn't urgent."

The maid left and Tullia, with her heart shattered, with
her head burning, read Adria's note.

"Dear Tullia, It was wrong of you to come. I would have
liked to see you too, but that's not possible. You knew it wasn't
possible and therefore that one shouldn't do these things. But
I forgive you. Go back to Rome, Tullia. I'm perfectly fine."

———————

3 But Tullia climbs the stone-filled street and
returns to the house again. She is not there to try another approach; she has no hope. She is there as a sinner filled
with shame. *One shouldn't do these things.* She goes when it is
dark, for no one must see her. She has the coach stop at the
entrance to the street and sends it away. Then she steps into

the street walking on her toes and looking about her, as if she were a thief entering a darkened house. She passes the small black door, turns the corner, and there is the first window. The shutter is open now, the window closed, but within the room, behind a drawn white curtain, there is light. Tullia envisions the bright light. *All that light,* said one of Adria's letters. *Clasped together, mother and daughter,* said another. But the last one, *One shouldn't do these things.* Yet it's a letter from Adria that has driven her into this darkness. *At night when I look out the window at my piece of the sky.* Is that her piece of sky up there? Long and narrow with a few small stars piercing the reddish mist.

Why doesn't Adria look out? The hours pass and the handful of stars in that narrow strip of pale sky change. It is useless to wait. Why cry? This same thing happened so many times when she was a child. With Remo there as well, two little children. But now Tullia is all alone. And Remo, who had wanted to keep his distance and live among strangers, doubtless by now has forgotten all about Tullia. It's as if Remo no longer exists. Perhaps he's still a child. She isn't. So much of her life has passed since then, so many years…how many years has Tullia been standing here hopelessly, staring at a piece of fading sky and at an illumined, opaque window? But how can she get herself to leave?

All at once Tullia's heart stops. Behind the window the lights have suddenly gone out. The window is no longer white, but dark. Perhaps now? Surely her mother turned out the lights in order to look out the window at her sliver of sky. Now…now. But it's important to be careful when she appears, not to call out to her, not to utter a sound. Yet there's no chance of that. Tullia knows that even if she wanted to call out on seeing her mother, she wouldn't have a voice. So she waits in the dark. She waits all night until it is no longer dark. The light she now sees is not in the window, it's in the sky, in that low hanging sky; it is a pallor seeping down from the roof and running atop and along the walls from one side to the other, a pallor straining to infiltrate the air, and it persists because it is almost morning. Therefore, someone will come by, and she must flee.

Tullia runs, head bent, leaping over stones like a mouse before a broom, racing down to the bottom of the hill, through all of Paris which is stretching its limbs, through the ashen light which in street after street is beginning to outline walls and roofs and curbs. Carts laden with greens appear, voices sound in the streets, the light becomes frightening, some of the voices now follow Tullia and, without her knowing how or why, cause her to run ever more frantically. She never remembered how she spent those hours and those days, how she got away, how she returned to Rome. Even in Rome she couldn't gain control of herself and went about Villa Adria like a wraith, without purpose or will. Finally, little by little, her will returned, her mind cleared and her heart reopened to the great song borne by every wind entering Rome. Her moods now reflected thoughts and images other than those of the luminous and silent window. Memories of Valoria and Ràmy returned. Tullia wanted to serve in the Red Cross. She pined away for months, almost a year in Roman hospitals, dreaming every minute of being in fighting zones. Unappeasable, she eventually overcame her uncle's objections and those of her friends, and was sent to hospitals along the front, where she worked day and night, was transferred from detachment to detachment, saw a hundred horrors and experienced a hundred exaltations. Although she received no salary, she didn't think as well of herself as she would have liked. A growing disquiet consumed her, an outrageously unjust dissatisfaction with herself, as if she senses she has an invisible destiny and no idea how to attain it.

She was in a small hospital in Friuli when it was overrun

and retreat became necessary. In the tumult of the first day, she felt a strong desire to be taken prisoner, and immediately as strong a sense of shame for having the wish. She was among the last to leave. Riding on a caisson, she traveled with a transport column under the low flight of airplanes, among sharp whistlings like the leaves of torn reeds. Subsequently, completely exhausted, she was transferred onto a truck where, despite its bumps and jolts, she lay inert for days, wakened from her torpor only by long, complicated series of explosions, red flashes that rose from a distant screen of poplars, long walls of flame that climbed to the sky and filled it with smoke.

Toward the end of the extraordinary, agonizing journey the column stopped on the right bank of the Tagliamento, hoping to camp there, but new orders forced it on instead. All about her there were curses and explosions, shouts, oaths, hunger, exhaustion, shattered spirits, despair, all of human life summed up in one compressed hell. On the road from the Tagliamento to the Piave she traveled with an Air Force lieutenant named Sammarco, who came from that area, who had lost none of his enthusiasm or energy, and who was able to comfort her. The remobilization of these rear guard troops came about more through the unofficial initiative of the scattered troops themselves than from orders. Sammarco and Tullia reached Treviso together and managed to join the first companies that had been restructured. He went to an air base on the left side of the road leading from Treviso to the Piave, toward Spresiano. Tullia joined a field hospital near Treviso. They parted with much warmth, promising to write to each other and possibly to see each other again.

Tullia spent the entire bitterly cold winter at that hospital. Sammarco wrote occasionally. In the spring, Tullia, who by now had been serving in advanced positions for two years, received notice that she had been relieved and that early in May she would be posted to Padova. From there she would be sent, so they said, behind the lines. The prospect tormented her beyond measure, and she wrote Sammarco a frantic letter. In answer, Sammarco told her he expected a two-day leave shortly and would come to see her.

◆━❋━◆

4 SAMMARCO KEPT HIS PROMISE. ONE morning a truck stopped in front of the hospital. Tullia was outside hanging linen in the sun. When she saw Sammarco getting out of it she ran toward him shouting with joy, a little girl again, as if in that moment all her years of suffering had been obliterated. Sammarco had two days of leave.

As happened wherever she went, Tullia was essentially in charge of the hospital. The medical officer had no objection to hosting the aviator's stay for those two days. Tullia asked Sammarco to tell her about his daily routine, and thrilled to hear about flights over enemy lines. They were days of great calm. Sammarco had made many solo flights.

"Did you drop many bombs?"

"Not even one. We fly in shifts to report on Austrian troop movements. With our reports and other information, we maintain a map of enemy front line positions that's as accurate as any map of our own positions. We've come across some peculiar and unexpected things. In the zone opposite our Armored Corps the enemy's front is very deep at the sides, but strangely attenuated at the center. There's a group of houses there, almost a village, just six kilometers from the Piave, still inhabited by civilians—peasants, who are somehow even managing to keep gardens in an area sheltered by a rise in the hillside."

"Italians? From the Veneto?"

"They're sort of a wedge. It's as if they were splitting a river,

273

making it go off to the right and left toward mountains or the sea, but here they're dividing the enemy columns that come down to supply the front line. And those movements are extremely important to us. If we know about them we can predict whether they're planning to attack from the Montello side or from the plain. But such things can't interest you."

However, they did interest Tullia, to the extent that they filled her mind all that night. She imagined herself flying, watching the slow displacement of masses of clouds or herds of sheep. And she imagined herself wandering amid the houses of those farmers, Italians, there in the Veneto, who with their families and fields existed solid as an island in the midst of a sea of enemy invaders. And real images appeared to her, images that Sammarco's words had evoked, but which were now deformed by fantasy. The strange ideas elicited by this tangle in her mind quickly took on a shape. The next morning she made her rounds early and by eleven was alone with Sammarco. At first she didn't tell him her strange ideas. Instead she asked, "When you flew over the enemy lines, didn't it ever occur to you to land there?"

"What for?"

"To get to our people. To talk to them."

"I'll tell you, as far as landing goes, I had an idea about doing it once. There are some abandoned fields north and west of that center section, halfway between the enemy camp and the houses. They're completely surrounded by trees that are leafless now, but their trunks are so intertwined that the site is completely hidden. I know every inch of that land. It's where I come from. Maybe with the right conditions you could get down there unobserved. But then what? It would be a worthless risk, a personal satisfaction, a vanity. First rule in war—don't take any unnecessary risks."

"Sammarco, I want to say something and don't interrupt me till I'm done. Promise?"

"Yes."

"I have an idea."

"What kind of idea?"

"A practical one. But be quiet now. In three days my time here will be up. I'm being rotated out. I'll have to go back to Rome or Milan, I don't know, some place far off. But instead, this is what I thought last night. Be quiet. I'll dress up like a peasant woman, you'll fly me to those fields and then go back. I'm still talking. At night I'll walk to that little village you told me about. I'll act like I'm from around those parts. But so I won't have to go into too much detail about where I come from, I'll say I got lost and pretend I'm a little out of my head. Quiet. Being right there I'll see the troops go by. There's no doubt I'll pick up information and see a lot more than you can from a plane. After, let's say a week, you'll come back to the field, land, and I'll give you my notes. Then I can either go back with you or stay a while longer and go on with my observations. That's the gist of the idea, an outline. You can fill in the details. Now all right, you can talk."

After a moment of silence Sammarco laughed. Then he looked admiringly at Tullia. Finally he spoke. "It can't be done."

"Why not?"

"For a hundred reasons. I wouldn't even know where to start."

"Well, tell me just one."

"The most elementary. You can't cross the barricade blockading the Treviso road, and the airfield is beyond that. Will that do?"

"No, it won't. To the right and left of the main road, the land this side of the barricade is completely flat so you can very easily pick me up in one of those fields."

"Then, no one would permit it."

"No one has to. The way things go in war, if something turns out well, everyone says they were in favor of it, including the people who wouldn't have permitted it."

Their discussion lasted for several hours, interrupted every so often by the rounds that Tullia made to see her patients, and resuming when she rejoined Sammarco, who tried in vain at each return to change the subject and divert her from her obsession. Obsession it was, and ever more insistent. And contagious as well for Sammarco, who, after running out of ways to counter her arguments, in the end no longer viewed the undertaking as impossible. So overcome was he by then that he had no sense of the responsibility he was undertaking. By evening, without being fully aware of it, he had altered and improved various aspects of the daring scheme. Having come that far, he could no longer turn back.

Tullia's tour of duty was over the evening of May fourth. On the morning of the fifth, she gathered her belongings, devoting particular care to wrapping a photograph in layers of soft paper. She placed the photo in a folder, which she tied with a ribbon and sealed. On its cover she wrote, "In case of my death, to be delivered as is, to my brother Remo wherever he may be. Tullia." She wrapped the folder along with other papers and personal objects into one package and gave it to a warrant officer on his way to Treviso, from where he could forward it to her uncle in Rome. She said good-bye to her patients, her medical officer and colleagues and, refusing offers of company, went alone on foot to the main road. She stopped the first truck coming from Treviso and had it take her to within a kilometer of the barricade beyond which only military personnel could pass. As prearranged with Sammarco, she headed into a field to the right of the road and took shelter behind a bush. She had some food with her and a bundle that contained a peasant dress which she'd obtained without difficulty. She took off her uniform and headdress and threw them into a ditch. Under her uniform she was wearing a thin, dark blue shift. Over it she put on the peasant dress, which went down to her feet, and tied a kerchief around her head. Hissing sounded in the clouded sky, then faded into the distance. As the first shadows fell, a rumbling noise grew close. The plane appeared and landed. Sammarco was agitated, but didn't dare a last attempt to dissuade her. He took out a map of enemy positions according to the latest reports, explained it, then gave it to her. All was rapid, precise and hushed. They took off, crossed the enemy lines, and passed above white crowns of exploding shrapnel that blossomed along their route. When the first stars appeared in the sky they landed in one of the fields hidden by the poplar trees. Night fell around them amid a deep silence. Bands of light appeared on the horizon, searched the skies, widening as they descended, then disappeared. Sammarco indicated the cardinal points to Tullia, then the direction toward the village. They were silent and felt themselves completely alone on the face of the earth. Sammarco whispered, "Here, in four days."

"Now go," she replied. He embraced her and kissed her eyelids. He waited to see her on her way, then left without incident.

With her heart beating evenly, Tullia set off immediately. The stars appeared brighter than before, and in a little while she caught a glimpse of the houses she had to reach. She walked a while longer, then lay down in a furrow and fell asleep. The first rays of sunlight awakened her.

Calm and rested, she resumed her way and in less than an hour was near the houses. She identified the gardens in the lee of the hillside, and saw in the distance Austrian soldiers harnessing a horse to a bread wagon with the aid of some peasants. She waited until they all left, then went on again.

A peasant looked at her, then blandly asked her where she'd

come from. Remembering her plan, Tullia tried to appear simple-minded. She asked him to repeat the question, pointed vaguely to the north and said, "From there."

Then she added, "I'm all alone. I don't have any family any more. I want to stay here and work."

The man shrugged. "There's just me and my wife," he said, and pointed to the first house. "Past us," he extended his arm, "there's two or three other folks. Every place else," he turned toward the south and described a circle, "there's soldiers."

"Austria's?" asked Tullia.

"Yup. Hungarians."

"But we're Italians."

"Sure, born right here. But you're not. Where're you from?"

Tullia sensed the peasant's distrust and realized she was forgetting to act her part. Her face dissolved into an expression of stupidity. "From there," she replied and repeated her vague gesture.

Then she asked, "Are there a lot of soldiers?"

The peasant looked heavenward. "It'll end," he said.

Two soldiers on bicycles rode up. They stopped and called out under a window of the house. A heavy woman appeared at the window and threw them a pack of cigarettes. The man ran up to them to get payment for the cigarettes. Neither of the two soldiers looked at Tullia. They were speaking an incomprehensible language.

"How do you understand when they want something?" Tullia asked the peasant.

"One way or another, they make it clear."

"Is there ever anyone who speaks Italian?"

"Sometimes."

Tullia was silent, then once again asked, "Can I stay and work for you?"

The peasant looked at her but said nothing. The woman

reappeared at the window and called to him. He entered the house and shut the door.

Tullia sat down on a rock, overcome with desolation and despair. The great enterprise was coming to nothing. She'd thought that getting here would be the most difficult part. It had been the easiest. Now she hadn't the faintest notion of how she might observe enemy troop movements, obtain information, or learn anything useful to pass on to Sammarco. She felt exhausted, drained. Even sitting up was too much for her. She let herself down on the ground and leaned back against some rocks as if she were on a bed. Lying there with her ear close to the ground, she heard a distant rumble in the earth. As it grew closer she made out the sounds of hoof beats and carriage wheels. She sat up halfway. Now she saw a cloud of dust which grew ever larger until it turned into a thundering horde, and finally into a column of field artillery.

It wasn't very long before the stony patches between the houses, and most of the level land beyond them, were crowded with weapons, pawing horses and soldiers who wanted to eat, drink and smoke. The peasant opened his door and motioned the soldiers in. Tullia saw that the house had been converted to a kind of inn, and began studying the soldiers' uniforms hoping to understand the significance of their badges, insignia and ranks, and to estimate the size of the contingent. She drew close to the peasant and following his footsteps entered the main room, a huge kitchen with a counter laden with bottles and dishes. In all the tumult Tullia began helping the heavy woman she'd seen at the window wash out glasses. After a few hours of commotion the soldiers began leaving; the columns reformed and started moving again. The peasant and his wife, with Tullia behind them, were now also outside, and Tullia began wandering about trying to set every detail in her head. The unit was moving west toward the Piave River, beyond the

Montello hill, to which Sammarco had ascribed such importance. The huge clouds of dust with all their noise receded
into the distance. Two officers had remained behind, as well
as a motorcyclist with a sidecar, two noncommissioned officers and three or four enlisted men. Tullia saw that one of the
two officers, a tall lieutenant, was speaking to the peasant and
that the latter was answering him. She walked closer to them,
managed to hear that the officer was speaking Italian, but the
conversation ended just then. The two officers mounted the
motorcycle, one in the sidecar, one straddling the seat behind
the driver. They drove off in the same direction as the columns. The two noncommissioned men and the few soldiers
stayed behind. The latter were sitting in the doorway of the house
smoking. Other peasants came in from the fields and headed
toward the more distant houses, followed by the soldiers. Now
Tullia approached her peasant again, at which moment his wife
came out of the house carrying an immense pot full of peeled
potatoes and walked slowly toward the other houses. One of
the two noncommissioned officers, a sergeant, speaking completely unintelligibly, came up to the woman, who stopped and
set the pot down. Laughing, the sergeant put his arm around
her waist, at which point the husband turned away with an air
of unconcern, and reentered the house.

Tullia saw the cheerful sergeant look around, then point to
her. The woman turned too and called out, "You," and motioned for her to come over.

When she was sure it was she they were calling, Tullia
rushed up to them.

Indicating the pot still on the ground, the woman said. "Take
it over there. To the second house."

"Right away."

The sergeant and the woman turned the corner, crossed a
rivulet at the edge of the field and disappeared behind a bush.

Tullia bent to pick up the pot. It was extremely heavy, but walking very slowly as she picked her way through horse dung, she reached the second house with the load.

A man came up to her and asked, "Who're you?"

"I'm with them," she answered, pointing to the house she'd just come from.

One of the enlisted men came for the pot and carried it into the house.

The man persisted, "But where're you from? I never seen you before."

Tullia's face went blank, and once again she made that vague gesture toward the north.

The man shrugged and walked away.

Tullia passed a group of soldiers digging a great square pit and thought it might be for use as an arms repository.

She returned to the first house. The corporal who was still sitting in the doorway of the house said a few words to her in Hungarian, looked her up and down rather contemptuously, then ignored her.

The heavy woman and the sergeant came back from behind the bushes laughing and in a while the husband came out of the house.

"That lieutenant," he said to his wife, "he told me that in a few days there's going to be lots of troops coming through here. We've got to get to town for supplies. He said they'd be back with empty trucks early tomorrow morning and we could use one of them."

Tullia jumped at this opportunity. "Can I stay?" she said to the woman. "You're going to need help."

The woman peered hard at her, then agreed. "All right."

A long, whining sound rose in the distance, quickly pierced the air over their heads, and faded away in the clouds to the north.

"Here it comes," the man said. "Let's get inside."

Immediately there were whistlings, fiendish screechings, piercing squeals, invisible bearings rolling around in the sky. Tullia stopped in the doorway and turned to see puffs of black soil rise from the distant fields, and white clouds exploding in midair. Now everyone left the kitchen for the next room, which was larger and had a number of sacks stuffed with dry leaves strewn across its floor.

The storm of explosions in the sky lasted for five minutes before finally subsiding. The two non-commissioned officers were speaking their native language.

"What are they saying," Tullia asked the peasant.

"Who knows?" He was listening to the noise now fading into the distance. "It's over. They must have spotted the artillery that moved up there. Now they're shortening their range."

"A lot's been going up there?"

"Enough."

"Only canons?"

"A little of everything."

"All in that direction?"

"A little everywhere."

Tullia didn't know what else to ask.

"And those two?"

"They're spending the night here."

Now everyone went outside again. The sun was setting, and the first light of evening on the greensward was as pale as dawn.

The couple and the two soldiers sat there doing nothing without the slightest sign of boredom. Empty time had no effect on them. Tullia, on the contrary, was consumed with impatience.

At dusk they all returned indoors. Dinner consisted of boiled potatoes and preserved meat that the soldiers had brought. After that, the two went into the large room, threw themselves down, each on a sack, and fell asleep.

The man and the woman took the largest sack, dragged it into the kitchen and stayed there.

There were three unused sacks in the large room. "Where can I sleep?" Tullia asked them.

"In there, if you want. On one of those sacks. Or there's a room upstairs." The man pointed to a wooden staircase in the corner of the kitchen. "But it's riskier up there."

"I don't care. I'll go up. Thanks. Good-night."

As soon as she entered the room Tullia locked the door as best she could and looked around cautiously. The house was quiet. Anxious to catch the last of the light, she loosened her peasant costume and from the bodice of her blue dress took the map Sammarco had given her. She had a small pencil. She wrote her first notes in tiny letters on the reverse side of the map: the date, May 6, colors and insignia, emblems and badges, the equipment she'd seen heading toward the Piave. She added the word "Hungarians" and thought, "Tomorrow will be even better and in four days the whole page will be full. Sammarco will have to take off immediately after landing. There won't be time to talk. Everything has to be in writing. He'll be pleased with what I've done and he'll want to take me back with him, but I'll stay here. By that time I'll be more experienced at it. Maybe there'll be troops that speak German and I'll learn a lot more." Filled with a sense of confidence, she replaced the precious paper in her bodice and fastened the peasant dress tightly around her. Then, fully clothed, so as to be ready for any eventuality, she lay down to sleep. Instantly, she began a review of her day but found it difficult to gather her thoughts. The sixth of May? I left on the fifth. That means yesterday morning, just yesterday I was still there in my hospital, all in white. Yesterday, just about this time, I was in the field. Sammarco had landed, but I was still there, among my own people. It was last night I got here with Sammarco. He kissed me and left. I'm all alone here. There's no one around anymore who's close to me. It's another world. How long ago? Her confusion about the passage of time upset her and at the same time exhilarated her almost to the point of intoxication. It gave her entire being a sense of lightness, of detachment, as though she had become an ethereal creature in the center of whose essence lay a great, simple, strange, yet weightless duty. And suddenly a sentence she hadn't thought of for so long. Yes, there it was. The heart of the matter: *I know that you will do something very wonderful in life, Tullia.* Who had ordered such a deed? The letter, Adria's first letter. Her beautiful mother. Now Tullia fell sleep.

Just after dawn she heard someone try the door, then loud knocking. She ran to open it. It was the woman.

"C'mon, get ready. The trucks are coming and we're leaving to pick up supplies. You'll stay here downstairs. I've got to explain things to you."

The morning was bright. When they reached the bottom of staircase the woman turned and asked. "What's your name?"

The question took Tullia by surprise. She hadn't prepared an answer, but there was no reason to give another name. "Tullia," she answered.

"That's not from around here, " the woman said.

"I'm from Rome," Tullia replied.

She realized too late that she'd spoken with a measure of pride, but the woman seemed not to have noticed.

She showed Tullia what was left of wines and tobacco, instructed her as to their prices, and went off with her husband when the trucks arrived.

Nothing happened all morning long. Seated at the edge of the field, for the first time in months Tullia found herself thinking constantly about her mother. Shortly after noon the motorcycle returned from the direction of the front and an officer got out of the sidecar. Tullia was pleased to see it was the tall officer who spoke Italian.

Reels of metal wire were unloaded from the cycle. Under the surveillance of the officer, a lieutenant in the artillery, the soldiers began to run the wire along the wall of the house, then brought it inside. They were planning to install a telephone in a corner of the wall behind the counter.

"Is there any wood around here?" the lieutenant asked Tullia. "Old boards?"

Tullia remembered seeing wood stacked in a corner of the room in which she'd slept.

"Upstairs," she said "I don't know if they're what you want. Would you like me to go up and get you one?"

The officer looked at her with some surprise. Was it her voice perhaps, her way of speaking—he himself wasn't quite sure why he was so surprised. He motioned to the soldier to go up and addressed the young woman. "Please don't trouble yourself. He'll get it."

And this time he was really amazed to have heard himself speak to her as he did.

While the men were working, with Tullia watching them and thinking of what she ought to ask and how she might begin a conversation with the officer, the motorcyclist came in and said something, after which the officer asked her, "Is there any motor oil?"

Tullia had no idea. For a moment she was at a complete loss.

"Look for some," the officer said and left with the other soldier to resume the work outside the house. With the Hungarian motorcyclist following her, Tullia searched under the counter, in a wall cabinet, everywhere she could think of, but found nothing. The motorcyclist grumbled loudly, then pointed upstairs as if to ask "How about up there?"

"I'll go look," Tullia said. She ran up the rickety staircase into the room in which she'd slept and began searching every cupboard. But the motorcyclist came upstairs too and was shadowing her every step, which she found extremely worrisome.

A few moments later the officer and the soldier who, in the process of unrolling and tacking down the wire, had been gradually moving away from the doorway of the house, heard a sudden shout from an upper window. They listened for a moment as the shouts grew louder, then recognized the motorcyclist's cursing and the young woman screaming *no, no* desperately. They rushed into the house just as the soldier came hurrying down the steps pushing the girl before him. One of her hands was pressed against the torn bodice of her dress.

The soldier uttered a few excited words to the lieutenant, which stunned him. Then there was complete silence. Finally, the officer ordered all the men out of the house. He sat down on a bench and stared at Tullia.

"I am sure," he began, "that you have some idea of what that soldier told me. That you're not a local woman, but without doubt a spy in disguise."

"That soldier attacked me."

"We're not discussing the soldier's behavior right now. Answer me."

"It's not true."

"Raise your arm. Don't make me do it for you."

Tullia realized that it was useless to refuse. She raised her arm. A long strip of the torn dress fell revealing the elegant blue sheath beneath it.

"He told me that he felt a paper in a pocket. Give it to me."

Tullia didn't move.

"Signorina, we are not now at a customs bureau where there are women to undertake certain tasks. I would have to take you to Headquarters, where no doubt some male or other, in no position to disobey orders, will be told to undress you. I hope you understand how offensive that would be to me. To avoid it, I beg you, signorina, to give me the clothes you've put on."

Tullia hesitated and he spoke again.

"I am not at all sure that you would encounter people there who would conduct that operation with consideration...that is, signorina, with the consideration which is your due."

With great dignity Tullia loosened and slipped off the coarse garment which fell at her feet. Standing erect in her thin sheath, she looked almost like a child. Impulsively, she pulled the kerchief from her head as well. Her dark hair was as smooth and shining as ever, her eyes more brilliant.

There was a long silence. Tullia felt neither alarm nor anguish at being caught. She was enclosed in a cold and quiet destiny.

She turned her back, reached into her bodice, withdrew her hand, then turned once more to face the officer, who was ashen. Tullia's arms hung limply at her sides. In one hand was her map, folded and refolded many times.

She did not extend her hand. The officer stood up, walked over to her and gently slid the map from her grasp. "Thank you," he whispered and returned to his seat. He unfolded it, and studied it, reading both sides. His face became grim. Then he refolded it and put it in his pocket. Tullia watched his every action as though she were looking into a valley from the crest of a mountain.

The officer pulled a notebook from his pocket, tore some paper from it and slowly wrote a report.

"I won't ask you how you got here, if you have any accomplices, or to whom you were going to give this. You wouldn't tell me anyway."

"Of course."

"I don't know if you're keeping your name a secret."

"No."

She gave it to him and he added it to the report. He put that into an envelope, along with Tullia's paper—the sheet of paper with Sammarco's map and Tullia's notes—for the sixth of May.

The officer then went to the window and called in the motorcyclist. He gave him some orders and handed him the envelope, whereupon the cyclist drove off toward the front.

"You'll stay in here until I get instructions from my commanding officer."

He saluted her crisply and left, closing the door carefully behind him. He ordered a soldier to stand guard at the house. Then he walked to edge of the field and began pacing back and forth.

After a while the truck that had gone in the opposite direction with the two peasants returned. The officer ordered them to unload their provisions in the second house.

Hours passed.

Eventually, a speeding motor roared ever closer from the front. The motorcyclist dismounted and handed the officer a message.

The officer read it and dismissed the soldiers. He ordered the sentry to bring out the young woman, then sent him away as well.

"I've received my orders," he told her.

He looked at her, then turned to stare at a yellow flower sprouting between two rocks at the edge of the road.

"Do you have any idea what headquarters has ordered me to do?"

"Yes."

"I'm obligated to tell you. You're to be shot."

Tullia had expected it. Yet she shuddered with sudden cold that shattered her, tore at her body as though she were about to deliver a child. From deep within her, a scream rose to her throat. She jammed her fist into her mouth, stifling the scream. The officer had moved away from her and was no longer looking at her. Tullia gasped, then regained control of herself. She sensed that all the color had drained from her face and that any minute now the man would turn and see her shameful pallor. A violent reaction called up by every ounce of will sent a wave of heat into her face. Then she called to him.

"Lieutenant!"

And asked, "When?"

He was looking at her now, as at a miracle.

"Tomorrow," he murmured. "Tomorrow at dawn."

"Why at dawn?"

"I don't know. That's the order. These things are always done at dawn."

"Well, I'm Roman," Tullia answered him. "So I want to be shot at noon."

Tullia discerned quite clearly that he would have granted her anything, even escape. But in that case it was he who would be shot.

"Is there anything you'd like until tomorrow?" he asked.

She paused before replying. " Nothing, thank you."

"There's something else I have to tell you," he said. "It will be done in front of everyone in the village. That's the order."

Tullia went back into the house and fell onto one of the sacks.

When she came outdoors the next morning, the sun was already quite high. The officer was waiting for her. "I don't know exactly what time it is, Lieutenant," she told him, "but the sun is fairly high. We can go."

Ten or twelve terrified village men and women stood rigid in the distance.

Tullia and the officer set off into the field. He pointed to a tree.

"Over there," he said and heard the voice issuing from his own throat as an inhuman sound. Four soldiers were following silently a few paces behind them. When they reached the tree the officer spoke again.

"Signorina, I want to ask something of you. Please don't refuse me."

"What is it?"

"Let us blindfold you. I know you won't want to. But I beg you."

At these words Tullia felt a mild sense of ease. She nodded her head.

With her back against the tree, her eyes blindfolded, and her arms hanging limply at her sides, an empyrean silence surrounded her.

Suddenly she felt an enormous terror that made her knees tremble dreadfully. She moved her arms slightly and her palms opened a bit.

But the Austrian officer saw nothing of this because he had turned away and was staring at the emptiest point on the horizon.

remo

---

1 (THIS STORY WILL HAVE TO WANDER dispassionately between heaven and hell.)

The hostess approached the small table at which Remo, Carmine Bonaccorsi, called Càrbon, and Càrbon's lover, Aloe, were still sitting. No one knew whether Aloe was a first name, last name or nickname. The sailors had all left and the hostess had finished wiping the greasy tables which now stood heavily in reddish, smoky shadows.

"Come on," she shouted. "Closing time. Pay up and go home to bed."

"We're waiting for Wilhelm," Càrbon said.

"He went home already."

They were all half-asleep. In fact, Aloe, on the bench between the two men, with her back against a bare wall, was sound asleep. A few worn playing cards were scattered on the table in front of her. The rest of the deck was still in her hand. Her head was on Càrbon's shoulder, but in her sleep, perhaps without even knowing it, her thigh was pressing against Remo's.

"Did you understand me?" the hostess pounded the table. "What do I have to do?"

"We're going," Remo replied, rising slowly, and pulling his hat down over his eyes.

Now Aloe raised her head. Her hair was as pale as flax, her eyes were blue and her hands dirty. "Five more minutes," she begged. "I'll tell *your* fortune too, Remo."

Bonaccorsi seized her wrist and twisted it. "No, you won't. All you do is tell lies. And you do it on purpose." Barely suppressed anger trembled in his voice. She had predicted that he would never return from the trip across the Atlantic which he was about to take.

Aloe stood up. She moved like a docile animal as she walked toward Remo, who had paid his bill and was waiting at the door. Càrbon paid quickly and rushed to take hold of her again. They all left the tavern. The hostess closed the door and followed them. The narrow, stone-paved street descended toward the port whose odors of tar and coal dust reached them on dark breezes. They had only to cross to the doorway on the opposite side. The hostess was carrying a lamp and preceded them up a staircase. At the first landing they walked along a narrow corridor lined with doors, where they mumbled goodnight to each other. When Remo reached his room, he entered, lit a candle, and lay down on his bed half-clothed.

He no longer felt sleepy. He was watching gloomy shadows flicker across the walls when he heard knocking, not on the door that opened into the corridor, but on another that led to an adjacent room. Without waiting for an answer, Wilhelm walked in and sat down at the edge of the bed.

"Things are really bad, Remo. First, the damn peace ruined everything. Now there's disasters, one after another. Today over at Neri's they impounded four packs of powder. Two of them were mine. We're going to have to make the best of it for a while. I've got a couple of things in the fire, but they'll take time."

Remo didn't seem interested. His long, blond hair and pale refined features came from a completely different world than the one which had produced Wilhelm's hard, square face and round, shaven head.

"You used to play the piano," the German went on. "I got

you a job. From five o'clock till eight. Playing dance music at the Rondinella. Very chic. Black tie. Close shave."

"Okay, "Remo murmured.

Wilhelm looked at him benignly. He pulled a letter from a pocket. "This came for you."

Remo put it aside without examining it. "How do you get the mail?" he asked.

"None of your business."

Wilhelm lingered a while longer in the hope that Remo would open the letter and disclose its contents. But Remo had dropped it on the bed and resumed studying the shadows which were now leaping wildly from wall to ceiling in the flickering candle light.

When Wilhelm stood up, Remo noticed a book in his hand. "What is it?" he asked.

Wilhelm showed him the cover. It was in German.

"*The Laocöon* by Lessing," he laughed loudly, then stopped and stared for a moment at Remo, who averted his eyes. Finally Wilhelm uttered a rushed "good-night," and almost fled the room.

Remo got out of his bed to lock the door between the two rooms, then got back on the bed and opened the letter. It said, "Sir, I am quite certain that this letter will reach you. I am the same person who wrote some time ago with the news of the heroic death of your sister, Tullia, which occurred almost a year ago under the circumstances I described. I will not repeat them now, because although you did not answer me, I have reason to believe that you did receive my letter. Your uncle was able to locate your address and, because I was coming to Marseilles for a few days, asked me to bring you a parcel found among your sister's effects that had been sent to him. The package is sealed and the note on it in signorina Tullia's handwriting says that in case of her death it should be delivered to her brother, Remo. Fearing that the package, whose contents I do not know, might go astray if forwarded in any other way, I am keeping it under my care. I will be in Marseilles for two days, three at the most. You can find me mornings before ten, or evenings between eight and nine, at the address below." This was followed by formal greetings and the name and address of a hotel in the Cannebière district.

Once more Remo looked about at the shadows, then he blew his candle out. Gradually, from the darkness around and within him, other more vivid shadows rose and stirred and pressed upon his heart. Betrayed ghosts, long dormant memories, burdensome shadows in his suffocating chest. Why were they reappearing now, tormenting him, who was so weak? Why were they keeping him from losing himself in a void? Gentle ghosts, doleful specters, and among them objects recalled as vividly as if they were real. At his back he felt the hard trunk of a tree that he, so little, was leaning against, completely exhausted. Tullia, still a child herself, takes his hand and makes him walk onward to Rome, toward a house. Even now Remo is tired, always tired, but not in the way he was then. Abruptly, in the flood of fragmented shapes streaming about him, another image becomes clear, solid and shiny. It is a hand mirror, Adria's mirror. One time, and one time only, when their mother was out, he and Tullia had entered her room with her maid. On the night table at her bedside they had seen the mirror with its polished frame and gleaming handle. For days afterward it had filled their fantasies and conversations. Now these images are being swallowed up in thick smoke, are dispersing and dissolving into a kind of music. Music? Music, like Tullia, is something from the distant past. Or, perhaps, neither ever existed.

Remo was in a bitter mood when he woke the next morning. The letter still lay on his bed. He thought of getting up and going to the hotel, but didn't stir. He knew it was too late and wanted desperately to have Tullia's parcel. He sought to recapture the flow of memories that had attended his sleep. He was drowsing again, was perhaps on the verge of recapturing them, when a cautious knock on the outside door woke him.

"Just a minute" he shouted, reaching quickly for the letter and, leaning over the edge of the bed, hiding it in the pocket of a jacket on a nearby chair. Then he called out, "Come in."

It was Aloe, timorous as a mouse.

Her presence made Remo uncomfortable, but she seemed not to notice. She appeared childishly shy and meek. Her voice, however, was thick and she smelled heavily of wine.

"I was afraid Wilhelm might be here," she said, looking around. "Remo, tell me if I have to take this. Wilhelm is giving Càrbon the little girl to take to America. He picked him to do it to get rid of him, because he's not bringing in very much. But he doesn't have to go. He says the girl's not for him, he wouldn't know what to do with her, and that as soon as he's turned her over he'll come right back. I don't care about any of that. But yesterday when I read in the cards that once he crosses the ocean he won't come back, and that he'll die soon, you thought I was saying that on purpose, making it up..."

"I?" Remo interrupted her. "I didn't think anything. What's it to me?"

"I know I'm nothing to you, Remo, and anyway you're wrong. But he thought so and he beat me last night because of it. Every night he's got some other excuse. Now it's this one. He says that I'm giving him bad luck saying those things. Only it's true, yesterday I really read it in the cards. He'll bring the girl over and then he'll die. I played the cards using his whole name, not just Càrbon, Carmine Bonaccorsi. And the cards said very clearly that Carmine Bonaccorsi was going to take a long sea voyage and when he got to the other side he'd die."

Boundless vacuity emanated from her singsong lamentation and shone in her suffering, childlike face.

Remo paid her no heed. He knew it was late and persuaded himself with complete injustice that Aloe had kept him from leaving for the hotel in time to get the package he wanted so badly. Now he would have to wait until evening.

The girl, who had been standing at the edge of the bed while she spoke, slipped down to her knees and with one hand reached for Remo's hand lying limply on the bed cover. The act irritated him beyond measure, but he lacked the courage to withdraw his own.

Aloe whispered darkly.

"We'd be great together, you and me, Remo."

Remo looked around the room and prayed for something to distract her. Aloe's hand and cheeks were burning.

"Say yes, Remo."

"I'm starting a job today," he murmured, just to say anything. "I'm going to play the piano. I don't remember where. But Wilhelm does."

As though he'd been summoned, a knock sounded at the inner door followed by Wilhelm's voice.

"Why is the door locked? Open up."

"Open it," Remo ordered. The young woman stood up and hurried to the door. Remo turned his face to the wall.

"What are you doing here?" Wilhelm shouted at her. "Get out."

Trembling, with her neck bent and her body hunched as though she were overcome by icy cold, Aloe left the room, dragging her feet and staring into space like a sleep walker.

Wilhelm turned to the young man.

Remo remembered that he had locked the inner door the night before so that he could read the letter. But he didn't feel like talking. Without turning his face from the wall, he defended himself. "I didn't know it was locked. Maybe Aloe did it."

"Who cares about Aloe? I know you've got nothing to do with her. She's Càrbon's business. Just remember the Rondinella at five today. Play dance music, mostly tangos. I came to check if your clothes are all right."

He lifted a suitcase from a chair, put it on the table, opened it and rummaged among clothing and underwear. Then, without preamble, without looking up, and feigning a lack of interest, he said, "I can't remember if I gave you a letter last night."

"You did," Remo said, then was silent, clearly indicating unwillingness to discuss the subject.

"You're making a mistake, Remo," the German said, jerking up his head and looking at him. "You're making a mistake not to trust me. There was a time it wasn't like this, when we were up there. It's the damn peace. Since the peace you don't trust me any more. There are things that still rankle me."

"Like what?"

"When we left Germany to come here, why'd you insist on taking the long way and going through Paris? And you had to be alone. What'd you do alone for two days in Paris? You never told me."

"I didn't do anything."

"Then why'd you want to go?"

"I didn't do anything in Paris. There's nothing else to say. I already told you."

"All I know is that you, who's always so easygoing, you're acting damn stubborn about this. And now…now you got a letter."

Remo rolled on to his back and closed his eyes.

Faced with the youth's resistance when he had come to expect submission, the German was completely at a loss. He took two or three steps around the room, unable to approach the subject again, to think of another subject, or to leave.

With his eyes still closed, Remo remained motionless on the bed. Inside, however, he was seething with impatience to be alone with the memories that had reawakened after such a long slumber, memories that his sleep had engulfed and that the arrival of Aloe and Wilhelm had prevented him from recovering.

The memories returned after Wilhelm finally left. They returned, but now they were filled with a bitterness that Remo in his very short, fatigue-filled life had never known. Now, beyond his memories of Villa Adria and his childhood, the German's words had recalled memories of his two days in Paris. When he and Wilhelm left the distant German city where he had been interned during the war, Remo had wanted to extend the journey so as to pass through Paris. He went there alone and just a few days later returned to his companion and their life of depravity.

He hadn't seen anyone in Paris. He had roamed the city without purpose because he was terrified of the only possible purpose. He had walked the city streets, driven by a melancholy fury. He knew that the street on which Adria had cloistered herself was in the neighborhood of the Sacre-Coeur, but he didn't go up there. He kept to the bottom of the hill, walking along the streets where the roads that descended the hill joined each other and from where the temple was visible. At various intersections he would stop to study the stark white cupolas. Paris street life, which had revived after the war and was whirling about with increasing velocity, rushed past the pale youth standing at the corner of Rochechouart staring upward. Staring in the same way as that long gone little boy stood nightly and stared through a slit into a glowing room, awaiting an apparition.

———————

2 REMO SPENT THREE HOURS at the Rondinella accompanying other musicians playing dance tunes. Through waves of harmony he contemplated the ballroom and the frenzied men and women dancing. The room lights were blinding, but after more than five years of semidarkness, the dancers wanted ever more light. Remo played as if in a dream. The only sensation he felt was overwhelming boredom. Every so often the boredom would be engulfed by a wave of hatred for the dancers, though this subsided quickly. While his hands produced music, his mind wandered, unable to fix upon anything. From behind the keyboard he studied the dancers at their pleasure. At one moment, however, he had the feeling it was he who was being studied. Indeed, a girl was staring intently at him over her partner's shoulder. Each time the pair passed the musicians, she would fasten her eyes on Remo while pressing herself more tightly to her escort. Remo avoided her glance and told himself, "This is the last time they'll get me in here." Every so often the violinist, while playing, would take four or five dance steps onto the dance floor and that also greatly annoyed Remo.

Nevertheless, when eight o'clock came, he was surprised at how quickly the time had passed. Outside, he almost regretted leaving the hall with its lights and well-dressed people. Filled with strange yearnings, he climbed the Cannebière to the hotel named in the letter, located its author, who turned out to be a young officer, and recovered Tullia's packet. All the way home he fumed and raged at his slavish dependence which would keep him from opening it for several hours.

Indeed, Wilhelm was waiting for him outside the house with a dark look on his face. "It certainly took you long enough to get back from the Rondinella."

The arrival of Càrbon and Aloe allowed Remo to escape

replying. The four walked up the street and went directly to their corner table in the back of the tavern. Càrbon kept tossing him dirty looks—he must have heard that Aloe had been in his room that morning. But Càrbon's state of mind wasn't of the slightest interest to Remo, who didn't utter a word all evening long. Càrbon and Aloe passed the time bickering. Once in a while Wilhelm would exchange a few words with the sailors at an adjacent table. More often, someone would come looking for him and he would get up and walk off to the side for a private conversation. The tavern was one of his regular business haunts. Returning from a conversation, he heard Aloe speaking to Càrbon: "Leave him alone. Can't you see he doesn't feel like talking?"

"I don't need you to defend me," Remo snapped at her. "Let him say whatever he wants."

Càrbon pounded the table, a saucer bounced and splashed liquid on Remo's black jacket. Remo wiped himself carefully with a wet napkin. He said nothing, but moved as far away from Càrbon as possible.

Càrbon tried once more to provoke him. "Now that you are in the employ of the patrons of the Rondinella, I see you have to keep your distance from us."

The image of those patrons suddenly thrust Remo into a distant world, elegant women and gracious gentlemen, Rome, Villa Adria, Villa Mayer, himself as a little boy and Tullia as a child, too. Tullia is so high up now. He cast his eyes down at the table to exclude everything but his own memories.

"And if you're·thinking," said Càrbon, advancing toward him, "of not answering just to rile me, that's fine with me. I can take care of you, you know, and right now, too."

He raised one hand and held it in the air. Aloe screamed. Remo, fearful, intuitively drew back and put his hands up to protect his face. But Wilhelm had caught Càrbon's arm.

"Cut it out, Càrbon, or I'll throw you in the gutter."

Aloe whispered: "Get out of here, Remo. Go on. It'll be better."

Remo seized the chance. He stood up and announced, "I'm going home to get some sleep."

Wilhelm still had a firm grip on Càrbon, who would have attacked again. Once Remo was outside the tavern and beyond the sight of his companions, he felt as lighthearted as though nothing had ever happened, as free as if he had escaped them forever. He went flying across the narrow street, climbed the stairs, entered his room, lit the oil lamp on his table and sat down. From an inside pocket he took out Tullia's packet.

It was a fairly large envelope tied with a ribbon and sealed. Remo held it in his hands for a few moments, then broke the wax seal and untied the ribbon. He proceeded slowly, savoring a deep and delicate pleasure.

He read the outside message again. "In case of my death, to be delivered as is, to my brother Remo wherever he may be. Tullia."

Remo felt a lump in his throat. Instantly he thought of his companions and the shame he would feel if they saw him crying.

He pressed his head between his hands to dispose of the intruding thoughts, then looked at those words again. A desire to kiss them took him by surprise, but he glanced around himself, unable to find the courage.

Finally he opened the envelope, tearing it as little as possible.

Within, there was a cardboard wrapped in layers of soft paper. He began to unwind the paper slowly. "Tullia," he thought, "a picture of Tullia." At the last layer he hesitated. "The last time I saw her, I was only twelve. When the war broke out, she was twenty-two, like I am now. I wonder if this will be a recent photo, or one when she was little."

He dallied still longer to put off the moment he would finally see the photograph. He asked himself which he would prefer, a photo of Tullia as an adult or as a child, the Tullia he never knew or the one he remembered. He couldn't decide. Smiling, he removed the last strip of wrapping.

The picture appeared. It wasn't Tullia. Beneath the circle of bright light cast by the lamp, there before his eyes was a photograph of Adria.

After the first numbing moment, Remo's wretched room was flooded with light. Trembling, he didn't dare touch the photo, but gazed at it as if he had been plunged into sunlight. It was Adria as he knew her all his life, as he'd seen her that last time when she had said, "my darlings." He smells her perfume, feels her soft arms around his shoulders, and the very instant her hand ruffles his hair.

Adria as she was, as she must still be, as she has always been and will always be for all eternity, Adria. Remo felt his heart opening, felt the cold that had inhabited him for years, that had dried up his feelings, suddenly vanish, felt his blood become bright and course through his veins as a wave of joy and tenderness. His mother, Adria, God. Remo is a child, he is finally a man, he is flying as if in a dream, one of God's own children. Remo is immersed in light and as pure as an angel.

Suddenly his blood ran cold.

Enthralled in ecstasy he had forgotten everything else—a sudden sound at the door filled him with terror. He leaped up to close the door and lock it in time to hide the sacred object. But just as he reached the door, it was already opening and he nearly fell into Càrbon's arms. He drew back with a shout.

"Don't yell, Remo. There's nothing to be afraid of. I came to make up with you, to apologize. I promised Wilhelm."

Remo regained control of himself. Standing at a distance from Càrbon, he carefully positioned himself to block the latter's view of the table.

Càrbon's words had relieved him. He chose his own carefully. "Of course, sure, with pleasure."

"Let's shake hands, Remo."

"Here."

They shook.

Càrbon sensed Remo's uneasiness, though not the reason for it. "Come on down," he said. "They're waiting for us to go have a drink together."

Remo hesitated. "Sure," he said. "You go on first, Càrbon. I'll be right down."

"Why?"

"It's just for a minute."

Càrbon refused to give in. "If you have something to do, I'll wait for you." His mood began to change. Remo's behavior was raising dark suspicions. "What's going on with you?" he asked. And as he moved forward and Remo retreated, Càrbon clearly saw terror in Remo's eyes.

"What do you take me for?" he shouted. He pushed Remo back and was suddenly standing at the illuminated table.

"No!" Remo screamed.

But Càrbon, having already uttered an "oh" of surprise, had rushed at the photo.

Remo felt the walls of the room toppling. He leaped at Càrbon like a madman, but the latter shoved him so hard that he slid along the floor to the opposite side of the room.

Dizzied by the blow, Remo couldn't immediately stand up. "Don't touch that," he cried in anguish.

Càrbon already had his hand out and a horrible grin on his face. For a moment, Remo saw him as though he were far in the distance and heard a rumbling about his head. And from within that rumbling came Càrbon's loud laughter and his voice, "Good-looking woman."

Remo, back on his feet, found himself close to Càrbon,

two steps behind him, as Càrbon was reaching for the picture with his other hand. A red flash darted across the room, a huge veil of flames whirled before Remo's eyes, and his hand was in his pocket closing around the knife and springing the blade. Now both of Càrbon hands were on Adria's picture. With one bound Remo was upon him, clutching a shoulder, plunging the knife into the center of his back and driving it deeply, to the hilt.

Càrbon screamed, gurgled, then was silent. His hands released the photograph and he fell heavily. All Remo saw was the photo. He dropped to the floor to retrieve it. On his knees, he swathed it quickly in its wrapping, ran to his suitcase and buried it at the very bottom, under everything else. He locked the suitcase, put the key in a pocket. Now he could breathe, could walk without staggering, and now he became aware of the deep silence around him.

He turned, saw the body on the floor and realized what he had done.

He took a few steps toward the corpse, and withdrew in horror. In a panic to escape the room, he couldn't find the door. With his back against a wall he dragged himself around the room, unable to take his eyes from Càrbon's body lying there, a half empty sack, with its back facing up and the terrible little knife handle protruding from it like a nail. He was sliding along the wall when he bumped into the iron bedstead and fell senseless and limp as a puppet, half on, half off the bed.

That's how Wilhelm and Aloe found him when they came upstairs, concerned about the delay. Wilhelm stifled the woman's scream with his hand.

"We've got to keep cool about this. Help me get Remo up. Into my room."

They carried him onto Wilhelm's bed. Wilhelm ran back to

lock the outside door of Remo's room. Remo regained consciousness, was delirious a few moments, then fell into a heavy sleep.

"All right, Aloe, don't leave this room. Lock the door and don't open it until you hear my voice. I'm going to get help because we have only two hours to get rid of the body."

---

3 TOWARD DAWN, WAKING FROM HIS deep slumber, Remo managed bit by bit to recall what had happened. He bolted upright in Wilhelm's bed, but Wilhelm and Aloe restrained him quickly and calmed him.

"Look Remo," Wilhelm told him, "you've got to keep your wits about you. You've made a huge mess for yourself, but there's no sense talking about it. Thank God we could get rid of him. Now we've got to get rid of you. That'll be easier. Where's your passport?"

Remo looked at him in total confusion. When he understood the question, he pointed to his jacket. Wilhelm took the passport. There was a small fireplace in the room. The German spread a newspaper in it, set it ablaze, then tossed Remo's passport into the flames. When it was completely consumed, he took another passport from his pocket.

"This one's Càrbon's. Carmine Bonaccorsi. That's you now. You are Carmine Bonaccorsi. The picture was taken when he was a lot younger and it's faded, so you won't have any trouble getting by with it. He was supposed to leave tomorrow on a merchant ship, the Damiana. You'll go with his name. He was going to deliver some goods to America, fake cargo, actually a kid, and turn her over to one of our men, who's expecting her. So you'll be the one who'll take her and hand her over. The kid's a minor, she doesn't have papers, so she's going to have to manage the best she can, someplace down in the hold or wherever she can grab some air. She's on board already. There's a sailor who's one of us. He'll tell you how to get her off in Buenos Aires, where to turn her over to André. I'll give you a letter later that says something about jute. Once you get there, since there's no way you'll be coming back here, André will probably send you to Boca or maybe to La Plata where he has a couple of houses of girls."

Remo looked about, dazed. Aloe was sobbing mindlessly, as though she might not even remember why she'd begun crying. Remo, suddenly stricken with fear, asked, "Where's my valise?"

"It's in there."

"Where?"

"Go get it, Aloe."

The young woman left the room and returned dragging the valise. Seeing that it was still closed, Remo felt calmer.

The German spoke again. "I'm sorry you're going, but there was nothing else to do. Tonight was the hardest part, but let's forget it. Take it easy now. You can rest up all day here. Tomorrow morning we'll see you off and that'll be the end of it."

So in a dawn filled with rosy mists, Remo sailed on the merchant ship Damiana, and was no longer Remo, but Carmine Bonaccorsi, known as Càrbon. And he was delivering an underage girl to André, a trafficker in white slavery overseas, in Buenos Aires, or perhaps La Plata—it makes no difference, because this isn't Remo. Remo no longer exists and we don't have to bother about Carmine Bonaccorsi, who's going off with either good or bad luck.

Remo was important to us, Tullia was important, Adria's husband was important. We've followed all of them to their final destinies. Now we have to see how Adria herself disappears, as we all will one day, from the face of the earth.

adria III

———◆◆◆◆◆———

1 TIME SILENTLY SMOOTHES ALL THINGS of the soul, but strikes violently at material things to keep them constantly moving. Water is sly and survives by flowing off or, subject to time's blasts in the ocean, by simulating great agitation. It is against solid objects, which expect to remain in place for eternity, that Time delivers its horrendous blows. Mountains and cities strive to embed themselves in the earth's crust. But, every so often, Time sends forth earthquakes to crush mountains and vents its rage against cities by putting restlessness in men's hearts and pickaxes in their hands. Buildings and houses which until yesterday seemed to be heavenly refuges in which to live happily until death, streets and squares which up to an hour ago were pleasant places to walk, all at once seem to men atrociously and unbearably constricted. Whereupon they reach for their pickaxes (unaware that it is Time, wanting everything to change and pass, which is inciting them and handing out the axes) and laboriously demolish houses to fill the newly freed spaces with even bigger houses— houses which their children and grandchildren will one day find equally uninhabitable and similarly destroy.

This is the way, to the rhythm of earthquakes and pickaxes, that the sacred history of the earth's surface proceeds through an infinity of centuries. And this is why, when the war was over, men returning to Paris from the eastern front decided that some of its districts were too squalid to provide habitation to a generation of heroes, and by dint of their pickaxes were in the process of demolishing them. One morning Adria received a notice that her entire street, including the house in which she had been secluded for twelve years, was scheduled to be destroyed by order of the highest Civil Authority. She was therefore bidden to locate another residence within a specified period of time. The blinds were all closed and the lights blazing in her three rooms when she received the extraordinary notice.

It didn't upset her. She tore it up and went on with what she had been doing, reading *Orlando Innamorato*.

However, everyone else on the street, including the poorer folk who lived there, became extremely agitated. Most disturbed of all were the people in Adria's service. They were anxious to know what she would do. But the mistress had no choice. She would have to leave this house. The issue consumed and troubled them. To leave the house and to find herself another one—at the very least she'd have to send someone else out to search, perhaps one of them, probably Albertina. But even if she relied on others to choose for her, she'd still have to leave the condemned house to get to the new one. Here, at last, was a change in their monotonous lives. They spoke of nothing else. People in neighboring houses came by every hour of every day, curious for news. Strange tales had circulated throughout the neighborhood about the woman whom no one had ever seen. Days went by. Everyone cursed the Authority's order and worried endlessly about the vicissitudes they would have to overcome in these already most difficult times. Adria's servants participated in the discussions along the street. They began to collect information on their own, so as to be prepared when the mistress assigned them the sensitive task. Another notice arrived. Albertina summoned the courage to mention it to Adria. Adria was still in bed. Through the curtains veiling her alcove, she replied: "There's time."

Albertina didn't dare persist. A new notice set the mandatory date. On the first of October the house would have to be vacant, ready for the first stroke of the pickaxes. Twenty days.

Now Adria began to think about the problem. She thought about it every day. She couldn't visualize any solution. Thereupon she stopped thinking about it until the day was almost upon her.

Her deliberations were simple and rapid. Adria would not accept the need to leave her house. To cede to that necessity would be to acknowledge it as superior to her own laws. Her own laws had overridden quite different forces than an ordinance promulgated by the City of Paris. Such an ordinance might consider itself a superior material power. But ceding to material power is the ultimate humiliation to a proud spirit.

Her submission, she thought, would have ruined everything. There was no way of doing it that would preserve the essence of the thing. No matter if she were to use the most incredible precautions, go out alone at night, cover herself with veils, the mere leaving, stepping past the door, walking again under the small black arch, would mean her ruination; the forfeiture not only of her travails of the past twelve years, but the complete destruction of the heroic edifice that was the glory of her life. This was the first time the word "heroic" occurred to her.

It was a strange phenomenon, her daily repetition of how things stood without the slightest variation, with neither a course of action nor a solution in sight, yet which nevertheless left her untroubled. She reconsidered the situation every day as a matter of habit, then immediately and effortlessly thrust it aside and resumed the normal activities of her life.

An unambiguous faith sustained her. She sincerely believed that a solution would manifest itself, perhaps at the last moment. And in that mysterious certainty she had not the least desire to know destiny's solution, nor the slightest impatience for the day to arrive. She had forbidden Albertina to mention the subject to her again.

Albertina and the other servants were living like survivors of a flood. Fatalism flowed down from Adria's rooms to the floors below and spread among them like a strange contagion.

Adria remained calm, but every day now she would review the story of her life. The canvas of past years unfolded like a placid drama; from the most distant and least accessible times, through her marriage; through the quiet years of her triumphs in Rome hopelessly scarred by Guarnerio's bloody madness; then the conversation with that agent of destiny, Giovanni Bellamonte; the distant death of Tullia and Remo's father; and the unexpected stirring of her soul in the remarkable epistolary exchanges with her daughter. She thought too of Atena, so quickly departed and lost to her, and the news of Tullia's death, and more recently of Remo's disappearance, then nothing, almost a return of stillness. Everything passed before her eyes—myriad details from this or that period—useless details abiding, who knows how, in a fold of memory.

The lucid images that accompanied her recollections roused nothing in her soul. She didn't judge them. She didn't collect or sort them. She had neither doubts nor remorse. The first of October drew closer.

Her entire staff, having lost patience with her, had looked after themselves and found new employment for October. The exception was Albertina, who was unwilling to make plans of her own until the last minute, and even then would never have forsaken her mistress.

For several days now, from morning till night, the pickaxes had been pounding from one end of the street to the other. Each day the noise grew closer. Only two or three houses to the right and left of Adria's were still inhabited. And on September 29th even those stood empty. The pickaxes were approaching. Adria's days, her thoughts, recollections and reading were encircled ever more tightly by the implacable advance. Now, even during the day she kept the blinds and shutters closed and every lamp lit. All day long their light poured through her rooms, striking the pale-hued surfaces. Adria pictured the world around her as an immense cloud of dust and heaps of crumpled mortar and bricks.

On the last day of September the ground floor was jammed with valises, trunks and parcels belonging to her servants who would be leaving the following morning. Even Albertina had packed her things, though she was convinced that she would be following her mistress somewhere. At eight o'clock on the evening of the thirtieth, as on every evening at that time, the noise of the pickaxes ceased. By nine, with the next morning's early departure in mind, everyone in the house was asleep except Adria. The telephone rang.

"Who is it?"

It was an unfamiliar voice, a man's voice.

"I'm a friend of Atena's. Do you remember her?"

"Of course."

"She's still in America. I met her there. She thinks of you often. And since I was coming to Paris she asked me to phone you and say hello for her."

"Thank you."

"And she thought that since I am going to stay here for some time, you and I could resume the kind of conversations that the two of you had before. Would you like to?"

"I'd be delighted."

"When?"

"I don't know.

"Tomorrow?"

"Perhaps."

"I'll phone you tomorrow."

2 AN HOUR LATER ADRIA FOUND HERSELF still sitting at the telephone table. She came to herself as though waking from a trance, and upon hearing her own voice speaking aloud: "No matter what, it's clear I am not leaving here tomorrow, or ever."

She had never before spoken aloud to herself. In the brilliantly lit room, the words sounded like a conclusion, but to what train of thoughts she didn't know and made no attempt to discover.

Then she spoke out loud once more, this time intentionally, after having curiously revised the sentence. "It's clear I'm never leaving here, dead or alive." After that, without undressing or turning off the lights, she lay down on her bed and slept heavily for about an hour.

When she woke she got out of bed.

The actions she undertook hereafter, though not preceded by any resolution, were precise and purposeful. She moved back and forth, working rigorously and meticulously without thought, just as a pilotless plane glides through the sky driven only by ethereal currents from the land far below. But I have no idea who, from what land, through what ether, guided her like that. I know nothing about Adria and I'm about to conclude her story without having been able to form a clear impression of her or to understand her behavior.

In any event, the first thing she did when she got out of bed was to make sure that the door in back of the bathroom through which Albertina came up to her quarters was locked. When she returned to her own room she locked the bathroom door itself, and for added security pushed a trunk against it. She paused for a moment, then turned into the alcove, to the place where a small door was built into one of its walls. She had closed it the day she'd moved in, so very long ago. She located the key and managed after much effort to turn and open the lock. It took even more effort for her to detach two heavily rusted bolts above and below the lock. Using a knife she managed to pry off the whole apparatus and open the door. Behind it was a staircase that led to an attic with a dormer window. A musty odor emanated from it.

She lit a candle and walked up the staircase. The dank walls smelled, the wooden steps creaked and sagged. Every so often the invisible thread of a spider's web brushed against her face. The patter of fleeing mice would suddenly sound, then fade.

When she reached the attic, the scurryings of mice increased. She could not open the large dormer window, but found a piece of wood in a corner and used it to smash a pane of glass. Cold wind suddenly blew in. Adria set the candle in a protected spot to shelter it from the wind. Then she broke every pane of glass of the window, from top to bottom, to admit as much air as possible.

She paused for a moment and thrust out her head to look into the dark night. She saw patterns of distant lights (it's the way Rome appears from the windows of Villa Adria, though there the air is softer). Closer by was a mass of roofs and thick walls, and high above all, a cloudy rust-colored sky without a single star.

She withdrew her head, picked up the dripping candle, and returning to her room set the small door to remain open, allowing air to circulate freely. The air that had rushed down with her and flooded the stairwell now reached the alcove in which Adria's large bed stood.

She positioned all the communicating doors between the three rooms so that they too were wide open.

Now her work became slow and deliberate.

She went in search of bound bundles of magazines and newspapers that she had collected over the years. She untied them and spread them under every chair, every curtain, everywhere there was upholstery or fabric. Most were under the rows of clothing, but she set a good many down under the full length of the bed.

Was everything ready?

A surprising thought stopped her as she was about to take the final step.

It was a thought she hadn't anticipated. She smiled at the heavenly spirit that had inspired it. Until that moment her heart had been quiet. Now it began pounding. Filled with joy and fear, she felt herself smiling.

She ran to a chest which she had never reopened and took out a box. She unwrapped the fabric that surrounded it, broke its seal and loosened the cover. The mirror within it, the beloved and condemned mirror, had been waiting for twelve years. By now Adria has truly earned this prize. Still she did not lift the lid, but set the box gently on the bed next to her pillow.

There is nothing else to arrange, Adria.

At this point her actions were swift.

She relit the candle and hurriedly set fire to the papers she had spread near every piece of fabric in the room. Before they burst into flames, she lit the papers under the bed. The fire was slow to take hold. She threw away the candle and lay down on her bed.

---

3 LYING THERE IN THE LIGHT OF EVERY glowing lamp, she put out her hand and, smiling at the joy she had promised herself, reached for the mirror. Thus, Adria once again

performed the most cherished and most profound act of her life of long ago. She leaned on her arm, turned a little onto her side, raised the mirror to the level of her face. As she'd done every evening until twelve years before, and as she hadn't done for the twelve years since, she looked long and hard at herself in the mirror of her simple life. Supporting herself on an elbow, she held the mirror out at full arm's length, brought it slowly closer, opened her mouth a little. She withstands the heat that is becoming intolerable, the sparks leaping here and there. What is this rush of bleak hissings? Tongues of flame from beneath, from above stream wildly around the door. Something shatters, the lights go out in a flash, the darkness is red, filled with roarings, the bed is a furnace, beams crumble and fall, the fire writhes between the walls, struggles, the house is a pyre besieged with screams. What are they screaming about over there? In the rooms where Guarnerio is going mad. It's time to get out of here. The entire street is screaming now. Thumps, the enormous blows of battering rams, pelting streams of water, interminable fallings. Then gray, a long sinking of gray into infinity, in which monotone mutterings hiss, and a sound, a distant sound, perhaps of bells, all the bells of Rome. The entire pile has fallen apart. There is a great deal of smoke, a few flames still escape the rubble and rise toward the reddish sky, which drops down and absorbs them. Out in the street the huge crowd can only cry out and watch. By the time the great jets of water had put out the last flames under the violet dawn, they are merely wetting down a pile of black ruins through which the horde rummages, pulling from it only ashes, charred lumps, and black bits of things that squeak.

I never could understand Adria nor form any opinions about her. But as no trace of her body was found, I fear that the flames on that last night of September consumed all of her, including her soul.